"IT SHOULD'VE BEEN ME."

Mandy covered her face with her hands.

"What was that?"

"It should've been me. Not that other woman. She should've got out of there alive. I should've died."

"Why do you say that?" said Capshaw.

"Because when she saw the guy down and me with my hands free, she started screaming—begging me to come help her. I could see her face in the moonlight—the fear in her eyes. I was that close to her." She paused and looked down at her hands.

"And?" McSwain said.

"I ran. I just ran and kept running, and I never looked back. I left that poor woman there with that maniac. She was only a few feet away—it might have taken a few seconds to untie her—but I didn't even try. I didn't think I had time. I ran away and left her to die."

LEFT TO DIE

Taylor Kincaid

AN ONYX BOOK

ONYX
Published by New American Library, a division of
Penguin Group (USA) Inc., 375 Hudson Street,
New York, New York 10014, U.S.A.
Penguin Books Ltd, 80 Strand,
London WC2R 0RL, England
Penguin Books Australia Ltd, 250 Camberwell Road,
Camberwell, Victoria 3124, Australia
Penguin Books Canada Ltd, 10 Alcorn Avenue,
Toronto, Ontario, Canada M4V 3B2
Penguin Books (N.Z.) Ltd, Cnr Rosedale and Airborne Roads,
Albany, Auckland 1310, New Zealand

Penguin Books Ltd, Registered Offices:
80 Strand, London WC2R 0RL, England

First published by Onyx, an imprint of New American Library,
a division of Penguin Group (USA) Inc.

First Printing, August 2003
10 9 8 7 6 5 4 3 2 1

 REGISTERED TRADEMARK—MARCA REGISTRADA

Printed in the United States of America

PUBLISHER'S NOTE
This is a work of fiction. Names, characters, places, and incidents either are the product of the author's imagination or are used fictitiously, and any resemblance to actual persons, living or dead, business establishments, events, or locales is entirely coincidental.

This novel is dedicated to the Rude Awakening Group in Longmont, Colorado—your presence makes the world a far more interesting place to be and my mornings a helluva lot more fun.

ACKNOWLEDGMENTS

Many thanks to my agent, Jennifer Jackson, and to my editor, Laura Anne Gilman, for their support, hard work, and encouragement.

Thanks to Jeffrey Miller of the Fairfax County Police Department in Fairfax, Virginia, who took the time to answer my questions regarding crime scene investigation.

And thanks to Donald Gould, whose knowledge of San Diego and the surrounding environs proved invaluable.

Chapter 1

What Mandy Sutorius liked about the Chula Vista Tap was that there were so many people getting shit-faced so fast, making so much boozy racket, and in general generating a kind of beer-addled, in-your-face chaos, that she could drink there for hours and nobody would remember she'd been there and nobody would know when she'd left.

On a calm night, there might be no more fights than take place on your average boxing card, a mere handful of drug transactions, and only one or two women who got hammered enough to flash their tits as they jiggled and pranced on the stained, sticky bartop. On a bad night, it was bedlam and bikers and blow jobs in the bushes under the palsied flicker of dull neon light. You could drop dead at your table and slide to the floor and nobody'd notice till they cleared the place out around two in the morning.

Mandy Sutorius was at the Chula Vista Tap on a very bad night.

Around seven she'd trudged in, surly and sullen, fresh from another telephone screaming match with her ex-husband, Kevin, over the kids, the court, and child support. She told herself she needed only one or two beers to mellow her mood, take the edge off the stress that rode the knobs of her spine like a constant wild itch, but here she was almost four hours later, still feeling like shit, but with the edge taken off the surliness and replaced by the first scrapings of fear, as she realized what time it was and what the consequences of her self-medication could be.

Nobody but the bartender noticed her leave, and to him she looked like half the chicks there, a peroxide blonde with brown roots and that old-at-twenty-five stare, a sour-eyed emptiness that could be temporarily filled with whiskey or the wrong man or both before the hollowness came back twice as strong.

In the packed parking lot behind the building, a drunken argument was breaking out between a couple of scruffy beer swillers. As Mandy wandered blearily past, one of them stopped shouting long enough to leer at her and make an obscene anatomical reference, and she shot back something equally uncivil and slid a hand into the pocket that contained her wallet and a canister of pepper spray. *Let one of the fuckers try something,* she thought, as she tried to focus her eyes around a dozen or so dusty brown beaters, all of which suddenly looked exactly like the battered beige Taurus she'd driven here in.

In the middle of the parking lot, she stopped, took a deep breath, and turned in a circle—a mistake, considering the world was already turning too fast on its own. She lost her balance, staggered backward a step, and collided with a slender woman wearing black denim jeans and a sleeveless white T-shirt who was just walking out between a couple of pickups. Her blond hair was scraped back off a round face spattered with freckles and clipped in a loose knot at the back of her head, and she looked scared and out of place in the parking lot of the Tap.

"Hey," Mandy yelled, "watch where the hell you're going!"

"Oh, sorry." The woman gasped, looking flustered although clearly it was Mandy who'd bumped into her. "I didn't see you."

"Well, look where you're going next time."

"I said I was sorry. I'm just trying to find my car."

"Join the club. Are you as shit-faced as I am?"

"Not shit-faced, just a little nervous. One of those creeps by the door said something nasty, and I got so rattled I walked in the wrong direction." She pointed across the lot. "I think I'm actually parked over there."

"What're you driving?"

"A gray BMW. What about you?"

"Your basic rust-bucket Taurus." She turned to scan the row of cars behind her and felt her stomach do a bob-and-weave maneuver at even that small discombobulation. "Oh, shit, I don't feel so good."

"Maybe you ought to go back inside. Have some coffee."

"Don't have time for that. I gotta find my damn car and get home. I—Oh, shit."

Her stomach clenched again and the world tilted. She bent over and heaved.

The woman fished a packet of tissues out of her pocketbook and handed some to Mandy, who swiped at her mouth. "Hon, you got no business behind the wheel. Why don't you call a cab?"

"I don't have time to wait for no cab. I gotta get home."

"In the condition you're in, you may not make it home. You don't care about yourself, at least think about the other people on the road. People with kids they may be going home to. You want to make some kid an orphan?"

To her amazement and shame, Mandy felt tears bubble up behind her eyes at the mention of children. In her drunken state, her emotions were magnified and close to the surface. Getting drunk had always had that effect on her—made her bawl over nothing at all. But this wasn't nothing. She thought about Emily and Dakota. Five hours earlier she'd stalked out the door, thinking that she'd be back in twenty minutes, her original intention having been to drive to the 7-Eleven for a six-pack. Somehow she'd ended up at the Tap, her two little kids all alone in the house while their piece-of-shit mother drank herself blind. Anybody found out she'd done this, she'd lose them for sure. They'd end up with Kevin.

Mandy realized the woman was right. She was too fucked-up to drive. She might get herself killed, or at the very least locked up for the night with another DUI on her record. She couldn't let that happen.

"Look, could you . . . I mean, I don't have anybody I can call to come out here this time of night. Would you give me a ride?"

The woman hesitated. "Where do you live?"

"Not too far from here. In I.B."

"Imperial Beach? That's not really the direction I'm headed in, but . . . sure, what the hell. I'll feel safer just knowing you're not on the road." She stuck her hand out. "Name's Billie. You?"

"Mandy."

"Pleased to meet you, Mandy."

Another barfly, pugnacious and paunchy, with a looking-to-kick-some-ass gleam in his eye, lurched out of the Tap. Billie cast an uneasy glance in his direction. "Come on, I don't want anybody to think we're looking for a hot date, us standing out here. Let's get in my car."

Wordlessly Mandy followed her, her mind spiraling downward in drunken loops. She wasn't worried so much about how she'd get back here to pick up her car tomorrow morning or about the job at Stellar Dry Cleaning that she'd lost the week before, or the rent that was due, but she'd started to obsess that, after their argument on the phone, Kevin had come to the apartment to continue the fight and discovered the two babies alone. He'd raise holy hell and get custody of the kids for sure. And the worst part would be knowing it was what she deserved.

Exactly what she deserved.

"Here you go." Billie unlocked the passenger-side door of a boxy, German-made car with an interior so spacious and plushly upholstered Mandy thought it could probably accommodate a homeless family of five. "If you need to barf again, let me know in time so I can pull over."

"I ain't gonna barf."

"Well, you never know." Billie reached back and unclipped her hair, which tumbled to her shoulders in thick, honey-blond waves. An expensive dye job, Mandy thought, feeling resentful because her own peroxided mane had a half inch of brown roots showing.

"So why the rush to get home? Husband due back from a business trip, baby-sitter out past her curfew?"

"Yeah, something like that."

"Which?"

"Either. Both." She pulled a face. "God, I hate throwing up. My mouth tastes terrible."

"Look in the console. There're some breath mints."

Mandy opened the console, pulled out an unopened tin of peppermint Altoids, and started to peel back the cellophane. As she did so, her eyes drifted down to the crevice where the passenger seat met the side of the console. Something shiny was wedged there—a gold coin or maybe a piece of jewelry. Something that looked like it could be worth something. Probably the woman didn't even know it was there, wouldn't miss it. Because Mandy had already decided this woman had it all—money, looks, a great car. One knickknack more or less wouldn't mean shit to somebody like her—if it did, she'd be taking better care of it.

Billie put the BMW into gear. The big car glided out of the parking lot, cutting off a pickup truck that honked in protest, and pulled out onto H Street.

"Not to pry, but I'm curious now—do you have a husband at home who's gonna be mad if you aren't back soon?" Billie asked.

"No. Used to, though." Mandy let her left hand slide closer to the niche where the coin or whatever-it-was was visible. "No-'count piece of shit. Thankful I'm shed of his sorry ass."

"Any kids?"

Mandy felt like she was being grilled and resented it, but maybe that was the price for the ride home, she thought. Maybe in return for the favor, Billie felt like she had the right to amuse herself with the details of her passenger's personal life. If that was the case, she wasn't going to get shit.

"No kids," she said.

"Lucky you."

"Why lucky?"

"Well, for one thing, you'd either be paying a sitter or you wouldn't be out enjoying yourself—well, maybe *enjoying*'s the wrong word—but you wouldn't be out on the town."

"Yeah, right."

The first tendrils of paranoia curled hotly along Mandy's spine. She sat very still, but her adrenaline started to buzz. Was the woman a fucking psychic? Did she know Mandy had two little kids left home alone? Was she a spy sent from social services? Mandy decided to ask a question of her own.

"The Tap—that don't seem like your kind of place. You go there a lot?"

Billie smiled again, this time without showing her teeth. "Off and on. It's the kind of place I got used to as a kid. Guess you could say my mom and dad were barflies. I grew up in El Centro and we had a bar about a block from my house that was a lot like the Tap. Several of them, actually."

"You mean you lived in a white-trash neighborhood is what you're saying."

If Billie was offended by the remark, she didn't show it. "We weren't all white—there was a Korean family up the block—and some of us were trashy, but not all. We were like people everywhere else—you had your good, your bad, your in-between, no more psychotics than your average neighborhood."

"Huh?"

"Joke."

Mandy slid her fingers down between the seat and the console, so she could feel the edge of the coin or the locket, whatever it was.

"So you cruise around in a sixty-thousand-dollar car, but you drink at the Chula Vista Tap—that's a hell of a jump, wouldn't you say?"

"Yeah, it is. Maybe too much of one, huh?" She shrugged and then gave a small smile. *"Il faut qu'une porte soit ouverte ou fermée."*

As though to punctuate whatever it was she'd said, she hit the gas and careened through a yellow light at the corner of Third Avenue and H Street, the BMW garnering appreciative glances from a couple of winos sharing a bottle of Thunderbird in the alley next to a Pollo Loco chicken joint.

The effect of the foreign phrase was to instantly piss Mandy off. She felt heat in her face and the alcohol working its evil alchemy, opening up floodgates of self-pity, paranoia, and insecurity. She'd barely scraped through high school and hated being in the presence of people who flaunted their education. They made her feel like a jerk and a rube.

Before she could think it through, she heard herself say, "Hey, stop the car! I want to get out!"

Billie's head swiveled around. Her eyes were wide, and she looked genuinely alarmed. "Why? What's wrong? Are you going to be sick?"

The woman's confusion pleased Mandy. A smirk crawled across her face. "What the fuck did you just say? You making fun of me? What the hell language was that you were talkin' in?"

"Oh, *that*! God, I'm sorry, honey." Billie looked stricken at having offended her new friend. "It's a French proverb that my husband uses sometimes. It means 'a door must be open or closed.' "

"Huh?"

"The idea is that there is no middle ground. That's all, honest. It just popped out of me after what you said about there being quite a jump between my two worlds. It kind of seemed appropriate."

"Don't see how it could seem appropriate if the person you're talking to don't understand what you're saying."

"You're right. You're absolutely right. I said as much to my husband the first time he used it on me. I apologize."

"So you weren't making fun of me?"

"Of course not. Why would I do that?"

Mandy's anger was rapidly turning into embarrassment. Now she *did* feel like a fool. "Sorry. I never took French. Guess I musta missed that day in school."

"Don't worry. I missed a few days myself."

They drove the next couple of blocks in silence, passing an assortment of fast-food joints, pawn shops, and hole-in-the-wall corner bars that made the Tap look high-class, until Billie said, "I always forget what a gas guzzler this car is. I thought I had a good quarter of a tank left, but if I'm taking you all the way to I.B, we'd better stop."

Mandy would've just as soon kept going, but said, "Sure. I need to take a leak."

Another block farther on, they spotted an Amoco station on the corner doing a brisk business. A Chevy low-rider was just pulling in loaded up with Chicano kids, Spanish music blasting out of the stereo, and Billie stopped at the pump behind theirs. While Billie filled the tank, Mandy got out to use the rest room. When she came out, Billie had paid for the gas and was going into the rest room herself. Mandy got in line behind two of the Chicano kids, who were buying big sacks of Doritos and six-packs of beer. She bought a hard pack of Marlboros. When her hand dipped into her back pocket for her money, she felt the cylinder of pepper spray pushed down next to her wallet and remembered the assholes who'd heckled her outside the Tap. She almost wished one of them would have tried something; she'd have liked to see the fucker's expression when she gave him a good blast in the face.

She paid for the cigarettes and went back to the car, which Billie had pulled around to the side of the station. She had time to light up and take a couple of quick drags before she saw Billie coming back from the rest room.

"I swear, I've got a bladder the size of a bean. I feel much better now."

"Me, too," said Mandy, a small smile in her voice as they drove off that only someone who'd known her for years would have detected. In her pocket was the gold object she'd just fished out of the crack next to the console. In the dark, she hadn't been able to tell if it was some kind of foreign coin or jewelry or what, but something told her it had to be worth something.

Hell, thought Mandy, feeling not the least bit guilty over having just ripped off someone who was doing her a favor, *that was easy. Maybe my luck's gonna change.*

Just as the thought went through her mind, two things happened in rapid succession. The first was that Mandy noticed an odor in the car that she hadn't been aware of before—a cloying, sweet fragrance that she associated with blue-haired old ladies tut-tutting and clucking in the front pews of the First Baptist Church of her childhood.

The second was that a man wearing a stocking over his head sat up suddenly from where he'd been crouched

down in the backseat and jabbed a small, snub-nosed
revolver into the back of Billie's neck.

"Oh, Jesus." Billie gasped. Her foot slammed the
brake and she twisted the wheel. The car swerved into
the oncoming lane, then veered back to the right. The
man leaned close and shoved the muzzle of the gun
under Billie's hair. He said, "Just do like I tell you, bitch,
and you might be okay. Make a left turn at the next
corner. There you go. Now left again. We're turning
around."

His squashed, horror-flick face clocked toward Mandy,
reading her mind, as he said, "Don't even fucking think
about jumping out. You'll be dead before your hand hits
the door handle."

"Don't hurt us, please," Billie said. "I've got money."

The man said nothing, but a harsh, wheezy sound that
might have been a laugh passed his lips.

"Just drive where I tell you."

A moment later, Mandy felt a round, cold kiss of
metal as Stocking Face rammed the gun into her cheek.

"What is it, you bitches out trolling for cock? Or
maybe the two of you's lezzie lovers?" He grabbed
Mandy by the hair and jerked her head back. "You look
like a slut. How much come you sucked down in your
life? Bet it could fill up a bathtub."

"Leave her alone," Billie said.

"Shut up!" Stocking Face roared, and whacked Billie
in the side of the face with the hand that wasn't holding
the gun. Her head snapped to the side. For a second
Mandy thought she was going to crash the car, but she
got it under control and kept driving.

The next ten minutes, while Billie followed the man's
directions, were the longest of Mandy's life. They left
Chula Vista and turned onto Bonita Road, heading east
and then south onto Otay Lakes Road. Mandy kept
praying someone in a passing car would see the gun
pressed to Billie's head, but the man kept it hidden behind his body. She thought of jumping out, but Billie,
probably out of nervousness, was going too fast and, in
an ironic twist of bad luck, the lights all seemed to
change to green as they approached.

On Otay Lakes Road, they sped south, past scraped, dust-bowl landscapes of tract homes under construction, before the road veered east again and they headed out into open countryside. Here, tall black hills crowded the narrow, twisting road, and the only headlights that penetrated the darkness were their own.

Mandy stared into the night, trying to see something that would indicate where they were. She glimpsed a sign for Lower Otay Reservoir and a few miles farther on, another sign that gave the mileage to Jamul and Dulzura, towns Mandy had never even heard of, that might as well have been in Bosnia for all she knew.

"Left here," Stocking Face ordered, and Billie swung the wheel, the headlights illuminating a dirt track that quickly became winding and rutted. In places, it climbed steeply into brush-covered hills. In others, it was almost too narrow to pass through—tree branches thumped the windshield and scratched at the doors.

Finally, at a place where the headlights revealed a clearing in the brush, Stocking Face told Billie to stop and give him the car keys. When she complied, he ordered both women to exit the car from the driver's-side door. Billie got out first, then Mandy, who deliberately took her time. Angered by her slowness, the man grabbed her by the hair with his free hand.

"Stop it!" Billie shrieked. To Mandy's horror and amazement, she lunged for the gun.

"Hey!" The man released Mandy's hair. His fist came up and he backhanded Billie across the face. She toppled across the hood of the car and lay there, gasping.

Still holding the gun on Mandy, Stocking Face reached into the backseat of the car and came up with a long coil of rope.

Despite her panic, Mandy tried to get a look at him. The fact that his features were flattened and misshapen by the stocking gave her hope—if he didn't want them to see his face, maybe that meant he intended to let them live—but she got a sense of his body. Maybe five-ten or -eleven, muscular. The scent she'd noticed first in the car was stronger now—not like any aftershave she'd ever smelled, a feminine scent, some kind of perfume.

"Both of you, walk ahead of me," he ordered. "And don't even *think* about making a run for it. First one moves too sudden gets a bullet."

With Billie walking ahead, they trudged off into the thick brush where larger trees—elms and sycamores and gnarled, bent oaks—loomed up over the scrub like thick phalluses emerging from pubic locks. Moonlight glimmered metallically across the trail and webbed the foliage in filaments of silver. Mandy's head spun with terror and the lingering effects of the alcohol still percolating in her system.

How much farther? she thought.

They walked for what felt like hours, but might have been as little as fifteen or twenty minutes. Suddenly Stocking Face grabbed Mandy and shoved her against a tree. He ground himself against her, let her feel his size and hardness.

He turned to Billie. "You try anything again like you did before and I'll kill you. Understand?"

Trembling, Billie nodded. Stocking Face stuffed the gun under his belt and bound Mandy's wrists together behind the tree. She felt the rope digging into her flesh, cutting off circulation.

He came around the tree, put his face to hers, and squeezed her cheeks between his thumb and index finger. "Lucky you, you get to watch. Try to enjoy it, 'cause you're next."

He aimed the gun at Billie. "Get naked. Everything. Off. Fold it neat. Lay it over by that tree."

The enormity of it hit Mandy then: They were both going to die, their bodies found buried somewhere maybe days or weeks from now. She would never see her children again. Never hold them or coo to them or cuddle them again. Her body might never even be found. Emily and Dakota would never know what happened to her, might grow up thinking she'd simply run off and abandoned them.

Her children would wind up with their father, who would create in Dakota his own callous indifference to the needs of anyone or anything outside himself while planting in Emily that perverse seed of self-loathing that, when she was older, would guide her unerringly into the arms and bed of a man as cruel as he. That would be the fate of her children. And for herself . . .

Fear lodged in her throat like a fistful of thorns. A terrible chill spread through her chest, and her blood seemed to turn to cold sludge. The pulverizing knowledge that she was almost certainly going to die cored her out, left her more acutely, terrifyingly sober than she'd ever been in her life.

All she could think was how desperately she wanted to live.

I'll change, she told God. *I'll do anything. Just give me another chance. Let me live.*

She started trying to work her wrists free, but found it was impossible—the rope wasn't tied into just one knot, but some complicated arrangement of several. She tried to get her fingers down into the pocket holding the pepper spray, but the little can was wedged too far down.

As Billie removed her clothing, Stocking Face moved up close to her. He wasn't holding the gun now, but something else, a tiny silver object that glinted in the moonlight. She heard a hissing sound and smelled the same scent she'd first detected in the car. Stocking Face was drenching Billie's body in perfume, moving the bottle up and down her body.

"Like this? You like it, don't you?"

Billie made a soft, whimpering sound.

"You're my little bitch, aren't you, Billie? I can do whatever I want with you. And you'll love everything I do to you, right? You'll beg for more."

Mandy must have made some involuntary sound, perhaps the beginning of a scream that she immediately bit back, because the man turned in her direction.

"Want some?" he asked, and sent a few puffs of scent in her direction. She shut her eyes and turned her face away, felt the unexpectedly cold tingle of gardenias on her cheek.

Then he turned back to Billie, who was naked now, shoulders hunched and arms folded across her chest.

In the darkness, she couldn't see what was happening to Billie, but she could hear the sound of flesh on flesh and Billie's moans and the man talking filth to her. She didn't let herself think of her children, because if she did, she knew she'd start screaming—hysterically, uncontrollably—and he'd have to kill her right then.

"You liked that, bitch?"

Mandy saw the man rising, heard the sound of a zipper going up. For a minute, she thought Billie must be dead. Then she saw her huddled down, her back against a tree, not fighting back at all now while Stocking Face tied her to the tree with the other end of the same rope he'd used to bind Mandy.

Oh, God, I'm next. She tried to will herself to be somewhere else, high up and far away in some remote corner of her mind, but she knew she had to be alert, to look for some chance to escape.

Stocking Face left Billie and came back to her. She didn't see the gun, but now he was carrying a knife. He held the blade to her face and dragged the metal down the side of her neck, around her ear, and under her throat.

"Which do you want inside you first—me or *him*?"

His mouth was inches from hers, his breath pristinely fresh, minty. She almost released a hysterical laugh—had he prepared for this as if he were going on a date?

Then the knife was gone, and he slipped behind the tree, began untying her wrists.

Now, she thought, *now.*

Her hand went to her pocket, found the spray canister, and inched it out with fingers numbed by fear and loss of circulation. Stocking Face grabbed her wrist and shoved her forward, not seeing the upward motion of her other arm as she swung the canister around toward his face.

It slid out of her trembling fingers and dropped to the ground.

Stocking Face halted. "What the hell was that?"

He bent down to retrieve the canister.

Mandy knew that she was going to die.

Chapter 2

Just before the phone rang, Ian McSwain was flipping ahead through the calendar, searching for a date two months in the future. Mid-October. Actually a little sooner than that. One month and twenty-six days. Nothing at all really, time-wise, he thought, when you've already sweated out almost two years. You blink your eye, and one month and twenty-six days have flown by.

The ringing phone jarred him out of contemplating the calendar. He snatched it up, superstitiously hoping that, because he'd been thinking of Lily, it might be her on the phone.

"McSwain and Capshaw," he said and waited a beat. Got silence for a reply.

"Hello?"

"Is this Mr. McSwain?" A woman's voice, soft and skittish-sounding. Not one he recognized.

"That would be me."

"The reason I'm calling, well, I kind of know Jenna—from the meetings and all."

"I see," said McSwain, as though that explained everything. His partner, Jenna Capshaw, was a recovering alcoholic—six years without alcohol. She still attended a lot of AA meetings, which seemed to be a breeding ground for lost causes who, from time to time, found their way to their office.

After another pause, the woman said, "Did Jenna mention I might stop by?"

"Guess she forgot. Were you calling to make an appointment?"

"Not exactly."

"Then . . . ?"

"Actually I'm across the street. In the phone booth outside the taco shop. I just wanted to make sure it was okay before I came by."

"It's kind of busy here now. Why don't you make an appointment?"

"It'll only take a few minutes."

McSwain glanced at the pile of paperwork on his desk and the even more intimidating mess on Jenna's desk, catercorner to his. He really didn't have time for this.

"Come on up," he said sternly.

"There is one other thing."

"What's that?"

"I came by yesterday, too, but I kind of lost my nerve. Actually, I wasn't sure how to get in. I couldn't find the door. All I saw was the door to Dave's Gym."

McSwain was used to that query. "That *is* the door. Just come in the gym and walk to the back. Anybody says anything, you're on your way to see us. There's a flight of stairs in the back next to the heavy bag. We're at the top of the stairs to your left."

"Oh." She sounded disappointed, like she had hoped for something tonier. McSwain was used to that, too. Some people didn't like the idea of having to walk through a smelly gym full of grunting, sweating, testosterone-fueled men when they went looking for someone to spy on their spouses, bring back a bail jumper, or snatch their kid back from an ex-husband currently residing in Romania. But less fancy digs meant less fancy prices, which made the temporary immersion in the wet gym sock smell a whole lot easier to deal with.

Not to mention, McSwain reflected, that being located in I.B. meant he could watch gigantic freighters, like floating cities, pass while he drank his morning latte at the Java Nook a few blocks up the street, or get splashed by a wave breaking over the seawall at high tide when he went jogging. Any lack of ambience in the neighborhood, the proximity to the gorgeous Pacific Ocean more than made up for.

"You still there?" he said into the silence at the other end of the phone.

"Yeah, I'll be coming up," said the woman, but her

voice lifted at the end of the sentence, turning it into a question.

"What's your—"

But she had already hung up.

Pushing back his chair, McSwain maneuvered around the side of his desk. He was a burly, broad-chested man who carried substantial muscle in his upper body and who moved with the alertness and confidence of one expecting to meet resistance at every turn and determined to deal with it. The beginning of a middle-aged paunch was starting to stake out its territory around his waist, and some gray had crept into his mustache over the last couple of years, but considering the high-stress nature of his work, he figured he was holding up pretty well for his forty-five years. The parts of him that some might have taken as evidence of a violence-prone career—the two-inch scar along one side of his jaw, the missing little finger on his left hand—were the result of injuries that had occurred long before he took up work as a private investigator, before he even got out of grade school, for that matter.

"Damn this thing," he heard Jenna say as he entered the second, smaller office and saw her leaning over the copy machine, glaring at it with a ferocity she usually reserved for lifelong enemies or clients who stiffed them on the bill.

"Problem?"

She looked up, short, curly hair framing a pale oval face whose only concession to adornment was a slash of coral-colored lipstick and the suggestion of eyeliner. She wore loose-fitting jeans, a man's workshirt, and biker boots with little silver chains across the heels. When she first joined the security firm where he was then working, McSwain had felt mildly guilty for thinking she looked like a dyke, until he got to know her and realized other people thought so, too, especially real dykes, who hit on her almost as frequently as guys.

She combed a hand through the tangle of chestnut hair that framed her face like some kind of wild foliage. "This thing's fucked-up again, Ian. We got any screwdrivers around, maybe a hammer?"

"Why, you going to fix it?"

She made a fist with her left hand—her dominant one—and mimed punching the machine. "Dismantle it maybe. Destroy it. Reduce it to rubble. But fix it? I don't know." She stood back, cocked her head slightly. "Don't tell me you came in here to copy something?"

He shook his head. "You got some woman coming up."

"I don't know. Do I?"

"It wasn't a question; it was a piece of information. She's on her way now."

"Who is she?"

"She didn't say and I didn't get a chance to ask, but she says she knows you from the meetings."

Capshaw's eyebrows did that almost imperceptible jiggle, meaning that she was attempting to access some interior file. Apparently she came up empty. "I don't know who—"

There was a knock on the outer door. McSwain went to get it.

"Mr. McSwain?"

The young woman extended a hand. She wore khaki shorts and a white T-shirt with a picture of a dolphin and the words *Sea World* on the front. Her brown hair was cut short and feathery, giving her round face an elfin appearance. From her right ear dangled a pair of small crosses, from her left a single gold hoop.

McSwain shook her hand. She glanced at him briefly, then peered past him into the office as though trying to determine if it was safe to go in.

He moved to one side. "Come on in."

"Where's Jenna?"

"Right here," said Jenna, coming into view and smiling in an overly enthusiastic way that told McSwain she had absolutely no idea who this person was.

Still looking as though she might bolt at any minute, the young woman came into the office and took a chair across from McSwain's desk. Capshaw took the other. McSwain leaned against his desk.

"We talked at the morning meeting last winter," the girl said to Capshaw. "I'd heard somebody say you were a private detective. I told you maybe sometime I'd stop by your office, and you gave me your card."

Capshaw's forehead creased briefly before recognition set in. "I remember you now—you look really different. Better, I mean. You changed your hair, didn't you?"

"Cut it short, yeah, and let the natural color grow out. Plus, after I quit drinking, I put on a few pounds. When I talked to you back in February, I'd only been sober a couple of weeks."

"Haven't seen you around lately."

"I got a job at Donut Delite over on Sweetwater, so I mostly hit meetings at night."

"I'm sorry my memory's not better," Capshaw said. "Your name's . . . ?"

"Mandy Sutorius."

"What is it you need us to do for you?" McSwain said.

Mandy sat a bit straighter, cleared her throat. "I need you to find someone."

"A missing person?" said McSwain.

"Kind of. I'm not really sure. One thing, though, I should tell you up front. I don't have any money."

"That could be a problem," said McSwain. "We don't work for free."

Mandy crossed her legs and swung one sandaled foot nervously, as though keeping time with an invisible metronome. "Finding this person might not take very long. I could pay you in installments or something."

"The person you want us to find," Capshaw said. "Who is it and why do you think finding them might not take long?"

The sandaled foot stopped swinging in midair. "The person I need you to find is a woman who I saw get raped. I figure it may not take very long because she's probably dead."

After that, McSwain and Capshaw kept silent and let Mandy tell her tale—the night at the Chula Vista Tap, the woman named Billie, the man wearing a stocking over his head who took them out into the woods.

"I thought I was dead," Mandy said. "I had the pepper spray in my hand, but I dropped it, and when the guy bent down to get it . . ."

She'd been talking nonstop for ten minutes and paused now to collect herself before going on.

"When the guy bent over to pick up the spray can, I

brought my knee up between his legs, and when that doubled him over, I brought the other knee up into his face."

"Way to go," Capshaw said.

"I didn't think it would work. When he fell down, I couldn't believe it. I've thought about it a million times, what I should have done. I should've grabbed his gun, but I wasn't sure where it was, and I knew he had a knife, too. If he grabbed me, I knew I was gone. I had on cowboy boots, and I kicked him in the head."

"You knocked him out?" McSwain said.

"Stunned him maybe. He had his hands up to his face like he was trying to pull the stocking off—I think I broke his nose with my knee, and then when I kicked him, the eyeholes in the stocking got moved around—but I knew if he got it off and I saw his face, then for sure he'd kill me." She looked up, almost hopeful, first at Capshaw, then McSwain. "I mean, I'm right, aren't I? I'da seen his face; he'd've had to kill me?"

Capshaw nodded, but McSwain figured she was thinking the same thing he was—a deal like what Mandy was describing, a rape that had clearly been planned, the fetishistic spraying of the perfume, this guy was going to kill both women anyway.

Mandy covered her face with her hands and muttered something McSwain couldn't make out.

"What was that?"

"It should've been me. Not that other woman. She should've gotten out of there alive. I should've died."

"Why do you say that?" said Capshaw.

"Because when she saw the guy down and me with my hands free, she started screaming—begging me to help her. I could see her face in the moonlight—the fear in her eyes. I was that close to her." She paused and looked down at her hands.

"And?" McSwain said.

"I ran. I just ran and kept running, and I never looked back. I left that poor woman there with that maniac. She was only a few feet away—it might only have taken a few seconds to untie her—but I didn't even try. I didn't think I had time. I ran away and left her to die."

"It's easy to be a hero in hindsight," Capshaw said.

"At least you were able to fight back and escape. A lot of people would have been paralyzed with fear; they wouldn't have been able to move."

"I've told myself that, too. I've turned it all different ways. Like what good would it have done Billie if I'd tried to untie her, but I was too slow, and the guy killed us both? And what did I owe her anyway? I didn't even know her. She was just a stranger who gave me a ride, and I was in the wrong place at the wrong time. I think the guy was out to get her and didn't realize I'd be in the car, too. The guy knew her name—I heard him call her Billie—maybe she'd done something to get him mad at her. Maybe she cheated on him or ripped him off."

"In your opinion, was this guy hiding in the backseat from the Tap on or did he climb in when you stopped for gas?" said McSwain.

"I think he got in at the Amoco station. That was when I first smelled the perfume."

"And you're sure you didn't use Billie's name before he did—either before you knew he was back there or during the attack?"

"I don't think so. But then, if it was someone she knew, wouldn't she have tried to reason with him? At least said his name?"

"Maybe, maybe not," Capshaw said. "She might have felt it was safer to pretend not to know who he was."

"When exactly did this happen?" McSwain asked. "Do you remember the date?"

"January eighteenth. It was a Thursday. The next day I bought a newspaper and looked for some kind of story, and I watched the local news for a week. I never saw anything about a body being found or a woman disappearing." She stared for a while at the detectives' licenses on the wall, the piles of paperwork. McSwain and Capshaw waited out the silence. "You think because there wasn't anything in the paper or on the news, that means maybe she didn't die?"

What McSwain thought was that it probably meant the body hadn't been found, but he kept that opinion to himself and asked a question of his own.

"I'm confused about something, Mandy. I can understand your panicking and running away—anybody might have done that—but why didn't you go to the police afterward?"

She winced like she'd been expecting the question, but still wasn't prepared for it. "First thing was, it took me hours to get back to the road and flag down a ride. I was still drunk and I couldn't find my way back to the road. There was a stream that I walked in—for hours, it seemed like—and it led to a dirt road and then finally back to Otay Lakes, where I hitched a ride. But by then it was almost morning. I figured whatever'd happened had already happened at that point."

Capshaw and McSwain looked at each other, silent. Mandy toyed with one of her earrings.

"That's not the real reason, though," she said finally. "The real reason is if I went to the cops, they'd find out how I ended up in that woman's car in the first place— that I'd been out drinking and left my two kids home by themselves." A note of defiance crept into her voice and she looked at McSwain almost challengingly. "You know what they could do if they found out I'd left two babies all alone while I went to a bar? You know what my chances would be of keeping my kids?"

McSwain, unmoved, said nothing. Capshaw shook a Parliament Lite out of the pack on her desk and lit it.

"No chance in hell," Mandy continued. "The state would take my babies is what would happen. And they'd end up with my ex-husband, who's a mean-tempered son of a bitch when things go his way and really bad when they don't, which is most of the time." She gave a short, rueful laugh. "I know what you're probably thinking, a match made in heaven, right? But I love my kids, and I couldn't take the chance of losing them. I couldn't go to the cops."

"So what do you think?" said McSwain. "If Billie's still alive, I guess that must mean she left her kids alone at home, too?"

Mandy looked up. "Huh?"

"Because she didn't go to the cops either, right? If she had, you'd have read about it in the paper and the cops would've been trying to track you down as a witness. First place they would've looked is the Tap."

"I haven't been back there since that night."

"But the point is, apparently Billie didn't go to the cops, either," said Capshaw. "You've told us why you didn't, but if she made it out of there, why didn't she?"

"Because she's dead," Mandy said. "I'm an idiot coming here. As soon as I left, the guy killed her."

"Probably," McSwain said. "That's usually the way those things work. But then again, you threw a monkey wrench into things when you got away, so maybe he panicked, too. Maybe he went back to the road, stole Billie's car, and got the hell out of there."

"And left her alive," Mandy said.

Capshaw nodded, but her expression said she believed the woman was still alive about as much as McSwain did. She drew on her cigarette and exhaled, fanning the smoke toward the partially open window. "If this has been troubling you so much, why didn't you talk to a private investigator before now? You waited all this time before coming here. Why?"

"I hoped I could just forget about it. That if I cleaned my life up and got clean and sober, that would be enough, but I can't stop thinking about what I did. I promised God if He'd let me live, I'd change, and I have. But sometimes I still feel like I don't deserve to be alive, like I need to punish myself. Last week I did. I got sick of the dreams where she's calling to me, so I said, To hell with it; I can't stand this; I'd rather be dead. I took the kids to my mother's and went to a bar. I stayed drunk for two days. Worst of all, I went driving around."

She paused as though waiting for some reaction before pressing on. "I was in a blackout, and when I came out of it, I was wandering around up at Torrey Pines."

"The nature preserve?" McSwain said. "Any particular reason why you'd go there?"

"As a kid, I used to ride the bus up there when things got bad at home. I used to think maybe I'd just go up to the bluffs and throw myself off." She gave a small, self-conscious laugh. "Dumb, huh? I was so hammered I don't know if I was looking for Billie or the shortest way down."

"So you think if you don't take some action to ease your conscience, you'll drink again?" Capshaw said.

"That, or go back to Torrey Pines and see what it feels like to fly. Either way, I end up dead. You know what they say; 'You're only as sick as your secrets.' I thought I could live with mine, but I can't. I need to know what happened to that woman I left in the woods. I *have* to."

She unzipped a pocket on her purse, pulled out the medallion, and handed it to McSwain. "I thought this might help you find out who she was."

"What is it?"

"I'm not sure. It was in her car."

"She gave it to you?"

Mandy shook her head. "I stole it. I know that was wrong, but I used to do things like that. I don't now."

"The 'S.S.' on one side," McSwain said. "I guess those could be the woman's initials. And either the middle initial is 'V' or the Roman numeral for the number five. But what the hell is that on the other side?" He passed the medallion to Capshaw, who put on a pair of wire-rimmed reading glasses to study it.

"It looks like some kind of puzzle," said Mandy, "but I couldn't figure out how to solve it."

"I wonder if somebody wants us to think they already did," Capshaw said. She gave the medallion back to McSwain. "Check this out. You've got what looks like a labyrinth and then one of those lines from upper left to lower right going across it, like you see on all kinds of signs, where all you've got is the symbol for whatever the forbidden activity might be—a crossed-out cigarette for 'no smoking,' a crossed-out dog for 'no unleashed dogs,' whatever."

"But just drawing a line through it wouldn't be solving anything, would it?" said Mandy. "And how would you solve it anyway? What's the point?"

"Well, normally you don't solve a labyrinth; you just go from the outer rim and work your way to the center and back out again," Capshaw said. "But what the significance is and why the line is crossed through it, I haven't a clue."

She took off her glasses and handed the medallion back to Mandy, who looked disappointed. "Don't you want to keep it? I mean, it's a major clue, right?"

"We haven't really said we'd take the case yet," said McSwain. "First of all, a lot of time has gone by. It's a cold trail. Second of all, we're pretty swamped at the moment."

"At the very least," said Capshaw, "we'll have to discuss it."

"Whether we agree to take the case or not, though," McSwain said, "you have to go to the police. Tell them what you told us."

Mandy rocked back in the chair. "No way! I thought the 'P' in PI stood for private. Private fucking investigators."

"If you're going to curse, can you hold it down a notch?" McSwain said. "The boys downstairs in the boxing gym don't go for that kind of language."

Mandy's lip curled. "Now you're making fun of me."

"I could be, but actually I'm not," McSwain said. "Guy who owns the gym's trying to recruit more women, give the place a better atmosphere. There's a sign of rules on the wall, if you had time to glance at it when you came through. Number eight is 'No swearing tolerated.' "

"Fuck that," said Mandy. "I'm not down there. I'm up here. And I ain't going to the cops. They find out what I did that night, they'll take my kids for sure."

"That's the chance you have to take," McSwain said.

A hardness came into her eyes that added ten years to her face. "Either of you got kids?"

"No."

"Then you don't understand. I know what you're thinking—you're thinking if my kids meant anything to me, why did I leave 'em alone in the first place, why was I out drinking when I shoulda been at home, and if I did do those things, it means I must not love them." She shook her head. "You'd have to be an alcoholic or a drug addict to understand. I love my kids more than anything, and I don't drink anymore—until last week anyway. I've done like I told God I would do—I've changed. But don't ask me to go to the police."

There was silence for a moment before Capshaw said, "Anything else you can think of? Anything at all that would help us decide if we might be able to help you?"

Mandy thought for a moment. "French."

"French?"

"She said something in French. Said it was something she'd heard her husband say."

"You know French when you hear it?" said McSwain, who wasn't sure whether he would or not.

"No, but I asked her. I got mad, 'cause I thought she was saying something about me. I made her tell me what she'd said."

"Which was?"

"Something about a door being open or closed. I remember, because when she told me what it meant, it didn't make any sense. I mean, what's a door got to do with anything? She said it's an expression her husband uses."

"She speaks French," said McSwain. "I guess that's something to go on."

Mandy glanced at her watch. "I'm working a double shift today, and I've got to get back. Here's my phone number and address." She pushed a folded piece of paper across McSwain's desk along with a couple of blue rectangles that looked like lottery tickets.

"What are these?" said McSwain.

"Coupons for a free breakfast at Donut Delite. It's kind of, like, you know, an advance."

"Well, what do you think?" Capshaw said when Mandy had gone.

"What I think," said McSwain, "is I hate cases like this. If we take it, we're gonna end up wasting our time, frustrating ourselves, and feeding into her obsession. If we don't, you're gonna make me feel guilty."

"I don't make you feel guilty. You do a good enough job of that on your own."

"Think she's telling the truth?"

"You don't?"

"I don't know. Hard to believe a person survives something like she described and doesn't tell anybody about it until this long after the fact. That's the first thing the police would be asking. Plus the fact that now you've got a second victim who, if she survived, evidently didn't go to the cops either."

"If she survived . . . that's a pretty big *if*," Capshaw said. "My bet is that she never left those woods alive, that her body's chopped up and buried in a bunch of different places in the woods or dumped into a river somewhere."

"That's how I see it, too. The kind of perp she described, he's not going to stop with just rape and his little perfume fetish. Covering his face, that was probably just for effect. I think he intended to kill both of them."

Capshaw stubbed out her cigarette in the ashtray on her desk. "Guys like that don't stop with one victim."

"Unless, of course, there was something about one of those particular victims—if Mandy's right and the guy knew Billie's name, then Billie was the target. Finding a second woman in the car with her could have been a bonus or a giant pain in the ass from his point of view."

"She seemed pretty sure he used the name without having heard it from her," Capshaw said. "That's the case, then the starting point of any investigation would have to focus on Billie."

"But Mandy was drunk and scared, so maybe she doesn't remember," McSwain said. "She might have used Billie's name at some point, and that's how the guy knew it. In that case, it could've been anybody, a random attack or somebody out to get Mandy. The ex-husband hires somebody maybe, so he can get Mandy out of the picture and take the kids. His friend sees her come out of the Tap, but before he can act, Billie gives her the ride. He follows, they stop for gas, etcetera, etcetera."

"If it was someone with a personal thing against either Mandy or Billie," Capshaw said, "that might be another explanation for the stocking. He didn't want to be identified, because he didn't plan on killing his victim—he was just into the power trip and the fun of brutalizing her."

"Maybe one of them was being stalked," McSwain said. "This Mandy, sounds like she got around a bit. How much you know about her?"

"Only what she told you today and the little bit I remember now from the meetings. Which I can't repeat outside those meetings. You know the drill; 'What you hear here, let it stay here when you leave here.' "

"Hear, hear," said McSwain, who wasn't entirely a stranger to twelve-step meetings himself. At Capshaw's recommendation, he'd been to a couple of Al-Anon meetings a few months back, thinking it might help him understand Lily, but found the litany of horror stories about alcohol- and drug-addicted loved ones had only confused and depressed him.

"Maybe we should talk to Mandy again," he said.

"That means we're taking the case?"

McSwain directed a beleaguered stare at his desk. "Well . . ."

"You want my opinion?"

"Like I won't hear it anyway?"

"I think we should pass."

"You do?"

"That surprise you?"

"Yeah, to tell you the truth, it does."

"Because she's in AA?"

"People who know you from the meetings have come here before, and you were always gung-ho to take on their cases—'Never turn away an alcoholic in need,' I heard you say once."

"I think that was referring to not turning away an alcoholic who wants to stop drinking."

"As opposed to what?" said McSwain.

"An alcoholic who's broke."

"Never seemed to bother you before."

"Maybe I've learned. Remember the guy who wanted us to help him find his missing wife, only when we looked into it, turned out she was at a women's shelter hiding from *him*? Or the woman who asked us to do a background check on her fiancé and got so upset when we told her he was already married that she went out and got hammered, then threw a screaming fit at the office? Not getting paid was the least of it; we were lucky we didn't get *shot*. I've gotten us burned one time too many trying to help out fellow alcoholics. I just don't want to go down that road again."

She eyed the piles of paperwork on McSwain's desk and hers.

"Not to mention the clients who *do* pay us and expect some results. We've got two skip traces, and that company over on Maddox—they sent us half a dozen background checks for people they're thinking of hiring. And they have to have that info back fast so they can make a decision."

"The background checks won't take much time," McSwain said. "The skip traces—we already know where one of 'em is, over at his mama's house in Pacific Beach just waiting to get picked up."

"So what are you saying?"

Before she could answer, the phone on McSwain's desk rang. He grabbed it, and tried to keep the note of disappointment from his voice when it wasn't Lily. It was two o'clock and her calls usually came in between two and three. Collect, naturally. McSwain's telephone bill was somewhere in the vicinity of a week's vacation in Aruba.

He chatted for a minute with the caller, an insurance company representative negotiating a settlement with a guy named Leonard Emerson, who reportedly worked part-time as a roofer when he wasn't appearing in court in a wheelchair. McSwain took a few notes, promised to call the man back, then hung up and turned to his partner.

"Yeah, I think maybe we should."

"Should what?"

"Take the case." Capshaw started to say something and he held up his hand. "You know and I know that if this guy grabbed Billie and Mandy at random, then this wasn't his first time and it won't be his last. Mandy got away because she was lucky. Billie probably didn't. Either way, I doubt if getting nailed in the nuts one time was enough to convince the guy to retire from raping."

"You don't mind that she can't pay?"

"Hell, no, I love poverty. It makes me feel noble."

"Plus I've never known you to turn down a damsel in distress."

"The least we could do is check with Hank Paris, see if any bodies have turned up."

"Or missing-persons reports," Capshaw said. "The kind of woman Mandy described—nice car, nice clothes, sounds like a decent person—she can't just disappear off the face of the earth without people looking for her."

"On the other hand," said McSwain, "what's a woman like that doing at the Chula Vista Tap?"

"You been there?"

"Picked up a skip there a few years ago. There was a fight in the parking lot before I even went in, and two guys got thrown out while I was there—and this was midafternoon."

"So the woman's out slumming," said Capshaw. "She's married, so maybe she's out to pick up a guy for a quickie before she heads home to hubby. Maybe hubby's out of town. More than likely, though, my money's on drugs. She went there to score."

"She also offered Mandy a ride, because she was too drunk to get behind a wheel. People out to score drugs aren't usually too quick to offer their services as the designated driver."

"Maybe Billie's the exception. Maybe she's a card-carrying member of MADD."

"As well as someone who goes to a seedy bar to score drugs?"

"Stranger things have happened. Wasn't Chula Vista where those three meth labs were busted last year? The Tap sounds ideal as a center of distribution."

"Could be," McSwain said, though he couldn't help but wince inwardly at the reference to methamphetamines. Lily's life had been all but destroyed—and his own along with it—by her addiction to the potent, euphoria-inducing stimulant. "Guess it couldn't hurt to check it out," he said tiredly. "First, though, I think I'll pay a visit to Hank Paris." He canted an eyebrow. "Unless, of course, you want to do it?"

Capshaw's eyes narrowed in mock disapproval. "Sure, I'd do it, but why torture the man?"

"S'what I figured."

"Give him my best, though."

"Always do." He looked past the paper pileup on his desk. "Where's that slip of paper with Mandy's number on it? If we're going to get involved in this, I'd like to have that medallion back."

"Oh, I wouldn't worry," said Capshaw, lifting the folded piece of paper off McSwain's desk and opening it up. Inside was the gold medallion with its crossed-out labyrinth.

"Guess she had a premonition," said McSwain.

Chapter 3

If the police department was trying to stay in close proximity to the criminal element of the city, then the location of SDPD headquarters was well chosen. Located east of downtown between Fourteenth and Fifteenth Streets, the imposing, concrete-and-glass structure sat like a sprawling bunker in the middle of several blocks of urban wasteland—empty lots awaiting construction, dilapidated apartment houses with barred windows and doors, and gone-out-of-business stores. McSwain flashed his badge at the reception desk and was routed upstairs to the third-floor Homicide division.

On the phone, Hank Paris said he could give McSwain fifteen minutes, which meant, if McSwain were lucky, he might get five. As he was heading toward Paris's office, the detective was rushing out, barking into a cell phone and carrying a Styrofoam cup that was dangerously close to sloshing coffee all over his wing tips.

When he saw McSwain, he made a hold-on-there gesture, glanced at his watch, and signed off on the cell phone, which rang again almost immediately. McSwain tried to be patient while Paris took the second call. He wandered back into Paris's office, a place so pristinely devoid of clutter, bereft of any and all extraneous objects, that McSwain wondered how he got any work done. He did notice something new, though—a framed photo of Paris's ex-wife and three kids that provided an unexpected personal touch.

"Sorry, McSwain, I don't have much time." Paris charged back into the room, set the Styrofoam cup down on a coaster, and started rubbing his jaw as though he'd just taken a mean uppercut. He was a lean, battered-looking man with a creased, sun-ravaged face and the haggard look of perpetual sleep deprivation. Even when he smiled, his flat, hard stare made McSwain think of an ex-con decked out in a well-tailored suit.

Briefly, he gave Paris a summary of Mandy's story.

"What I need," he concluded, "is to find out if there's been any missing-persons report filed for a woman answering this description or if a body's turned up."

"I need to talk to this woman," Paris said.

"She won't talk to the cops."

"Has she got an outstanding warrant or something? She use drugs?"

"Not that I know of. She just doesn't trust the police."

"Then I can't help her."

"No one's asking you to help her, but I thought you'd want to know about the perp. He sounds like the kind of guy you might be hearing from again."

"As far as missing persons, I'll have to check. As far as bodies, I can tell you nothing's turned up matching this woman's description. But I'm interested in a number of things in her story—the guy's MO, the way she was tied to the tree, the weird thing he did with the perfume."

"You run into anything like that before?"

"The perfume, no, but then again, we weren't checking for it. Perfume's mostly alcohol, so it wouldn't last long. And even if Forensics finds perfume on a woman's body, unless there's some reason to believe otherwise, they're going to assume it's just what she happened to be wearing when she was killed.

"But as far as the other stuff . . . well, you read the papers—we've had three women in the past eighteen months that were raped, strangled, and trussed in elaborate bondage positions either prior to or after death. Nothing simple about the knots this guy used to tie them, either. They were complicated, had to take him some time."

"Maybe he was a sailor," said McSwain.

"Or a Boy Scout. Which is what we've been calling him."

"The prior victims, were they murdered outdoors?"

Paris shook his head. "Only the second one, a day laborer named Jeanne Pendergast. Dark-haired woman, early thirties. She was living in a homeless shelter and was supposed to report back every night after work. When she didn't show up, nobody thought much about it—figured she went off on a bender, hooked up with some guy, whatever. A group of bird-watchers found her nude body in some underbrush. Coroner said she'd been trussed up so tightly you could have stuffed her body into a bread box."

"I remember reading about Pendergast," said McSwain. "Any chance Forensics noticed if she was wearing perfume?"

"This was last summer during that heat wave. She smelled to high heaven, but it wasn't Chanel."

"You said there were two others."

"One was killed in the spring prior to Pendergast. An unemployed mother of three named Dendra Gleason. Blond hair, early twenties. She was found in the basement of an abandoned house in Pacific Beach. The other one, Harriet Wynn, was a cocktail waitress with a heroin habit. Similar to Gleason in that she was found indoors—a vacant apartment building."

"Both bound as elaborately as Pendergast?"

"Yeah, but Forensics said it appeared they'd been tied up, then untied for the rape and strangulation, then tied again—more creatively—after death. Pendergast, on the other hand, was tied up while she was still alive. Unconscious, possibly, but alive." Paris shrugged. "Our boy likes knots."

"Wynn, when was she killed?"

"Late October. If this is the same guy, then your client and her friend would have been his fourth assault that we know of, and the first time with more than one victim."

"And he's bold enough that he doesn't mind killing outdoors, but he takes victims into abandoned buildings, too," said McSwain. "They were alive when they went in?"

"According to Forensics, yeah."

"Wonder how he gets them to go in there?"

Paris shrugged. "Your guess . . . maybe by force, held

a gun to their heads. Maybe offered them money or drugs. As far as we know, none of the women did any hooking, but two of them were low-income and liked to hang out in your dirtbag-type bars. Maybe not real particular about the company they kept."

"I'd like to take a look at the forensics reports of the three victims," McSwain said. "Could that be arranged?"

"I'll work on it," Paris said, "but I need to talk to that girl. If this is the same guy who killed these other women, then her friend's probably dead, but she's the only person we've got who had a run-in with this guy and lived to tell about it."

"She didn't see much," said McSwain. "It was night; she'd been drinking; he was wearing a stocking."

"Tell you what," Paris said, "I'll run a check for a woman matching the description of the second vic, but you talk that girl into coming in and making a statement."

"So between you and me," said McSwain, "you think there's any chance this Billie woman made it out of those woods alive and just didn't go to the police?"

Paris rubbed a hand across a stubbled jaw that still bore the scars of old acne. "Anything's possible, but if your girl's telling the truth, I'd say there's another body out there somewhere we need to be looking for."

"She said Billie was taking her home to I.B. from Chula Vista when they stopped at the Amoco station. Then the guy pops up in the backseat and makes them turn around and go east, ending up out on Otay Lakes Road, headed toward Jamul. Exactly where they turned off the main road, though, she's not sure. After they stopped, the guy walked them through the woods for maybe half a mile."

"Any chance she could find the place again?"

"I asked her that. She's willing to try, but she doesn't think she could find it. When the guy was marching them into the scrub, her mind was pretty much on the gun at her back."

"You said after she got away, she ran through the woods till she came to a road and then hitched a ride. Anything that would help us find the person who picked her up? He could verify her story, maybe even remember where it was that he stopped for her.''

McSwain shook his head. "She said it was a guy in an SUV, but she doesn't remember the make or anything about the driver. She told him she'd run her car into a ditch and needed to get to a pay phone so she could call her mother to come pick her up. Which is what she did, apparently, but her mother wasn't home or wasn't answering the phone, so she called a cab from a convenience store in I.B. Got home about dawn, slept for twelve hours, tried to convince herself it was all a bad dream.''

Paris rubbed his jaw. "I still don't see why—"

"There is something else, though," McSwain interrupted. He described the medallion with the labyrinth and the initials S.S., leaving out the part about how Mandy'd come to acquire it. "Does that mean anything to you?"

Paris shook his head. "The labyrinth? Didn't that have something to do with Greek mythology?"

"Yeah, guy named Theseus. I looked it up. Killed a bull-headed monster who lived in the labyrinth. Went home a hero.''

"Greek mythology, who the hell knows? My ex-wife's into goddess jewelry. She sculpts these busty little figurines out of some kind of Play-Doh shit, hangs them on a chain and calls them Athena amulets. Takes them around to craft fairs. Sells a shitload of the things, or so she says.''

"Goddesses, huh?" said McSwain.

"So why not a labyrinth is all I'm saying? Doesn't necessarily mean anything that would help us find this woman.''

"I thought maybe if my client could sit down with a sketch artist, they could come up with a drawing. Fax it to police agencies around the country.''

"Based on what?" Paris said. "Your secondhand account of what some girl supposedly said? For all I know, she's on drugs. A mental case. Bring her here to be interviewed and then we'll talk about a sketch artist.''

Paris checked his watch for the third time in as many minutes. "Don't let me keep you," McSwain said.

"Sorry, McSwain, I got a partner out sick and an abscessed tooth I'm gonna have to take a pair of pliers to if I can't get to the dentist today."

McSwain slid back his chair. "Well, thanks for talking. You'll run that check and let me know if anything turns up?"

Paris nodded, got up from his desk, and headed for the door. McSwain walked out with him.

When they reached the point in the hallway where they were about to part company, Paris said, "How's Jenna these days?"

McSwain had to conceal a smile—he'd just won a bet with himself. It had been almost three years since his partner and Hank Paris had carried on a short-lived affair that seemed to have meant more to Paris, who was fresh out of a divorce, than to Jenna. He didn't know the details of the breakup and didn't want to; only that Jenna had ended it and Paris had apparently never stopped resenting her for doing so.

"Jenna's doing good."

"She seeing anybody?"

"I don't know. She doesn't share much personal stuff."

"Figures."

"I'll tell her you said hello." He turned to leave and got a few paces down the hall before Paris called him back.

"McSwain?"

He turned around. "Yeah?"

"Do me a favor. Don't."

Outside SDPD headquarters, the breeze had changed direction. Even at this distance from the water, McSwain realized he could smell the ocean. Not the sewage-tainted odor that occasionally emanated from the beach near his office in I.B., but ocean as it was meant to smell: fresh, invigorating, briny. When he and Lily had lived north of San Diego in the house in Leukadia, he used to jog on the beach every day and see spectacular sunsets from the window of the upstairs bedroom. In Leukadia, he'd weighed twenty pounds less and got a headache only if he sparred too many rounds with the wrong guy at Dave's Gym. Now the headaches came with the regularity of telephone solicitors wanting him to switch long-distance service—anytime after four o'clock in the afternoon, he was prey to them.

He glanced at his watch, saw the headache hour was only a half hour away, and decided to try to forestall it by courting indigestion instead. He bought a hot dog from a Hispanic vender with a pushcart, heaped it with relish and onions, and watched a pair of tanned, sleek young women gliding past him on Rollerblades, each radiant with the kind of perfection McSwain associated with only two things: airbrushing and youth.

His cell phone rang as he was getting back in the car. A quick glance at caller ID told him it was from Lily, and for a moment he was warmed, not just by the sun streaming in the Monte Carlo's driver's-side window, but by a small wave of pleasure. After almost two years of their living apart, Lily still had the power to do that to him. Sometimes he thought that made him a lucky man, other times that it only proved, as Jenna put it, that he was so deep in denial he might as well be on a boat trip through Egypt.

He punched a button on the cell phone and the recorded voice he now knew as well as his own mother's went into the familiar spiel: "You have a collect call from an inmate at the California Institute for Women. If you want to accept the call, you can push one; if you do not want to accept the call . . ."

He pushed the appropriate button, then rolled the window all the way down, so he could still smell the sea, and, if he closed his eyes and listened only to Lily's voice and not the traffic whizzing past, pretend he was still back in that bedroom in Leukadia.

"Honey, hi!" It pained him that she always tried to sound so cheery, so *up*—as if she were calling from a day spa or on her way back from aerobics class. He knew it was an effort she made for his benefit, to keep him from worrying about her. Lily had suffered from depression for most of her life. More than once, he'd seen her sink into that place she called her "black hole," that dark night of the mind where hope does not exist and just getting through another day feels like running a marathon through Death Valley. At times in his life, McSwain had experienced deep grief and crushing sadness, but he knew little of the soul-numbing depression that Lily described.

Now he tried to sound as upbeat as she did—failing badly and knowing it—as he said, "Hi, Lil. How you doing?"

"Same old, same old, what can I say? Hey, what happened yesterday? You said you'd come."

"I know. I got tied up. I'm sorry."

"It's okay. Probably better you weren't here anyway. Becky drove up."

"Your sister?"

She laughed gently. "No, Ian. One of the other dozen Beckys we know. Yes, my sister, who else?"

"I thought she told you she has to do a couple of Valium just to get up the nerve to walk into a prison? Like as soon as she steps inside, there'll be a riot and she'll get taken hostage," he said, thinking that in such a scenario, he'd pay the ransom to whomever would keep her.

"Well, people have their quirks," said Lily. "You should know, Ian. You're claustrophobic."

He grumbled something.

"Anyway, I was happy to see her," Lily went on. "She and Tim just got back from a cruise. A month down the east coast of Africa. Athens to Cape Town."

McSwain shut his eyes, had visions of his sister-in-law showing snapshots of her and her husband romping on some exotic beach in God-knew-where, while Lily spent her days sewing dresses in the prison workshop, lucky if she saw the sky.

"Nice for Becky," he finally said.

"Look, forget Becky. And don't go thinking I'm jealous of her and Tim's lifestyle, because I'm not. I'll be perfectly content if I just see you this afternoon. Think you can make it?"

"I'll do my best, Lil. I can't promise, though. Jenna and I are working a new case."

"Try, Ian. Visitors that come late, you know they have to send somebody to go get whoever it is they're visiting, and you can grow old waiting. I don't have to tell you.

You know how it is; the guards don't like to have to make a special trip. They drag their feet sometimes just to be mean."

"I'll do my best, Lil."

"I know you will, honey. But it won't just be me that's disappointed if you don't make it. You know that real tall guard, Alicia?"

"Yeah, I do. Got a nice smile. Not a sourpuss like some of them."

"She thinks you're hot."

"Me?"

"For a middle-aged white guy."

"Isn't that racist?"

"It's ageist, too, but you'd rather she didn't notice you?"

"Hmmm. Well, on behalf of all middle-aged white guys, tell her I'm flattered."

"Tell her yourself when you get up here this afternoon. We'll neck like horny teenagers and I'll tell you how hot I think you are." She gave a soft, sultry laugh that made McSwain ache.

The girls on Rollerblades skated past the car again, glorious in all their Lycra-spandexed splendor, legs endless, manes wild. He caught a whiff of sweat and floral perfume, felt overwhelmed with longing.

"God, I miss you, Lil."

"I miss you, too."

"Everything we used to do . . . little things . . . making pancakes together on Saturday morning, renting a movie and snuggling up on the couch, driving up to Encinitas and eating lobster at that place where none of the waitresses speak English. I took things like that for granted before."

"But you never took me for granted. You were a wonderful husband, Ian. I was the one who fucked up."

He could hear the self-recrimination in her voice, a kind of bottomless sadness that always lurked just below the upbeat exterior she tried to project. It frightened him, the knowledge that she still carried within her that capacity for bleakness and despair and self-hatred. He was convinced that what had made meth so attractive to her in the first place was its promise of temporary elation and energy, a manic and short-lived joie de vivre that was, in the last analysis, anything but.

"It's in the past, Lil. Once you're out of there, we don't ever have to think of it again."

"How many days now?"

"Fifty-five. No, fifty-four. Too damn many, I know that."

"Not so many now. I can't believe you keep track."

"You don't?"

There was a pause where, in the background, he could hear someone yelling and someone else laughing harshly, a sound that was ragged and sharp, like the chops of an ax.

Lily said, "Does it scare you sometimes, thinking about how soon I'll be out? How soon our lives can go back to the way they used to be?"

McSwain started to say that, for better or worse, their lives would never be the way they used to be. You didn't get sent to prison for drug possession—or have a spouse who got sent up—and think anything would ever be the same. Hopefully, someday, with all kinds of hard work and luck and the grace of God, things might be good again, even better, but they would never be the same.

"You getting out, no, it doesn't scare me at all. It makes me goddamned joyful."

Her voice got small. "Sometimes it scares me."

"Why?"

"I want so much for things to be different now. I want to be a good wife to you. I don't want to drag you down."

He started to say she'd never dragged him down, but knew she'd catch the condescension and resent him for it.

"It's going to be hard," she went on. "Having a new house, getting used to each other again. I mean, not just us, Ian, other people, too. Our families. Everybody that knows what happened."

"Everybody who knows what's happened will be thrilled to see you come home. Anybody who doesn't feel that way, to hell with 'em."

"I always admired you for that, Ian."

"For what?"

"Being able to not give a damn what people think. I've never been that strong."

"You're strong. If you weren't strong, you'd never have survived this."

"I'm not as strong as you think, Ian."

There was a pause, during which McSwain had the feeling she was trying to work up her courage to tell him something, but his own fears about what that could be prevented him from wanting to press.

"About the house, Lil," he began. "I don't know if . . . There may not be a decent house we can afford right away. This is southern California. Prices out there would scare off Bill Gates. It may take some time."

She gave a wry laugh. "Well, if there's one thing I've learned in here, it's how to wait."

The cell phone filled with static, but at her end, Lily must not have heard, because she kept talking. McSwain caught only bits and pieces of sentences that slipped through the static occasionally, like a swimmer's head glimpsed above waves: "housing market . . . out of . . . release date . . . promise me."

He raised his voice. "You're breaking up on me, Lil."

"Love you . . . hon . . . talk to you soon."

"Yeah, see you tomorrow, Lil. I love you, too."

He hung up, plugged the cell phone into the charger, and thought of Lily hanging up the pay phone at her end and walking back to her cell. Her pod, actually—that was what they called them these days, in the places that passed for your finer correctional institutions.

He tried not to think about Lily's release date—too distracting—and the affordable house he was trying to find—too depressing. Instead, as he took the ramp onto the interstate and headed south toward Chula Vista, he thought about the woman who'd been raped and was probably dead, and, either way, about the very slim chances of finding her.

Chapter 4

As soon as he saw the Chula Vista Tap, the headache that had been stalking McSwain for the last half hour pounced with full force and began rending his frontal lobe like a lion on a gazelle. A squat, windowless rectangle covered with peeling green paint, it sat on the corner of Third Avenue and H Street and had the grim, spartan look of a reformatory or a housing unit in some remote penal colony. At four o'clock in the afternoon, there were only a few vehicles in the parking lot behind the building—most of them junkers, Harleys, or pickup trucks sporting bumper stickers that proclaimed the driver's constitutional right to shoot anybody, anytime, anyplace.

McSwain drove past, then left the Monte Carlo on a side street half a block away, and walked back, coming in through the rear entrance off the parking lot.

Inside the Tap, the darkness contrasted blindingly with the sunlight outside, and McSwain stood for a moment, letting his eyes adjust to the sensation that he'd just stumbled into a troglodyte's lair. When he could see again, he made his way past the pool table and pinball machine and took a seat at the end of the horseshoe-shaped bar. From his vantage point there he surveyed the clientele, which was primarily male and consisted of older, down-and-out types who looked like they might be one shot away from an aneurism, and younger, muscular blue-collar workers with the fuck-you stares and belligerent body language of men who were either currently out of work or only a paycheck or two away from entering the ranks of the unemployed.

"Son of a bitch, oughta blow his goddamned brains out," snarled a female voice with a three-pack-a-day rasp.

McSwain looked toward the other end of the bar and saw that the bartender, a lantern-jawed woman with dyed, jet-black curls, was talking to one of two TV sets positioned at angles above the bar. A teary-eyed woman in a red leather skirt and a pound or two of mascara was babbling about her boyfriend while beneath her a caption read: *Women Whose Husbands Slept with Their Sisters*. The bartender continued to harangue the screen, ignoring her patrons just as many of them ignored the TV, but stared into their drinks with the intensity of soothsayers getting a preview of doomsday.

"Take a shotgun and blow his balls out his asshole, that's how you handle it, honey," she snapped and turned around, directing at McSwain the kind of cynical gaze that suggested that he, being male, was somehow responsible for the wrongs being recounted on-screen. "What'll you have?"

McSwain ordered a draft. When the bartender brought it, he passed her a twenty and said, "Keep the change."

The big woman eyed the bill as though unsure whether or not to be insulted, causing McSwain to wonder exactly what it was she expected him to want in return. The images that came to mind were so repugnant he found himself glancing up at the TV, where the wronged sister was still bawling, and then down the length of the bar, where a bearded guy with the body of a sumo wrestler and legs like lollipop sticks was just settling himself on a stool. He was about the same height as McSwain, but twice as wide. He glared at McSwain, then at the bartender, and then at the TV, as though trying to decide which pissed him off most.

"I'm looking for a woman who was in here one night about the middle of January," McSwain said. "Wonder if you might be able to help me."

The pad of fat over the bartender's eyebrows furrowed. "What are you, a cop?"

"I'm not a cop. I just want to ask you some questions."

She gave a curt nod.

"The woman I'm trying to find is named Billie. Mid-thirties or so, slender, blond, shoulder-length hair. This one night she wore black jeans and a white T-shirt, and her hair was clipped up in the back."

The bartender glanced at McSwain's wedding ring. "She your wife?"

"Not my wife, just someone I need to find. A nice lady—kind of person who might give a ride to somebody who'd had too much to drink."

"A nice lady," the bartender said, grinning around the words. "Mister, you want a nice lady, try the church up the street." She directed a glance at a scrawny, gray-faced little man a few stools down from McSwain. His lank, bristly hair looked like it hadn't seen shampoo in days, and the jailhouse tats on his biceps were so faded and old they bled into the surrounding skin. "Hey, Milty, seen any ladies in here?"

Milty chuckled, showing teeth that leaned and toppled into one another like tipsy conventioneers. He poured a shot glass into his beer and said, "Of the night maybe."

"T'other kind."

"Aw, hell, Darlene, ain't no other kind. Some might tell you otherwise, but with their legs in the air, they's all the same."

"The woman I described," said McSwain, reclaiming the bartender's attention, "think you'd remember her if you'd seen her?"

Darlene's jowly neck compressed into rolls. "If she came in a few times, maybe. Woman in her mid-thirties and still decent-looking? Around here they peak at eighteen, and it's downhill from there." She glanced back at the TV, where the traitorous sister was explaining her side of the triangle to a chorus of boos from the audience.

"Back in January, how many other bartenders were working nights?"

Before she could answer, Milty wagged a finger in McSwain's face. Pronouncing each syllable with painful effort, he said, "One question I gotta ask—"

"Milty, shut the hell up!" Darlene scrunched her face

and picked at a pimple at the side of her neck. "Three bartenders if you include me, but I'm the only one still works here, and I don't remember anybody like you describe."

"What happened to the other two?"

"One's in jail and the other had some ex-wife troubles and took off."

"So they come and go?"

"Yeah."

"How about waitresses?"

"Look around. You see any food being served besides pretzels? We don't got no waitresses."

He started to ask another question, but before he could get it out, the bearded mountain at the other end of the bar brayed, "Hey, Darlene, how much they paying you to watch the TV?"

"About as much as they pay me if I don't watch it."

"Can I get another drink here or what?"

"Hold your horses, Merwyn." She took down a high-ball glass and filled it from a bottle of ouzo, added a shot of Jose Cuervo, and then ambled the length of the bar with the ponderous steps of one lugging a forty-pound weight.

When she made her way back, McSwain said, "How about a young woman named Mandy Sutorius? She come in here much?" He gave a brief description of Mandy as Jenna'd said she looked at the meeting back in February, rail thin and her hair bleached blond.

Darlene shrugged. "Any night, you got a dozen girls look like that."

"This woman has a couple of kids."

Milty's chin jerked up, a bleary connection being made behind his watery blue eyes. "Mandy?" He looked around as though she might have just walked into the room. "You talkin' about Randy Mandy? Always yak-kin' about her rugrats?"

McSwain nodded. "She been around in a while?"

Milty rubbed a bump on the bridge of his nose. "Naw, I figured she'd moved back in with her old man. That, or maybe got herself 'rested."

"Why? Was she doing something illegal? Did she come here to buy drugs?"

"Hey!" Darlene's head jerked around so fast McSwain heard the tendons in her neck pop. "What kind of a place do you think this is?"

"A fine establishment, to be sure."

Darlene scowled and blinked at the same time, as though dimly aware she was being mocked but uncertain exactly how.

She glared at Milty, and he seemed to wilt as she waddled down toward the other end of the bar.

Milty covered his mouth and whispered, "You don't want to piss her off."

"I'm doing my best to be charming. Now just between us, did Mandy come here to score?"

"Naw, nothin' like that, just . . . she sure liked her liquor. Sometimes she ran outa money before she got a good buzz, and a guy might buy her a few rounds if she was friendly. She was a real friendly girl, you know. So I thought she might've, you know, gave head to the wrong vice cop or somethin'."

He gave a high, cackling laugh. McSwain turned away, thinking of the neatly dressed young woman who'd come to his office and trying to shake off the image of what she'd been like in her previous life. Which hadn't been all that long ago, he reminded himself.

"When was the last time you saw her?"

"Not since last year. I remember 'cause I'd just had my hernia operation. I was still hurtin' and she bought me a Seven and Seven." He winked at McSwain. "Don't happen too often a gal buys me a drink. Thing like that, I remember." He stopped, squinted, took a pull from his beer. "Remember, yeah. Something I wanted to ask you; can't think now what it was."

"How often do you come in?"

"Hell, he's in here so much, the stool's shaped like his butt," said Darlene. She reached for McSwain's beer glass, but stopped when she saw it was still full. "Big drinker, ain't you?"

McSwain took out a card and handed it to her. "If this woman Billie comes in, give me a call. There'll be money in it for you if I find her or anybody who knows anything about her."

Darlene held the card at arm's length and squinted at it.

"Mr. Ian McSwain," she said, pronouncing each syllable as though it were coated with tar. "So you're a private detective."

"That's right."

"And you pay people to give you information about other people?"

"Sometimes."

"Well, fuck you, Mr. P fucking I." She stuck her chin out belligerently, ripped the card into quarters, and spat at the pieces as they fluttered to the floor.

"Guess you got something against private detectives," said McSwain. "What is it; you were married to one?"

Darlene's nostrils flared. "You know what a PI is? They're all cheats, sneaks, and scum. Dicks who can't make it as cops or even night watchmen, the fucking bottom feeders who've failed at everything else."

"In some cases, that's true," said McSwain. "I'm not one of those, though."

"Oh, no?" Darlene looked up and down the bar, raising her voice in competition with the TV. "This private dick here says he's not one of the bottom feeders. Anybody here believe that?"

Milty leaned over, grinning absurdly, and stage-whispered, "I remember now what I was gonna ask."

"Shut up!" bellowed Darlene.

Out of the corner of his eye, McSwain saw Merwyn shift in his seat and lean forward like a man ready to make a move. Milty must have read the body language, too, because he slithered off his bar stool and crept toward the back of the room with the exaggerated care of a man walking on sponges.

"The name Mickey Celeste mean anything to you?" said Darlene.

"Yeah, I know him."

"Yeah, you do know him. I remember your name. You're the one come in here and hauled him away. It's 'cause of you my son's doing hard time."

"I'm sorry about your son," said McSwain, although remembering Mickey Celeste, a third-rate drug dealer

and con man, he thought prison was the only fit place
for him.

Darlene reached under the bar, a move surprisingly
swift for so burly a woman, and came up with a sawed-
off baseball bat.

To his right, McSwain was aware of Merwyn easing
off his stool and moving between him and the door. He
glanced at Darlene and she tossed him the bat. He
caught it and moved in closer.

Heads snapped around like they'd been whiplashed.
For the first time, light glittered in the liquor-dulled pu-
pils of the men at the bar. Their flat eyes lit with antici-
pation and malice. They looked like caged sharks
watching chunks of meat tossed into the water: alert,
avid, malevolent.

McSwain stood up. "Before you use that bat, you
might want to take some things into consideration."

Merwyn gripped the bat with both hands. He took a
couple of short swings, like a batter getting warmed up.

"First of all, why the hell should you risk a prison
stretch because Darlene here raised a kid as lazy and
stupid as she is?"

A couple of sour smiles cracked the faces of the men
at the bar.

Darlene's already florid face flushed deep crimson, but
whether it was pure rage or the humiliation of knowing
what he'd said was the truth, McSwain didn't know.

"Second, if you weren't so tanked up, you might have
figured I'd have this. . . ." He brought his right hand
inside his jacket, letting Merwyn see the Smith & Wes-
son .38 Chief clipped to his belt.

"Fuck that," Merwyn said with a sneer, raising the
bat. The man was aching to charge him. Flecks of spittle
clung to his beard.

"Throw that down," said McSwain. "There's nothing
going on here worth getting a kneecap blown off for."

He gestured with the gun.

Merwyn glanced around as though looking for backup,
but at the sight of the .38, his buddies seemed to be
taking renewed interest in anything elsewhere. He
cursed and let the bat fall.

"Now back off. Anybody wants to come after me, you

can send your hospital bills to Darlene. I'm sure she'll be happy to pay."

He reached behind him for the door handle, yanked it open, and stepped outside, then stood to the side of the door waiting to see if anyone followed.

No one did.

He started back toward his car. As he passed along the side of the building, Milty came careening out at him from behind a Dumpster, clutching onto McSwain for balance and breathing whiskey into his face.

" 'Fore you go, gotta ask you that question."

"What?"

"Don't tell Darlene. She'd have my nuts on a fuckin' platter."

"There's a diner a ways up," said McSwain. "How about a cup of coffee?"

"Coffee?" He looked as though the beverage were unknown to him. "Hell, no! Wouldn't want to ruin my buzz before happy hour."

"Suit yourself. What's the question?"

The guy worried a patch of raw skin on the inside of his elbow. For a minute McSwain thought he'd forgotten what he was getting ready to say.

"About this gal name of Billie, you say—what the hell is it she does in bed makes guys so hot for her cooze?"

"What are you talking about? You know her?"

"Not personally, but I seen her. Day or two after New Year's, was a blond woman in here and a guy wantin' her to leave with him. He called her Billie. When she wouldn't go with him, he grabbed her by the arm and tried to pull her outside, so the bouncer comes over, tells him to leave."

"Did he?"

"Yeah, but you could tell he was steamin', and the woman looked scared. They had a history; you could see that."

"What did this guy look like?"

"Younger than you are, a lot thinner, but muscular. Had on one o' them tight shirts like the fags wear to show off their pecs. Had a mustache, black hair shaved close"—he paused, snickered—"had this big dick floppin' between his legs like I never seen before in my life."

"His penis?" McSwain said. "You saw it?"

"In the john, yeah. He was at the urinal next to me earlier that night." He held up a hand, teetering slightly. "Don't get me wrong; I'm not the kind makes a habit of checkin' out guys in the john, but this one, man, it was the size of a goddamned firehose and—check this out—it was tattooed."

"Tattooed?"

"Stem to stern, s'far as I could tell."

"Were there other tattoos on his body?"

"None I could see."

"When they were arguing, did the woman call him by name?"

"Unless his name's asshole, I don't recollect."

"Was this the last time you saw the woman?"

"No, saw her once after that. Couple weeks later. She was alone, just sitting at a table, having one o' them chick drinks you don't see women order much here, kind of a pink, sissy drink."

"She leave alone?"

"I don't know."

"How about the guy she was arguing with? Ever see him again?"

"Never. But he was a horny motherfucker, you could tell. He wanted that gal bad. Steam was blowin' out his nostrils when he left."

"Tell you what, you see either one of those people again, call me." McSwain dug in his wallet, produced a card. "It'll be worth some money, I promise."

He turned away, felt Milty's nails digging into his shirt sleeve, and resisted the visceral impulse to shove him away. "Yeah?"

"Hey, hold on, you never did answer my question— this woman Billie, the other guy wanted her and now you want her, too—is she some kinda great fuck or what?"

McSwain checked his watch as he got in the car and saw that it was later than he'd realized. Even if he drove like a maniac—which was the generally accepted standard on San Diego freeways—he wouldn't make it up to Corona in time to do more than peck Lily on the mouth before visiting hours were over. The worst part was, he couldn't call her to say he wasn't coming and apologize, because prisoners couldn't get incoming calls. He'd have to wait until she called him the following day.

Tomorrow, he thought, but the idea of Lily sitting there, waiting for him and being disappointed, weighed him down like a month's worth of bills. He was debating whether to try to drive up, after all, just as his cell phone rang. It was Jenna, her voice more subdued than usual with what McSwain had come to understand over the years was contained excitement.

"Are you still at the Tap?"

"Just leaving. Where are you?"

"Downstairs at Dave's ogling the hard bodies. I can't figure out why he has trouble getting women to join—they should pay him just to let them come in and leer."

"Is that what you called me for?"

"Not entirely. Where are you?"

McSwain honked and swerved around a Toyota straddling two lanes. "On the trail of a guy with, and I quote, 'a dick the size of a firehose.'"

"All by yourself? Like hell you are!"

"Only kidding. But I did want to ask you something—didn't you tell me you dated a guy a few years ago who worked in a tattoo parlor?"

"Eddie DeVito, yeah. He did the barbed wire around my ankle and . . . a couple of others."

McSwain tried to rein in his imagination. "Think you could find him?"

"Maybe. Why?"

"The firehose? According to a guy who claims to have seen it, the entire penis is tattooed."

"They *do* that?"

"Apparently so. But I would think it's unusual enough that whoever the tattoo artist was, he might have talked about it. Somebody in the business might know something."

"No shit. I'll see if Eddie still works at the same place."

"Great."

"You going up to Corona?"

"Too late now."

"Lily's gonna be disappointed."

"Hey, it's a two-hour drive. Not like running to the 7-Eleven."

"Okay, okay, don't get defensive. Think you could come over here?"

"Why?"

"Because while you've been out researching penises, I've been on-line. Ian, I think I found it."

"What?"

"Our labyrinth."

Chapter 5

Except for her own, the hard bodies Capshaw had talked about were all gone by the time McSwain arrived. The gym was closing up in twenty minutes and only two men remained—a puffy-jowled middle-aged accountant type with flabby, soft-looking biceps who was puffing away on one of the heavy bags, and a skinny teenager pawing at the speedbag like a cat batting at a catnip toy on the end of a fishing pole.

Dave Marquette, the gym owner and the only pugilist McSwain had ever met who'd studied Shakespeare at Oxford and who evinced a scholarly glee when conversing about the historic tomes in the Bodleian Library, was on the phone in his office. He was a stocky, dark-haired man with python arms and the thick Southern accent of his native New Orleans. When he saw McSwain, he put the phone down and beckoned him in.

"Hey, want you to meet someone." He indicated a heavyset older man with droopy, basset-hound jowls and a nose with as many twists and turns as a circular staircase. "Ian, this is Ricardo Delgado. He's my new night-watchman. I told him you and Jenna keep a couple of file cabinets down here, so if he wakes up and sees somebody rummaging around in the storage room, not to go for my gun."

Of the dozens of firearms Marquette owned, McSwain wondered which one he was referring to. He also guessed the reason Delgado had to use one of Dave's guns and not his own was that he was either a convicted felon, out on parole, or possibly unstable to the point where no gun shop would sell to him. In the five years that he'd known Dave Marquette, half a dozen different "night watchmen" had bunked on the sofa in Dave's office for anywhere from a few nights to a few months— it was the euphemism Dave used when trying to give a hand to someone who otherwise would be in jail, a homeless shelter, or sleeping on the street.

"Ricardo was a trainer for George Foreman," said Marquette, and launched into a detailed account of Delgado's fighting career, which sounded to McSwain a lot like Hobbes's definition of the average human life— "nasty, brutish, and short."

Marquette loved to talk boxing even more than he loved to discuss the merits of various handguns. He would have gone on all night, but McSwain excused himself to go talk to Jenna, who was working out on a heavy bag next to the stairs. She wore baggy shorts and a blue jogging bra. Her skin and hair were as wet as if she'd just stepped from the shower, and she hit the bag like she genuinely hated it.

She saw McSwain and threw one last combination, then held out her gloved hands so he could help her unlace.

"You look pissed off," McSwain said.

"Only at myself. I called the tattoo shop where Eddie worked, but he's not there anymore, so I got out my old address book and buzzed him at home. When I told her my name, his girlfriend said Eddie'd talked about me, and from her tone of voice, I gathered he wasn't telling her about my expertise as a gourmet cook. She said she'd tell him I called, but I'm not holding my breath." She dropped the gloves onto a shelf with others lined up according to size and began unwrapping her hand bindings. "Feel like a trip to La Jolla tomorrow?"

"Is that where our labyrinth is?"

"I don't know about a labyrinth, but there's a guy there we need to talk to. Tell me, does *The Stromquist Solution* mean anything to you?"

McSwain thought a moment. "Vaguely. Wasn't it some kind of theory in mathematics or physics that won the Nobel prize a few years ago?"

"Nice try, Ian. It's the number eleven book on the *New York Times* best-seller list, up from number fifteen two weeks ago."

"Is that what the S.S. on the medallion stands for? A book title?"

"You got it." Capshaw finished unwinding her bindings and hung them on a peg next to the gloves. "Come on; let me show you."

McSwain followed her upstairs, through the main office, and into the computer room. "I spent all afternoon checking out Web sites involving labyrinths—believe me, I had no idea labyrinths were such a hot topic."

"They are?"

"Evidently. There's the most famous one, of course, the labyrinth in Greek mythology where the bull-headed monster, the Minotaur, received human sacrifices. But there's also labyrinths painted on the floors of some churches—the Cathedral of Chartres is one of them. Pilgrims follow the path of the labyrinth into the center and then back out again. A labyrinth is laid out the way a spiral occurs in nature—think of a cross-section of a chambered nautilus shell or the rings made when you throw a pebble into still water. You walk a labyrinth slowly and meditatively as a kind of spiritual exercise. That's why the builders of a lot of medieval churches included them in the floor plan and why people still walk them." She paused. "I know what you're thinking—what has this got to do with *The Stromquist Solution*."

"Actually I was wondering what they do with the chairs."

"The chairs?"

"Every picture of European cathedrals I've ever seen, the entire floor looks like it's taken up with chairs. You wouldn't be able to see a labyrinth if it was down there, let alone walk it."

"You want to see a labyrinth?" said Capshaw. "Take a look at this."

She typed in an address, hit a key, and the Mac went to work. After a few seconds, a book cover appeared on the screen: a red labyrinth on a white field with the title *The Stromquist Solution* in black letters bisecting the labyrinth at a diagonal, upper left to lower right. Below that, the author's name: Leland H. Stromquist.

"That's the labyrinth on Mandy's medallion," said McSwain.

"Right. Except on the medallion, the labyrinth is crossed out by a plain line. For the book cover, the designers have gotten a little fancier and printed the title across the line."

McSwain leaned closer to the computer while Capshaw hit another key. The screen changed, this time showing a close-up of a dark-haired, middle-aged man with a close-cropped beard, narrow face, and that fierce, piercing stare that McSwain associated with stage magicians, con artists, and TV evangelists.

"Apparently he's not just a writer, but a motivational speaker, too. Travels around giving lectures and seminars on how to streamline your life by getting rid of most of the people in it." She reached around the computer, brought out a copy of the book featured on the screen, and handed it to McSwain. "I've only read the first couple of chapters, but I'd have to say what he calls his Ten Principles for Personal Freedom are very inspiring—if you want to live the rest of your life in the Gobi Desert."

McSwain scanned the inside of the bookjacket and read aloud: " 'The family is the birthplace of fear, repression, and mediocrity. Mandatory and unquestioning loyalty to family, friends, and origin are society's most insidious traps. John Donne wrote that no person is an island. He was wrong. We are all islands—alone, adrift, and reaching toward the past.' "

He closed the book. "Heartwarming. Guy must be a hit at Thanksgiving dinners."

"And guess what? He's based in La Jolla."

"Ritzy neighborhood."

"Yeah, so wear your best suit, because I think we ought to drop in and pay him a visit."

"So you think because Billie had a medallion with the Stromquist emblem or whatever it is in her car, this connects her in any significant way? Why should it mean anything except that she's one of however many people who bought the book and this Stromquist guy's line?"

"That's what I thought, too—until I read more of the Web site. There's more to this than just the book, Ian. There're lectures and seminars, too. A kind of hierarchy of achievement. For completing different courses, you get certificates of completion, but for completing everything—all the seminars and courses—you get a medallion like the one Mandy stole. A fifth-level medallion."

"And only a smaller, select group of people make it to that level?"

Capshaw shrugged. "I don't know. Maybe Stromquist's new on the motivational speaking scene, and his book's only just begun to take off. Even if he doesn't remember a blond woman named Billie who took all the seminars, she's got to be in his computer."

"It's worth a try," said McSwain. "Tomorrow morning?"

"How about afternoon? I called Stromquist Headquarters posing as a reporter wanting to schedule an interview. The woman who answered said to call back tomorrow after one, that Stromquist will be in his office then."

"Sounds good. Maybe I can call my realtor in the morning, see if she's come up with any more houses I might be able to afford that aren't out of state."

"Seller's market these days?"

"Not according to my realtor." He forced a smile. "I did look at a place in Carlsbad I might be able to swing. It's not as nice as the old house, but there's room for a garden out back and if you stand on the roof, you can actually see the masts of sailboats going by. I'm talking to the bank to see if I can qualify for a loan." He paused. "I really want everything to go right this time. I want Lily to be happy."

"Don't you think just being with you again will be enough to make her happy?"

"I hope so, but . . ."

The silence hung in the air between them. "You worry too much, Ian. These things tend to work out better if you don't try so hard."

"She's my wife. I can't *not* try."

"I'm just saying if you care so much about another person that pleasing that person starts to consume your life, sometimes it . . . backfires."

"Is that what happened with your marriage? The one you told me lasted eighteen months?"

"No." She glared at him, and he felt small and stupid

for trying to hurt her because she'd raised a possibility
he didn't want to think about, that too much of him
might be invested in Lily's getting out and in his hopes
for their future together. He knew Jenna didn't like to
talk about her long-ago marriage, so he was surprised
when she continued.

"Actually when I was married I don't think I cared
nearly enough. Or if I did, I didn't know how to show
it." Her voice got very small. "The way things ended, I
still don't know if I was to blame for it or not."

"You never told me how it did end."

She jabbed a few keys on the computer, exiting
quickly.

"Badly, Ian. Very badly."

According to the weather report, the entire coast from
Point Loma up to Carlsbad was socked in with fog, but
sunlight cast a golden glow over La Jolla's bistros, art
galleries, and boutiques. It reinforced McSwain's private
conviction that La Jolla was another world, and fog was
simply not permitted to exist here.

Beside him, Capshaw sat slumped in the passenger
seat, frowning and muttering under her breath as she
turned a page in *The Stromquist Solution.* As McSwain
searched for a parking place along La Jolla Boulevard,
she slammed the book shut, making a face like she'd
gotten a whiff of spoiled meat.

"What?" said McSwain.

"Want to hear one of this Stromquist guy's gems? 'Religion crucifies common sense.' "

McSwain considered it. "Well, the wording's strong,
but maybe he's talking about zealots with explosives
strapped to their backs, abortion-clinic bombers, that
kind of thing."

"I don't think so, Ian. I think he means that 'love thy
neighbor' is for wusses, and only do unto others before
they do unto you."

"And this guy's a hit on the motivational-speaking
circuit?"

"Doesn't exactly restore your faith in humanity,
does it?"

"What faith?"

He turned the corner onto a one-way street, spotted a parking place halfway up the block, and headed for it. At the same time the driver of a Ford Explorer in the next lane had the same idea and speeded up, preventing him from claiming the space.

"Now, you see, right there," said Capshaw, "that's an example."

"Of what? Poor city planning? Urban congestion?"

"No, hesitance to—quote—'assert one's entitlement'—endquote."

"To a parking place?"

"Right."

"What about the other guy's entitlement?"

She shrugged. "His problem."

"So what should I have done, raced the guy for it?"

"You wanted it, didn't you?"

"Not enough to risk his hood up my fender, no."

"But you didn't get what you wanted."

"It was a parking place, not a seat on the last lifeboat leaving the *Titanic*."

"Same principle, though."

McSwain rounded another corner just as a lime-green BMW was pulling out of a parking spot on his right. He pulled in, reached to cut off the motor, then looked at Capshaw. "You want, I could keep circling the block till I see the guy who took my space and punch his lights out. Is that what Stromquist recommends?"

"I don't know. I haven't gotten to the chapter on payback yet."

"There is one?"

"Not yet, but I wouldn't be surprised." She tossed the book onto the dash. "Seriously, though, I'm glad I bought this. I need something to prop the back door open so I can hear the phone when I'm out in the yard."

"That bad?"

"Let's just say if this guy had lived in fifteenth-century Italy, Machiavelli would've had some stiff competition."

"What a treat if we can meet him in person."

If the man's headquarters were any indication, McSwain decided the displaying of ostentatious wealth must be another of Stromquist's guiding principles.

Stromquist Headquarters occupied the entire top floor

of a three-story building on the corner of trendy Nautilus Street, where designer shoe stores, exotic art galleries, and eight-dollar-a-cup cappuccino bars prevailed. The first floor housed the Bank of Switzerland, the second was devoted to something called the Elite Language Academy.

On the third floor, subdued lighting, bright abstract murals, and a sonata by Bach greeted visitors as they stepped off the elevator. An elegantly attired receptionist with platinum hair coiled in a bun and a perfectly painted face looked up and smiled as they entered. Her mouth was the same shade of red as her nails, which looked sharp enough to draw blood.

"Ian McSwain and Jenna Capshaw to see Leland Stromquist," McSwain said.

The woman, who wore a small gold name tag that said *Fern,* consulted a dayplanner. "And your appointment would be?"

"We're private detectives," he continued, "investigating a missing person who we believe was associated with the Stromquist organization."

The receptionist's smile didn't falter. "And what would make you think that?"

"That's something we need to discuss with Mr. Stromquist."

"He's in a meeting. You'll have to wait."

"We can do that."

McSwain took a seat at one end of a sectional sofa while Capshaw perused a rack displaying tapes of Stromquist's lectures and brochures for his speaking engagements and seminars. He thumbed through a copy of *Architect's Digest,* but most of his attention was on the other people in the waiting room as he tried to get a feel for the type of personality attracted to Stromquist's self-help program.

Across from him sat a heavy young woman with straggly blond hair caught back with a band and a posture so erect that she might have been perched on a wire. She toyed with her hair, curling strands of it around a chubby index finger. To her right, a middle-aged man in Levi's and a chambray shirt hissed instructions into a cell phone the size of a cigarette pack. Stress gouged his face like old war wounds. To McSwain, he looked like a man whom life had passed over, but who hadn't quite realized it yet.

But it was the guy next to the cell phone talker that grabbed his attention.

Buff, tanned, and Nautilus-toned, the guy looked young enough to be in college, but sophisticated enough for a fashion ad in *GQ*. He had long, wheat-colored hair tied back in a ponytail and pale, predatory eyes that surveyed Capshaw like a potential real estate investment. He wore an expensively tailored suit that probably cost more than McSwain's monthly rent, and a pinky ring with a stone in it that looked like a garnet or an opal. The ring caught the light every time he raised his arm to consult his Rolex, which he did frequently and ostentatiously.

While McSwain was contemplating the dozen or so good reasons to hate this guy, a slender black woman in high heels and a pink suit came in and summoned the man with the cell phone. Ponytail looked up and tried to make eye contact with her, but to McSwain's surprise, she looked through him as though he were glass.

The woman's failure to acknowledge him appeared to agitate Ponytail into action. He lunged to his feet and charged the reception desk like a TV cop about to kick down a door. "I'm tired of waiting, Fern. He knows I'm here. I insist that he see me."

The red-lipped receptionist played with a pen. "Him?"

"Mr. Stromquist. Now." He emphasized the word *mister* in such a way that it came out sounding derisive.

"I'm sorry," said the receptionist, and from the tone of her voice, it sounded as though she genuinely was. "I'll page him again in a few minutes. Okay, hon?"

Ponytail took a deep breath, as though trying to compose himself. He muttered something McSwain couldn't make out and stalked back to his seat.

"Mr. Capshaw? Ms. McSwain?"

McSwain looked up to see a solidly built man who appeared to be in his mid-to-late thirties. Dark hair receding off a high, shiny forehead, a sharp nose with a prominent bump at the bridge. Dishwater-blue eyes.

"You've got it backward," said Capshaw, extending a hand.

"Ms. Capshaw. Sorry. I'm Richard Moxley, chief of security for Mr. Stromquist. You're here about—did I get this straight—a missing person?"

"That's right."

"Okay, well, Mr. Stromquist has a little time between appointments. He says he can see you if you'll keep it brief."

Moxley ushered them into a large corner office with a sweeping view of the Coronado Bay Bridge and Point Loma. Contemporary decor with a touch of the nautical—scrimshawed whale's teeth displayed in a glass case and a large replica of a frigate atop a bookshelf.

Leland Stromquist, seated behind a teakwood desk the size of a small barge and talking on a cell phone, barely glanced up as they came in. He was a slender, wiry man with graying black hair and goatee, and the clipped, rapid speech of one used to being in charge. He wore a pearl-gray silk shirt, matching pants, and an expression of vexed disdain that McSwain guessed was probably permanent.

"Sit down. He'll be with you in a minute," Moxley said, and stepped outside, closing the door behind him.

As soon as he'd left, Stromquist snapped the cell phone shut, a sound like a tiny guillotine falling. Without acknowledging his visitors, he strode past them and stepped out into the hall.

A moment later, Moxley reappeared, looking chastised, and posted himself wordlessly inside the door.

"Richard, please don't leave me alone with these people."

"We're not dangerous," said McSwain.

"Unless we need to be," said Capshaw.

Stromquist went back behind the big desk as though seeking a bulwark between him and his visitors. "You're the people claiming to be private detectives?"

"We are private detectives," McSwain said.

"So you say." Stromquist's frown deepened, and he massaged his goatee. His bright, fierce little eyes went from McSwain to Capshaw and then downward, toward a top drawer of his desk, then back to Moxley again. "Did you ask them for ID?"

"No."

Stromquist shook his head in disgust. "Jesus, man. A child would know to ask for ID." He looked at Capshaw and McSwain. "Do you believe I pay this man to protect me?"

Moxley's face remained impassive as he stared out the window behind Stromquist's head, but he shifted his feet uncomfortably. "Mr. Stromquist, I just thought—"

"Well, don't, Richard. Trust me, it isn't your strong suit." He studied the IDs Capshaw and McSwain were proffering. "These mean nothing. A child could get these over the Internet."

"That may be true," McSwain said. "However—"

"All right, sit down. I don't have much time. Be succinct."

"Succinct is our middle name," Capshaw said.

"My secretary said this has something to do with a missing person. Who's missing? More important, why would it have anything to do with me?"

"It probably doesn't," said McSwain, "but apparently the person we're trying to find was affiliated with your organization."

Briefly he described Billie, the car she was driving, the medallion his client was in possession of, and Billie's whereabouts on the night that the medallion had been lost, leaving out further details. As he spoke, he was aware that Stromquist fidgeted and seemed to have difficulty keeping his eyes off the desk drawer.

"Our client would like to return the medallion to its owner," said McSwain. "That's why she contacted us for help."

Stromquist steepled his fingers, adopting the look of a trial judge about to deliver an unfavorable verdict. "Richard, on second thought, I don't think you're needed here after all. Step outside, would you?"

Wordlessly, Moxley left the room.

Stromquist having dismissed his lackey, McSwain was hoping for some revelation, but instead Stromquist continued in a pedantic tone. "A medallion, you say? Do you have any idea how many medallions have been given out since I began these seminars? Anyone completing one of the seminars gets one. That would put the number at this point in the thousands."

"I've been reading some of your material," said Capshaw, holding up one of the brochures. "If I understand correctly, there are five levels of achievement outlined, and these levels correspond to five seminars that can be taken, the first seminar being the most basic, the fifth the most advanced."

"That's right."

"Then I would assume however many people take the first seminar, considerably fewer proceed through all the way to the fifth?" She unzipped a compartment in her purse and produced the medallion. "There's a Roman numeral five on one side of this—that means it was given to someone who completed the final seminar?"

Stromquist took the medallion and examined it as though he'd never seen one before. His expression didn't change, but the muscles of his jaw moved like marbles under the skin. "The woman you want to return this to, you don't know her name or anything more about her than what you've told me?"

"We were hoping to learn more from you," said McSwain.

"Let me get this straight. You said this client of yours—"

"—came into possession of it through a misunderstanding," said McSwain.

"And what is your client's name?"

"We have to keep that private."

McSwain tried to redirect the conversation. "What we need is a printout of names for all fifth-level female seminar graduates in the San Diego area."

"I can't give you that."

"Could you tell us why not?"

"For one, client confidentiality. Some people taking the seminars prefer it be kept private. Second, since you won't give me the name of *your* client, I must assume there's a reason for this—either your client stole this from its rightful owner and is suffering a belated attack of conscience or there is no client but some other, less palatable reason why you're trying to find this woman." He raised his head in a way that was designed to look imperious but more resembled a bantam rooster trying to see over a fence. "Either way, I can't help you."

"Hold on," said McSwain. "This woman was the victim of a crime. If she is or was involved in the Stromquist organization, that's irrelevent to us except as far as it helps us find her."

Stromquist's eyes narrowed and his gaze again veered toward his desk. "A victim of what kind of crime?"

"She was raped," Capshaw said. "She may have been murdered. But if she's alive, it's important we find her. She might be able to help the police get a dangerous criminal off the street."

"Raped? Possibly murdered?" For a millisecond, Stromquist seemed dumbstruck, as though some fundamental law of his universe had been contradicted and he was trying to fathom the ramifications. Then, like one who suddenly catches on that he's the victim of a practical joke, he began to laugh.

"Pardon me if I don't get the joke," Capshaw said, "but what the hell is so funny?"

"Well, clearly your coming here is some kind of . . . I mean, what is this? Did that nut Kreski send you? You're not on the level, are you?"

"Who's Kreski?"

Stromquist gave a dismissive wave. "Doesn't matter. I just thought—"

"Maybe we should start again from the beginning," said McSwain. "The part where we show you our credentials as private detectives and tell you we're investigating a case. Or maybe we should just hang around outside the elevator and start interviewing everybody who shows up here. See if one of your 'students' might remember this woman."

Stromquist raised his hands in a conciliatory gesture. "Now, now, I didn't say I wouldn't help you."

"Yes, you did," Capshaw said. "You said it would violate client confidentiality."

"Well, I'm making an exception," Stromquist said, "but only because I'm so sure your possibly murdered woman isn't going to be a match with anyone who's taken my seminars. I'll ask Fern to go through the files and see if any fifth-level graduates are in their thirties and go by the name Billie. Then I'll get back to you."

"When?" asked McSwain.

"When I can."

McSwain got to his feet. "We'd appreciate promptness. We don't want to have to come back."

Capshaw held out a hand. "The medallion, please?"

"Oh. Of course." Stromquist seemed to have forgotten he was holding it.

"We'll be waiting to hear from you," McSwain said, handing Stromquist a card. "Oh, one other question. I'm curious, Mr. Stromquist, why you need a bodyguard?"

"I think anyone in the public eye requires protection these days—myself more than most, as I generate a certain amount of controversy. Surely you know better than anyone how many deranged people there are in the world."

"Wonder if he's one of them," Capshaw said in a low voice as she preceded McSwain out the door, where Moxley had posted himself like a Buckingham Palace guard. Rather than go back into Stromquist's office, he fell into step behind them.

"Hope Mr. Stromquist didn't give you guys a hard time. He can be a real prick."

"Isn't that the theme of his book," Capshaw said, "how to be a real prick and succeed beyond your wildest expectations?"

Moxley shrugged. "I wouldn't know. I've never read it." He paused, then added, "Private eyes, huh? I always wanted to be a private eye."

"We hear that a lot," said McSwain. "It's not as glamorous as you think."

"Yeah, it is," Capshaw said. "We just don't like to admit it." She handed Moxley one of their cards. "Why don't you hang on to this, just in case."

"In case what?"

"In case you hear something, see something, in case a woman named Billie waltzes in here one day saying she lost her medallion and wants another."

Moxley's head bobbed up and down. "Sure, of course. I'd like to help any way I can." He started to say something else, but Stromquist opened the door behind them, clearing his throat loudly.

"Richard, I think they can see themselves out."

Moxley exhaled a muted curse. His high forehead

darkened a shade, but he turned and walked back up
the hallway toward Stromquist.

Back in the reception area, the too-good-looking guy
McSwain had mentally dubbed Ponytail sat with his legs
spread apart, elbows on knees as he appeared to study
his face in the shine of his Gucci shoes. When he saw
Capshaw and McSwain, he turned to the receptionist
and said, "These people are leaving. See if I can go
back now."

The receptionist pursed her lips, picked up the phone,
and whispered into it. She nodded, then turned back,
looking pained. "He says not today. He overbooked his
appointments. Maybe tomorrow . . ."

The knobs of Ponytail's aristocratic cheekbones
burned fuchsia. "Fuck him then." He turned quickly,
almost colliding with McSwain as he barreled out of
the office.

Capshaw caught McSwain by the arm. "Wait, I'm
going to buy some tapes." She selected a couple at random from the display rack, took out her wallet, and approached the reception desk.

"Oh, no charge," said Fern, handing Jenna a couple
of brochures as well. "You never know—you might
come back one day to take a seminar. Have either of
you read his book?"

"In the process," Jenna said, and Fern beamed as
though she were showing off pictures of her
grandchildren.

"The guy who just left," McSwain said, "he looked
angry enough to chew nails. Mind if I ask why?"

Fern glanced up the hallway toward Stromquist's office and lowered her voice. "Well, he was hoping to get
his job back. He got fired a few weeks ago."

"And with such a sunny disposition, imagine that!"

"It's sad, though. I feel bad for him."

"Why's that?" asked Capshaw.

"Well, he *is* Mr. Stromquist's son."

"And Dad canned him? For what?"

"I'm not sure. I've really said too much already."

Before either of them could ask anything else, a sleek
young couple with the monied aura of trust-fund kids got
off the elevator and Fern turned her attention to them.

Capshaw pocketed the tapes, and they took the elevator down. "What do you make of that guy?"

"The old one or the young one?"

"Either."

"Well, the old guy, I'd say, as a motivational speaker, the only thing he'd motivate me to do is punch him in the mouth."

"He sure seemed to have a change of heart when you started describing Billie."

"Yeah, enough to send Mr. Chief of Security packing."

"That desk drawer he kept looking at—think he had more than breath mints in there?"

"Wouldn't be surprised."

"Something else that bothered me—he seemed awfully quick to jump to the conclusion that the medallion had been stolen. Why would he think that? Wouldn't it be more natural to assume the owner just lost it?"

"I thought so, too, but then he's the type who expects the worst in people."

The elevator door opened and they exited past a group of Japanese who were entering the Elite Language Academy.

Outside the building, Capshaw paused to light a cigarette. When she spoke, her voice almost disappeared on the warm breeze wafting in from the ocean. "The laughing when you told him the woman we're trying to identify was raped and possibly murdered. That was fucking bizarre."

"Out of character, too. He doesn't seem like the type who shocks or surprises easily."

"You thinking what I'm thinking?"

"That he knows or thinks he knows who Billie is, but finding out what happened to her caught him by surprise. Or the only surprise was that *we* knew about it?"

"Which would be enough to shake him up either way."

They walked to the car, where Capshaw took a last drag off her cigarette before tossing it to the curb. "So what now?"

"I think we ought to talk to Mandy again." He glanced at his watch. "She should be at work now, but maybe she can take a break. I want to find out if she knows anything about the guy who was seen harassing Billie."

"The firehose?"

"Him, yeah."

McSwain hit the release button that unlocked the doors to the car, and got in.

"God, Ian, is that sunburn on the back of your neck or are you blushing?"

"It's hot, if you haven't noticed."

"Oh, I've noticed."

They sat in the car for a minute while McSwain got out the card with Mandy's phone numbers on it and rang Donut Delite on his cell phone. On what seemed like the fiftieth ring an annoyed-sounding woman answered the phone and said Mandy hadn't come in that day; she'd called in to say one of the kids was sick. He then called Mandy's home number and got a busy signal.

"She must be home then," said McSwain. "You've got her address. Let's head over there." He pulled out into traffic as a silver Rolls-Royce slid seamlessly into the spot vacated by the Monte Carlo. "So let me ask you something."

"Shoot."

"Why'd you buy the tapes of Stromquist speaking?"

"Hey, listening to him at night might help my insomnia." She reached into her bag, pulled out one of the cassettes she'd bought, and tucked it into the pocket of McSwain's jacket. "I got the impression the guy didn't like us too much. Maybe it wouldn't hurt you to listen to him either."

"Why's that?"

"Stromquist's Principle Number Seven: 'Investigate your enemies.' "

Chapter 6

A maroon Buick was stalled in the turning lane at the intersection of Delaware Street and Imperial Beach Boulevard, tying up northbound traffic for a couple of blocks. A one-armed man wearing rolled-up khaki shorts and a green-and-beige camouflage jacket was taking advantage of the situation. He strolled among the rows of cars, holding out a can for donations, occasionally exchanging a brief word with those who rolled down their windows and gave or directing a sour glance at those who didn't. Behind him, propped against the curb, a hand-lettered cardboard sign read: *Lost Arm in Gulf War. Out of work and hungry. Please give.*

Something about the man, maybe the jut of high cheekbones under leathery skin or the slicked-back black hair, struck McSwain as familiar. He turned around for a quick double take, but the light had changed and the man was crossing the street to cruise eastbound traffic.

Capshaw, walking next to McSwain, shortened her stride. "Something the matter?"

"No, just . . . oh, I don't know . . . thought I'd seen that guy somewhere, that's all. Can't place him, though. Now it's going to bug me."

"The only thing bugging me is why Mandy's phone has stayed busy ever since we left La Jolla."

"She likes to gab?"

"Yeah, but I don't like it. Could be her phone's off the hook."

"Yeah, I thought of that, too."

The address Mandy had given them was a four-story,

yellow stucco apartment building near the corner of Seventh Street and Grove Avenue. It was wedged between a music store called Freedom Guitars and Second Hand Jones, a used-clothing shop. Inside, the hallway smelled of kitty litter and cooked cabbage. A bank of mailboxes next to the stairs showed an M. Sutorius on the third floor. McSwain led the way.

Behind the door of 4B they could hear a kind of low-grade commotion, a child crying against a background of TV or voices, maybe both. He knocked on the door.

"Go away!"

"Mandy? It's Ian and Jenna."

There was a long pause. Then Mandy said, "Mr. McSwain? Jenna?" in a tone of voice suggesting that, up until that moment, she'd believed both of them to be trekking through Outer Mongolia.

"Can we come in?" said Capshaw. "We need to ask you a couple of questions."

"Sure, be right there."

"Guess we caught her at a bad time," McSwain said after they'd been standing in the hall for a couple of minutes. Jenna stepped closer to the door, her nostrils flaring as she sniffed the air. McSwain wasn't sure what it was she smelled, but he could tell by her expression she didn't like it.

Finally Mandy opened the door looking flustered, almost near tears. A blond baby with a runny nose was clinging to one hip, sniffling and clutching at a strand of her hair. At the sight of two strangers, he scrunched up his small red face and started to scream.

"Come on now, Dakota, don't. They're friends. It's okay." To Capshaw and McSwain she said, "Come on in, but excuse the mess. Dakota's got a cold, so I stayed home from work. Don't suppose I could talk either of you into baby-sitting?"

"We do enough of that already," Capshaw said. "Every time we have to transport a bail jumper."

"Yeah, but at least they don't cry all the time."

Something clicked briefly in the back of McSwain's mind, but he ignored it for the moment. "You'd be surprised."

"Yeah, maybe I would." She shifted the child on her

hip, fussing self-consciously with her hair and looking at McSwain as she said, "I must look like shit. I've been up all night with him."

"You look fine," said McSwain.

She smiled and used the back of one wrist to push the hair off her face. "Sit down. I'll be right back."

The living room was clean and sunlit, furnished in thrift-shop decor and littered with LEGO blocks and dozens of the bright plastic toys that McSwain recognized as the kind that came free with purchases from several fast-food chains. There were lots of photos of the blond baby that Mandy had been holding when she came to the door and a slightly older child, a toddler with brown hair and a cute underbite that gave her face her mother's elfin appearance. McSwain could see cartoons playing on a TV screen in the next room. He also smelled the faint, sweetish aroma of pot and realized that was what Jenna had detected as they waited outside the door.

When Mandy returned a few moments later, her hair was brushed, and she'd put on a streak of pink lipstick. She still carried the baby in one arm, but now a second child, a little girl, held on to her other hand. The girl wore tiny Farmer Johns over a blue LEGOLAND T-shirt with white flowers stitched around the neck. Her curly brown hair was caught back with barrettes.

"This is Emily," Mandy said, clearing some LEGO blocks off the plaid couch so she could sit down. "She can say her alphabet already. Can't you, Emily?"

The little girl giggled and put part of her hand in her mouth.

"She's cute," Capshaw said. "How old is she?"

"Two and a half. Dakota's almost a year. Both really smart kids, really good. Not like I was at all."

While McSwain was wondering how Mandy could have come to form that opinion, Capshaw said, "Your phone's been off the hook. Any reason for that?"

"Yeah, the telemarketers. You know how they can be. I just got tired of the calls and—"

"Don't telemarketers usually call in the evening?"

"Yeah, but . . ." She glanced toward the back of the apartment.

"I guess I must have took it off the hook and—"

From further back in the apartment they heard a harsh, hacking cough. Then a woman's slurry smoker's voice yelled, "She took it off the hook 'cause I kept calling. I got a right to call my own daughter, don't I? But she didn't want to talk to me. That's why I had to come over."

Mandy winced and said, "Oh, fuck."

"I heard that. Fine way to talk in front of children." A fleshy, round-faced woman with white-blond hair and a sweaty, pockmarked forehead stood grinning at them from the doorway. She wore a loose-fitting pink smock over beige tights and carried a rhinestone-studded tote bag slung over one shoulder. An unlit cigarette dangled from one hand.

"My mom," Mandy said. "Kelly Rohrbach."

"Pleased to make your acquaintance." The woman swayed toward McSwain, extending a red, puffy hand. When McSwain moved forward to give the hand a perfunctory shake, he got a lungful of the smell that emanated from her: a head-splitting combination of gin, perfume, and pot.

"Mr. McSwain and Ms. Capshaw are detectives, Mom. They're helping me find somebody."

The woman looked blank for a moment, then hooted. "A new husband, I hope. That last loser . . . hell, I coulda done better myself, and that's not saying much."

"Mom, please, you need to go home."

"You hear that!" Kelly braced her fists on her hips and turned toward Capshaw, who was already backing away from her. Failing to find any empathy there, she turned her small, red-rimmed eyes on McSwain. "She doesn't want to talk to me. Doesn't want to let me see my own grandkids."

"Mom, I never said that."

The woman went on, her voice rising. "Thinks I'm not up to her standards 'cause I still have a beer or a Bloody Mary now and then. Miss Perfection here, thinks she's so high and mighty now that she joined up with those teetotalers at AA and gave up booze for self-righteous bullshit." She turned back toward Mandy and said with a sneer, "You were a lot nicer when you was just another goddamned drunk. Anyway, I'm out of here. Just don't come crying to me when you get fired for missing work and it's 'cause you wouldn't let me stay with the kids."

She hoisted the tote bag higher on her shoulder and made her way to the door with the exaggerated caution of one walking on shards of glass. She missed on her first try for the knob, grabbed it on the second attempt, and walked unsteadily out into the hall, slamming the door behind her.

Mandy sank down onto the couch, the children crowding against her. Emily hid her face under her mother's arm. Dakota's round blue eyes were riveted on the spot Kelly had occupied just before she went out the door. Mandy said in a small voice, "Mom's not usually like that. You caught her on a bad day."

"She's not driving, I hope?" Capshaw said.

Mandy shook her head. "No, lucky me, she lives in the apartment house across the street. The kids are usually in day care, but with Dakota sick, I had to keep him here at home. She saw my car out front and started calling. That's when I took the phone off the hook. So she came over—"

"You let her come in in that condition?" Capshaw said.

"She didn't seem too drunk when she got here," Mandy said. "But she probably brought a pint in that bag. The joint, she was smoking that in the bathroom just before you guys knocked."

"This isn't a twelve-step call," Capshaw said, "so I'll keep the lecture brief. But having drunks around—especially drunks who happen to be your mother—is risky for you and dangerous for your kids. You're not doing her any favor either by putting up with her bullshit."

"I know," Mandy said. "I used to leave the kids with her when I went out drinking. She can't get used to the idea that things have changed."

"Well, things could always change back. I'm not trying to be mean, Mandy, just telling you the truth."

Mandy nodded, but an awkward silence, punctuated only by Emily's sniffles, hung in the air between them. " 'Scuse me a sec." She got up and returned with two Tootsie Pops. Dakota ignored the treat and continued to stare at the door his grandmother had just slammed behind her, but Emily snatched the candy with the desperation of the famished and popped it into her mouth. Her brown eyes looked huge as saucers and she seemed to be sucking the candy with the intensity of a chain smoker taking a drag.

"Me and the kids' dad used to argue a lot, and Emily gets scared when she hears people yelling," Mandy said. "I've told Mom to keep her voice down, but she forgets." She turned to Emily and said, "It's okay, honey. Grandma's not mad at you. She just talks loud sometimes." Pulling the child onto her lap, she smoothed the girl's hair back where it had come loose from the barrette and gazed into her upturned face with such pure adoration and, at the same time, such heartfelt sadness that McSwain felt like an intruder.

Finally, with Emily nestled into her stomach, her eyes starting to close, Mandy said, "I'm almost afraid to ask. Did you find Billie? Find out what happened to her, I mean?"

"No," said McSwain, "but we might be closer. A guy at the Tap—someone named Milty—remembers a man arguing with a woman we think might have been Billie right after New Year's. We don't know his name, but he had a mustache and dark hair that was shaved down to a stubble. A tough-looking guy, very muscular."

"That could be a lot of people."

Capshaw leaned forward to look at Emily and saw she was asleep before going on. "One thing that sets him apart from your average thug—his penis is tattooed."

"What?"

"Milty saw him in the john," McSwain said. "It's the kind of detail that would be hard to forget."

Mandy's face clouded as she processed this. "So what are you getting at? You just assume I've had sex with every freak ever walked into the Tap?"

"Nobody cares who you might or might not have had sex with," Capshaw said. "All that matters is that we identify this guy."

"Yeah, well, I think I'd remember that kind of tattoo if I'd seen one. Anything else?"

"One more thing," said McSwain. "Did you ever hear anybody at the Tap mention something called *The Stromquist Solution*?"

"The what?"

"It's a book written by a motivational speaker named Leland Stromquist," Capshaw said. "We went to see him the other day. The medallion that you took from Billie's car probably means that she or someone she knew took one of his seminars."

"I never heard of it," Mandy said. "As far as anybody at the Tap talking about it, forget it. Intellectual stuff, that doesn't go over real big there."

"This isn't an intellectual book. More like self-help."

"You mean like the books on Oprah's recommended list?"

"Probably not this one," said McSwain.

"Here, this'll give you a better idea." Capshaw took the brochures she'd gotten at Stromquist Headquarters out of her purse and handed one to Mandy. "Maybe something in here will remind you of something you heard at the Tap. You never know. Sometimes people who get heavily involved in some organization try to convert others."

"Yeah, like what Mom says I try to do with AA," Mandy said, smiling faintly.

"I guess we'll be going then," McSwain said.

"You're not giving up, are you?" said Mandy, looking suddenly unsure. "I mean, because I told you I never saw that tattoo?" Tears started to seep from the corners of her eyes. "Look, to tell you the truth, I don't know if I've seen it or not. I was drunk out of my mind whenever I was at the Tap. Maybe I did see it . . . I don't know." She rocked Emily on her lap and turned her face away. "That's what makes everything in the past so terrible—I never *know* what I did or I didn't do."

Capshaw went to the sofa and sat down beside her. "You had blackouts, didn't you?"

Mandy nodded. "All the time. People used to come up to me, tell me something I'd done or said; it was like they were talking about somebody else." She sniffed loudly and wiped the wetness from under her eyes. "So many things I don't remember, and the one thing I wish

I didn't—that poor woman calling for help—I remember that like it happened this morning. Every detail. I dream about her, I hear her voice. I see her everywhere I go."

"You see her?" Capshaw said.

"Women who look like her. The other day I followed a woman who was leaving Rite Aid, because I thought it was Billie. I had Emily and Dakota with me, and I ran to catch up with her, yelling at her to wait. When she finally turned around, she was, like, fifty years old. She looked scared, too, like she's thinking this screaming woman dragging around two little kids must be straight out of the psych ward." She stared at the dust motes spinning in a band of sunlight that slanted across the sofa. "Sometimes I just wish I could die, so I wouldn't have to hear her calling for help every time I go to sleep."

"Hey, don't talk like that," Jenna said.

"It's the truth. Sometimes I feel so guilty about what I did, I wish I was dead."

The words sounded genuine enough, and McSwain's heart hurt for her. Instead of leaving right away, he and Capshaw spent another fifteen minutes talking to Mandy, until she seemed calm enough that once more they stood up to go.

"God," said Capshaw as they walked toward the stairwell, "it scares me when I hear—"

A piercing shriek came from Mandy's apartment. They both turned and raced back. Capshaw shoved the door and it snapped open. "Mandy! What is it?"

She was sitting on the sofa where they'd left her. Emily was still on her lap, but now the little girl was yowling in response to her mother's scream, and Mandy was staring at Stromquist's brochure like she'd seen the date of her death written on it. She pointed to a photo on the inside. "It's her. Billie. Her real name's Virginia Stromquist. She's this guy's wife."

"I just wonder if Mandy's only seeing what she wants to see," McSwain said as they were leaving Mandy's apartment building a few minutes later. He was walking slowly, holding the Stromquist brochure and staring down at the photo of the woman Mandy had identified as Billie. The woman's blond hair fell to her shoulders, and her smile revealed teeth whitened to the brilliance of a ski slope, but most of the rest of her was obscured by her husband, Leland, who stood behind a podium with one hand raised theatrically.

"She did say she was predisposed to seeing women who resemble Billie in lots of different places," said Capshaw.

"But if it is her, it means Stromquist's lying through his teeth. No wonder he acted weird when we mentioned rape and possible murder. He knew it was his wife we were talking about. The only question is, Did he react that way out of shock, because it was all news to him, or because he didn't think anybody but him knew?"

"A return visit then?"

"As soon as possible. See if you can find out Stromquist's schedule for the next couple of days and where he lives. I'd like to see him on his home territory next time."

"And ask him if he just forgot to mention that he's a widower?"

"Something like that."

McSwain stopped suddenly, folded the brochure into thirds, and slipped it inside his jacket.

"What?" said Capshaw.

McSwain looked around. "I just remembered something I meant to do. Wait here a sec."

He crossed the street to where the one-armed guy was still soliciting donations from cars stopped at the intersection.

"Frankie, hey, how's it going?"

The guy started to smile, then frowned. "Who—"

"Hell of a thing, war," said McSwain. He held up the hand with the missing finger. "I mighta gone to 'Nam myself 'cept for this."

The man stared at the four-fingered hand as light dawned slowly in his eyes. "McSwain, look, I—"

McSwain slammed the guy backward, yanked the combat jacket up over his head, and twisted the left arm it had been concealing. Frankie yelped as McSwain applied more pressure.

"That's just phantom pain, right, Frankie? Gotta be,

since this arm I'm about to break off and whack you over the head with isn't really here."

"Jesus, McSwain, you're fuckin' killin' me."

He gave the arm a final twist and then let the man go. "I see you pulling this scam again, Frankie, I'm gonna do you a favor and bang you up so bad a twisted arm's gonna be the least of your worries. Then you can beg legit."

As he crossed the street, he saw Capshaw smiling. "Jesus, how did you know?"

"When you mentioned baby-sitting bail jumpers a few minutes ago, it jogged my memory. I had the pleasure of this one's company on a twenty-hour drive back from Topeka a few years ago. He had both his arms then, 'cause I cuffed 'em."

"Jesus," said Capshaw, "a fake amputee. What's the world coming to?"

"God only knows," McSwain said, "God only knows."

Chapter 7

After leaving Mandy's place, McSwain dropped Capshaw off at the office, saying he'd be back in a couple of hours. The episode with Frankie had inspired him to swing by the Bonita Road neighborhood where Leonard Emerson, the supposedly wheelchair-bound defendant in a current court case, was reported to be augmenting his income with roofing work. He also felt the need to take a break from Mandy's case, but found himself mulling it over anyway as he drove. If Mandy was right and Virginia Stromquist was really Billie, did that mean Leland Stromquist was protecting his wife from further trauma or covering up what had happened? On the other hand, he reminded himself that Mandy, by her own admission, was predisposed to seeing Billie in many different places.

Unfortunately, the insurance-scamming roofer was apparently taking the day off, but McSwain enjoyed the drive along quiet, steeply curving streets lined with handsome, beautifully landscaped houses set along streets with names like Bronco Court and Mustang Drive. Many of the homes had the red tile roofs, arched entranceways, and courtyards typical of the Spanish style that was Lily's favorite. He stopped in front of a house with a For Sale sign and debated whether or not to take one of the flyers from the box out front, then decided against it. Whatever such a house would cost would be far more than he could afford.

He got back to the office in the late afternoon and took in the final rounds of a sparring match in Dave's

Gym between a lanky Hispanic kid with a solid left hook and a black kid who seemed adept at avoiding it. Eventually Dave stepped in and called the match a draw, although privately McSwain thought the left-hook guy was the winner.

He went upstairs to the office to find Capshaw at her desk. She was talking on the phone and gave him a thumbs-up when he walked in. A minute or so later, she thanked whomever she was talking to, adding that yeah, she'd be careful, and hung up.

"So what's the news on the roofer? Did our paraplegic experience a miracle cure?"

"Either he took the day off to practice his wheelchair technique or he was fixing roofs in some other neighborhood."

"Well, maybe this'll cheer you up. I've got good news and bad news."

McSwain cleared a space and sat down on the edge of his desk. "And?"

"The good news is that Eddie's girlfriend told him I called, after all. That was him on the phone. He says the person we're looking for is a tattoo artist who owns a place called Xtreme Ink in National City—unless, of course, there's more than one guy whose penis is tattooed like a diamondback rattlesnake."

"So what's the bad news?"

"The bad news is that Eddie says the guy's name is Danny 'the Deacon' Tibbs and that he is one vicious dude."

"Danny the Deacon? That's not bad news. That's a disaster."

"You know him?"

"Only peripherally, but I was hoping to keep it that way."

"A tough-guy tattoo artist?"

"The tattooing is in addition to the Deacon's other activities—prostitution, loan-sharking, drugs. He's not the top guy in his organization, but he does a lot of the dirty work. Plus he's got entrepreneurial ambitions. Besides Xtreme Ink, he owns a topless joint called VaVoom."

"Xtreme Ink and Xtreme Kink?"

"That about sums it up, yeah."

"How do you know him?"

"Back when I first worked for Maverick Security—
before you came on board—we were hired to protect
a guy named Harry Orlando who'd rolled on Danny,
hoping to get Danny out of the way and take over
some of his action. The DA couldn't make the charges
stick, though, and Danny walked. On top of that, the
police didn't provide Harry with any kind of witness
protection program. So he was in deep shit, to say the
least, and he came to us. We got him set up out of
state, new name, new business, but then he decided to
come back to San Diego for his son Kevin's wedding.
Thought he could get in and out without Danny ever
knowing."

"Big mistake, huh?"

"Yeah." McSwain went to the half-open window and
raised it all the way, looking past the row of run-down
businesses across the street to the dark blue seam of
ocean that was just visible if he stood on his toes. "Actually Harry Orlando arrived at the church and made it
back to Vegas alive and well. But Kevin never showed
up. His body got fished out of the Batiquitos Lagoon a
couple of days later—shot in the back of the head before
he even got to go on his honeymoon."

"Jesus." Capshaw sucked in her cheeks as though inhaling an imaginary cigarette. "So if Billie was mixed up
with a character like that, then what happened to her
was almost inevitable?"

"That or something equally awful."

"You think Tibbs was the guy hiding in the car?"

"Him or a cohort. The sadism in the attack, that
sounds like his style."

"But what about those other women Hank told you
about, the ones the Boy Scout killed? If they were done
by the same person who attacked Mandy and Billie, and
if Tibbs is that guy, does that mean he's gone from being
just your average sociopath to a raving psychotic? That
now he's a serial killer?"

"Seems unlikely," said McSwain. "From what I've
heard of him, Tibbs is capable of anything, but if he

killed someone it'd be for money or revenge, some kind of personal gain, not for thrills. Then again . . ."

"Maybe he's expanding his repertoire?"

"Scary thought."

"Shall we check him out?"

"That depends," said McSwain. "How crazy are we?"

"I guess that depends on how dangerous Tibbs is."

"Plenty," said McSwain, but he was grabbing his jacket.

They took Capshaw's vehicle, a late-model green Subaru with Nevada plates. Rush hour was approaching, and Interstate 8 was clogged with traffic. Frequently a gap would open up in another lane, which would immediately precipitate a competition by several other vehicles to occupy it. Frequently Capshaw was the winner of such contests, but the lanes she fought her way into always seemed to wind up moving even slower than the ones they'd just squeezed their way out of.

She stomped the pedal and cut in between two semis.

"I'm worried about Mandy, you know. That mother of hers—"

"Not exactly June Cleaver."

"I hope Mandy doesn't drink or use because of her."

"You think she'd do that? I mean, except for the one slip, she's got, what, six months of sobriety?"

Capshaw's eyes clocked to the side. McSwain couldn't tell if she was smiling at him or grimacing in exasperation. "You still don't understand addiction, do you, Ian?"

"Do I understand why anyone would destroy their lives by teaspoonfuls—no, I don't. It doesn't make any sense to me."

"Even with Lily?"

"*Especially* with Lily."

"You could go back to Al-Anon."

"I don't think so. The people there didn't seem to have a clue. They just bitched about all the shitty stuff they had to endure because their loved ones wouldn't stop drinking and drugging. They kept insisting their husbands and wives wanted to quit, were trying to quit, even occasionally *did* quit. They just couldn't stay quit."

"That's addiction, Ian."

"That's insanity."

She gave a rueful laugh. "There's a difference?"

McSwain felt a sudden rush of irritation and the urge to say something sarcastic and hurtful, but he felt ashamed of the impulse and squelched it. Besides, they were taking the exit ramp now into National City, a sprawling industrial section between downtown San Diego to the north and Bonita and Chula Vista to the southeast.

Xtreme Ink was located in the kind of neighborhood you wouldn't want to cruise through without locked doors and rolled up windows. If you could do it in a Humvee, so much the better. Danny Tibbs's place of business occupied the first floor of what appeared to have once been a grand Victorian, now gone to seed, in a neighborhood where double dead bolts and barred windows were as normal as fern bars and Perrier in Coronado. Next door was a tarot reader and a Santería supply shop. A sign outside advertised Conchita's Bridal Boutique on the second floor, but the boarded-over and broken-out windows indicated Conchita had long since wedding-marched her way to another neighborhood.

Inside the shop, the walls were covered with flashy designs and photos of proud tattoo owners showing off elaborate artwork. Some of the designs were the traditional type—American flags and eagles, skull and cross-bones, *I Love Mom*s—but others were real museum pieces: a man's entire back tattooed with a Four Horsemen of the Apocalypse scene that resembled a Dürer etching, a woman whose breasts and belly were the canvas on which a parasol-twirling geisha smiled down at a samurai warrior who'd set aside his sword to kneel in front of her. McSwain was impressed with their intricacy and beauty.

Less impressive was the fleshy, almond-eyed woman wearing toreador pants and a crimson leotard who sat behind the counter, chewing gum and flipping through a copy of *TV Guide*. She stopped reading and eyed them with the wary suspicion of one accustomed to unexpected visits by the police and worse.

"Help you?" She stood up and leaned her forearms on the counter. A wildly colorful profile of a woman's face surrounded by Medusa-like tentacles covered her exposed chest from collarbones to cleavage.

"Danny Tibbs in?" said McSwain.

The woman's sour look remained unchanged. "Danny don't do walk-ins, mister. You want a tattoo, you get on a waiting list. Right now, it's six to eight weeks."

"Tell him it's about a friend of his, a woman named Billie from the Chula Vista Tap."

McSwain heard what sounded like a moan coming from behind a dark curtain at the rear of the shop. He and Capshaw exchanged glances.

The woman ignored the sound and yawned around her gum. "It won't make any difference who you know or not, but I'll tell him."

When she disappeared through a door behind the cash register, Capshaw took the opportunity to peek behind the curtain.

She turned back a moment later, eyes wide. "Ian, check this out."

He stepped into the spot where she'd been standing and peered into the room beyond. It was twice the size of the one they were now in and contained fifteen or twenty chairs arranged in front of a raised platform. A nude man stood on the platform in front of a long-haired woman wearing a bustier and a rubber skirt so short it impinged on her pubic hair. Unlike the woman, the man appeared completely hairless. Even his pubic area had been shaved. The woman moved back and forth in front of him, gesticulating dramatically while he remained still, arms folded behind his head, legs spread. Scarlet stripes descended the length of his bulging triceps and zigzagged along his torso and legs. For a second, McSwain had the disconcerting impression that he was seeing a man bleeding profusely from a multitude of wounds. Then he realized the red stripes were actually ribbon and that the woman was wielding a needle, piercing the man's body at various points and sewing the ribbon to his skin.

He stepped back from the curtain just as the leotard-clad woman returned, glaring. "Go on back."

Behind the door she'd just exited, they found a narrow room smelling of incense and lit up like an operating theater. A cabinet along one wall displayed tattoo and piercing equipment. On a table in the center of the room lay a woman with short, white-blond hair and tattooed breasts whose size and jut could only have been the result of a plastic surgeon with a Barbie-doll fetish.

Danny Tibbs was bent over her, working on her washboard abdomen, his big hands encased in thin latex gloves. Although the room was cool, sweat glistened in the hairs of his closely shaved scalp and beaded in the folds of his neck. He wore blue sweatpants and a black, sleeveless T-shirt that emphasized biceps every bit as impressive as the woman's chest.

When McSwain and Capshaw entered, he raised his head and stared at them. His eyes were large and deeply set, giving him a contemplative, almost monkish look. They could have been striking were it not for the fact that they were also as black and void as craters on the moon.

His tattoo equipment was unlike any McSwain had ever seen. Instead of the standard electronic needle, he was using a six-inch metal rod, pointed at one end and coated with pigment from clay jars lined up along a shelf next to the table. These he tapped into the woman's skin in minute increments.

"Don't be shy." He straightened up, revealing rows of abs like small paving stones, and indicated the woman on the table. "Have a look. She doesn't mind."

McSwain gave the woman's exposed torso the most cursory glance, saw a design that was at once exquisitely done and galvanizingly lewd.

Tibbs patted the woman's hip. "Take a break, Vi."

The woman sat up languorously, as though clearing her head from a deep sleep or a fix of quality smack. She looked around as though trying to decide where she was and made eye contact with McSwain. "Like what you see?" When there was no answer, she exchanged a small smirk with Tibbs, rose from the table, and undulated through a door next to the display cabinet.

Tibbs watched her. "One of my masterpieces."

"Lucky girl," said Capshaw.

"Oh, she is."

"Unusual technique you've got there."

"Yeah, I hear that a lot. Ever heard of the yakuza?"

"The Japanese Mafia," said McSwain.

"Best tattoo artists in the world. In Japan they use bamboo rods to tap the ink in, but I like the steel ones—easier to keep sterile."

"The yakuza, aren't they the ones who go in for the full-body tattoos?" said Capshaw.

"Art in the flesh," said Tibbs. "When those guys die, they strip the skin off and preserve it. The tattoos outlive the owner." He peeled the gloves off and dropped them into a trash bin beside the table. "So what are you two anyway, cops?"

"Private detectives," said Capshaw.

"Private dicks, huh? Ever seen my work before?"

"Only in the morgue," said McSwain.

Tibbs's huge mouth parted in a Jagger-esque grin. "A tattooed stiff?"

"No, just a stiff."

"Did said stiff have a name?"

"Kevin Orlando."

"Orlando." Tibbs rubbed the bristles alongside his jaw with the tattooing rod.

"Harry Orlando's son."

"Yeah, I remember now. Kid who got shot on the way to his wedding. That was a shame. Bummer for the bride. How'd you hear about it?"

"I was at the wedding. Working for Harry."

"No shit, a security dick. Well, you boys did a good job. Last I heard old Harry was alive and raising his grandkid in north Vegas. You see Harry, give him my best. Tell him I got a long memory. Someday that grandkid of his might take a swim in the same lagoon his old man did."

"We're more interested in a woman named Billie," McSwain said. "How you know her and where we can find her."

"Billie, Billie, a bitch named Billie," Tibbs said in a loopy singsong. "What makes you think I know where she is? Or that I even know who it is you're talking about?"

"Why else would you have been willing to see us?"

"Comic relief?"

"You had an argument with a woman you called Billie at the Chula Vista Tap back in January," Capshaw said. "The bartender threw you out. We've got witnesses."

"Yeah, right. You hang around the barflies in that dive long enough, you'll find witnesses who swear they saw pink giraffes giving blow jobs on the bartop."

"Funny, the bartender didn't look like a lush, and he remembers you very well." said McSwain, who figured Tibbs had no way to know he was lying.

"That so? Then did he also tell you I left like a gentleman and didn't come back?"

"Not that night anyway."

Tibbs looked unamused. He folded massive forearms across his chest. His shirt was cut low, and McSwain saw no tattoos on his chest either. He wondered if the most remarkable tattoo was also the only one.

"So what is it, you working for Billie's old man? Is that it? 'Cause from what she said, he didn't sound like the type who'd have the balls to come see me himself. He'd send some two-bit rent-a-dicks."

"We're not working for her husband," said McSwain, "and we don't care who she slept with or when or how many times. We just want to find her."

"So the question is why? The question then becomes which one of you wants to fuck her." He looked from Capshaw to McSwain and then back to Capshaw for a long, leering stare. "You're pretty hot, but you look like a dyke."

"I'm not a dyke," Capshaw said, "but meeting men like you just might make me reconsider."

"Well, don't, hon; you're as cock crazy as the woman you're trying to find. You may eat pussy now and then, but it's dick you got on the brain."

Capshaw smiled. "Hey, hon, at least I have a brain."

"So where's Billie now, Tibbs?" said McSwain.

"How would I know?"

"You were dating her?"

"I was fucking her."

"At your place? Her place?"

"She was more your sleazy-motel type."

"She got a last name?"

Tibbs rubbed the tattoo rod between his hands as if he were trying to start a fire. "Who says I even remember, or that she even told me? We hooked up a few times; that's all I know. I wasn't exactly taking notes on her personal history."

"Where'd you meet her?"

"She was pulling a train at a truckstop and I got in line."

"Keep it up, Tibbs."

"Oh, I will. I find you two amusing."

"This woman may have been murdered," McSwain said. "We find out she was, you're the one we're siccing the cops on. Then you may not be so amused."

"That night at the Tap," said Capshaw, "what was the argument about?"

"The length of my dick. I told her it was twelve inches, but she didn't believe me. Said it was more."

"Did you go there together? Or had you followed her there?"

Tibbs flipped the tattoo rod, caught it, flipped it again. "We bumped into each other. Just one of those things. Kismet." He smiled as he threw the word out, apparently assuming neither would have expected him to know it. "Look, I know you're working for her old man. I'da known you people would come sniffing around, I'd've snapped a few pictures of her with her ass in the air. I can't blame her old man for checking up on her, though."

"And why's that?" said McSwain.

Tibbs tapped the rod faster, warming to the topic. "Know how crack whores act when they gotta get their pipe filled? Any hard-core, gutter alkies? 'Cause that's how she sucks dick, this bitch—like she's fucking addicted, like her next breath of air's coming out the end of my cock." His bottomless eyes fixed on Capshaw. "I can tell when a woman's hungry for it like that, when she can't get enough of it. I can see it in their eyes."

"You know what you remind me of?" Capshaw said.

"A rattlesnake. And I just love to cut the heads off rattlesnakes."

Tibbs looked unfazed. "I'd love you to try." He flipped the tattoo rod in the air, caught it, and said, "Hey, you haven't asked yet. By this time most people have."

"Asked what?"

"How I got to be Deacon."

"Maybe we already know," Capshaw said, "or maybe we aren't interested."

"Well, you should be. It'd give you an idea who you're fucking with."

"That may be the crucial difference between us and the woman named Billie," McSwain said. "We *do* know who we're fucking with."

"Maybe you don't. Ever hear of an upstanding, churchgoing citizen named James Bell?"

When neither of them responded, Tibbs went on. "He was into an employee of mine for fifty grand and didn't show much interest in working out a payment plan. So one night I show up at his house with a briefcase and a Bible, tell him I'm the new deacon from his church making a call. He lets me in, I bash him in the head with the brick I got inside the Bible. Then I break both his arms. And while he's out, I plug in the tattoo equipment I got in my briefcase, and I go to work. Let's see, how did it go—I tattooed *Thou* on his forehead, *Shalt* and *Not* on his cheeks, and *Steal* on his chin. Then I left. Took him two years and a shitload of laser surgeries before he could leave the house in the daylight. And I been called Deacon ever since."

"Cool, Tibbs," McSwain said. "You must be proud of yourself. A real badass. You did that to a guy owed your stooge money, what'd you do to a woman who told you to get lost? Maybe hide in her car one night, rape her, and terrorize her friend?"

"Sounds like fun, but I don't need to do that. Women don't tell me to get lost."

"Maybe this one did," said Capshaw.

"You find her, you ask her, hon."

"Oh, we'll find her—even if you killed her—*hon*."

Tibbs ran the tip of his tongue along his fleshy lower

lip. He laid the tattoo rod on the table in front of him and folded his arms, a stance that made the veins in his arms stand out like cords. "Let me give you a tip. I'll let you two stroll in here and fuck with me once"—he paused and looked directly at Capshaw—"and you, babe, I might even let fuck with me twice—but no return visits from you, McStain or whoever-you-are, or you may be leaving here with some body modifications you weren't planning on." He looked pointedly at McSwain's left hand. "You got only nine fingers now—you might wind up with just five or six."

"I'm shaking, Tibbs."

"Yeah, that's what Harry Orlando said. Now he's got a kid in the grave and a grandkid on borrowed time." He picked up the tattooing rod and started around the side of the table. McSwain saw Capshaw's left hand slide behind her, going under her shirt. Tibbs saw it, too. He stopped, looked at McSwain, "What? You gonna let the bitch shoot me?"

McSwain didn't answer. Capshaw said, "Why not? You just gave me a good enough reason."

"What? Harry Orlando's fucking grandkid?"

"No, you called me a bitch."

Tibbs shot her a look that could have halted a charging bull, but he stopped his advance. Capshaw brought her hand out from behind her back.

"We'll be seeing you, Tibbs," said McSwain.

"Yeah, well, for your sake, you better hope you don't." He flipped the tattoo rod and caught it. "In my line of work, you hear things, you know? I might be able to hurt you in ways you can't even imagine."

McSwain paused and looked back, saw Tibbs's black eyes pulsing with the malevolent energy of one who genuinely likes inflicting pain and does so for the mindless glee of it. He felt the blood churn in his chest and fought the impulse to hammer the grin off Tibb's face with the butt of his gun, before he turned and followed Capshaw out the door.

On their way out, Capshaw paused in the outer room and said to the woman behind the counter, "The human pincushion in the next room, what the hell's that about?"

She sighed as though the question taxed her faculties to the limits, but finally answered. "We do performance art here on weekends. They're rehearsing. You like the ribbon, you should see what she does with a tub of Vaseline and a few strings of pearls."

Chapter 8

As soon as they got back to Capshaw's Suburu, she lit a cigarette and took a long drag, followed by a sigh of such satisfaction it sounded positively postorgasmic. McSwain had the feeling what she really wanted was to smoke two or three at one time.

"You know what scares me most about Tibbs," she said as they drove back to the office, "is how much I wanted him to give me a reason to shoot him."

"He has that effect on a lot of people, I expect," said McSwain. "That stuff about not knowing Billie's last name or where she lives, I don't buy that. Whatever Tibbs had going on with her, if it was more than a one-night stand, he would've made it his business to find out something about her, look for something he could exploit."

"Besides her body?"

"That would be just the start."

"When he was talking about what he did to James Bell—*bragging* about doing it—I kept wondering if maybe he had a gun on him, if I could shoot him and claim self-defense. Like killing him in cold blood would've been the correct moral choice." She dangled her left arm out the window, brought it back in for a quick drag on the cigarette. "You ever feel that way?"

"Somebody like Tibbs? Would I want him to bypass the Go to Jail card for the one that says Go Directly to Morgue? Sure I would. I just don't act on it."

"Me, too, and it scares the shit out of me."

"That you wanted to kill him or that you knew you couldn't act on it?"

A small shiver rippled up her right forearm. "Both."

A few minutes later, when they pulled up in front of Dave's Gym, Jenna said, "I don't know about you, but I'm beat." She looked at her watch. "It's almost seven, and I could use a meeting. If I hurry, I can make the happy-hour group at the Alano Club over on Coronado."

"Want to grab dinner later?"

"Can't. I got a friend coming over."

"Mind if we exchange vehicles then?"

"A Suburu for a Monte Carlo? Sure, but why?"

"It's gonna be light for a couple more hours. Maybe I'll swing by Emerson's place again. I don't think anyone in the neighborhood's noticed my car, but having a vehicle with Nevada license plates couldn't hurt."

"Sure, no problem."

McSwain handed her the keys to the Monte Carlo and she got out, flicking the remains of her cigarette into the gutter as she walked around the front of the car. She leaned into the window. "You work too much; you know that, don't you?"

"Keeps me from thinking too much."

She started to say something, seemed to change her mind, glanced down at her right hand as though surprised to see a cigarette wasn't in it. "You're not planning to go back to see Tibbs, are you?"

"Not today anyway. I was thinking I'd go check on Emerson."

"Just remember I don't want you making any return visits to Tibbs without me, okay?"

And not without the right equipment, he thought. An idea had come to him after leaving Xtreme Ink, but he didn't share it with Capshaw. After she dropped him off at his car, he put in a call to the Plum Crazy Saloon, where a friend and ex-con named Blackjack Ames tended bar.

He explained to Blackjack what he needed, then grabbed a burger at the drive-through window of McDonald's and went back to the Bonita neighborhood he'd visited before. While he was sitting behind the wheel, pretending to read a newspaper while watching the roofer's home through a hole in the paper, he mulled over the visit to Tibbs. The guy was capable of rape, he had no doubt, but would he take the risk of abducting not just one woman, but two? For that matter, if he was the rapist, why would he even admit he'd had an argument with Billie at the Tap when the word of witnesses recalling something that happened six months in the past was worth about as much as last week's weather report?

He was jarred from his thoughts by a dark green Chevy Blazer with two occupants that pulled into the carport of the roofer's home. McSwain picked up his Nikon with the telephoto lens and snapped half a dozen photos of the burly Emerson exiting the passenger side door with his arms full of groceries and heading around the side of the house with the jaunty stride of a man in the full bloom of health. His lady friend followed, also laden with grocery bags, and he held those, too, while she used a key to unlock the door of the house.

"What d'you know, a miracle cure," McSwain said to himself, as he imagined the look on Emerson's face when the insurance company showed the photos to him and his lawyer.

Grateful to have gotten at least one thing accomplished, he drove to a quiet residential neighborhood on Calla Avenue in north I.B. He found street parking for the Suburu, got out, and stopped at a mailbox outside an ornate wrought-iron gate. He took out a couple of bills, a flyer for a new Italian restaurant, and a letter from the bank, which he tore open first and read by the light of the street lamp. The news wasn't good—another *we'd love to give you a loan, but only when you're making so much money you don't need one*—from yet another bank. This one had been his last hope. No way in hell was he going to be able to swing that house in Carlsbad now.

Whatever satisfaction he'd derived from getting photos of a hale and hearty Emerson evaporated, leaving him feeling drained and angry. He hated telling Lily they wouldn't be able to afford a house, hated most of all the implication that he was a less than adequate provider, which, in turn, seemed to imply he was also less than adequate as a man. He knew that was bullshit, but it tapped into old fears—the sound of his mother sobbing at the kitchen table, because his father had lost his job at the auto factory and an eviction notice had been posted on the door. His father's shortcomings as a wage earner before he finally took off for good and his mother's anger and resentment at him for it had been a central motif of his childhood, one he was loath to repeat in his own marriage.

Instead of heading directly home, on impulse he crossed the street and walked half a block north to St. Francis Church on the corner. McSwain rarely attended Mass, but he dropped in at least once a week, often late at night when the church was officially closed. He'd become close to the priest, Father Takamoto, when he did free surveillance work shortly after moving into the neighborhood and rounded up the teenage vandals who were breaking into St. Francis for late-night Ecstasy parties, presumably enhanced by the presence of the statue of Saint Teresa in her own, non-drug-induced ecstasy. McSwain had lamented the necessity for keeping churches locked at all—since personal crises seldom waited for business hours and, for most people, the most nightmarish angst usually came late at night. He thought they should be open on a twenty-four-seven basis. Father Takamoto couldn't oblige him by leaving the church unlocked, but he gave him a key to a basement door that led to a staircase up to the rectory.

When he felt depressed or agitated, he found the atmosphere of the church soothing and restorative—the calming half-light that painted the interior of the chapel in gray-browns and charcoals, the flickering of the votive candles, the exotic, faintly festive scent of incense. As was his custom, he lit a couple of candles, one for Lily and one for his mother, and dropped a few bills into the collection box before he slid into a pew and knelt to pray.

God, please keep Lily safe and get her out of there. Let her be happy with me this time. Let our life together be enough that she doesn't have to use drugs.

But what if she does? his mind countered.

She won't.

How do you know?

She just won't. She's learned her lesson.

Oh, really? Once an addict, always an addict.

When the mental nagging kept interrupting his prayers, he gave up and trudged back up the street toward an imposing Tudor-style house that dwarfed the carriage house behind it. The carriage house was McSwain's. He rented it from the gay couple who owned the Tudor. He'd told Craig and Mark that he was looking for a house, and they were undoubtedly expecting him to move. If he'd changed his plans, he ought to let them know.

He wondered if Lily could be content living here and considered whether there was any point in continuing to look for a house within his price range or if it would be better to wait, address their finances after she was released and they could sit down and discuss it together.

As he was making his way up the graveled path that led from the main house to his own, there was a rustling in the ficus bush to his left. Something leaped out, brushed past his ankle, and then tore off in the direction of the koi pond in Craig and Mark's garden.

"Evening, Ghandi," McSwain said to the retreating shape.

The big black-and-white tom ignored him. His mission was accomplished, and McSwain wondered how long he'd waited there for his quarry to pass. The nightly stalk and pounce had become a ritual now, and McSwain almost expected it. The first time he'd nearly jumped out of his skin until he realized it was his landlords' cat, Ghandi, the first animal McSwain had ever known who had a sense of humor.

He unlocked the top and bottom locks to the back door and let himself into the kitchen. Tossing the mail onto the counter, he got a beer from the refrigerator and the fixings for a pastrami-on-rye sandwich, which he made on the butcher-block table. Dinner prepared, he took the food upstairs to the bedroom and turned on the news.

Two hours later, half the sandwich remained uneaten, the TV was still on, and he felt no closer to sleep than when he'd first gotten home. Annoyed at himself, he cut the TV off, found the Stromquist cassette tape Jenna had given him, and popped it into the stereo next to the bed. At first he found Stromquist's pontificating grating, but the man spoke with an impassioned, theatrical cadence that he had to admit garnered attention.

The talk was divided into several sections that corresponded to Stromquist's Principles for Finding Personal Freedom. "Free yourself from the ties that bind" was the one Stromquist was now speaking about. The general thrust of it seemed to be how to undo the hard-wiring that goes on in early childhood, the parental and societal messages that often decide a person's destiny, but McSwain found the underlying message unsavory— it seemed to be that parenting was basically on a par with slave owning.

"A Detroit mother tried to sell her five-year-old son to a convicted pedophile so she could buy money for crack," Stromquist was saying. "A father in Philadelphia beat his eight-year-old daughter to death when she ignored his demand to turn off the TV set. Extreme cases? Of course they are. And if your parents were that bad, you wouldn't be here listening to me tonight.

"Often it's the desire for ego gratification that motivates people to become parents. Maybe your parents saw you as a thing, not an individual. Maybe they wanted a smaller version of themselves or unquestioning obedience to their authority, or maybe they wanted a child to use as an ally or a pawn against the other spouse. And if they did—and let me tell you that it's likely that they did—then the message transmitted to you was that you're not good enough, you aren't okay, you exist to serve and—bottom line—whether psychologically or physically, your parents had the power of life and death over you, and on some level, *you knew it and were afraid.*"

McSwain felt a surge of anger out of all proportion to what Stromquist had just said. He found himself thinking about his mother, Catherine, whom he visited two or three times a year at the retirement home in Sacramento, where she shared an apartment with her second husband, whom she'd acquired at the admirably active age of seventy-four. He told himself that, like any good son, he loved his mother and had forgiven her for everything—all in the past, water over the dam—and tried to suppress the nagging voice that said he was a patsy and a sucker and that, in some perverse way, Stromquist was absolutely fucking right.

Irritated, he reached over and hit fast-forward, moving ahead to another part of the tape before hitting play. What he heard then made his eyes snap open. He sat up in bed, hit the rewind button, and listened to what Stromquist had just said. After listening to it a third time, he grabbed the phone, got a number from Information, and dialed it.

On the fourth ring, Dave Marquette's sleepy voice answered.

"Dave? It's Ian. Sorry, did I wake you up?"

"Jesus, it's after one A.M. What is it? Something wrong?"

"No, but . . . didn't you tell me you studied French lit in college?"

"A little, but—"

"I want you to listen to something—"

"—that was twenty-five years ago."

"—and tell me what you think it is." He held the phone next to the tape player and hit play. Stromquist's voice, soft and strangely mellifluous, repeated what McSwain wanted Dave to hear.

"It's French."

"Yeah, I know it's French, but what's it mean?"

"You woke me up for this? Jeez, I don't know. Play it again."

McSwain rewound, hit play again.

"Okay, okay." This time Dave sounded more awake. "It's a French saying. There is no middle ground. Literally, a door must be open or closed."

McSwain was silent.

"Got anything else for me tonight—term paper, homework assignment, crossword puzzle maybe—or can I go back to bed?"

"Yeah, sure. Thanks, Dave. You've helped a lot."

"Yeah, Ma always said my education would come in handy. Guess she was right."

They hung up, and McSwain hit speed-dial for Capshaw's number. On the fourth ring, the phone was picked up. He heard sheets rustling and a small thunk that sounded like someone had dropped the receiver.

"Yeah?" Capshaw's voice sounded husky and slightly breathless, like she'd been interrupted from something more than sleep.

McSwain remembered then that she'd said a friend was coming over and felt suddenly embarrassed. He knew so little of Jenna's personal life that sometimes it was easy to assume that, like him, she didn't have one.

"Sorry to call so late, but I found something."

"Okay, hold on a sec. I'm going to take this in the other room."

He heard more rustling, a male voice saying, "Who is it?" and Capshaw whispering something that he couldn't make out. She giggled softly and hissed "Stop it" in a way that made clear that whatever the man was being asked to stop doing had been decidedly pleasurable. Seconds later, she picked up another phone, waited a beat, then said, "I got it, Ray."

The "Ray" in question hung up the phone. McSwain felt irrationally irritated. He didn't know if this was because he was anxious to talk to his partner and didn't like having to wait or because being forced to confront the reality of someone else's sex life made his own lack of one more galling.

"Yeah, Ian, what's up?"

He bit back the urge to use the opening she'd just given him to say something smart-ass. "Those cassette tapes of Stromquist giving his spiel—I listened to the one you gave me."

"And?"

"Mandy was right. Stromquist's wife is the woman who gave her the ride."

"How do you know?"

"Remember Mandy told us Billie used a French expression that she attributed to her husband, something about a door? Well, Stromquist ends his talk saying something in French, only he doesn't bother to translate it—guess he figures his audience should be Sorbonne-trained at the minimum. I called up Dave and let him listen to it. He says the idea is that there is no middle ground, but literally, it means 'A door must be open or closed.' "

"Dave speaks French?"

"A man of many talents."

"Apparently. So we were right thinking maybe Stromquist was just playing us. He had to know it was his wife we were talking about."

"Which means it's important to pay him another visit as soon as possible," said McSwain. "Try catching him at home this time. If he's hiding something, our visit the other day may have spooked him. We don't want to give him more time to get rid of evidence or leave town."

"You think he's our guy?"

"If he is, I doubt if he actually did the deed. He's the type who would have hired somebody. Maybe payback for her having an affair with Tibbs."

"So if she's alive, where is she? And why wouldn't Stromquist admit it was his wife we were talking about, when he had to know?"

"Maybe she never told him she'd been attacked and our telling him about it came as a shock. Or maybe he knew, but he thinks he's protecting her?"

"Or protecting himself."

"That's possible, too."

"So we'll pay him another visit tomorrow?"

In the background, McSwain heard the click of a door opening. He didn't know if Jenna had opened it herself or if Ray had decided to see what was taking her so long. He realized suddenly that it was very likely she was naked while they had this conversation.

"Ian? I asked you—"

"Yeah." He was suddenly anxious to get off the phone. "We'll see if Stromquist can produce his wife safe and sound. If not, he may be making his next motivational speech at a cell block."

Chapter 9

After finally falling asleep around two A.M., McSwain woke early, put on sweats without bothering to shower, and got to the office in I.B. before seven. Dave's Gym didn't open until ten, but since it offered the only access to the office, McSwain and Capshaw had keys to the front and back doors, as well as free use of the facilities. Today, before he could even put his key in the lock, Ricardo appeared, unshaven and wearing dungarees he'd apparently slept in, and opened the door for him. Whether Ricardo was actually holding the door open or the door was holding up Ricardo was in question, though. The gin fumes that came off him punched McSwain in the face like a left hook.

Fortunately, Ricardo seemed more interested in going back to sleep on Dave's sofa than in making small talk, so McSwain put on the coffeemaker, changed into his workout clothes, and went a few rounds alternating between the heavy bag and the speedbag. He then did a hundred sit-ups and fifty push-ups and returned to the heavy bag for a few more rounds.

It was eight by the time he finished showering, threw his workout clothes into a duffel bag to wash later, and put on one of two sets of dress pants, shirt, and sport coat that the dry cleaner up the street had sent over the day before. He filled the time until nine by checking his voice mail—nothing urgent there; a software company up in Del Mar wanted a background check on a potential new executive, and Delta Insurance was calling to remind him that Emerson was due back in court for a ruling on his settlement in less than two weeks, a message that made McSwain smile.

Just after nine, he dialed Stromquist Headquarters and was put through to the receptionist, Fern, who told him Mr. Stromquist wouldn't be in the office until that afternoon.

By the time Capshaw arrived a few minutes later, he was on the phone to a woman named Ellen Fried, who worked in Voter Registration. Ellen's eight-year-old son had disappeared a few years back, and McSwain had traced him to the home of her ex-husband in an Atlanta suburb. Since then, she had always been happy to help him out when she could.

McSwain hung up, brought Capshaw up to speed on what he was doing, and was halfway through his second cup of coffee when Ellen called back.

"That's what I figured," he said, jotting down the address she'd found for him. "I'd've been surprised if he lived anywhere else."

He thanked Ellen and hung up.

Capshaw raised an eyebrow at him over the rim of the double espresso she'd bought at the Java Nook up the street. "Well?"

"Stromquist has a home in Rancho Santa Fe." He read her the address, but she was already reaching for the street map guide in the bookcase next to her desk.

"Want me to check the reverse directory, get a phone number so we can find out if he's home?"

"Let's take our chances," McSwain said. "We know he's not at the office. And who knows, maybe the mysterious Mrs. Stromquist's at the house?"

They took I-5 north to Lomas Santa Fe and turned east into Linea del Cielo, winding through hilly countryside dotted with orange groves and horse farms. Fifteen minutes later they arrived at Paseo Delicias, the main drag of the old monied community, lined with an array of chic boutiques, jewelers, and gift shops. Rancho Santa Fe had been an enclave of the ultrawealthy since the nineteen twenties, but had remained mostly unknown until the cult members of Heaven's Gate decided it would be the perfect spot for a mass suicide in 1997.

McSwain cruised slowly through a two-block shopping district lined with late-model Mercedes, Lexuses, and Porsches to Del Dios Highway, a curving two-lane road that passed equestrian trails, orange groves, and golf courses. Most of the residences were set back out of view of the road, locked away in gated and guarded enclaves.

About two miles north of the town center, Capshaw spotted the address they were looking for posted on a mailbox in front of a flower-lined driveway that led to a gated wall. Next to the gate was a small guardhouse with a man stationed inside.

McSwain made a U-turn and pulled into the driveway. The guard stuck his head out. He looked young, with a gawky frame and prominent Adam's apple. McSwain surmised he was one of those who'd tried to get into the police academy, but failed to make the grade for whatever reason.

He flashed his ID. "We're here to see Leland Stromquist."

"Mr. Stromquist expecting you?"

"We had a meeting with him at his office recently. This is just a follow-up."

The guard looked unconvinced, but dialed a number and spoke into a cell phone. He nodded and turned back to McSwain. "Housekeeper says no one's expected." He hesitated, then spoke into the phone again.

"You're sure, Mr. Stromquist? Okay, then."

The guard shrugged, hit a button that opened the electronic gate, and motioned them through.

For about a quarter of a mile, they followed a road shaded by eucalyptus trees and expensive-looking imported palms. Finally, at a point where the road curved over the top of a rise, the red tile roofs of what at first appeared to be several houses came into view. Then the soaring eucalyptus trees were replaced by hedges and they could see a single sprawling white, Spanish-colonial mansion with arched windows and a gracefully columned portico.

Capshaw pulled into the circular drive behind a burgundy Corvette and a citron-yellow Lamborghini.

With Capshaw in the lead, they went to the door, a heavy, wooden Sante Fe style that looked capable of repelling a horde of attacking huns. She eschewed the brass lion's-head knocker in favor of an ornate bell to one side of the doors.

A few moments later the door was opened by a short, round Latina wearing a red apron and carrying a mop.

"Is Mrs. Stromquist in?"

"Who's calling?"

Capshaw told her. The woman's brow furrowed, giving her wide face a look of suspicion and consternation. "She's not here. If you like, I can take a message."

"What about Mr. Stromquist?" Capshaw asked.

"He's not here either."

"But he just told the guard to buzz us in."

From inside the house, McSwain heard the scuffling sound of slippers on a hardwood floor.

"What's this, Javiera? Are you giving these nice people a hard time?"

The maid's head jerked up. The folds of fat around her neck began to compress so that her head appeared to draw in toward her shoulders, turtlelike. She stepped out of the way, and a man who appeared to be at least a foot taller than she but close to the same weight leaned into the doorway. McSwain recognized him as the impeccably dressed young job applicant who'd been waiting in Stromquist's office the day before—Stromquist's son. This morning his look was considerably more casual. His long hair dripped water, and he wore a white terry-cloth robe over a pair of black swim trunks. Beads of water gleamed on bronzed, muscled flesh so perfect it might have been airbrushed. His eyes, a deep violet-blue like the color of fine Dutch china, flashed first to McSwain and then settled on Capshaw.

"You're the private detectives from the office the other day. The old man let you see him ahead of me just to get my goat."

Jenna stuck out her hand. "Jenna Capshaw and Ian McSwain. Thanks for buzzing us in."

"Josh Stromquist. And it was my pleasure. I wanted to talk to you the other day, but my temper got the better of me. It does that sometimes." He smiled ingratiatingly. "Now the question is, What can you do for me?"

"Maybe you could do something for us first," said McSwain. "We need to talk to your father or mother."

"You've got a better shot at the old man. My mother's dead."

"Mrs. Stromquist is dead?" Capshaw said. "But your father told us—"

"Oh, God, you're talking about Virginia? She's not my mother. She's the bimbo Dad married when I was eighteen." He shook his head in amazement. "Please, you impugn the Stromquist gene pool."

"Your stepmother then, where is she?"

"Who knows? On her back someplace, I guess." He laughed and, turning away from the door for a moment, shouted back into the house. "Hey, Javiera, make me a Bloody Mary, will you? I feel the need of liquid sustenance."

When he got no response, he yelled out, "Never mind. I'm leaving anyway. I'll make my own when I get home."

"You don't live here?" Capshaw asked.

"Here? Of course not. I just come over here in the morning to do a few laps in the pool. My own place is up the road on the property. You want to talk to the old man, he's over that way. Come on; I'll take you."

"We want to talk to him alone," McSwain said. "Just point us in the right direction."

"Now, what kind of hospitality would that be, sending you two off alone? You might get lost. Look, I'm going to do you a huge favor. Come on; I'll escort you myself."

"What about your liquid sustenance?" said Capshaw.

"Plenty of that at my place. I'll whip up a pitcher of Bloody Marys and we'll talk business." He gave what McSwain figured was meant to be boyish grin, but if so, it was that of a boy with larceny in his heart and a gun in his back pocket. "I just might have some work for you two."

"And we just might not be interested," said Capshaw.

"Oh, I doubt that," said Josh, and winked at her.

Outside on the porch, Josh shed his robe as sleekly as

a stripper sliding out of a G-string, flexed his chest and biceps as he squinted up at the sun that surely must be shining only for him, and led them around the side of the house to a golf cart.

"Something I don't get," said McSwain, as they got into the cart. "Looks to me like your father won't give you the time of day as far as employment, but he lets you live here on his property? How old are you anyway, at least twenty-five?"

Josh's hands tensed on the wheel, and he seemed on the verge of exploding—which was exactly what McSwain had in mind—but he controlled himself and flashed a smile that was dazzling in its combination of menace and sun-drenched good looks.

"Hey, what can I say? Some people have a hard time leaving the nest."

McSwain looked at the late-model luxury cars in the driveway and the tennis courts visible up ahead. "I can see where this could be a tough nest to leave."

They passed the pool and tennis courts and crested a slight rise, below which they could see a paddock with horses grazing. Beyond that they entered a wooded area where the road was lined with fern pines and twisted junipers. This eventually opened up into a wider road with orange groves on both sides.

"Nice little spread you got here," Capshaw said, when they'd covered a quarter mile.

Josh turned around, grinned at her. "Time you get to the end of the property, you're not even in the same zip code."

"Leland's always lived here?"

"Naw, back in our poor days, before he wrote *The Sucker Solution,* all we had was a little place near the Cove in La Jolla, worth less than a mil. Then when the book hit it big, that's when he decided he needed a fiefdom."

Capshaw leaned forward, rested her arms on the front seat of the cart. "You don't think much of the book, I take it?"

"No, I think it's a great book, an inspired book, be-cause"—he gestured at the passing landscape with one arm—"it pays for all this. But it's for suckers who pay big bucks for seminars where my father basically tells them what to do with their lives, what to keep and who and what to trash. And believe me, Dad doesn't have a lot of respect for the way most people lead their lives. There's not a lot he advises them to keep."

He swung the golf cart hard to the left. They passed through a stand of trees, and emerged on the front lawn of a two-story, blue stucco house set on the crest of a hill that overlooked, from the brief glimpse McSwain got, an impressive hedge and more orange groves. If seclusion was what Josh was after, he had it here—the eucalyptus trees along one side of the house were set so close that deep shade fell over most of the front, their upper branches spreading out across the roof and almost obscuring two small dormer windows.

The garage door was open and a forest green Jaguar was parked inside.

Josh scowled at the empty slot next to it, hissed an epithet, and got out of the cart.

"Something wrong?" said McSwain, but Josh was already striding around the front of the cart, heading for the front door.

He went in and they followed, through a minimally furnished living room and into a hall that opened up into a TV and exercise room. An entertainment center took up most of one wall. The rest of the room was filled with fitness equipment, the most striking of which was an inversion device from which a blonde in black tights and a pink spandex leotard dangled upside down. She smiled, her face flushed from her inverted position, and gave a small wave.

"Samuella, what are you doing here?"

At once, the smile inverted, too. In one lithe movement she brought her arms up and curled forward until the table tilted and brought her back to an upright postion. She then freed her feet from the ankle clamps and stepped forward.

"Nice way to talk to me after the other night, you piece of shit."

"How'd you get in?"

"You left the door open."

"I *know* that; I mean how'd you get onto the property? Where's your car?"

"On the road out back, asshole. What, you think I can come in third in a woman's triathlon, but I can't climb over a fucking fence?"

"Where's Daphne?"

"Is that her name? The little bitch with the Valley-girl accent and the shitty car? She left."

"You fucking cunt."

"Hey!" The blonde raised one hand and extended her middle finger. "Screw you, Josh. I am so fucking out of here."

She shoved past him, biceps popping up like billiard balls under the toned skin, slamming the door on her way out.

Josh said, "Hey, wait a second," and went after her, paying no more attention to Capshaw and McSwain than if they'd come to deliver a pizza.

McSwain turned to Capshaw. "Are we so fucking out of here, too?"

"Fucking better be."

They appropriated the golf cart while Josh was having a screaming match with Samuella around the side of the house, his voice the louder one but her invective laced with more creative obscenities, and drove down the hill past stands of mulberry and juniper trees until they reached the hedge. There they left the cart and walked alongside the towering green wall, which was so dense it looked virtually impenetrable and rose over a foot above McSwain's head.

Capshaw said, "You don't suppose this thing is . . . ?"

"A labyrinth?"

"And here I thought it was just a metaphor."

Fifty feet farther on, they came to what looked like the end of the hedge wall and saw, up ahead, a couple of pickup trucks and a white Buick LeSabre. Beyond the trucks, the hedge continued—it hadn't ended, he realized, but merely made a ninety-degree turn.

Beside one of the pickups, a couple of Hispanic kids, boys who looked about seven or eight, were playing with a toy helicopter and plastic tank. The boy with the helicopter kept attempting a landing while the other one tried to run the helicopter down with the tank.

Beyond the children they saw four men, two of them on their knees, attacking the hedge with shears. The other two, Stromquist and Moxley, observed from the sidelines. Stromquist was saying something to one of the men. He leaned down and pantomimed clipping with his hands. Moxley looked in the other direction, but he was turning slowly. His turn brought him around so he was staring directly at Capshaw and McSwain.

There was a moment when Moxley's face was completely without expression, a blank, unblemished cipher, as though he either didn't recognize them or was peering through them as though they were glass. Then his pencil-thin lips formed a smile and he said something to Stromquist, who straightened up, squinting in the bright sun. There was no immediate expression on Stromquist's face, either, but McSwain could feel the anger contained in the rigid and unmoving tension of his body. Finally he seemed to come to some decision and strode forward, his demeanor that of a man used to having any and all obstacles move out of his way.

"How did you get past the gate?"

"Your son told the guard to let us in," Capshaw said.

Stromquist shook his head. "How predictably stupid of him."

McSwain saw Moxley watching them. Even the two gardeners had stopped work and were sneaking glances. He lowered his voice. "We need to talk someplace private."

Stromquist took a deep breath, then turned back to Moxley.

"It's all right, Richard. I'll deal with this." To McSwain he said, "We can talk here, but this had better be brief."

They walked back toward the road to the point where the hedge made its first turn.

"You lied to us the other day," McSwain said. "The description of the woman we gave you, her car, everything—you knew it was your wife."

Stromquist stood so straight he seemed to add an inch in height to his diminutive frame. "What did you expect me to do? Two complete strangers who claim to be private detectives show up at my office with some outlandish story that's obviously designed to upset me—how was I to know what your motives were? At the very least, I had to make sure you were legitimate. Fortunately, I have a private investigator who once took one of my seminars, and he was happy to do a background check on both of you."

"And?" said McSwain.

"I still don't know your motives, but I do know you've been duped. I spoke to Virginia last night. She's never heard of a place called the Chula Vista Tap, let alone been there, and she certainly hasn't been attacked by anyone."

"Then you're saying the similarities to your wife are all a coincidence?"

Stromquist smiled as though McSwain were a dimwitted child. "No. I'm saying your client is either deluded or is some sort of malicious troublemaker with a vendetta against Virginia or myself. If the latter, I must say it's not only creative but extremely sadistic—to plant the idea in my mind that my wife was raped after leaving a sleazy bar where she was using a fictitious name."

"And the French quote that the woman attributed to her husband?" Capshaw said. "We heard a tape where you use the same expression in one of your talks."

"*Il faut qu'une porte soit ouverte ou fermée?* I use that expression in a lot of my talks. Anyone who heard me and had a passable knowledge of French could have quoted me and attributed it to anybody."

"And your wife never used the nickname Billie?"

"Why would she? It isn't her name."

"Where is she now?" Capshaw asked.

"Out of the country. And that's all the information you're going to get. You've bought into what appears to be some sort of sick practical joke. Whether you're involved in it or just stupid enough to believe it, either way, I don't want you harassing her."

The shrieks of the children playing nearby grew louder, and Stromquist frowned as he waited for the noise to subside. "In any event, I have your card, and I asked my wife if she wanted to talk to you. She said that unless you want to reveal the full name of the client who's perpetrating this fantasy and allow her to meet with this person, then she has nothing to say to you except to leave us alone."

He turned and shouted back toward the gardeners. "Will you get back to work, please? *Trabájete, por favor?*" He looked for Moxley, who was leaning against the LeSabre, shaking a cigarette out of a pack of Lucky's. "And Richard, keep an eye on those kids, will you? I didn't give my permission for these people to bring their children out here. It's not a playground."

"Which brings up another question," Capshaw said. She indicated the hedge. "What, exactly, *is* that?"

"If you've read my book, you shouldn't have to ask."

"A labyrinth?"

"I've been known to call it that, but strictly speaking, it's a maze. You know the difference?"

"A labyrinth is designed to enlighten, a maze to confound."

"Very good. You've done your homework. Although in this case, I'd have to differ with you, nonetheless. What you see here is a maze, yes, but it's purpose is first to confound, then—for those who persevere—to enlighten."

McSwain nodded toward the hedge. "Mind if we take a look inside?"

"Not at all. You won't become enlightened, but you might learn something."

With Stromquist leading the way, they walked to one of the corners where an opening about three feet wide had been cut into the hedge. It was visible when they were in front of it, but almost impossible to see otherwise, because of the way it blended in with the hedge wall behind it.

Stromquist turned left and walked about ten feet. They were in a corridor composed completely of greenery, narrow enough that they were forced to walk single file. McSwain tried to see through the hedge, but it was too thick. He might as well have been trying to peer through a wall. Stromquist passed by an opportunity to turn right, then took the next turn a few paces farther on. Almost immediately he turned again. McSwain got the feeling they were doubling back.

He was surprised at the intensity of the claustrophobic feeling the place gave him—worse than being inside an elevator and almost as bad as the MRI he'd once suffered through. He reminded himself he was outdoors— all the air he could want—but his palms already felt like he'd dipped them in warm water, and sweat traveled down his neck and the backs of his thighs. The sun had been shining, but now, as if to increase his discomfort, a cloud bank pressed in. The corridor they were moving along grew grayer, the anvil-shaped clouds sinking lower, pressing out the air.

He was just about to make some excuse for wanting to leave when Stromquist stopped and seemed to deliberate before making a turn. McSwain glanced at Capshaw, but her attention was focused on Stromquist. He guessed she was doing the same thing that he was, trying to memorize the succession of turns.

"I won't take you in any farther," Stromquist said. "The entire area is too big. And if I took a wrong turn, we might need Richard to come get us out—he knows the way. But this gives you an idea."

"I think it raises more questions than answers," said Capshaw. "If I've got this straight, people who make it to your fifth seminar go through the maze. Do you give them a bag full of bread crumbs or a ball of twine before they go in?"

Stromquist smiled. "I'm sure some wish we did." He turned and started leading them back out the short distance they'd come. "I use the labyrinth—which as you pointed out is, technically speaking, a maze—as a kind of real-life metaphor, and I use it only with fifth-level students. They go into it alone, taking tokens or mementos of whatever they wish to jettison in their lives— maybe photos of a spouse or of family, something that symbolizes a job or career path they want to change. They take these items to the center and discard them in a pit. Then they find their way back. I tell you, it accomplishes more than years of therapy. It gives closure to the finality of things left behind."

He stopped and plucked at an errant bit of greenery, McSwain fighting the urge to grab the guy and shake him, yell, *How the hell do you get out of here?* "People in our society are conditioned to hang on to things, places, and people. This is a rite of initiation that facilitates letting go."

"Even of their families?" Capshaw asked.

Stromquist cocked one graying eyebrow. "*Especially* their families. Society has put the family on a pedestal, made it something sacred. It's not. In many cases, the family is nothing but a genetic quagmire pulling people down."

"That's a message that must piss off a lot of people," said McSwain.

"Let me guess. You're one of them?"

"I can think of worse things than being loyal to your roots."

"Depends on the roots."

"Then you're saying—"

"Anybody ever get lost in here?" said Capshaw.

"Getting lost is part of the point. Students enter here believing all they're going to do is walk a labyrinth. They aren't told it's a maze. They discover that for themselves."

"Fun and games, huh?" said Capshaw. "Anyone ever give up?"

"A few panic and yell for help. Then Richard will go in and lead them out. Most tough it out, though, even if it takes them all night, and they emerge stronger people because of it."

"You send people in here at night?" said McSwain.

Stromquist's smile was so laced with malicious glee that McSwain had to control the impulse to backhand the grin off his face. "It's not all that dark. We wait for a full moon."

They came to a break in the hedge wall and strolled outside. For McSwain, the dead blue sky suddenly filled with air again. His lungs filled, and he could breathe.

Moxley was leaning against one of the pickups, gazing at the trees and lighting a cigarette in a meditative way that, for a moment, made him seem more the lord of the manor than Stromquist.

Ignoring him, Stromquist went on. "Most people never question their allegiances to family, country, origins. This provides a means for them to discard their albatrosses, so to speak. If it were easy, though, they wouldn't value it."

McSwain started to ask if anybody ever decided to discard Stromquist's bullshit rhetoric, then remembered the night before when, listening to the tape, he'd experienced a bitter moment of agreement.

Stromquist glanced pointedly at his watch, a Rolex with tiny diamonds circling a black face. "I've already given you more than enough time." He turned toward Moxley. "Richard will see that you have no trouble finding your way out." He turned away, then seemed to remember something. "Oh, McSwain?"

"Yeah?"

"The other day I noticed you wear a wedding band. Since you're so interested in my wife, I told my PI friend I wanted to learn about yours. I must say I was shocked that a man presumably working on the side of the law would be married to an incarcerated felon. I don't know you, McSwain, and I don't particularly like you, but a word of free advice nonetheless. Being married to a drug addict is like being married to a train wreck. Lose her. For your own good."

McSwain felt a surge of superheated blood flood his forehead and neck. He felt Capshaw's hand on the back of his arm and fought to keep his voice calm. "A word of advice to you, Stromquist. Get your wife to give us a call. Fast. For your sake."

Stromquist held his gaze for a moment, then gave a small smirk, and turned away.

Moxley walked with them to the golf cart. He got behind the wheel while Ian and Jenna sat in the back.

"So Stromquist says his wife's out of the country," Capshaw said. "Is that true?"

"Far as I know," Moxley said. "They have a condo someplace in Mexico, but seems like she's the only one who uses it. Supposedly she's an artist, but I don't know—was my wife taking off on her own like that she wouldn't be my wife for very long, know what I mean?"

"You've seen her recently?"

"Oh, sure, recently as last week. What, you didn't think . . . ? Hey, Stromquist's a weirdo who likes to play head games, but he wouldn't, you know, hurt her, that's what you're thinking."

"But you don't know where she is now."

"Not for sure, no. Anyway, I'm the last one she'd tell. Way she looks through me, you'd think I was a window. My girlfriend, too—Helen came by once to pick me up after my shift and ran into Mrs. Stromquist. Helen's a little on the heavy side, and Mrs. Stromquist made some snotty comments about her size—told her fat's not a glandular disorder; it's a gluttony disorder. Poor girl left here in tears."

"Are you Stromquist's only bodyguard?" asked McSwain, trying to redirect the conversation.

"No, there's another guy. Bailey Adams. You want to talk to him?"

"We'll see," said McSwain. "Why's Stromquist need bodyguards anyway?"

"Well, you've met him. You can see how he could rub some people the wrong way. Hey . . ." He twisted around to look at McSwain, "I had martial arts training and I know how to handle myself with a firearm. You ever think about expanding your business, I could be, you know, a real asset, know what I mean?"

"Right now, I think we're going to stay a two-person operation," said McSwain.

"You'll keep me in mind, though, right?"

"Sure."

They reached the driveway and Moxley stopped the cart next to the house. McSwain got his address and phone number in case he needed to talk to him again, which seemed to bolster Moxley's mood—apparently he thought McSwain might be considering him for work.

"So apparently Stromquist's wife is alive and well," McSwain said as they were in the car passing back through the gate, "at least if Moxley's being straight with us."

"But is she really Billie? If she is, then she's either lying to Leland or he's lying for her."

"And if Billie is Virginia Stromquist, then we've got another woman who didn't go to the police when she was assaulted. Is she protecting someone? Maybe Leland set up the whole scenario for some sadistic reason."

"What about the stepson?" Capshaw said. "He sure seems to have some animosity toward Virginia."

McSwain glanced in the rearview mirror, where a green Jaguar was bearing down on the car. "Speak of the devil."

Chapter 10

The Jaguar flashed its lights twice. McSwain checked the mirror again, then put on his turn signal and pulled off onto the shoulder as the Jaguar glided to a stop behind them. The driver's door opened and Josh Stromquist emerged. Since they'd left him having the swearing match with Samuella, he'd changed out of his swim trunks and was now wearing tan shorts and a white Izod shirt. He tried to smile, but battling a triathlon finisher, even verbally, had definitely sapped some of its wattage.

Capshaw and McSwain got out of their car and walked back to meet him.

McSwain was still furious at Leland's remark about Lily and was looking for someone to take it out on. He had to remind himself this might not be the person or the place.

"Hey, why'd you guys take off like that?"

"Your lovers' quarrel got old fast," Capshaw said. "In spite of the fact that it sounded like you were losing."

"Hey, she's nothing but a psycho-slut stalker I met at a bar. No reason you two had to run off."

"You wanted to talk to us," said McSwain, "you could have caught us on our way back from the labyrinth."

"You kidding? And have Motormouth Moxley see me and report back to the old man? Don't think so." A car passed and his eyes clocked to the side, as though he were worried he might have been followed. Satisfied that it was neither his father nor Moxley, he went on. "You want to find the bitch, right?"

"Are you talking about Virginia Stromquist?" said McSwain.

"Who else? You want to talk to her or not?"

"What we want first," Capshaw said, "is to establish that she's okay."

Surprise registered on Josh's face. Either he was an accomplished actor or he truly had no idea what she was talking about. "Why wouldn't she be okay? Hey, what's going on? Has something happened?"

His acting wasn't so good after all, McSwain decided. The attempt at seeming concerned rang patently false.

"When did you last see Virginia?"

"Couple of weeks ago, I'd say. Then I drove up to Burbank, spent a few days with a lady I'm seeing. When I got back, Leland said she'd gone down to Mexico."

"She goes there often?" asked McSwain.

"Well, officially, Virginia claims to be an artist, says the landscape down there inspires her. Some kind of Georgia O'Keeffe thing. I'll tell you what impresses her—it may be south of the border, but it ain't Mexico."

"We don't much care what she's doing down there," Mcswain said. "We just want to find her."

Josh grinned broadly. "How bad?"

"You know where she is?"

"I know where she *probably* is. You find her, though, I want something in return."

"Gee, I figured you for the kind of guy who just does things out of the goodness of his heart," said Capshaw.

"What is it you want?" said McSwain.

"You do surveillance, right?"

"Sometimes."

"I want photos. Good-quality eight-by-ten glossies of Virginia in the most pornographic positions you can catch her in. Audio to go with it earns you a bonus."

Capshaw took a pack of cigarettes from her pocket and shook one out. "Not to burst your bubble, but your father doesn't seem to be the kind of guy that photos would impress."

"Yeah, I know, jealousy is a useless emotion and all that crap. Believe me, it's an act for the marks who buy the book and come to the seminars. He's as jealous as the next guy—why do you think he's so cavalier about not knowing where she is or what she does? If the truth that she was screwing around hit him in the face, he'd have to *kill* her or something." He saw the looks on their faces and said, "Just *kidding,* for Christ's sake. What, you people got no sense of humor?"

"So you want to bust up your father's marriage," said McSwain. "What does that get you—a bigger chunk of the family fortune?"

"That—plus the personal satisfaction of knowing I got that gold digger's hooks out of the old man and . . ." He waved a hand in front of his face and frowned at Capshaw. "You mind not polluting the atmosphere?"

"We're outdoors," said Capshaw, but she blew the smoke away from him on the next exhalation.

"You know, judging from the way you were cooling your heels in your father's office the other day, I wouldn't count on inheriting anything, wife or no wife," said McSwain, "or was treating you like the prodigal son just another act?"

"Just a power trip for the old man. I got in a little hot water with a chick a while back, and he gets off on thinking he's busting my balls. It won't last, believe me. Nepotism's his middle name. I'll be back on the payroll by next week."

"So where's Virginia?"

"First, do we have a deal? You find her shacked up with somebody, you photograph her? The nastier the evidence, the more money you'll make on the deal."

McSwain glanced at Capshaw, who shrugged. "If she's with someone, we could take photos. But we're not going to be staking the place out for a month, if that's what you think."

"Just photograph what you find. Ten to one, it'll be a *Portrait of the Artist with Her Legs in the Air.*"

"Okay," said McSwain.

"Great. Leland owns a condo at Las Estrellas in Ensenada. Second floor on the back; I don't remember the number. If she's not there, try the area bars. She likes to drink Tecate and scope out the local bullfighters."

"How do you know this?" McSwain said, and knew immediately that Josh had been waiting for the question. He smiled broadly, maliciously. It was a smile McSwain recognized—the smile of the schoolyard bully or the thug cop.

"I know because I've been there with her when she's got those legs in the air. Believe me, it's quite the view."

"So you're just another one of her fucks," said Capshaw.

"Hey, you have a nasty mouth. I like that in a woman. It means her mouth's probably nasty in more ways than one."

"Sleeping with your daddy's wife makes you a very fucked-up little boy," said Capshaw. "Freud would've had a field day."

"Yeah, well, fuck Freud." He took a step back, fanning his face. "Jesus, stop blowing your carcinogens at me. Another thing, I know what you're thinking. I've told you where Virginia is; now you don't have to do shit. Even if you don't care about the money, that wouldn't be smart. Don't fuck me over. Don't even think about it. You don't want me for an enemy."

McSwain felt the anger he'd been holding back for several minutes now surge to a boil. He stepped forward, grabbed the front of Josh's shirt with both hands, and slammed him back over the hood of the Jaguar. At the same time, he hoped that no cars would be coming by to witness what probably looked like a road-rage incident.

"Believe me, you don't want me for an enemy, either. But if you threaten me and my partner again, that's exactly what I'm going to be." He leaned forward and forced Josh back even further while putting his face inches from his. "You got that real clear?"

He let go and stepped back. Josh straightened up slowly, never taking his eyes off McSwain. "What are you, some kind of nut job?"

"Yeah, that's right. And you don't want to set me off or you'll find out just how much of a nut job I can be."

"Yeah, well, I'm sure the tough-guy routine plays well in some quarters. Just don't push your luck." He took a step backward so he could reach the door of the Jaguar without turning his back on McSwain. "Just get me some photos, doctored or otherwise, I don't give a fuck. Got it?"

"We're not really going to take pictures for that creep?" Capshaw said when they were driving back through the Rancho Santa Fe shopping area.

"Hey, I'm a man of my word," said McSwain. He shrugged and navigated a sharp turn where the road passed by a horse farm with a piebald stallion grazing out front. "But if I forget to load my camera, what're you gonna do?"

Capshaw laughed and lit another cigarette. She then lowered her window a few inches to let the smoke blow outside.

McSwain looked at his watch. "It's still early. We can get down to Ensenada if we go now."

"Doesn't that mean we'll have to swing by the office, put our guns in the safe?"

"We'd better, yeah. And unless you want to take your car, I want to pick up a rental."

"What, you don't trust the Tijuana drivers?"

"Too many bad experiences. This way I won't worry."

"You realize this may be a waste of time. I mean, come on, do you trust that guy to tell us where Virginia Stromquist really is? If he just wants incriminating photos, he could hire any PI firm to do that."

"True, but why would he send us on a wild-goose chase? If we're assuming Virginia's the woman we're looking for, he's got to know we'll find her sooner or later."

"You think Josh could be the guy who hid in the back of the car that night? If it was him, then there's a motive for Virginia not to go to the cops. She might be too afraid of him or of what it might do to her marriage."

"As well as a reason for her to hang out in Mexico when he's practically living with them."

They passed an upscale convenience store trying to disguise itself as a boutique or a branch bank, the red tile roof gleaming like spit-polished leather, muted, buff-colored walls blending in perfectly with the muted, buff-colored neighborhood.

Capshaw looked at him. "Want to stop and get a bottle of water?"

"No, I'm okay."

"You didn't look so good when Leland was giving us the grand tour. I thought maybe it was too much sun."

"Touch of claustrophobia, that's all." He shrugged, trying to make light of it, hoping she'd let it go.

"You're okay in elevators, stairwells, though."

"This was different. It was an enclosed space, but outdoors."

"That's worse?"

"For me it is." He found himself glancing at his hands on the steering wheel, at the whitish nub on the left one where the little finger used to be. It had been sliced off so long ago that he rarely thought of what had happened except in moments like these. He realized Jenna had said something, but he hadn't heard her.

"Sorry, what?"

"I asked if something happened to you to cause it."

He felt her eyes on him and stared at the road. "No, it's just how I am."

For the next mile or so, while they drove by palatial homes sealed away behind high walls and gates, they stayed silent. McSwain turned the radio to a Spanish station he sometimes listened to and tried to see how much he could pick up from what seemed to be a weather report and an ad for a car dealership, but his mind was on the case more than his Spanish.

Capshaw finally said, "What Stromquist found out about Lily, it made me wonder if he researched me, too."

"I don't know. Maybe. What, you worried about skeletons in your closet?"

"I meant, you know, my marriage."

"Probably not. Yours was a long time ago and ended in divorce. He can't use it to twist the knife with you like he can with me and Lily."

"Well, maybe he could." She tilted her head to blow a fresh stream of smoke out the window, but the car was rounding another curve and most of it blew right back in. "Larry and I never got divorced."

McSwain glanced at her. "You mean, you're still—"

"Oh, no, no." She lowered the window a few inches more and tossed the rest of the cigarette out the window. "Larry and I weren't divorced because he committed suicide. Twelve years ago this month. It was on my mind more than usual, I guess, because of the time of year. Then when Stromquist said what he did about Lily, all I could think was that he was going to hit me with Larry next."

"It's nothing to be ashamed of."

"Neither is having a wife who's in stir, but it stabs you right in the gut when you hear it. I can tell."

McSwain nodded. A Spanish voice was talking loudly about the birthday of someone named Miguelita. He reached over and cut it off.

"You never told me exactly what happened with you and Larry. I just assumed . . ."

"I let almost everyone think he and I got divorced, because it seemed easier. Easier on me, I guess."

McSwain wasn't sure if he should press her for details or not, so he said nothing. Eventually Capshaw said, "Larry's big mistake was he got clinically depressed back in the days before half the world was on antidepressants and the other half was in therapy. He didn't think it was manly to be depressed. And I didn't confront him about the fact that he was barely able to function, sitting up all night staring at the TV. So I'd have a drink and tell myself he'd snap out of it and to be thankful he was at home at least and not chasing around after women.

"Tuesday nights, he'd get home from work before me and he'd put out the garbage to be picked up the next morning. We'd argued over it a couple of times when he forgot. And this one Tuesday, as I was leaving the house, he told me I'd have to put the garbage out myself that night. I figured this was just one more thing he didn't feel like doing so I said, yeah, whatever, I do everything anyway so why not this, too, something like that. When I came home from work, he was gone. And he stayed gone till the next morning, when the cops came and said his body'd been found in the park a few blocks from our house. He'd shot himself. I didn't even know he had a gun, but he'd bought it a few weeks before."

She lapsed into silence and reached for another cigarette.

"Jesus, that must've been tough," said McSwain. "You were what, twenty-four?"

"Twenty-five. The funny thing was, I was so angry at him, like it was me he'd murdered instead of himself. Then I got to thinking how lonely he must've been, to be that unhappy and not even tell the one person he should have been able to talk to." She lit the cigarette, took a long drag, and leaned her arm out the window. "Except I wasn't there; I was locked away somewhere inside my head, with all my expectations of what marriage was supposed to be like and what a good husband was supposed to be like. Sometimes I still feel like I pulled the trigger as much as he did."

"That's giving yourself a lot of power."

"Yeah, a shrink once told me that, too. That, and a lot of other things." She blew a ribbon of gray smoke out the window and stared at a pair of smartly dressed young women in riding gear trotting their horses along a bridle path.

After his unwillingness to talk about his claustrophobia, McSwain found himself wondering if her sudden self-disclosure was an unconscious ploy—*I'll tell you my darkest secret if you'll tell me yours.*

But what she said was, "Maybe Stromquist's book isn't all bullshit, you know. Looking out for number one, steering clear of intense emotional involvement. Maybe that's the smart way."

"Wouldn't be much of a life, would it?"

In the silence that followed, he found himself thinking of Lily, asking himself if knowing her, loving her, was worth the price of these last two years. He decided unequivocally that it was—people made mistakes and nothing was irrevocable except the final, tragic mistake that Jenna's husband had made.

After a while, he reached over and turned the radio back on. A love song was being sung, but he couldn't make out the words.

Chapter 11

After stopping at the office to lock their guns in the safe, Capshaw went across the street to the taco shop for a burrito and coffee while McSwain drove up the street to Imperial Beach Rental Cars. There, a kid named Ramon, who looked almost old enough to have finished high school and was trying to grow a beard to prove it, rented him a blue Acura. He left the Monte Carlo on the lot, then swung back by the taco shop to pick up Jenna, and they headed south on I-8.

A few miles north of the border, McSwain saw the road sign that always caught his attention, the type of sign he'd never seen anywhere else in the world. It showed three people in profile, a man, woman, and child, holding hands as they ran, leaning forward as if against an invisible wind. The message was clear: Watch out for illegals darting across traffic. It always got to McSwain, the fear and desperation that made such a sign as necessary and normal as a deer-crossing sign would be on highways in upstate Vermont.

Traffic moved fairly smoothly through the border into Tijuana. He skirted the heavily congested thoroughfares leading into the city as much as possible. The prevailing atmosphere of Tijuana, a typical bordertown mix of shabbiness, struggle, and greed, had always depressed him. He took the Old Highway in favor of the interstate, which was faster but also, in his experience, more congested. Once past Tijuana, it became a pothole-ridden, two-lane affair lined with beer joints flashing signs for Tecate beer, fake-Moorish style hotels, and a proliferation of generic pottery shops. A few miles outside the tourist town of Rosarito Beach, they passed a checkpoint manned by municipal police in green uniforms who eyed the car without interest before waving them on. The police carried long, rifle-style guns that looked like M-16s. McSwain knew it was illegal to bring firearms into Mexico, but the sight of such conspicuous weaponry made him more aware of the absence of his own .38.

Farther south toward Puerto Nuevo, the shops and hotels became sparse. Other than men making cinder blocks by the side of the road, there was little to see. Deep arroyos and gulleys choked with weeds gouged the land on either side of the road. McSwain could see the distant ocean, but it looked pale and bleached out, like a mirage.

At Puerto Nuevo, Las Estrellas Resort and Condos rose like a sand sculpture in the middle of a block of seafood restaurants, art galleries, and the garishly red-roofed Club Morena health spa, whose sign claimed it to be the most exclusive in Baja. A smooth, sand-colored wall encircled the three-story building, but the front gate was open. McSwain drove in and parked among a dozen or so vehicles, most of them rentals bearing California tags. Capshaw went inside and reported back that there was a bank of mailboxes, but nothing with the name Stromquist.

"She's here, though."

"How do you know?"

"There was a kid out back scooping bugs out of the pool. He didn't know anything at first, but when I offered him ten bucks, he remembered a blond lady who lives in two-eight. He said she left here a couple of hours ago. Alone and on foot."

McSwain felt buoyed. "How hungry are you?"

"Not very. I had the burrito."

"You want to stay here, keep an eye out? I'll check out the bars and the restaurants, grab something to eat, and come back if I don't spot her. Then I'll take over."

"Fine."

McSwain first checked the small eatery at the Club Morena and the Califia Restaurant across the street, where he sat at the bar and wolfed down a fish taco and a Coke. The place was about half-full, but except for the bartender and two bejeweled American women using a calculator to total up their check, all the patrons were men. Two other seafood restaurants on the same block proved disappointing.

At the end of the block, the tiny La Costa Restaurant was crowded with laborers just getting off work and a sprinkling of what McSwain took to be ex-pats—foreigners who seemed at home and didn't stand out like the typical tourists. In one corner, a mariachi band played at a volume designed for a room several times larger than the one it was in. He took the last seat at the bar and ordered a Tecate, which was brought to him with a coaster and a basket of chips. He stayed there a half hour, but saw no one resembling Virginia.

Around seven, he left the last restaurant/bar in a three-block radius and walked back to the car. To his surprise, Jenna wasn't there, but her cell phone was. Thinking she wouldn't have gone far, he unlocked the car using the spare key and got inside.

An hour passed, then two. It was dark, and McSwain began to get worried. Had Jenna spotted Virginia Stromquist and followed her? That was the best explanation he could think of, and he hoped it was correct. On the other hand, she'd have to know he'd returned to the car by now and was worried about her.

Another hour. McSwain knew he should stay with the car, but he was just about to go look for Capshaw anyway when her face appeared outside the passenger-side window. He hit the lock-release button and she jumped inside.

"What happened?"

"Just drive. I don't think anyone saw me, but I want to be sure."

McSwain started the ignition and pulled away from the curb. "What are you talking about? Where've you been?"

"Inside the Stromquists' condo all this time."

"What?"

She tossed the hair back off her forehead, which was stippled with sweat. "I waited here an hour; then I figured what the hell, why not go inside and look around?

I went in through the back way, walked up the fire escape, and used my lockpicks to get in."

"Why the hell—"

She raised a hand and kept talking. "So it's fairly ordinary in there—a few framed pictures of Virginia and Leland, some expensive-looking abstract sculptures that I'm pretty sure they didn't buy in Tijuana. Closet full of women's shoes and clothes—unless she's got a lover who's a cross-dresser, no men's stuff as far as I could tell. There is sexual activity going on, but it may be solo—couple of vibrators, the electric and the battery-powered kind, in a drawer by the bed, tube of K-Y, and some soft-core porn magazines. She does paint, and not bad, too—a seascape up on an easel and some other paintings on the walls with her signature. Nothing to indicate the kind of Orgy Central Josh seemed to be hoping we'd find.

"Anyway, I'd just finished looking around when I heard somebody coming—Virginia maybe; I don't know for sure. There was a garment bag at the back of the bedroom closet, and I crouched down behind that. Whoever it was came inside, turned on the TV set, and lit a cigarette—I could smell the smoke, and it was giving me a nicotine fit. Whoever it was had on flip-flop sandals, too, and they seemed to be pacing around—I think they were going to the window behind the easel, looking out, then walking back to the sofa again. The TV stayed on, but after a while I realized I hadn't heard any movement for at least half an hour, and my calf muscles were cramping so bad, I was gonna have to crawl out of the closet if I didn't move soon, so I snuck out and peeked into the living room and there was nobody there."

"So it's definitely Virginia's place?"

"Yeah, there were receipts for some credit-card purchases with her signature—mostly art supplies, but one from a liquor store for over a hundred dollars' worth of booze. Gal either drinks a lot herself or entertains. Bare essentials in the refrigerator—a minimalist lifestyle, I'd have to say. Oh, and her makeup—"

"Makeup?"

"Yeah, she's got a ton of it—the bathroom looks

like she cleaned out Esté Lauder—and a couple of jars of really heavy-duty foundation—the kind of stuff a stage actress might use, even somebody wanting to cover up a skin condition, like eczema or maybe serious scarring."

"And you're sure whoever came in didn't know you were there?"

"How would they have known?"

"I don't know. Maybe you moved something, left something out of place. Virginia or somebody else came in, then realized something didn't feel right, got spooked, and left in a hurry, without bothering to cut the TV off."

"I think you're reaching."

"And I think it would've been a lot better if you'd followed the plan."

"What plan?"

"That you'd stay in the car and watch the building. If you saw her go in, we could've just knocked on the door."

"We can still do that."

Up ahead he saw a Chinese restaurant with its neon light on and turned into the lot, coming to a stop at the rear of the half-full parking lot. Capshaw had grabbed the lighter from the car console and was lighting a cigarette.

"Why did you have to break in? You want us both to end up in the slammer in Tijuana?"

She threw back her head and blew a long stream of smoke out the window as though trying to exhale her frustration.

"I thought I could be in and out in five minutes. It was just bad luck."

They sat in silence for a minute. A group of young, inebriated partiers stumbled out of the restaurant into the parking lot, piled noisily into several different cars, and roared out onto the main road, one barely avoiding a collision with a much larger vehicle, some kind of upper-end SUV, that was turning into the lot.

Capshaw gave an exasperated sigh. "So what now?"

"Well, we still haven't found out for sure if Virginia Stromquist is the woman who gave Mandy the ride that night, but I'm not comfortable going back and banging on the door to ask her after you've made an illegal entry. I think we should just go home."

"Jesus, Ian, I'm sure I got in and out without being seen."

"As far as you know."

"What, you think Virginia Stromquist watched me sneak out of her apartment, but was too stunned to say, 'Hey, lady, what the fuck are you doing?' "

"No, but what about the boy cleaning the pool who knows you were looking for her? If he or somebody else saw you inside the building or even coming out of her condo, there's no reason to think he wouldn't say something to Virginia, maybe hoping to get a tip for it, if nothing else. Assuming that was even Virginia who came in."

"Who else would it have been?"

"I don't know, but it sounds like they were waiting for someone—you said it sounded like they kept looking out the window. Maybe it was Virginia the person was waiting for."

"I think we should go back to Las Estrellas. At the very least stake the place out again."

"Have you ever been in a Mexican jail?"

"Have you?"

"No, and I want to keep it that way."

He pulled out of the parking lot, turned north, and headed back along the Old Highway paralleling the sea. There were no streetlights. Here and there, a flicker of neon from a restaurant or bar cut through the darkness, but after they left Ensenada the car's headlights were the only light that sliced through the blackness.

"You know, it's too bad we can't wrap this up the easy way," said McSwain. "Moxley's so eager to be accommodating—we get him to give us a call as soon as Virginia comes home—then we use a telephoto lens to get some close-ups and show them to Mandy. Assuming that Virginia is Billie, Mandy ID's her, she's satisfied that the woman she left behind is alive and well, end of story."

The headlights illuminated a pothole the size of a tire. McSwain swung the wheel, managed to veer around it.

"Except, of course, we can't do that," said Capshaw.

"No, we can't."

"For starters, I'd like to know why Stromquist was so unwilling to put us in contact with his wife or even admit that her nickname's Billie? What's he hiding?"

"Maybe nothing. Maybe he's scared of bad publicity. He knows she's screwing around and doesn't want to risk us selling a story to the tabloids."

"Jeez, is he that famous?"

"In his own eyes, he probably is."

As McSwain slowed for another pothole, Capshaw's right foot pressed an imaginary brake. "Assuming Virginia is Billie," she said, "then she's our best lead in finding this guy before he rapes and maybe murders someone else. I think you're right that she's protecting someone—especially if the perp in the car that night knew her name. And if there's a chance that this guy is the Boy Scout, then— Ian, watch out!"

A pair of bright, red-tinged eyes appeared suddenly in the road. An animal—a cat or small dog—stared into the headlights and then darted away as McSwain spun the wheel so violently the car almost lurched off the road.

Capshaw braced herself against the dash and then twisted to peer out the window. "It's all right; it's okay. Whatever it was, you didn't hit it." She settled back in the seat. "Thank God."

As she spoke, something crashed into the Acura from behind. A taillight shattered. They were both slammed forward against their seat belts. The Acura skidded across the lane and onto the shoulder while McSwain fought to control the wheel. Before he could right the car, the vehicle behind them speeded up and rear-ended them again.

McSwain went with the skid. The Acura careened along the rutted shoulder before veering back into the right lane. He hit the gas and the car surged ahead. In the rearview mirror, he saw the high beams of the pursuing vehicle come on.

"Christ, he's not letting up," Capshaw said.

McSwain thought he saw her hand brush automatically at the back of her belt, where she would have carried her SIG Sauer if she'd had it on her. For a second, he thought of his own gun in the safe at the office. But there was no time for regrets; the vehicle behind them roared forward.

"Hang on," he said, and braced for another crash, but it didn't come. Instead the vehicle behind them—the same oversize SUV that had entered the restaurant parking lot soon after they did, McSwain thought—came roaring up alongside them in the left lane.

McSwain floored the pedal, trying to move ahead of the truck. He kept an eye out for lights up ahead, either an oncoming vehicle that would force the truck to pass or drop back from the left lane or some sort of business that was open. He saw nothing, and the road was becoming narrower as they came into the desolate stretch between Ensenada and Rosarito Beach.

The truck crashed into the Acura's left bumper. Metal screeched and sparks shot from the grille. The car was knocked sideways, where it careened along the flat expanse of dust and scrub before McSwain was able to regain control and get back on the road.

The truck roared past and accelerated, its brights slicing the dark like a scalpel.

"Jesus," McSwain said, letting his breath out. He felt like he'd been holding it since the truck first came up on them.

"What the hell was that?" said Capshaw.

"More than a bad case of road rage, I'd say."

"No shit, he was trying to kill us."

McSwain slowed the car, trying to assess the damage. Even with the car doing forty-five, the wheel was pulling hard to the left, and he was sure the rear left tire was blown. There was a spare in the trunk, but he didn't feel like pulling off onto the shoulder to change it. They'd be sitting ducks that way. Maybe when they got to Tijuana . . .

The truck thundered out of the darkness on their right. It struck the side of the car, caving in the front bumper and slamming them sideways. Even wearing his seat belt, McSwain felt his head and shoulder thud against the window. The car skidded sideways, tires screaming as it clung to the shoulder before pitching over the edge. McSwain felt the air leave him as his air bag deployed, punching him in the torso and face like a huge boxing glove. Then the car rolled. It was upside down, sliding, then suddenly righted itself before it flipped one more time and jolted to a halt upside down.

He opened his eyes and stared into darkness that seemed absolute as a grave. He was hanging upside down in his seat belt harness, his arms dangling over his head, fingers brushing the roof of the car. He heard a sound that he thought was his ears ringing and then realized it was waves pounding up on the shore not far away. Lights began to dance at the edge of his vision. He knew he was in danger of passing out. Perhaps worse, he was in danger of panicking—memories of his mother's whimpering pleas and of his own blood gushing onto the roof of another overturned car surged into his mind. He fought them down and started struggling to free himself.

"Jenna, you okay?"

She didn't answer at first, but her hand brushed his and she briefly clasped fingers with him and squeezed. Then he could hear movement as she, too, tried to extricate herself from the harness. Suddenly she gave a sharp, pained cry. "My right hand, I think it's broken. Shit, I can't get out of this thing."

"Can you open your door?"

"I don't think—" The words caught in her throat. "No, I . . . my hand's pretty bad."

"Okay, hang on. I'm going to do something."

He swung his legs up and forward as he unhooked his seat belt and did a clumsy backroll onto the interior of the roof.

On the road above, a vehicle passed. He held his breath for a second, but he could tell by the sound of the motor that it wasn't the truck that had run them off the road. He knew whoever was in the vehicle going by couldn't see them, but for an instant the headlights illuminated the inside of the car, and he could see Capshaw's face. Her eyes were shut, and her skin had a slick, waxen sheen.

He waited a beat on the chance the driver of the car might actually see them and stop, but it kept going.

"Ian?"

"Yeah."

"That guy might come back."

"That's why we have to get out of here." He twisted around and positioned himself just below her. "Put your weight on my back and unhook the belt. I'll lower you onto your right side."

"Okay. Here goes."

He heard the belt snap open and she toppled onto him. He broke her fall, turning her to the right as gently as possible, but he felt her whole body clench against the pain of being jarred.

"How bad?"

"I'm okay." He heard a scrabbling sound, and a handle being worked. She cursed quietly. "The door's jammed."

"I'll try this one."

He ran his hand along the inside of the passenger door. The impact of the crash had caved it inward and dislocated the handle, making it useless. He leaned back and swung his legs around, aiming his feet at the door.

"Close your eyes. I'm going to kick out the window."

There was a dull pop. A bullet ricocheted off one of the tires. Another careened off the exposed undercarriage.

"Into the backseat—get down," said McSwain.

The shots seemed to be coming from above and in front of the car, meaning the shooter was probably descending the embankment that the car had rolled down. McSwain figured he'd pulled off somewhere that the truck wouldn't be seen and come back on foot. He also seemed to be firing blindly, maybe hoping to flush them out into the open if they were still able to get out of the car.

Capshaw crawled under the top of the driver's-side seat and McSwain did the same on his side. He had barely squeezed through when another bullet exploded the windshield and glass fragments showered the inside of the car. He drew his legs up to his chest and kicked the back window. Nothing happened. He kicked again, feeling the impact in both knees. The glass groaned and popped out in a single piece.

"Come on!"

Another shot screamed off metal. It sounded much closer. The shooter must be almost down the embankment. He grabbed Capshaw's good hand, and they ran in a diagonal toward the water. He knew the shooter would reach the car any second. As soon as he realized they weren't in the car, he'd come after them.

As they neared the surf, the hard-packed sand began to turn mushy. McSwain could see the pale streaks of whitecaps marching forward atop ink-black waves. Above the hiss of the water, he heard another gunshot, then the sounds of squealing metal and shattering glass. He realized the shooter had reached the bottom of the embankment. Unable to tell in the darkness if they were hiding inside, he was firing into the car.

Capshaw grabbed his arm. "Over there!"

At first, he couldn't see what she was pointing to. His night vision wasn't as good as hers, and he was staring at black against blacker. Then, as they got closer, he made out a hulking shape a hundred or so yards up the beach. From that angle, it looked to him like a section of wall. As they ran toward it, though, the object became clearer—a cistern that had been excavated and abandoned.

As they ducked inside, Capshaw reached down and unclipped a .22 from the ankle holster she was wearing under her jeans.

"I thought you put your guns in the safe."

"One of them."

They crouched inside the cistern and waited, but heard no more gunshots. No one came after them. McSwain decided to take a chance. "I'm going up to have a look around."

"Take the gun."

"No, keep it."

He crawled out of the cistern and part of the way up the embankment, planning to take a quick look around. Reaching the top, he was about to hoist himself up when light exploded in his eyes. The muzzle of a gun was rammed into his ribs and a voice shouted at him in Spanish. When he didn't respond right away, a second voice said in heavily accented English, "Hands up and throw down your weapons. You're under arrest."

Chapter 12

A bored-looking police captain at a roadside station in Ensenada listened to their story of being forced off the road and shot at. He seemed convinced it was a case of road rage fueled by the other driver's inebriated fury at McSwain over some slight—real or imagined—that had occurred on the road or in a bar earlier that evening.

Attempted murder over some imagined driving infraction might not be normal, but neither did he seem to think it improbable.

Fortunately the fact that Jenna had a gun in her possession didn't complicate matters—she'd had the presence of mind to strap the revolver back in her ankle holster as soon as she realized it was the federales Ian was talking to.

Around five in the morning, after giving their statements for what seemed like the tenth time and being told that they would be contacted on any developments in the case, they were told they were free to go. McSwain found a pay phone and a coffee machine dispensing black sludge that might have been brewed the week before. He gulped a cup of it anyway, then called the emergency 800 number for the rental company. He reported the accident and asked for a replacement car to get them back over the border. It was the middle of the night and he was in Mexico—he could tell the woman on the other end had to fight not to laugh at his request before she told him "No way, buddy," and hung up the phone. He then tried calling a few of the local taxi services listed in the battered phone directory, but got only answering machines or busy signals.

Finally he waylaid a patrolman going off-duty and persuaded him, for fifty dollars, to drive him and Jenna to the border, where they walked across around seven in the morning and found a cab. He dropped Capshaw off at her home in Ocean Beach, making her promise to have her hand attended to, then debated whether to head home or to the office. He knew he needed to shower, shave, and get something to eat, but he decided to swing by the office first, just to satisfy himself that everything was all right.

It wasn't.

Two police cars and an ambulance were double-parked outside Dave's Gym.

An imposingly large female cop stationed at the door informed him the gym was closed, but he flashed his PI's ID and told her his office was upstairs and she nodded him through. As he came in, two EMTs were bringing Ricardo out of Dave's office on a stretcher. Ricardo's head was bandaged, but his eyes were open and he looked alert. When he saw McSwain, he mouthed, *I'm sorry, man,* and held up both hands in a whaddaya-gonna-do gesture.

"It's okay," McSwain said as the stretcher swept past. He didn't know what had transpired, but the fact that Ricardo was apologizing to him for something put a hard, clammy knot in his stomach.

Dave was standing next to the ring, talking to a tall cop with a receding hairline and acne-scarred skin. He saw McSwain and said, "Ian, where you been? I've been calling you."

"It's a long story. What happened here? Ricardo . . . ?"

"He's got a knot on his head, but he's okay. I've seen him look a lot worse at the end of ten rounds."

"You work here?" said the cop, who wore a tag on his uniform that said Roussin.

McSwain still had his PI ID in his hand and held it out. "I rent the upstairs office from Dave."

"Oh, yeah, the PI." Roussin pronounced the initials as though *private detective* were a few rungs down the ladder from *hooker.*

"What happened?" said McSwain.

"Looks like somebody broke in who thought the building was empty," said Roussin. "This guy . . ." He looked at his notes.

"Ricardo Delgado," said Dave.

"Delgado heard something, came out of the office to investigate, and got whacked over the head. How long you rented here, Mr. McSwain?"

"Little over three years."

"Work alone?"

"I have a partner. Jenna Capshaw."

Roussin went through a few more questions before McSwain had a chance to ask what was uppermost in his mind. "My office," he said, "how much damage?"

Dave was rubbing the back of his neck as though he were the one who'd been clobbered. "Pretty well trashed, but I couldn't tell if anything was taken."

"Shit, what about—"

"Don't worry. The files you keep in the storeroom down here are fine. So's the safe. After he'd ko'd Ricardo, the guy didn't even bother checking out what was in my office. He just went through yours like a hurricane and then split."

McSwain felt a wave of relief take the edge off some of his anger. He knew that would be temporary—that as soon as he saw the damage upstairs he'd want to kill someone—but the more important thing was that the case files hadn't been touched.

"Go on upstairs," Roussin said. "There's a detective up there. You can look around and tell him what's missing."

As it turned out, there wasn't anything taken that McSwain could see, but the level of chaos was such that it might take him some time to determine that for certain. His gut feeling, though, was that nothing had been stolen, that the files in Dave's back room had been the real object of the break-in.

The detective, a heavyset black man who introduced himself as Sullivan, was dusting the outside of the desk drawers for fingerprints, and answered McSwain's question before he could ask it. "I'm not getting any prints, and I'd expect to at least find some of yours. There's nothing on the doorknob either. This guy wiped everything down." He straightened up, knees popping like those of a much older man. "Any idea who might've done this?"

"In my business, could be a lot of people," said McSwain, although he suspected it was the same man who'd run him off the road, then been scared off when the federales showed up. With light traffic at the border that time of night, the gunman could've made it back to Imperial Beach in two hours, easy. He didn't want to go into that, though, with the detective. "You might talk to a guy named Danny Tibbs who owns Xtreme Ink in National City. He and I had a little run-in recently. See if he's got an alibi for last night."

Sullivan tilted an eyebrow. "Deacon Tibbs? Believe I've heard that name a time or two. We'll check it out."

McSwain became peripherally aware of a phone ringing nearby. He traced the sound to a corner, where he found the cordless phone partially buried under a pile of unopened mail that the intruder had swept onto the floor. He expected it to be Jenna, but the voice on the other end belonged to Hank Paris.

"We got another one."

McSwain was momentarily nonplused. "Huh?"

"The Boy Scout. He did another one."

"Shit. Where?"

"Same area your client described being taken to. Few miles west of Jamul." He gave directions to the scene, which McSwain hastily scribbled down.

"I'm on my way. You'll be there?"

He heard the weariness in Paris's voice. "Unfortunately so."

Chapter 13

Before leaving Dave's Gym, McSwain opened the safe, took out his .38 in its holster, and put it on. He also took Jenna's 9mm SIG Sauer, which he slipped inside his jacket. He then called her on her cell phone and found her in her car, driving to the walk-in clinic in Palm City to have her hand checked. After filling her in on the events at Dave's Gym, he told her about Paris's call. She told him her hand could wait and pulled off the road so she could take down the directions to the crime scene.

McSwain headed east on Otay Valley Road toward Jamul. He passed a number of identical-looking subdivisions sprawled out over the low humps of bare, sun-scorched hills and then drove through an area of wooded slopes that hadn't yet been scraped raw by developers. Rounding a curve, he pulled over next to a cluster of black-and-whites on the shoulder. Capshaw had made it there first; her Suburu was parked a few yards ahead on the opposite side of the road.

Parking his car beyond hers, he trudged up one side of a rock-strewn trail paralleling a drainage ditch. Beer bottles, crushed-out cigarettes, and used condoms gave evidence that teenagers used the area for partying. At one point, the trail narrowed down to no more than a couple of feet and was flanked by scraggly bushes as high as his head. The effect was that of a natural tunnel—he could see only directly ahead of him and then only a few feet. If this was the where the murder victim had been marched to her death, he could scarcely imagine a more desolate and frightening trek.

He emerged from the tree-lined path to be confronted

by a pair of officers, a short, swarthy Hispanic with a name tag that said Riviera, and an older, barrel-chested man named Clemson. About a hundred yards farther on, he could see yellow crime-scene tape, and beyond that, a dozen or so police officers and detectives. When he headed that way, the cop named Clemson blocked his path.

"That's as far as you go, pal."

"I'm with Detective Paris. He called me out here to take a look."

Clemson shot a bored look up the hillside and turned to Riviera. "You want to go check on that?"

Before Riviera could comply, they saw Hank Paris striding toward them. He jerked his head curtly and barked, "It's okay; let him through."

Clemson hesitated. McSwain got the impression he saw the crime scene, any crime scene, as his personal turf, but then he shrugged and stepped out of the way. McSwain made his way up the hill to where Paris was standing. The detective wore tan pants and a blue shirt with mud on the cuffs of his rolled-up sleeves. One hand clutched a handkerchief he'd been using to cover his mouth and nose.

"You're late. Forensics is finishing up," Paris said, then added, "Jenna got here ten minutes ago."

McSwain nodded, not really interested in who'd won the race to the crime scene or the fact that Paris apparently resented having to deal with Jenna without McSwain there as a buffer. He stepped over the yellow tape and looked down a steep, weedy slope that ended in a shallow drainage ditch. Something was lying in the ditch, but from this vantage point it didn't look like a body, not an intact one, anyway. He found himself wondering if the killer could have possibly sawed the victim in two. Queasiness churned in his stomach as he started to descend the slope.

"Hold on."

He turned back to Paris, who was staring down at the ditch as though still trying to assimilate what he was looking at. "I just want to make something clear—I wouldn't have called you out here if I didn't think your client may have had a run-in with this guy and lived to talk about it. The woman down there in the ditch wasn't so lucky. You see this, maybe you can convince her to come talk to me."

McSwain nodded. From his vantage point on the slope, it still appeared to him that at least half the body was missing. "Did he . . . was she mutilated?"

"Take a look."

There'd been rain recently and the slope was slippery as they descended. The pungent, intensely repellent odor of decomposition was becoming apparent, too. McSwain was glad he'd thought to bring a handkerchief.

The forensics team that Paris claimed to be finishing up was still collecting and bagging evidence. A photographer shot pictures of the body and the surrounding area while detectives scoured the underbrush behind the drainage ditch. Beyond this area, he saw Capshaw taking notes as she talked to a female police captain.

"Any ID?"

"Nothing yet. There's been a lot of destruction to the facial area." He grimaced and brought a hand up to one side of his face. McSwain remembered the toothache, wondered if anything had been done since he last saw him, figured it hadn't. Paris went on, "Animals, you know. Coyotes and foxes up here. We'll probably have to go with dental."

McSwain moved closer and then stopped. The smell hit him full force—the olfactory equivalent of a kick to the face. He clamped the handkerchief to his nose.

"How long's she been here?"

Paris nodded in the direction of a lanky, stoopshouldered member of the forensics team who was using tweezers to place something in a plastic bag. "Hector over there says a week to ten days, give or take."

McSwain stepped closer. The woman's dark brown hair had been braided once, but now most of it had come loose and floated in the inch or two of filthy water in the drainage ditch. Animals had been at the face, but the bloated and discolored limbs appeared, for the most part, intact.

He could see now what had been done to her and why he'd mistakenly thought part of her body was missing. The woman lay on her back with her legs brought up to her chest, knees bent, and crossed at the ankles, a position that left her obscenely accessible to her killer. A thick rope was wound around her ankles and looped around her neck, then knotted between her breasts. Another rope encircled her waist. McSwain couldn't see her arms, but they appeared to have been yanked back behind her. Clearly her killer had enjoyed arranging her—perhaps gotten more gratification out of applying the bondage than the actual killing.

He turned back to Paris. "This was done before or after she was killed?"

"Before, probably—which means this one's different from the earlier victims that were tied up after death. They do the autopsy, they'll know for sure. The ME can make an incision in the tissue to look for bruising that would indicate she wriggled around, tried to free herself. But Hector says you look close enough, you can see the abrasions on her wrists where the ropes burned her."

"Which means she was either unconscious when she was being bound and woke up later and started struggling or the killer intimidated her into holding still while he tied her up."

"Forensics will be able to tell us if there was battering to the skull, but I'd say he intimidated her into cooperating. A limp body, don't see how he could have held the legs in that position and tied them at the same time."

McSwain considered that. "Unless there were two?"

"I doubt it. This type of killing, it's usually one guy acting out his own sick shit. But we'll know more after the autopsy."

"The other Boy Scout victims, were they tied like this?"

"All different. Each one very elaborate, meticulous; the guy took his time." He looked away from the body to stare at the bruise over McSwain's eye. "What the hell happened to you two, anyway? Jenna's hand is messed up and you look like you been spending too much time in that boxing gym under your office."

"Car accident."

Capshaw came over. From the way she and Paris avoided eye contact, McSwain guessed whatever encounter they'd had before he'd arrived had been less than cordial. She held an unlit cigarette in her left hand, turning it over and over in her fingers, obviously dying to light up. Her right hand was wrapped in an elastic bandage that extended from below the knuckles to midway up her forearm.

"You can't smoke at a crime scene," said Paris.

"I'm not smoking."

"Thought you were planning to quit?"

She shot him a look. "The plan changed."

"You'll never quit smoking. Give up the cigs, you might put on weight. You'd never let that happen; you're too vain."

"Jesus, Hank, lay off, will you?"

"The body, who found it?" said McSwain.

Paris turned his head sharply, as though just remembering there was a corpse only a few feet away. "Couple of sisters, twelve and fourteen. They were walking the family dog before school and came down here so it could run off the leash. The dog started barking. That's when they saw it."

McSwain shook his head. It was hard enough seeing something like this when you were an adult who'd seen dead bodies before. But to be a kid and come upon such a thing . . . he couldn't even imagine.

Two members of the forensics team, the man named Hector whom Paris had pointed out and a heavyset Asian woman whose perfume had obviously been applied in the faint hope of canceling out the stench of decomposed flesh, were using gloved hands to gingerly turn the body onto its side. The photographer moved in to shoot pictures from that angle.

From the way her arms were positioned when he'd first seen her, McSwain had assumed the woman's wrists were tied, but the killer had used a much more complex restraint. The rope around her neck extended down her back, where it was knotted between her elbows and then used to bind her wrists in a crisscrossed position similar to that of her ankles. It was a position that had to have been excruciating for the woman, and, for her sake, McSwain found himself wishing that Hector could be wrong about what the abrasions on her wrists meant, that she'd been trussed up like this after she was already dead.

"Her clothing—anybody find it?"

"Nothing yet, but we're looking. He didn't kill her here, though. He did her somewhere up on the hill and then rolled or dragged the body down."

"If the perp sprayed her with perfume," Capshaw said, "any chance Forensics could still find trace amounts?"

"This much decomposition and exposure, no chance," Paris said. "Anyway, perfume's mostly alcohol. It would've evaporated."

"If you find the clothing then . . ."

"We find the clothing, then maybe there's a chance. I'll tell you right now, though, I'll be surprised if we do. My bet is the perp took the clothes with him, destroyed them or ditched them in a Dumpster somewhere."

The forensic techs had moved the body onto its side on the stretcher and covered it with a sheet. They were taking it up to a waiting ambulance. McSwain got another blast of death stench and, in its wake, the lingering odor of the Asian woman's fragrance. He hoped if any trace of perfume was found on the corpse, it wouldn't turn out to be hers.

He watched the techs carry the stretcher uphill and the unnatural lump that the feet made under the sheet. It looked like whoever was under there might still be alive and trying to kick her way out.

"The officer I was talking to a minute ago," Capshaw said, "she told me one of the Boy Scout victims had her ankles tied to a broom handle. Has he used objects like that before?"

Paris's eyebrows bunched and he rubbed the side of his jaw as though it was paining him more than ever. "That information wasn't supposed to be leaked. I assume it won't go any further."

McSwain and Capshaw both nodded.

"He used the broom handle on Harriet Wynn, the woman whose body was found in an abandoned building. Her ankles were bound to either end and her wrists were behind her back, tied to the handle. He'd bound her breasts, too."

"Her breasts?" said McSwain.

"Above and below the nipples. Tight enough to do significant tissue damage if she'd lived."

"Besides the bondage, anything else that ties the killings together? Does the perp take souvenirs?"

"Not body parts, that's what you mean. Only thing we think might've been taken was from Wynn. Night she was killed, she stopped in a bar, had a drink with a woman friend named Carol Yates. When we interviewed the woman, she mentioned that Wynn was wearing a necklace that night, some kind of Hindu symbol she wore all the time. It wasn't on the body, though, which means the perp might have taken it or, more likely, it was torn off in a struggle between her and her killer."

McSwain pulled out his notepad and added this to the other information he'd already jotted down. When he heard Paris curse, he looked up to see a photographer with a camcorder shooting down from the top of the hill.

"Shit, here they come," Paris said. He turned to Capshaw and McSwain. "The media's going to be all over this. I've got to give some kind of statement. And you two, you're not supposed to be here. In fact, you never were here."

"Got it," said Capshaw.

"Take care of that tooth," said McSwain.

Paris grimaced. He started up the hill, then turned back. "You get that girl of yours to come in and make a statement. She doesn't want to, give her an idea what you saw here today. Change her damn mind."

When they got back to where they'd parked their vehicles, Capshaw lit the cigarette she'd been fondling for the last twenty minutes and took a long drag with her eyes shut. McSwain didn't smoke, but at moments like that he sometimes wondered if he wasn't missing something. When she finally exhaled, much of the tension in her body seemed to flow out along with the smoke. "Okay, Ian, I'll see you back at the office." She started to get into her car.

"Whoa, hold on there." He put a hand on her arm.

"What?"

"I'm the one going back to the office. You're going to the clinic to get that hand x-rayed."

"Ian, our office has been trashed. I've got to get in there."

"Forget it. I'll take care of the office. Your hand looks like an old baseball glove. Get it looked at."

"Yeah, well, first time in my life I feel lucky to be a leftie. It's my right hand, so it can wait." She blew a long plume of smoke, following its upward coils with her eyes. "Whoever broke in, they didn't get what they wanted, did they?"

"I don't think so, no."

"Which brings up a question—what *did* they want?"

"Well, if it's some other case, who knows? The burglar could've been somebody we once put away looking for information on who hired us, a stalker trying to find out where an ex-spouse or girlfriend currently lives, any number of things. But if there's a connection between what happened last night and the break-in, then I'd say he was looking for the case file on Mandy."

"Who she is and how to find her."

"I'd say so."

"Which means whoever it was won't give up. He'll try again."

"Not at the office, but yeah, somewhere."

"Probably the same guy who ran us off the road. While we were dealing with the federales, he was crossing back over the border and breaking into our office."

McSwain nodded. "It looks that way."

"Okay, I'll go to the hospital, but when I'm done, I'm going to do some checking up on our boy Josh. He's the one who sent us down there to find Virginia. Ten to one, he was either the guy driving the truck or paid someone to do it."

"Or Tibbs," said McSwain. "I think he lied about not knowing where she lived. For all we know, he could've been the one paying her a visit while you were in her condo."

"Oh, before I forget"—he reached inside his jacket and took out the SIG—"thought you might want this."

Capshaw lifted an eyebrow as she took the SIG and slid it inside her jacket. "I see you waited to give this to me until *after* I've seen Hank. What, you don't trust me?"

McSwain shrugged. "Never know with you two."

"Yeah, the way he carps at me, you'd think we were still sleeping together."

"That's a pretty cynical view of relationships."

"Yeah, well . . ." She dropped the cigarette on the ground, crushed it out. "Hank looked like shit, didn't he?"

"He had a bad tooth last time I saw him. I don't think he's been to a dentist."

"No, I meant . . . in general. Since I last saw him, he's really aged."

"Haven't we all?"

"Gee, thanks, Ian. You always know how to cheer me up."

"Anytime."

She gave a wry smile. In the bright sunlight he could see the small scar at the edge of her upper lip and flecks of green in her eyes. He didn't like the surly way that Paris acted whenever Jenna was around, but maybe—if the guy had never gotten over her—he could understand.

Chapter 14

After leaving the crime scene, McSwain debated whether to return to the office or go home for breakfast and a much-needed shower. He had decided to return to the office—the only thing he felt he could get down anyway was coffee, and why worry about showering when the only people he was likely to come in contact with were the sweaty pugilists in Dave's Gym?—when it occurred to him that whoever had trashed the office could also have found out where he lived and paid him a visit.

With that in mind, he changed course immediately and headed home. Along the way, he checked his cell phone for messages. There was a message from a security company wanting some background checks done, a long, rambling message from Mandy apologizing for her mother's behavior and urging him to stop by her place of work for free coffee and doughnuts anytime, and a short, love-you-honey-I'm-doing-fine message from Lily, who told him she was borrowing a friend's illegal cell phone to make the noncollect call. He hated to think of Lily violating any rules when she was this close to freedom, but still he played the message over three times just because it made him feel good. There were also four hang-ups, the fourth of which was the last thing on the tape. He tried to trace the number using star 69 and got a recording saying the call had been blocked.

Back at home, he was hurrying along the cobblestoned walkway when Ghandi pulled the hide-and-pounce trick from the bushes.

"Got me, Ghandi," he said to the black-and-white cat, who meowed and rubbed against his ankles.

The front door to the carriage house was locked, just as he'd left it the morning before, the interior undisturbed. Relief flooded through him and, with it, deep weariness. His body ached from the battering it had taken inside the overturning Acura. Worse was the impact of seeing the Boy Scout's victim, an image he was unable to shake from his mind. He wanted to talk to Lily, but knew he was unlikely to get a call from her this early in the morning. They hadn't talked the day before, though, so he was sure she'd call this afternoon.

While he was trying to decide how much, if anything, he'd tell Lily about recent events, he put on a pot of coffee. Then he went upstairs, stripped his clothes off in the bedroom, and took a shower with the water as hot as he could stand it, letting the stinging needles pepper his back and shoulders. He was leaning back into the spray, rinsing shampoo from his hair, when a noise came from downstairs at the front of the house.

He froze with his arms up over his head, shampoo streaming down the sides of his face. The hot water pouring over his neck and back seemed suddenly cold.

He tried to recall the details of his entry into the house only minutes before. Had he turned the dead bolt on the front door after he came in? He couldn't remember. Had he been so relieved to find no one had broken in that he'd forgotten that most obvious task? Had Ghandi slipped into the house when he opened the door, and was he the cause of the noise downstairs?

His first instinct was to turn off the water, but if someone was in the house, that would draw their attention. Leaving the water running, he slowly moved out of the shower and peered out into the bedroom. Saw nothing. Grabbing a towel from the bar overhead, he wrapped it around himself and moved out into the bedroom. His .38, still holstered, was on top of the bureau where he'd laid it before getting into the shower. Now he removed it from the holster and bent down to pick up the pair of boxer shorts he'd thrown on the floor. Letting the towel drop, he managed to step into the shorts while still holding the gun.

There was another noise now, what sounded like the soft thud of shoes on the carpeted floor.

He held the .38 in both hands as he moved toward the bedroom door and into a short hallway. To his left stairs led down to the living room, dinette, and kitchen. Cautiously, he began descending.

At the bottom, he could see that the longer leg of the L-shaped living room as well as the dinette and kitchen were unoccupied. Beyond that, the room made a ninety-degree turn into an area that McSwain had transformed into a reading nook—an armchair and bookcase set facing a bay window that looked out over the garden. He realized now that, in addition to offering a modicum of seclusion, the reading nook was an ideal location for an ambush.

Keeping his back to the wall, he crossed the living room. He was just about to make the turn into the reading nook when a crash came from behind him. He whirled and charged toward the kitchen in time to see Ghandi perched atop the counter next to the stove. Below him on the tile floor a drinking glass lay broken in several pieces.

He swore softly and retreated into the living room. Almost as an afterthought, convinced Ghandi had been the source of the original noise, he checked the reading nook.

And recoiled as if he'd seen a corpse sitting there.

"You aren't going to shoot me, are you?"

A woman with wide green eyes and a tentative smile sat in the armchair in front of the window. She wore a patterned ankle-length skirt, a white, sleeveless blouse, and white, high-heeled sandals. She'd taken a pillow from the chair and was holding it on her lap.

McSwain made no move to lower the gun. "Put the pillow on the floor. Slowly."

"What? You think I've got a gun?"

"Just do it."

Using the tips of her fingers, she scooted the pillow over her knees onto the floor. Her lap was empty. "I wish you'd put that gun away. I'm afraid of guns."

"And I'm afraid of strangers who show up in my house unannounced."

"Even a woman?"

"Especially a woman. Now who are you? What are you doing here?"

"Put the gun down and I'll tell you."

But by then he'd recognized her from her picture in the brochure.

"Virginia Stromquist."

She nodded. "Do you make it a practice to leave your door unlocked, Mr. McSwain? Doesn't seem very wise. I knocked first, but when there wasn't an answer . . ." She nodded at Ghandi, who had followed McSwain into the living room and now leaped up on the windowsill. "I assume that's your cat. He seemed to know his way around."

Her gaze wandered slightly, then returned to his face. He was suddenly, acutely aware that he was standing in front of a woman he had never met in his life wearing nothing but boxer shorts. "Look, whatever your reasons for being here, I'm glad you are. I'm going upstairs to get dressed. Don't go anywhere."

"Want to handcuff me to the kitchen table? Just to be sure?"

"I think I'll trust you."

When he came back downstairs a few minutes later, he found Virginia making herself at home in his kitchen. She'd gathered up the pieces of the broken glass and dropped them into the trash and was pouring herself a cup of coffee. She took a sip and little lines crinkled at the bridge of her nose.

"You make terrible coffee."

"So I've heard. The spoon stands up by itself. I need it like that, because I haven't been getting much sleep lately."

"That makes two of us then." She carried the coffee back into the living room and sat at the end of the sectional sofa, fiddling with the gold clasp of a small leather shoulder bag. McSwain sat across from her on the ottoman. "The boy who does the gardening said a dark-haired woman with terrible Spanish and the most striking eyes was in Ensenada asking about me yesterday. Except for the Spanish, my husband described your partner that way." She lifted her coffee mug and fixed cool

green eyes on McSwain. "You, he described less flat-
teringly. In any event, shall I assume you and your partner—Jenna Capshaw, isn't it?—were at the condo at Las
Estrellas yesterday?"

McSwain nodded. "Your husband said you weren't interested in talking to us, but we felt it was important to
change your mind."

"So you were snooping around?"

"If you want to call it that."

"Was I under surveillance?"

"For a little while."

"Did you—this may seem like a silly question—but
did either of you see anything suspicious?"

"I'm not sure I know what you mean."

Virginia lifted the coffee cup to her mouth, took a
tentative sip, then exhaled through her nostrils as though
trying to rid herself of some unpleasant scent. "I spent
most of yesterday in Tijuana, shopping, hitting a couple
of museums. I got home about ten. I think someone
came into the apartment while I was gone, probably
during the time you and Ms. Capshaw were down
there. Actually I know someone was there, because
they left something behind."

McSwain was taken aback. While his first thought was
that she had to be talking about Capshaw, at the same
time, the Jenna that he knew could walk across a snow-
bank without leaving tracks. He couldn't imagine her
having left evidence of her presence inside the condo.
"What was it you found, Mrs. Stromquist?"

Virginia snapped the clasp of her bag open and shut
several times in rapid succession. McSwain noticed that
pale sweat stains had formed under the arms of her
white silk shirt, which surprised him—Virginia Stromquist didn't strike him as the type of woman who
sweated at all, let alone to excess.

"I think maybe this was a mistake," she said. "I
shouldn't have come here." She clutched the bag in one
hand, uncrossed legs so long and evenly tanned it was
impossible to think she ever wore hose, and started to
stand up.

"Hold on," said McSwain. "Whatever your reasons
for coming here, before you leave, I need to know some-

thing, and I need the truth. Last January, two women who'd just left the Chula Vista Tap were abducted in their car and taken to a remote location. One of those women—a woman who called herself Billie—was raped. Was that you, Mrs. Stromquist?"

She turned her face away, but before she did, their eyes met for a second, and the look in her eyes was enough to give McSwain his answer. It was a look he had seen before—on the faces of people who'd just found out the child they'd hoped was only missing had turned up dead or the spouse they'd thought one day was coming home would not be back. Her chin crumpled inward as though her teeth were no longer sufficient to give shape to her mouth, and her body seemed to clench against some vividly remembered pain.

She put both hands to her temples and lowered her head while a tremor, like a tiny electric shock, passed through her shoulders.

McSwain wanted to touch her, to comfort her in some way, but knew there was no comfort to be had for what she must be feeling. After a few moments he said, "You've got to tell me what happened, Mrs. Stromquist."

She took a deep breath. When she looked up at him, he thought he saw vast resources of strength underneath the despair in her eyes. "I thought I could run away from this. I thought that just surviving it had been enough, that nothing else would be asked of me."

"The man who attacked you is still out there. I think there's a chance he may try to hurt you again."

"I know. That's why I came here." She shook her head. "Actually I went to your office first, but when I saw the police cars outside, I kept driving. About an hour later I came back and talked to someone named Dave. I convinced him I was an old friend from out of state and got him to tell me where you live."

"Congratulations. Maybe you should be the detective."

"Dave seemed like a nice man. Don't be mad at him. I guess maybe my college acting classes finally paid off." She shut her eyes and took a long sip of coffee. McSwain could see the muscles in her throat working. "You were right about me. I was assaulted last winter by a man who hid in the backseat of my car. I haven't wanted to think about that night, but I guess now I have no choice."

"You were calling yourself Billie?"

She nodded. "It was my nickname when I was a kid. For some reason, my mother was convinced she was having a boy, and William was the name she'd decided on. Then I came along and still Ma called me Billie—especially when I was doing something she thought unladylike."

"And your husband doesn't know about the nickname?"

"There's a lot that Leland doesn't know." She toyed with her purse again, her long, dark pink nails plucking at the clasp. "He was very upset after your visit the other day. He wanted to know if I'd been attacked and kept it a secret from him."

"And?"

"I told him it was nonsense, that your coming to see him must have been somebody's idea of a sick joke. It's what I'll continue to tell him."

"That's your choice, Mrs. Stromquist, but—"

"That young girl I gave a ride to . . . Mandy. She's the client supposedly trying to return a medallion to me, isn't she? I was relieved to find out she escaped. I'd thought that man might have caught up with her and killed her."

"She thought the same thing about you. She felt a lot of guilt about leaving you that night, and she hired us to find out what happened to you."

A small crease appeared between Virginia's eyes. She blinked rapidly, as though trying to absorb this. "Guilt? She shouldn't feel guilty. She probably saved my life."

"How so?"

"When she hit that man and ran away, he pursued her. She lured him away from me, gave me enough time that I was able to get my wits together, untie myself, and get out of there."

"Before we go on," McSwain said, "would you object if I tape-recorded this? You have my word I won't share it with Leland."

"Or the police?"

"That's up to you, Mrs. Stromquist."

A small smile played at one corner of Virginia's mouth, and she tapped a finger against her upper lip. Her expression was so pensive and knowing, so subtly seductive, that for a moment McSwain felt as though he were still wearing only boxer shorts—or less. "You seem like a trustworthy person, Mr. McSwain, but appearances can be deceiving. So no, I would not be comfortable being tape-recorded."

"Any objection to my taking notes then?"

"That's fine."

"Hang on then."

He returned from the kitchen with a pen and a yellow legal pad. "Tell me what happened that night."

"Call me Virginia," she said. "After all, like it or not, you're going to know a great deal of personal information about me." She then repeated for McSwain basically the same story that Mandy had told, how she'd met Mandy in the parking lot of the Tap and given her a ride, how they'd stopped for gas, at which point the man in the ski mask must have climbed into the backseat of the car. Her version of events after that was the same, too, except she either deliberately omitted or forgot to mention the assailant spraying her with perfume.

"When Mandy escaped, I started trying to work my hands free. I knew he could come back any minute. And I could hear him crashing around in the woods, but then it got quiet. I thought maybe he'd caught her and killed her and that he was on his way back for me. Finally, though, I got my hands free and put my clothes on and ran back to my car. There was enough moon that I could see to find my way back. When I got to the car, I realized I didn't have the keys—the man had taken them—so I used the spare key that I kept in a magnetized box behind the front tire. Leland had a speaking engagement out of town that night, and so I drove down to Ensenada—I felt safer there—and stayed for, oh, I don't know, two or three days. Most of that time's a blur because basically I just drank and slept. When I sobered up, it all seemed like a horrible dream."

McSwain felt as though he were having a repeat of the same frustrating conversation he'd had with Mandy. "You didn't go to the police."

"I know. You have to understand that"—Ghandi came nudging up against her shoe, and she bent to pet him—"first of all, I'd been drinking at this sleazy bar, hobnobbing with people who aren't exactly the cream of society. Even if I wasn't there to pick up a man— which I wasn't—who's going to believe it? They'd say I was cheating on my husband and got what I deserved. Leland's in the public eye, the big motivational speaker telling people how to improve their lives. How would it look if the whole world were to think his wife's cheating on him—even if that weren't the case?"

McSwain thought about the argument with Danny Tibbs, which seemed to imply something more than a mild flirtation was at stake, but let it go.

"Mrs. Stromquist, I have to ask this—the man who raped you, was it someone you know?"

She shook her head. "He wasn't familiar to me, what with the stocking over his face and the darkness and the fact that I was scared out of my wits. . . ."

"Not even his voice?"

"No."

"What about the fact that he knew your name? That he called you Billie?"

Her eyes clocked to the side, searching her memory for a split second before she looked back at him. When she did, her eyes were bright and hard, like polished gems. "I don't know what you mean."

"Mandy said the assailant called you Billie."

"She did? I don't recall him doing that, but I guess it's possible. What I do recall is that Mandy said at one point 'Billie, do what he says,' something like that. He might've heard her and used my name himself, but if he did, I don't remember it."

"Mandy says she does."

"I wouldn't trust her memory. Remember she was almost falling-down drunk. That's how I ended up giving her a ride in the first place."

"What about the BMW you drove that night? Even

now there could still be evidence inside—hair, clothing fibers, maybe something the man dropped without realizing it. What happened to the car?"

"I couldn't stand to see it anymore, so I traded it in."

McSwain tried another tack. "While you were in the Tap, did you talk to anyone in particular? Notice anyone watching you or behaving suspiciously?"

"We're talking months ago. No, I barely remember anything before getting into my car. And that, I wish I could forget."

McSwain jotted something down in the notebook. "Can you think of anyone who might want to scare the hell out of you? Maybe stop you from going to places like the Tap, fall into the mold of what some might call a more traditional wife?"

It took her a moment to realize what he was getting at, but then anger flashed in her eyes. "You mean Leland? My God, no! You haven't read his book, have you?"

"It's on my list."

"Rule number three: 'Clinging kills.' He's talking about all relationships, but especially marriage. He wants me to be independent."

"Does that include having lovers?"

After a long pause, she shook her head. "No. No, that would humiliate him. Leland's desperately insecure."

"He had me and my partner checked out by a PI. Is there any reason to think he hasn't done the same with you? Possibly had you followed?"

"If he did, I hope he paid them well, because they'd have been bored out of their minds."

McSwain cocked an eyebrow. "Meaning?"

"Mr. McSwain, in the eight years of our marriage, there've been exactly two—two—dalliances, both of which I deeply regret now. When I go to a place like the Tap, it's because, believe it or not, I enjoy the atmosphere. I grew up in El Centro, and my origins aren't what you'd call refined. My parents were the kind of people who saw nothing wrong with taking a four-year-old kid to a bar. I'd drink soda and whirl around on the bar stool till I got dizzy and fell off and then I'd pretend I was drunk. Everyone thought it was hilarious. Leland wouldn't be caught dead in a place like the Tap, so I go by myself. Is that so terrible?"

"Your stepson seems to think it is. He also claims to have been one of your 'dalliances.'"

She made a face. "I'm not surprised. He's an arrogant liar, with nothing going for him except a rich father and a pretty face. And when the pretty face gets a little bit wrinkled and the pecs aren't so firm anymore, that's it for him. Of course he'd say he'd been to bed with me. The only person Josh hates more than his father is me."

"Why's that?"

"Leland controls the money, and in Josh's eyes, I control Leland. Which means I control the only thing he really values. That makes me the enemy."

"Does he dislike you enough to try to hurt you? Or pay someone to hurt you?"

"You mean could he have been behind what happened that night? No. Josh is bullying and totally self-involved and a whole laundry list of nasty things, but would he do something like that? Never—he wouldn't have the balls." She reached down, adjusted the strap on one sandaled foot. "I believe whoever hid in my car that night was a stranger to me. Unless he's caught for something else and confesses to other crimes, I doubt we'll ever know who it was."

"And you won't help the police try to find him?"

"I can't do that, no."

He felt exasperated. "Then why'd you come here?"

"Well, for one thing, I thought I'd better prove I was alive and well before you started digging up the yard to try to find where Leland buried my body. I mean, it's always the husband who did it, right? But seriously, there's another reason."

She looked down at her hands, which were clasped around the coffee mug as though afraid someone would snatch it away. "Last night, when I realized someone had been in my apartment, I was so frightened, I couldn't stay there. I drove up to Rosarita Beach and got a room at the old hotel there, and I sat out on the porch and looked at the water and tried to decide what to do. I knew I couldn't go to the police with what I'd found, but . . ."

McSwain was still puzzling over what kind of game she was playing. If she knew Jenna'd been inside the condo, she was taking her sweet time saying so. And what his partner could have left behind to tip Virginia off to her presence, he couldn't imagine.

She reached into the purse she'd been fiddling with and pulled out a plastic Ziploc bag. Opening it up, she took out what looked like a gold ring about the size of a dime and handed it to McSwain. "Stupid me, I picked this up before I thought there might be fingerprints. In case you haven't seen one of these before, it's not an earring."

He turned the small gold loop over in his palm. "Where'd you find this?"

"It was on my pillow last night." She smiled wryly. "A pornographic variation on the tooth fairy, I presume."

She held the Ziploc bag out, and McSwain dropped the ring back into it. "Mrs. Stromquist, are you acquainted with a man named Danny Tibbs?"

Her eyes widened. "How did you—"

"A witness saw you and Tibbs having an argument at the Tap early this year. My partner and I dropped in on him the other day. He admitted knowing you under the name Billie and said you'd had an affair, but that it was over. Was he telling the truth?"

A tremor pulsed in the small blue vein at her temple. When she spoke, her voice was low, almost a whisper. "Yes, yes, he was. It's been over since that night he followed me to the Tap and we had the argument you're talking about. As soon as I realized what kind of man Danny was, I stopped seeing him."

"And he knows about the condo in Mexico?"

"Yes. Unfortunately I was stupid enough to take him there once." She looked down at the coffee mug, grimaced. "God, I must be exhausted. There's enough caffeine in this stuff to jump-start a car, and I don't feel a thing. I'm going to get some more. Want any?"

McSwain shook his head. Hearing someone downstairs and then finding Virginia Stromquist in his living room had given him enough of an adrenaline buzz that he'd feel wired for the rest of the day.

When she came back and took her seat again, he said, "Have you been to Xtreme Ink?"

She looked puzzled. "It sounds like some kind of underground newspaper."

"Danny Tibbs owns a tattoo shop in National City. He's got a showcase full of jewelry for body piercings. Some of them the kind you've got there."

She nodded grimly. "He showed me a labial ring early on, after one of our meetings at a motel. He called it a 'pussy padlock' and said he wanted me to wear one. Of course, I told him he was crazy, I'd do no such thing. Then when I found this, I knew, of course, he'd left it— either that or someone from what he calls his 'Mexican Mafia.' "

"Assuming it was Tibbs, how'd he get inside your condo? Did he come in through a window, door?"

"Door."

He thought of Jenna using her lockpicks on that same door and wondered how she could have failed to hear Tibbs breaking in if it was he who'd been in the apartment with her.

As though she were reading his thoughts, Virginia said, "I need to add something to that, but I'm embarrassed. It's going to sound incredibly . . . stupid. Danny would've been able to come in easily enough. I keep a spare key under a ceramic urn at the front door of the building. I remember using it the time that Danny and I went to my condo."

A question occurred to McSwain. "Does Danny Tibbs smoke?"

She looked unsure. "Why do you ask?"

"You knew him intimately. Don't you know whether he smokes or not?"

"I've seen him light up on one or two occasions."

"How about you? You smoke?"

"No, I don't see—"

"Just curious. Look, why don't you tell me about you and Tibbs? For starters, how did you hook up with him? He doesn't seem like your type."

"Only in some areas."

A hint of color rose in her cheeks, darkening the

freckles that dotted her face like grains of sand. He had the feeling she wanted him to ask her what areas those might be, that she was baiting him to cross some unspoken boundary.

He waited until the silence between them became too heavy and she began to speak. "Danny and I were in first class together on a flight from Vegas to San Diego last fall. Leland's a big fight fan and there was a title fight at the Bellagio. I told him I'd go with him to Vegas, but not to the fight. I hate boxing; I think it's barbaric. Anyway, we were supposed to fly home together the next day, but Leland started winning at blackjack. He was on a roll, and when Leland's on a roll, there's no stopping him. We had an argument, and I decided to fly home alone. And Danny was flying home, too—he'd been to the same fight. We got to talking, and he told me he was an investment banker." She saw McSwain's expression and pulled a face. "Yeah, I know. That's like me telling people I'm a Saudi princess. Anyway, I was attracted to him, so I chose to believe what he said. By the time I found out everything he'd been telling me was lies, I'd already slept with him. I tried to break it off then, but—"

"Danny doesn't deal well with the word *no*."

"To put it mildly. The last time I saw him was at the Tap. He got aggressive, wanted me to leave with him. The bartender threw him out."

"Did Tibbs know about the house in Rancho Santa Fe?"

"No, I let him think I lived in Ensenada and made my living as an artist. I told him my last name was Clarion, my first husband's name. As far as Leland or our home in Rancho Santa Fe, he knew nothing about that."

"But how did he find you at the Tap the night the two of you argued unless he was following you? It wouldn't have been hard for him to find out where you lived. All he'd have had to do was look in your purse when you were in the bathroom or check your license plates out at the DMV. Or have someone follow you when you left one of your trysts."

"If he knows where I live, then it's not just me I have to be worried about. He could harm Leland, too." She bunched and twisted a handful of her skirt, avoided McSwain's gaze. "Did I bring this nightmare on myself? Did Danny send someone to attack me that night?"

"I don't know, but it's a possibility I think we have to seriously consider. And you need to talk to the police."

"I won't do that." The pitch of her voice escalated so suddenly that Ghandi, who'd been lolling in a puddle of sun near her chair, jumped up and scooted out of the room. A sullen, cowering quality flickered across her features, aging her by ten years. "What I said earlier, about not wanting to embarrass Leland, that was just part of it. If I go to the police and they catch the person who raped me, I'll have to testify against him. Believe me, I know what lawyers do to women in a situation like that. They paint the rapist as the poor, persecuted victim and the raped woman as some kind of demented shrew."

"I think you're exaggerating," McSwain said evenly, and realized at once it was the most inflammatory thing he could've said. The look she gave him made him think that, had she been holding a gun, he'd've had a bullet between the eyes.

"*Exaggerating? That's* what you think? How many courtrooms have you sat in when a rape victim was on the stand? And even if you have, I'll bet you were a witness for the defense or a friend of the defendant." Her voice vibrated with rage and the blue vein at her temple started to throb again. "You know what the lawyers do? They make the victim describe every nasty, humiliating detail—right down to how many pubic hairs she plucked out of her teeth. And God forbid if the woman's vagina wasn't full of abrasions when the doctors examined her. Do you know what that means, if the vagina isn't abraded after a rape?"

He stayed silent, waiting for her to tell him. "It means she was lubricating while she was being raped. To the jury, to the defense attorney, that means she *wanted* it."

"An intelligent jury knows that's ridiculous," said McSwain.

She rolled her eyes. "An intelligent jury. Now there's a fucking oxymoron if I ever heard one."

"Look, Mrs. Stromquist, whatever personal traumas you've been through to make you feel this way, I'm sorry for that. The fact remains, whether it was Tibbs who attacked you or somebody else, it's likely he'll attack other women. Probably he already has. He's got to be stopped."

"Then stop him."

"What do you mean?"

"Just what I said. Stop him. I know it was Danny who left the ring in my condo, so start with him. Make sure he never comes near me again. If it turns out he's also behind the attack on me and Mandy, so much the better. Two birds with one stone."

"Mrs. Stromquist, I'm a private detective. There are some things I can do. But I'm not the police."

"Just make Danny Tibbs leave me alone." She leaned forward, and there was a hardness in her eyes, an opaqueness, as though some inner light had gone out of them. "Don't forget, Mr. McSwain, this is really your fault. Your going to see Danny, questioning him about me—that made him angry. He wanted to send me the message that he hasn't forgotten me, that he can get to me whenever he wants to. You and your partner set that in motion." She glanced at her watch. "I haven't slept in two nights, and Leland's expecting me to go with him to a book signing tonight. I have to go."

"Wait," said McSwain. "One more question. You said you'd had two affairs during your marriage. Who was the other one?"

"Oh—*that.*" She pronounced the word with a mixture of scorn and embarrassment. "It was an afternoon with my ex-husband about a year after Leland and I were married. Phil had called me, very upset. He'd been dating one of his students—he's an art history professor at UC—and it had gotten back to the dean. The shit was hitting the fan and he was panicking, afraid he might lose his job. I agreed to have lunch with him for old times' sake, and one thing led to another. That was it, the one time. We both regretted it—at least, I know I did."

"Are you sure about that? Maybe Phil had a stronger attachment to you than you realized."

She shook her head. "Phil's a sweet, kind man, but he's weak; he lacks self-confidence—that's one reason I divorced him. His entire criminal career consists of a handful of parking tickets."

"And that's bad?"

"No, it's very commendable. But dull."

"Well then," said McSwain, "guess we don't have to worry about Phil."

She picked up her bag and stood up. "Look, I realize I can't ask you to go outside the law, Mr. McSwain. But I came here because I don't want any more surprises on my pillowcase or anywhere else. Whatever you can do to keep Danny Tibbs out of my life, I'd be extremely grateful. And I'd write you a check that would reflect that gratitude."

"I'll keep that in mind, Mrs. Stromquist, but I don't think I can help you. I think this is a matter for the police."

Her gaze was so cold McSwain was surprised there weren't ice crystals on her lashes. Without a word, she picked up her coffee mug and carried it into the kitchen, where she rinsed it out and put it in the sink. McSwain walked her to the door.

Halfway down the porch steps, she paused, fished in her purse, and handed him a card with her name and the phone numbers for the house in Rancho Santa Fe and the condo in Ensenada. "This isn't for you, Mr. McSwain."

"No?"

"Not unless you decide to have a talk with Danny Tibbs on my behalf. It's for the young woman I gave the ride to—Mandy. Tell her to stop feeling guilty. And if she ever wants to talk or meet somewhere so she can see me in the flesh and reassure herself that I really did survive . . . well . . . she'll know how to reach me."

"I'll tell her that."

He watched as Virginia made her way along the cobblestoned path and out toward the street, and he thought about what she'd said about surviving. Somehow he had the feeling she always did.

Chapter 15

A few hours after McSwain saw Virginia Stromquist to the door, he was sitting at an outdoor table at Anthony's Seafood Grotto, watching the sun slide under the horizon while samba music blasted briefly from a passing dinner-cruise boat loaded with celebratory tourists.

Capshaw, sitting across from him, was using her left hand to toss croutons to a seagull perched on the pylon by their table.

Rather than go back to face the cleanup in their office, they'd agreed over the phone to meet at Anthony's, near the Star of India, the majestic schooner that was now a nautical museum. McSwain found he was ravenous, devouring a hearty serving of crabmeat and lobster along with a couple of St. Pauli Girl beers while filling Capshaw in on the visit from Virginia.

"So Virginia thinks our visit to Tibbs got him so riled up he decided to drop in on her with a token of his esteem," McSwain said. "If that's the case, then the fact that somebody also tried to kill us the same night seems like a pretty big coincidence."

Capshaw toyed with her blackened grouper, forking a piece toward her mouth, then putting it down. "If Tibbs was the person who came into the condo while I was there, he could've also spotted you sitting in the car, decided to follow us, and run us off the road."

"*If* it was Tibbs. You said the person in the condo smoked a cigarette, but Virginia doesn't smoke, and I thought she acted unsure when I asked her if Tibbs did. Like it wasn't a matter of knowing the answer so much as giving the right one."

"You also said the ring was left on Virginia's pillow, but nobody came into the bedroom while I was there; I'd've heard them. So the person would've had to leave and then return later, which doesn't make sense."

"Unless Tibbs or whoever it was was waiting for Virginia," said McSwain, "and that's why he kept going to the window to look out. You said that's what it sounded like he was doing."

"But a stalker who breaks into her place, then hangs out to smoke a cigarette and watch TV? That's pretty damned comfortable, if you ask me."

"Maybe Tibbs *was* that comfortable. He'd been to Virginia's condo before; he'd slept with her there. Maybe he had a sense of ownership. A lot of stalkers do—that's why they stalk."

"So you're suggesting that the day after our visit to Xtreme Ink, Tibbs breaks into his ex's apartment, leaves a souvenir to either scare her out of her wits or turn her on—who the hell knows which he thought it would do—and possibly tries to kill us as a bonus. Or sends a flunky to do it. Pretty ballsy of him either way."

"Pretty stupid, too. Maybe he still thinks Virginia's husband was behind our drop-in, that us claiming to be trying to find her was just a ploy to pump him for information."

Capshaw plucked a crouton out of her salad and tossed it to the gull, who swooped up and caught it in midair. "I know you and Tibbs have some history with the Harry Orlando case. I know he's a sociopath and a sadist, and who knows, maybe the rattlesnake on his dick means he's also a closet masochist, but trying to kill us . . . I mean, come on, Ian, would he have a motive to do that?"

"Maybe he doesn't need one. If he spotted either one of us outside the condo, he could've seen that as an opportunity."

"Spur-of-the-moment homicide?"

"Why not?"

"You think he was the one in Virginia's car that night, trying to give some payback for her dumping him?"

"No, she would've recognized him. But he could've had someone do it. I just wish we knew if Mandy's right about the guy knowing that Virginia was calling herself Billie. She said she told Tibbs her name was Billie Clarion, Clarion being the name of her first husband. On the other hand, if Mandy's wrong—and Virginia says she is—then it was probably a random attack and we're wasting our time focusing on people in Virginia's life."

Capshaw bent down, pulled a small spiral notebook from her handbag, and flipped it open. "But on the assumption that we're *not* wrong and that the attacker might have known Virginia by the name Billie and called her that, I did a couple of background checks on Moxley and the other bodyguard, Adams. Adams served as a SEAL in the marines and his record's as clean as a whistle. Moxley's been divorced twice, was arrested twice for shoplifting, and did a month in jail for the second offense, but that was almost ten years ago, and since then, nothing."

She flipped a page in the notebook. "When we get to Josh, though, it gets more interesting. Turns out he's more than just a self-infatuated creep and Leland's prodigal son."

A family group of a mother, father, and three young kids along with several elderly relatives crowded past. One of the kids bumped into the table, sloshing water out of Capshaw's glass and upsetting the kid's mother, who started to scold. "No problem; no harm done," Jenna said, blotting up the water with a napkin.

When the family had gone past, she turned back to McSwain. "In the past four years, two different women have had restraining orders issued against Josh. In one of those cases, the woman evidently had a change of heart. She and Josh went back to court to request that the order be lifted, and it was."

Mcswain started to say something but she held up a hand. "Wait, it gets better. Three months ago, a nineteen-year-old woman named Marisol Larkspur accused Josh of date rape. He was arrested, got out on bail, and a trial date was set. Before anything could happen, though, the woman changed her mind."

"Sounds to me like Leland's wallet entered the picture."

"Exactly. Maybe that was the reason Josh got fired.

Getting hit with a rape charge would certainly be a good reason to have him fade out of the picture for a while."

"You make photocopies of the documents?" said McSwain.

"Yeah. In the car."

Another gull showed up, and Jenna tossed him a crouton.

"I'd like to talk to this Marisol Larkspur," McSwain said. "Also the other two women who got restraining orders."

"I'll take care of that. Interestingly, the woman who dropped the restraining order moved up to Seattle, but Marisol and the other one are still here. Oh, and one other thing—I called Stromquist Headquarters a few minutes ago and talked to Fern. She said both Leland and Josh left for a speaking engagement Leland's got in Temecula tonight. Apparently Josh is either back on the payroll or had some reason for wanting to tag along with Dad."

"So if he was the guy who tried to kill us last night and the one who trashed our office, he's been a busy boy."

"I have a feeling Josh is the type who misses a night's sleep now and then."

"I don't know," said McSwain. "He seemed like a sleaze, all right, but a killer? Virginia seems to think he's a cad who's out for his father's money and who lied about sleeping with her, but that he's fundamentally harmless."

"Yeah, tell that to Marisol Larkspur. And who's to say Virginia isn't lying herself? If she'd sleep with Tibbs, she wouldn't be shy about bedding her stepson; I'd bet on it."

"You think Josh is a more likely candidate than Tibbs for whoever ran us off the road."

She flipped another crouton to a gull, who caught it in midair before soaring away. "Josh was the only person who knew we'd be in Ensenada last night. Maybe his telling us where to find Virginia was a setup. He could've driven down there before we did and spotted the car. On the other hand, I have to admit I don't see him as the type to charge down an embankment firing shots at two people he has every reason to think may be armed and are capable of shooting back."

McSwain sipped his beer. "Maybe he figured us for law-abiding types—one of us, anyway—who wouldn't bring weapons into a country where they're illegal."

Capshaw rolled her eyes. "That gun could've saved our asses."

"I agree with you, though: Josh seems a lot likelier to hire somebody to do his dirty work."

A waitress in a ruffled white skirt and a blue top with a pelican pin on the lapel stopped and leaned over the table. "I'm sorry, hon, but there's a rule against feeding the gulls. They bite people and crap all over the tables."

"Sorry," Jenna said. She turned back to McSwain. "I'm going to see if I can find Marisol Larkspur and the other woman with a restraining order against Josh. I'd also like to track down Phil, the first husband, see if he seems as mild-mannered as you say Virginia painted him." She started to reach for her drink with her right hand, sighed and set it aside, then used her left. "But we're forgetting the one good thing in all this—Mandy doesn't have to obsess about whether Billie's alive or not. Have you called her yet to give her the good news?"

"Why don't you do it?"

"Because Virginia didn't show up in my living room."

He thought for a minute. "I'd rather you called her. Since you know her from AA, it seems more appropriate, and it'll give you a chance to talk to her about her mother's drinking, too."

"You want me to call her, because you think she's got a crush on you, isn't that it?"

"What?"

"The way she looks at you, the way she rushed off to fix her makeup when we were at her house the other day. You're afraid she'll hit on you."

He drained his beer and tried to laugh it off. "I'm afraid of death and cancer and psychos running around with automatic weapons, but I'm not afraid of women hitting on me. Unfamiliar with it, yes, afraid, no."

"Okay, then. Sure. I'll give her the good news. And tell her Virginia said to call her if she ever wants to talk."

"Somehow I doubt she's going to take Virginia up on that. The only thing they've got in common is a nightmare."

"Yeah, that's how I see it, too."

He saw that Jenna'd finished eating, pushed his plate away, and looked around for the waitress. "I've got to run by the rental company before they close and fill out some more paperwork about how their nice new Acura ended up totaled in a ditch in Mexico."

A distant look had crept into Jenna's eyes. He knew whatever she was thinking about, it wasn't the wrecked Acura. "What about Tibbs? Do we pay him another visit and strongly suggest he stay the hell away from Virginia? And from us?"

"Like that's going to stop him?"

The waitress came by with the check, and McSwain left a couple of twenties on the table. They got up and started threading their way through the closely packed tables. At the door McSwain glanced back. A gull had landed on the table and was struggling to carry away a dinner roll three times the size of its head.

Outside, the sun had guttered out like a drowned candle, and a moist breeze smelled of rain and the damp promise of summer storms. As they waited for the light so they could cross the street, a trolley car with *Haunted San Diego Tours* on the side passed by, the tour guide at the front decked out in ghoul makeup and a coat and hat gray as a crematorium. McSwain couldn't hear what the guide was saying, but from the smiles and laughter of the tourists crowded on board, they must have been getting their money's worth.

"You didn't answer my question," Capshaw said as they walked back to their cars.

"What question?"

"About Tibbs. What to do about him."

"I guess I haven't decided myself."

Capshaw lifted a brow in a quizzical gesture that McSwain knew meant she didn't believe him. "Ian, you're not going to do anything stupid, are you?"

"Do I ever?"

For an answer, she jabbed an elbow into his ribs so hard a couple of tourists at the back of the Haunted San

Diego tour stared like they were witnessing a mugging—although who they thought was mugging whom was up for debate.

"Was that a yes?"

"Just promise me you won't go back to see Tibbs without telling me, because I'm going with you."

"Or Tibbs may be the least of my worries?"

She smiled. "You got that right."

Before going into Anthony's, McSwain had turned off the ringer on his cell phone, but he checked it as soon as he got back to his car, after he and Jenna parted company. There were three messages, one from the car rental company wanting more information about last night's accident, and an irate one from Josh Stromquist demanding to know why his two earlier calls to the office in I.B. hadn't been returned. The third message was from a woman who didn't identify herself at first, but didn't need to. The dull rasp of her voice scraped the back of McSwain's skull like a cold spoon coring out a grapefruit. His sister-in-law, Becky.

"Hello, Ian. I was up to Corona to see Lily this afternoon, and she wasn't looking so good. She told me you haven't visited her in . . . well, you don't find time to get up there very often. Your work and all." McSwain noted the sarcastic emphasis on the word *work*.

"Anyway, I think she's seriously depressed and nervous about getting out. I thought somebody should tell you, because she won't do it, and it sounds to me like you aren't up there enough to notice it yourself." A pause, Becky allowing time for that to sink in.

"You know, Ian, maybe it would be a good idea for Lily to move in with Tim and me for a while when she gets out. Just so she'll have somebody to keep an eye on her. Yeah, well, that's it. I've said what I wanted to say. Oh, yeah, this your sister-in-law." Another pause. "But I figure you knew that, right?"

McSwain stared at the phone, feeling sucker-punched and furious. He felt scolded, diminished, and immediately wondered what Becky had been telling Lily—that he was a bad husband? That she deserved better? Knowing Becky, that was probably the least of it.

Until Lily went to prison, she and Becky had never been close, but Becky seemed to need a cause beyond that of busting her husband Tim's balls, and Lily, the wayward sister, drug addict, and incarcerated felon, had given her one. Before that, McSwain had met Becky only a couple of times, at family functions Lily felt obliged to attend, but she always went out of her way to give the impression that he wasn't good enough for her sister, that Lily could've and should've done better in the husband department. She was a tall woman with a harsh laugh whose shape always reminded McSwain of a lemon lollipop—a huge, puffy helmet of blond hair perched atop a straight, stick-shaped body.

Now here she was calling to take him to task for not visiting Lily enough. Worse, acting as though Lily might actually consider moving in with her and her husband, Tim, a psychiatrist with a two-million-dollar house in Laguna that was on its third incarnation, having been destroyed once by mudslide and once by fire. Of the major natural disasters endemic to coastal California, McSwain figured the only thing Becky and Tim had missed so far was an earthquake, and that was probably next.

His first impulse was to call Becky back and tell her just what he thought of her idea about Lily coming to live with her and Tim, but she had an unlisted number, and he figured that was probably for the best. Having it out with Becky over the phone was the last thing either he or Lily needed.

He debated what to do next. Finally he decided there was nothing he *could* do, that it was better to just let it go for now and bring up the subject of Becky's phone call with Lily when he went up to Corona the next day.

He drove back to the rental car company, had a brief, semicivilized discussion with two different managers about the events that had led to the demise of the Acura, and filled out enough forms to make a stack as thick as a phone book. When he left there, he was too keyed up to go home, so he drove back to Dave's Gym, where he changed into workout clothes and pounded the heavy bag till his arms ached.

Around nine-thirty, when Dave was getting ready to

close and the heavy bag was winning more rounds than McSwain was, he took a shower and changed back into street clothes, checked the office upstairs to make sure the new locks had been installed, and headed for the door. Dave was saying good-bye to his last student, a young woman who couldn't have weighed over ninety pounds and had biceps that stood out like tennis balls under her tanned skin.

He turned to McSwain and said, "I almost forgot. Somebody dropped something off for you about an hour ago." He went into his office and returned with a flat, padded envelope about the size of a hardback book. McSwain's name was printed on the front, but that was it.

"Who left it?"

"I don't know. I was in my office between eight and nine, and when I came out, I saw it there by the door."

McSwain felt a queasy fluttering in his stomach. He went into Dave's office and used a letter opener to rip open the end of the envelope, then shook the contents out onto Dave's desk. A small sheet of paper, lined as though it had been torn from a loose-leaf notebook, dropped out. It made a metallic ping as the thing attached to it hit the desk surface.

McSwain picked it up, saw that someone had taped a ring identical to the one Virginia'd gotten to one side of the paper. On the other side, the message read: *Give this to your wife up at CWI.*

He stared at it, felt the blood hot and prickly at the back of his neck.

"You okay?" Dave said.

"Yeah, I'm fine." He folded the paper and slipped it into his pocket.

Dave followed him out the door. "You don't look fine. Where you going?"

"To see a man about a tattoo."

Chapter 16

Darkness had obliterated the last streaks of amber and saffron from the sky as McSwain drove north on Bonita Road, passing through Chula Vista on his way up to National City. Underneath the 805 overpass, he made a ten-minute stop at the Plum Crazy Saloon, where he drank a Heineken and paid the bartender, Blackjack Ames, for the tattoo gun he'd ordered after his and Jenna's visit to Xtreme Ink. Blackjack had done a stretch in Lompoc for assault and armed robbery, where he'd become proficient at creating crude jailhouse tattoos using a gun rigged up from the fan from a blow dryer, a syringe, and ink from a ballpoint pen. The one he sold to McSwain was about the size of a .22 and fit neatly into McSwain's hand, although he had to practice a few times on the bartop to get the hang of it, and even then the thing jittered in his hand like teeth chattering.

After leaving Plum Crazy, he took the freeway east to National City. Xtreme Ink was closed up tight, the place tomb-black when he drove by. An iron gate had been pulled down over the front door and windows and secured with a lock as big as a serving dish. He saw no sign of Tibbs's car with the Deacon vanity plates. In the alley behind the building, the only vehicle was a maroon Chevy with a couple of thuggish-looking teenagers leaning against the dented hood, making some kind of transaction that probably wasn't an exchange of baseball cards.

After satisfying himself that Tibbs wasn't there, he decided to check out Tibbs's other place of business, one he was familiar with from his time on the Harry Orlando case. He left Xtreme Ink and drove half a dozen blocks south, making a right at an abandoned warehouse that had once housed a combination flea, produce, and meat market. Except for a couple of streetlights, the only illumination came from VaVoom's neon sign, the two "O"'s fashioned like breasts with scarlet tassels trailing from the centers. Appropriately enough, the club occupied the three-story tile-and-gray-siding building next to what had originally been the meat market. Windowless except for a couple of small, boarded-up rectangles at the back and with a broad roof flat enough for skateboarding, it had the ominously unfinished look of a structure whose occupants are always a phone call or a police siren away from disappearing to parts unknown.

He cruised past the lot behind the building and parked the Monte Carlo in the open area where the Saturday-morning flea market used to take place. Before getting out, he removed the .38 from its holster and locked it in the trunk of the car, then tucked his purchase from Plum Crazy under his belt, checking to make sure his sport coat covered the bulge.

Then he got out of the car, feeling a tug of reluctance at leaving it in a neighborhood where an upper-end car unattended stood about as much chance of remaining unpilfered as a lost wallet, and cut through the alley toward the club. He passed two sleeping bags piled so deep in newspapers and plastic garbage bags that it was impossible to tell if their owners were actually asleep somewhere inside the twin mounds or not, cut through a passage between VaVoom and the south side of the warehouse, and approached a front door painted so brightly silver, it might have been wrapped in aluminum foil.

The thick-necked brute guarding the door must've thought he looked like your average horny middle-aged guy out for a night on the town, because, to his relief, he was barely searched before paying the cover charge and making his way to the bar next to the stage. Only one girl was dancing there, although the cloverleaf design indicated as many as four could perform at one time.

He took a seat next to the stage and ordered a Scotch

from a platinum blonde with Nefertiti eyes who tried hard to interest him in a magnum of champagne. She had a wide mouth as red as a gunshot wound, and tired blue eyes that looked used-up and old. The rest of her looked depressingly young.

The woman on the stage looked even younger—she was wearing a plaid Catholic girls' school uniform, knee socks, and black patent-leather shoes, and her dark chestnut hair streamed down her back in a loose pony-tail. As McSwain sipped his Scotch, she shed the footwear and socks, then the shirt, and finally peeled out of the blouse, leaving her in a satin G-string and bra that could have easily been tucked into a shot glass. She turned her back, spread her legs, and bent forward, scraping red nails down the insides of her thighs, lush hair forming a dark pool on the stage in front of her.

The blonde with the taste for champagne came back with his Scotch. "My name's Amore," she purred. "It means love."

"Love, huh?" said McSwain, thinking how unconducive the setting was to anything remotely resembling it.

She walked two fingers along his shoulder. "You know, you look pretty stressed. A Scotch might not be enough."

"Prob'ly not."

Her eyes lit dimly with some bleached-out emotion that might have once been enthusiasm, but had long since faded into the most apathetic of hopes.

"I can give you all the relaxation you need."

"Yeah?"

"Upstairs we got rooms. Nice and private." Her eyes clocked upward and to the side as she recited the list of enticements. "Mirrors on the ceilings, four-poster beds. You like more action, I got some hot girlfriends who just love to party."

McSwain chugged half his drink and pushed back his chair. "Maybe you should give me the tour then."

They ascended a tightly curving flight of stairs whose very circuitousness would go a long way toward impeding a hasty exit and entered a hallway with doors spaced every ten feet or so. A small, rabbity-eyed man who looked like a worried CPA at tax time was leaving one room. Amore started to enter the room he'd just vacated.

"Hold on," said McSwain. He took two fifty-dollar bills from his wallet. "How about we call it even right now?"

She stared at the money with those glazed-over eyes, then shrugged blandly. "You don't want to see the room?"

"No."

"You don't want to see what Amore can do?"

"I'll take Amore's word for it."

She ran a hand up his chest, but as a frisk, it was fortunately even less thorough than what the bouncer at the door had done. "Some guys don't want to do nothing, you know. Just want to talk about what's going on with them, their wives, work, whatever, you know what I'm saying?"

McSwain opened his jacket and flashed his PI ID just long enough for her to get a glimpse of something official-looking. Her mouth formed a small, surprised 'O,' like a guppie reaching out for a piece of food.

"How 'bout you tell me where your boss is, know what I'm saying?"

"My boss?"

"Danny Tibbs. I know he's here."

She looked toward the end of the hall where a small alcove opened up into a flight of metal stairs.

"Up there?"

She nodded blankly. "I never told you nothing."

"I got that."

She turned away, then added, "You don't know what you missed."

"Oh, I think I do."

He was moving toward the stairs leading to the third floor when his gaze was diverted by movement above him. It was the reflection of a woman emerging from one of the rooms, her image caught in an oval mirror of the type used in convenience stores to detect shoplifters, set at an angle high on the wall. She was topless and wore a tiny red taffeta skirt that barely covered her pubic hair. Gold hoops pierced her tea-colored nipples. A bright sheen of fear hovered in her dark eyes, and

McSwain thought at first that for some reason his presence there in the hall had alarmed her. Then he realized she wasn't looking at him, but past him.

He spun around to see Danny Tibbs striding toward him, his face set in a murderous scowl. He wore a skintight silver T-shirt that showed off his weightlifter's physique and carried a .357 Magnum, which he jammed into McSwain's ribs.

"You just can't stay away, can you?"

"You sent me a present for my wife. People do things like that, I like to drop by. Reciprocate if I can."

"You're fucking dead, you know that?"

"We're dead when we come into the world, Tibbs. Life's a terminal illness. You haven't figured that out?"

"Upstairs." He poked the gun into the small of McSwain's back and shoved him forward. They ascended the metal stairs to the third floor, where Tibbs directed him into an office that smelled as though a dozen chainsmokers had just departed after spilling a bottle of gin. A bank of windows covered the far wall, where, McSwain guessed, the action down below could be observed through a one-way mirror. A hefty blond guy with a cigarette dangling between his lips sat at a desk counting out bundles of money and totaling it up on an adding machine. Next to him stood an ashtray of the kind often found outside hotel elevators, a couple dozen cigarette butts sprouting from its sandy surface.

"Take a break, Ben," Tibbs said. "A long one."

The guy ground his cigarette into the sand in the ashtray, placed his palm on top of the mountain of cash like a dog owner reassuring his pet he'd be back soon, and hustled out of the room.

"I gotta admit you surprised me," Tibbs said. "I didn't think you'd have the balls to turn up again. But since you have, the question is, What do I do with you?" He walked to the door, turned the lock, and then moved to the window, where he gazed down for a moment until a smile curled the corners of his thick mouth.

"You look down from here, you don't see the second floor, you know; you're looking right down on the stage. I like to keep an eye on my girls, see the action. Guy like you comes up here and attacks me—we get into a scuffle and I throw the guy through one of these windows, I can see something like that happening. Make a hell of a mess on the stage, but what the fuck—it'd put the fear of God into some of the help around here." He glanced at his watch, a gold Rolex. "Now all I have to figure out is what to do with you until we close up."

"Then let's talk," said McSwain. "We got time to kill."

"Some of us more than others."

"That note you sent with the package? About my wife? What the hell did that mean?"

"That I know she's pulling a stretch at CWI—girl who used to work here's doing the same thing. Prison's the most dangerous place on the fucking planet, McSwain, even a ladies' country-club joint like your wife's in. I can get to her. I kill you, and if I still don't feel the kind of peace in my soul that comes with a righteous hit, I may go after her. You have pissed me off royally. Just doing you may not get it all out of my system."

"So you're gonna kill me?"

"Fuck no, I thought we'd have tea."

"Funny, Tibbs. By the way, do you smoke?"

"What?"

"I asked, Do you smoke?"

"You kidding? I value my health."

"Too bad. I don't usually smoke, but I could sure use one now."

Tibbs's jerked his head toward Ben's desk. "He's got a pack of Salems over there. Help yourself."

McSwain found the pack next to the adding machine and shook out a cigarette. "Shit, I don't have a light on me. Do you—"

"Fuck, you think this is what, a convenience store? I don't know. Lighter oughta be on the desk somewhere." He chuckled. "Just don't get any ideas about setting the money on fire."

"The lighter, yeah, here it is."

He put the cigarette in his mouth and turned away from Tibbs as he bent toward the desk, straightened up with the lighter in his left hand, the right one down by his side. "Hope this doesn't give me lung cancer."

Tibbs actually cracked a smile. McSwain stepped forward and flung the fistful of sand he'd scooped from the ashtray into his face.

Tibbs's arm went up, shielding his eyes. McSwain grabbed his other arm and wrenched the gun out of his fingers while twisting his wrist back so hard he heard tendons snap.

He kept his grip on Tibbs's hand, forcing him down, then dug his knee into his back and slammed him face-first onto the floor.

"You say you value your health—make a sound, and you won't have any health to worry about. Understand?"

Tibbs nodded.

"Now crawl—slowly—over to the wall next to the desk."

When Tibbs balked, he cocked the gun and the man started to crawl. McSwain kept a knee in his back, letting up the pressure just enough to allow him to wriggle along.

When they were close enough to the wall for what he wanted to do, he reached into his jacket, pulled out the tattoo works, and plugged the cord into the wall over Tibbs's head.

Tibbs tried to sit up. "What the fuck are you—"

McSwain pressed the needle into his cheekbone. "So how about it? You want to tell me what you were up to in Mexico the other day?"

"I wasn't in Mexico."

"No? What about the labial ring you left on your ex-girlfriend's bed? What the fuck about that?"

"You're crazy, McSwain. This is fucking assault."

"Sure it is. After I break both your arms, maybe you can dial nine-one-one with your tongue."

"Fuck you!"

"That's the way you want it, fine."

He kept his weight on Tibbs's spine, held the needle under his ear, and flicked the trigger. The crude machine began vibrating wildly. Tibbs screamed and bucked as blood streamed down his neck.

A dark blue patch, amoeba-shaped, grew next to the hairline.

"Jesus, stop!"

"What is it, Tibbs, you one of those guys get hard

stalking women who've dumped them? What else you do besides break into Billie's apartment, huh?"

He let up with the tattoo gun. Immediately Tibbs tried to crawl forward, grabbing for the leg of the desk. McSwain raised his elbow and smashed it down on the crown of Tibb's head as he jammed the tattoo gun under his eye.

"You gonna talk to me, Danny, or should I practice my tattooing technique on your face? Maybe something like you did on James Bell—Thou Shalt Not Fuck with McSwain? Or maybe something more abstract, a few zigzags and tic-tac-toe-type designs, do a little coloring outside the lines. What the hell, not like you were pretty to begin with."

He hit the trigger, but the needle had barely made contact before Tibbs hissed, "Stop, enough, okay!"

"I'm just getting started."

"I didn't break into Billie's condo. Had a buddy of mine lives down in Tijuana do it. I just wanted to remind her I'm out here, that I haven't forgotten about her. That nobody brushes off Danny Tibbs."

"What about the package you sent to Dave's Gym? You still thinking to hurt my wife? I swear to God, Tibbs, you come near her and I'll fucking kill you. You got that?"

"Yeah, yeah."

McSwain got up, yanked the cord to the tattoo gun out of the socket, and threw the whole apparatus into the wall. He then picked up the .357 he'd taken from Tibbs and stuck it under his belt.

Tibbs got to his haunches, crouched there for a second with his hand to his face, checking for blood, then stood up. He looked at the gun in McSwain's hand. "Unless you plan to use that right now, don't think this is over. No fucking way. And you can tell your partner and that cunt Billie and your cunt wife I said so."

"Leave them out of this, Tibbs."

Tibbs's elastic-looking lips twisted into a snarl. "You blew it, asshole. You fucked with the wrong guy. One way or another, you'll pay for this—maybe you, maybe somebody you care about."

McSwain pulled out the .357 and backhanded Tibbs

across the jaw. He heard bone break with a sound like someone stomping on kindling. Tibbs's legs crumpled and he slithered down the wall.

Before he left, McSwain used the butt of the gun to knock a hole in the one-way mirror overlooking the stage. He grabbed a couple of bundles of cash, ripped the rubber bands off, and pushed wads of money through the broken glass. When the noise from down below assured him that bedlam had broken out, he made his departure.

Chapter 17

Most of the time, McSwain looked forward to his trips to Corona, not just the time spent with Lily but the drive, too. It gave him a break from work, a chance to think, and an opportunity to listen to his favorite Spanish radio station playing love songs with lyrics sufficiently repetitious and limited in vocabulary that he could actually understand some of them. Today, though, he gripped the wheel like he wanted to throttle it as he replayed the events of the previous night in his head. The violence of what he'd done to Tibbs didn't concern him. What bothered him was whether or not it was enough to deter Tibbs from making good on his threats against Virginia, Jenna, and Lily.

If McSwain's experience with people like Tibbs was any indicator, he knew it wouldn't. The only violence that deterred vermin like that was a bullet banging around inside their skulls. On Jenna's side was the fact that she almost always carried a weapon, that she was a good shot, and, more important, that she'd have no compunctions about shooting. As far as Lily, being in prison offered little protection if Tibbs really wanted to get to her, and once she got out, she'd become an even easier target. It was Virginia Stromquist, though, whom he judged the most vulnerable. He wondered if, in his effort to help her—and hell, really, what he'd done was mostly to protect his wife—he'd actually put her in more danger, if by attacking Tibbs he'd almost guaranteed retaliation.

With these thoughts stewing in his mind, he arrived at CWI's sprawling complex just as visiting hours were beginning and joined the queue of people waiting to get

in. The line crept along at a pace only slightly slower
than ice melting while each visitor went through the ritual of signing in, locking away all personal items in lock-
ers provided for that purpose, then passing through a
metal detector under the watchful eyes of a couple of
guards. A pregnant woman in line ahead of McSwain
kept setting off the metal detector, even though she
wasn't wearing jewelry and had relinquished her change.
Finally one of the guards asked if she was wearing an
underwire bra. The woman said that she was and then
hurried off to the ladies' room to remove it.

McSwain found himself growing impatient with the
time-consuming procedure of just going through the for-
malities—he thought of the irony that getting into a
prison sometimes seemed almost as hard as getting out—
but he knew that the tedious routine was necessary—
visitors trying to smuggle in drugs or other contraband
were a constant problem in any correctional facility. Just
the week before, Lily had told him, a man was caught
trying to bring his wife a packet of cocaine tucked into
his briefs—a guard had grown suspicious when she saw
white residue caught in the teeth of his zipper.

Finally, though, the line picked up speed and he
passed through a clanging metal door into the visiting
area. Lily was sitting at a table with a couple of other
women. When she saw him, her eyes widened and she
let out a little gasp of surprised pleasure that sent a
ripple of sadness through McSwain's chest—clearly she'd
had doubts that he would make it today even though
he'd assured her he'd be there. She'd had her hair cut
since his last visit. It cupped her head in lush, dark gold
waves that fell just past the curve of her jaw.

She threw her arms around him and kissed him hard,
then leaned back and looked at him and gave another
small gasp, this one anything but pleased. "Your face . . .
what happened?" She turned his face to the side and
ran the backs of her fingers over the bruises.

"Got in a fender bender down in Mexico. It looks
worse than it is."

"What were you doing in Mexico?"

"Just some follow-up on a case Jenna and I are working on."

"The car . . . is it as banged-up as you are?"

"I was driving a rental. No big deal. The insurance is going to take care of most of it."

"Some fender bender," she said, but she didn't press. Instead she led him over to a small table with a couple of straight-backed chairs and pulled hers next to his, sitting as close as possible.

"You're right on time. I'm proud of you." She ran a hand up the side of his neck, turned his head toward her. "My hair, do you like it?"

"Yeah, it's a nice change."

She frowned as though he'd said something critical. "I can grow it out again if you don't like it."

"It's fine, Lil. It looks good."

A silence thin and impermeable as a cellophane membrane hung between them. She sighed and took his hand and leaned her newly shorn head on his shoulder. Underneath the regulation green dress, identical to what all the other women were wearing, he could feel the sharp jut of her hipbones.

She took a deep breath. "I talked to Becky. She told me she called you. Are you upset?"

"Yeah, she left a message," he said, relieved that she knew and had brought it up.

"And? Are you upset?"

"I was pretty pissed at the time, yeah, but I'm over it."

Her eyes narrowed. Flecks of amber, like dark, angry sparks, roved in the irises. "She won't do it again. I reamed her a new asshole, let me tell you."

"She's worried about you, that's all. She probably meant well."

She put a hand in the center of his chest and feigned giving a hard push. "Is this my husband talking or have you stolen Ian McSwain's body? Because never would the man I married stick up for Becky."

"Yeah, I know. Sometimes I surprise myself, too. And I was mad as hell when I first got her message, because I felt like she was accusing me of being a bad husband— which we both know she thinks I am anyway."

"That isn't true."

"Sure it is, Lil. She made it clear from the first she thought you could've done better. A week before the wedding and she was trying to set you up with that Swedish periodontist her husband fishes with."

"Oh, God." Lily covered her mouth and giggled. "I'd forgotten all about that. I met the guy once, the famous periodontist; did I ever tell you? About five-four, and I've seen billiard balls with more hair. My God, what was Becky thinking?"

"Who the hell ever knows?"

"So what was her message anyway? She gave me her version, but I'd like to know what she really said."

"Something to the effect that I wasn't visiting you enough—"

"This is true, but it's still none of her damned business."

"—and that I should be concerned because you seemed, I don't know, depressed, and I know depression's something you struggle with, even though you don't let me see it."

"I'm in prison, Ian. People in prison tend to be depressed."

She squeezed his hand so hard he felt the bite of her nails in his wrist, but he couldn't bring himself to pull away. "I think you try too hard to be cheerful for my benefit, Lil. Maybe Becky saw you on a day when you weren't trying so hard. Or maybe you just don't put up a front for her. Seriously, is something going on? Is there something you need to tell me?"

She exhaled a long, slow sigh, like air leaking out of a balloon, and leaned her head on his shoulder again. He got a faint whiff of the jasmine scent in the shampoo she used. "A few nights ago I dreamed I had one of those little candy machines that used to be popular, a PEZ dispenser. This one looked like a duck. You hit the duck's bill and a candy was supposed to drop out, only every time I did that, what dropped out was a tablet of meth. And pretty soon the stuff was just erupting out of the duck's mouth, a whole mountain of meth, and I took a capsule and another one and then I stuffed my mouth full and it felt . . . wonderful . . . like dying but without any pain, without any fear."

He stared at a crack in the ceiling that zigzagged like a mark of Zorro, little flecks of plaster missing at the edges of the "Z." "It was a dream, Lil. People dream all kinds of shit."

"I wanted it so much, though, Ian. I thought I'd gotten past that kind of craving."

"Jenna says the cravings come back now and then. That's normal."

Her spine stiffened slightly. "Jenna's only an alcoholic. What does she know?"

He bit back the urge to dispute that and let it pass.

After a while she said, "It's been almost two years, Ian."

He told himself she had to mean two years since they'd shared a bed, two years since they'd had sex, even two years since they'd last held hands and kissed in private, without the intrusion of other eyes, but what she said next was, "Almost two years since I've gotten high."

He couldn't help himself. He pulled away from her.

She looked up at him, the hurt sparkling in her eyes as she recognized it in his. "I don't mean I want to get high. Just that I get nervous sometimes. Thinking about getting out, readjusting to life on the outside, a free life where I can go where I want, do what I want, except I can't use. The drugs are still out there, but I can't use."

"Using's what got you here."

"I know that."

Her apprehension and almost wistful sadness made him nervous, and he tried to change the mood. At the same time he realized, with a pang of guilt, that this was probably why she tried so hard to be cheerful—because she knew he found that easier to deal with than the truth.

"Only forty-nine days till we can be together."

"I can't believe you still count the days."

"You don't?"

Some of the tension leaked out of her muscles. "I love you, Ian."

"I love you, too."

"We'll make this work."

"Damn right we will."

"How's the house hunting?"

He was expecting that, too, although the question still left him flustered, like a student who knows he's going to be tested yet still comes to school unprepared. "I haven't really had a chance to look at anything the last few days. There's that new case Jenna and I are working on and . . . well, to tell you the truth, Lil, there's not a lot in our price range that I think we'd be happy with."

He paused, hoping she'd say something, but she used his own technique and waited him out until finally he continued. "I was thinking it might be best if we stayed in the carriage house, at least for a few months. My landlords are great—I think they'd be okay if we stayed on a month-to-month basis. Then when you get back to work, maybe we'll be able to start looking again."

"But I thought you'd found a house up in Carlsbad?"

"I did, Lil, but the bank . . . they took a look at my finances and decided I wasn't such a great bet on a loan. When there're two people working, it'll be a better financial picture."

She looked down at her hands, twisting the fingers together. He saw she'd started biting her nails again—several of them were chewed ragged and looked red and painful.

"Ian, when I get out of here, I'll still be an ex-con on probation. If you think I'll be offered any high-paying positions, you're dreaming. I'll be lucky to get something at minimum wage."

"I know it won't be easy, Lil, but I thought you could talk to your old boss at Exabyte. She was always more than fair. Maybe if you—"

She cut him off with a laugh and a dismissive wave of her hand. "Kay? I don't think so. She's washed her hands of me."

"You don't know that."

"Oh, I believe I do. If you must know, I wrote Kay a letter a few months ago. Putting some feelers out in case she'd be willing to take me back. The note I got back was so cold there was frost on the envelope."

"Oh. I'm sorry to hear that."

"Well, so was I."

A couple across from them started kissing passionately, the woman's leg creeping up onto the man's thigh. Lily's gaze lingered on them a moment. Before she turned away, he saw the want in her eyes, an intensity of hunger he'd never seen there before, even in the midst of lovemaking. He wondered if she felt as miserably alone at that moment as he did.

"Lily, look . . ." He took her hand and folded it between his own. "We'll get a house. That will come in time, but that's not what's important. The important thing is that you'll be free again. We can start rebuilding our life."

"And you don't think having a home of our own is part of rebuilding that life?"

"I think a house will be icing on the cake, and we have to be patient. In the meantime, the carriage house I'm living in is perfectly nice. There's a garden you could almost get lost in, and a koi pond, and I've told you about Ghandi the ninja cat. . . ."

He waited for some agreement on her part, but it was as though she hadn't heard. "Things could be different if you would just consider what we've talked about before, another line of work. You're not too old for a career change, Ian. You've got a degree in business. You could do so many things."

"Lily, please. You know I'm not going to do that."

"Why do you have to be so stubborn? There's nothing wrong with making more money." He started to say something, but she was on a roll now, pressing on. "This case you and Jenna are working on. Just out of curiosity, how much are you being paid?"

"It's not a lot, but—"

"How much, Ian? I want to know. You used to always say you and Jenna were going to raise your rates, concentrate on more corporate stuff. Is that what this case is?"

"We've been doing a lot of background checks and some insurance fraud," he said, and went on to quote a few figures. All the while hating himself for tap-dancing around the truth this way.

"That's the new case then? The background checks?"

He was stuck. Back when Lily was first arrested and the extent of her drug abuse had come to light, they'd had a long talk and promised they wouldn't lie to each other again. Not about the big things, not about the little ones. McSwain had been guilty of his share of deception, too. There'd been a flirtation with a client that crossed the line into something more serious. Ultimately, they'd both agreed that if truth had played a bigger part in their marriage neither her drug use nor his straying would have had a chance to take root.

"Actually the new case is something Jenna and I agreed to do gratis."

He was going to continue, explain it to her, but she turned her face away in the manner of a woman who's just been propositioned in the most humiliating manner. When she turned back to him, tears gleamed in her eyes.

"No wonder we can't afford a house. And as long as you find it rewarding to work for nothing, I'm sure we never will be able to."

"It's only one case, Lil. We've got others that pay very well."

"You're always so eager to give away your time and energy. Who is this client, anyway? Is it a woman?"

"Yes."

"Oh. Then that explains it."

"Lil, that's not fair. If you'd just—"

It went on like that for a while, the conversation circling around and around, a downward-spiraling dance of discord and frustrated expectations. McSwain finally gave up and got to his feet, feeling amazed and saddened that after looking forward so much to seeing his wife, he was now eager to leave.

At the door, he made a last attempt at ending the visit on a positive note. He pulled her against him and whispered into her jasmine-scented hair, "I love you, Lil. Don't forget that. If I don't always make you happy, it's not for lack of wanting to."

The pause that followed was so long he wondered if she was going to answer at all. Finally she said, "I love you, too, Ian. And God knows, I haven't made you happy these last few years. I should be grateful that you've stuck by me at all. Any other man would be long gone by now. I know you must have thought about it. I know you must have wanted to at times."

He was astonished that she'd think such a thing.

"We'll make this work, Lil. We love each other; that's all that really matters, right? That's all that counts."

But as he was walking back to the car, he found himself wondering if he was just whistling in the dark, if love was only the start of what they needed.

Chapter 18

On the trip back to San Diego, McSwain cut almost forty minutes off the trip. Unfortunately, turning I-8 into his own personal Indy 500 did nothing to help him outrun his own mind, which was what he most wanted to escape.

He kept going back over the visit with Lily, her impatience with getting a house, his anger at himself over not being able to provide one. He knew where some of those feelings came from. Growing up in Phoenix, his father'd gone through prolonged periods in which riding his Harley and partying took precedence over earning a living. At Christmas, or whenever it came time to send pictures to the relatives back east, his mother would dress him and his brother Andrew in their best clothes and march them next door to their neighbor's nicely kept ranch house. There they would pose, grinning like idiots on the front steps of a house they'd never set foot in.

The sting of those episodes, his mother's shame about being poor, and her bitterness at his father for keeping them that way, had taken root under McSwain's skin. It always burned in his gut like an old ulcer when he was unable to provide something Lily wanted.

And when he thought about her fears that he would leave her, a different kind of guilt burned like tiny blisters behind his eyes, because he'd lied to her about never having considered filing for divorce. Not when she'd first been arrested—he'd been too caught up in meeting with lawyers and organizing her defense to even think of the bigger picture—and not now, when she was so close to freedom. But sometime along about the start of her second year at CWI, when he and Jenna were going through a slow spell as far as caseloads, he'd started spending time at one of the neighborhood bars, a cozy hangout where a lot of the clientele seemed to be starry-eyed couples who gazed at each other with the kind of feverish lust you just wanted to hose down, and the self-pity had set in like stomach flu.

So he'd flirted a bit, sniffed guiltily around the edges of adultery, and found to his dismay that the only thing lonelier and more nerve-racking than being without Lily was pretending he could substitute someone else for her and it would be okay.

Dwelling on the contradictions of it all depressed him and made his foot heavier on the pedal. He was just south of Temecula, on the outskirts of San Diego, when he reached for his cell phone to check for messages.

There was one from Jenna, saying she was at the office and that he should give her a call, a couple more that were inquiries from potential clients. A fourth call came from an obviously inebriated Josh Stromquist, whose formerly demanding tone had now changed to sloppy conviviality. He wanted to know how the quest for compromising photos of his stepmother was going, and described the kinds of shots he wanted in pornographic detail.

The only call of interest to him was Jenna's, but before calling her back, he decided to follow up on something he'd intended to do all day. Leaning over, he rummaged in the console for the card where he'd written Richard Moxley's address and phone number and managed to read it and dial while executing a number of lane changes—a feat he knew other drivers did all the time and which he considered only a little less foolhardy than driving with your eyes shut. He doubted he'd be able to reach the bodyguard at his home number this time of day, but to his surprise, Moxley picked up on the second ring.

"Yeah?"

"Richard? Ian McSwain."

"Ian, hey! How's it hanging?"

"Not bad, Richard. If you've got some time, I'd like to sit down together, go over a few things."

"About the case?" From the enthusiasm in his voice, McSwain might have been calling to tell him he'd just won the Lotto. "Hey, sure, be glad to. Happy to help out."

In the background, he could hear a woman talking, a sexy, little-girl voice that sounded like butter melting.

"Can you hang on a sec?" Moxley said.

"Sure."

McSwain could hear the woman's voice, then Moxley's, in animated conversation before Moxley came back to the phone.

"Sorry to keep you waiting, Ian. Hey, look, Helen and I were just on our way over to Coronado Hospital. She's got physical therapy. I'll be hanging out there for the next couple of hours. Wanna meet me in the cafeteria in, say, half an hour? It'll be a chance to get to know each other, and, you know, talk some shop."

"Sure, I'll see you then."

The phone rang as soon as he hung up. It was Jenna, calling from the office. She'd just gotten off the phone with Marisol Larkspur and wanted to fill him in. "I got her at work. She's an accountant with a law firm in La Jolla. She met Josh at one of Leland's seminars. Basically, she says they went out for a while, and he was a controlling son of a bitch, but when she tried to break it off, he went ballistic. She says he slapped her, threatened to come back and really mess her up if she didn't continue the relationship. You know, typical stalker type."

McSwain sighed. "Whatever happened to candy and flowers?"

"I guess some guys think a black eye and a broken jaw make a more lasting impression. Anyway, she got the restraining order and Josh faded out of the picture. That's about it. But for what it's worth, she thinks he's dangerous and that date rape would be the least of it. Speaking of dangerous characters, did you give any more thought to the Deacon?"

"Actually we had a little chat last night."

"What?"

In the silence that followed, he could hear the phone

line hum with her anger. Finally she said, "You went to see Tibbs? After you told me you weren't going to do anything stupid?"

"I don't think I actually said that, but in any event, what I did wasn't stupid; it was necessary." Briefly, he told her about the contents of the envelope left at Dave's Gym the night before.

"Tibbs admitted he sent somebody down to Virginia's place. The idea was to break in and scare the shit out of her as payback for our visit. Plan B, if she wasn't there, was to just leave her the ring and come back another day."

"Was Tibbs the one who ran us off the road?"

"He claims not."

"You believe that?"

"I'm not sure what I believe."

"How'd he know about Lily?"

"Circles he runs in, it wouldn't be hard. And remember the way the papers ran it—'Wife of local PI caught in meth bust.' "

"Yeah." She sounded sorry she'd asked.

"I'm on my way to meet Richard Moxley. Want to join me?"

"Hate to miss it. I always like hanging out with people who think being a PI is second only to being a rock star."

"Who said anything about its being second?"

"Yeah, well, I'll have to pass. I'm trying to track down Virginia's ex-husband. There's a Phil Clarion who teaches art history at San Diego State. I've left him a couple of messages, but so far no word. And I'm trying to get hold of Hank. He never gave us a callback on that body out on Otay. I want to see if there's been any ID."

"You talk to him, ask him if we can take a look at the forensics report."

She gave a sharp laugh. "You dreaming? It's almost like you think the guys at Homicide might want to cooperate with us."

McSwain was well aware that the majority of homicide detectives, including Paris—hell, even the majority of cops—considered private detectives to be a lower life-form, only a rung or two up the ladder from the bail jumpers and con artists they were often trying to track down.

"Well, give it a shot anyway. Use your charm."

"Charm doesn't work on Hank. A blunt instrument maybe, charm no."

"Whatever it takes."

McSwain had always loved the view from the Coronado Bay Bridge, a sweeping span that carried traffic to and from Coronado Island. Today the bay was dotted with motor yachts and sailboats taking advantage of clear skies and an easterly breeze. Farther on, he saw an aircraft carrier, about as long as two football fields, docked at the naval base. What always got to him, though, besides the view, were the signs posted along the bridge with the 800 number for suicide counseling, testament to the number of desperate souls who'd ended their lives on the bridge and the countless others destined to attempt it. He wondered if the 800 number had ever turned anybody back. Wondered what kind of pain a person would have to be in to think that last, long leap could solve anything.

The hospital was just on the other side of the bridge next to the Coronado Island Marriott. He parked in the lot and walked back to the main entrance, stopping at an information desk just inside the front doors to ask how to get to the cafeteria. The elderly woman who gave him directions noted the bruises on his face and asked if he wouldn't be better off heading to the emergency room. McSwain told her all he needed was a good meal.

"Don't know why you're going to the cafeteria then," she called after him.

The cafeteria was located down a flight of stairs at the end of a hall where the odor of fried food mingled disturbingly with the smell of Pine-Sol and a variety of medicinal scents. McSwain didn't see Moxley until the man called out to him. He was sitting at a table along the far wall that was partially blocked from view by a column. It was the seat McSwain would have chosen himself if he wanted to see who came through the door before they saw him.

He made his way around a table full of men and women whom he assumed, from snippets of conversation he picked up, to be doctors discussing the relative merits of Antigua versus Saint Kitts. Moxley smiled broadly and rose to meet him. He wore black jeans and a striped hot-pink-and-black shirt of the kind favored by country-western stars and rodeo riders. Against the muted white and cream tones of the cafeteria and the subdued clothing of almost everyone else, the brilliance of the outfit was startling, a peacock at a convention of wrens.

"Sorry to ask you to come all the way out here, Ian," he said as the two men shook hands and sat down, "but when Helen has her therapy, I never know how long she's going to be." He gestured to the tray in front of him, which contained a plastic cup with a seafood salad and a glass of iced tea. "Want anything to eat? They've got great chocolate pudding, and the crabmeat cocktail's actually not too bad if you don't have any loose dental work."

"I'll pass," said McSwain. "Actually this shouldn't take long. Sorry to hear your girlfriend's not feeling well, though."

Moxley shrugged. "Oh, Helen's okay. It's just . . . she's got some glandular stuff going on, thyroid problems, and her blood pressure's way the hell higher than it oughta be. She's got a good attitude, though. At least she lets 'em poke her and prod her. Me, I hate doctors. You ask me, half the time the cure's worse than the disease." He forked some crabmeat into his mouth. "So, Ian, you give any thought to what we discussed the other day?"

McSwain was nonplussed as to what he was talking about.

Moxley went on enthusiastically. "You know, about me doing some work on the side for you and Jenna. Sort of like an apprenticeship, if you will."

"I don't think so. We don't really have enough business to farm anything out."

"What, you guys don't want to expand?"

"Guess we're just not growth oriented."

"Well, Ian, my man, you can't run a business that way."

something else, right? Is somebody trying hurt her? Is that why you wanted to find her the other day?"

McSwain was just about to deflect that question when Moxley's head jerked up and he scrambled to his feet with such haste his glass of iced tea almost tipped over. "Hey, here's my gal now."

McSwain twisted around in his seat and saw an enormous woman with flushed pink cheeks and light brown braided hair coiled around the sides of her head. An obese milkmaid to Moxley's urban cowboy. She wore a violet top over cream-colored pants and stood in the cafeteria doorway, looking left to right with the rapid, vexed glances of a convenience-store clerk watching candy bars go out the door inside the coat pockets of teenagers.

Moxley waved and she came tottering over, dabbing at her eyes with a wad of tissues as she launched herself into his arms. For a second it looked as though both of them might collapse in a pile, as Moxley's muscular body braced to take the woman's weight. When they finally disengaged, Moxley said, "Ian, this is my fiancée, Helen Croft. Honey, this is Ian McSwain, the private investigator I told you about."

"Pleasure to meet you," she said in that breathy, dark velvet voice that McSwain had heard on the phone. He realized that, on the basis of the voice, he'd pictured her as slim and sexy, and had to laugh inwardly at his predictable male assumptions. She lowered herself into a chair next to Richard's, fanning herself with one small, manicured hand that looked as soft and boneless as a child's, a treasure trove of gold bangles jingling at her wrist. When she moved, her whole body, in fact, seemed to ring musically with the soft clinking and clanking of jewelry—a set of ornate earrings dangling from each lobe and several necklaces cascading off the immense shelf of her bosom, one of which, a silver filigree design, was made up of what looked to McSwain like little squiggles and fishhooks.

She clutched Moxley's hand with the urgency of someone about to be hauled up back into the lifeboat after tumbling overboard. "This is the last time I'm coming here. That physical therapist *hurt* me. When I told her my back doesn't bend in that direction, she yelled at me and said I wasn't trying hard enough. She was so rude. That's it; I'm never coming back."

Moxley patted her hand in a placating gesture and gazed into her eyes. "Honey, you said that last time."

"Well, I mean it. I won't put up with this kind of abuse."

"You don't have to, hon."

"I won't."

She sniffled into the tissues. Moxley looked at McSwain, lifted his eyebrows, and gave a small whaddaya-gonna-do kind of shrug that Helen didn't see.

"You want me to talk to the physical therapist, hon? Set her straight about how she can treat you?"

"No, no. You're sweet, Richard, but I can stand up for myself." She turned her flushed, tear-streaked face to McSwain. "I put up with abuse from my ex-husband for fifteen years, and when I walked out that door, I said no more—that's it—never again will I allow myself to be mistreated." She used one bangle-laden wrist to nudge back a strand of hair that had come loose from one of the braids and looked fondly at Moxley. "Now I've found a man who treats me like a queen."

"Honey, you deserve it. Remember, though, if you quit therapy, it's going to look bad when you go to court for the settlement."

She gave a forlorn sigh. "I guess you're right. Always something else to contend with, isn't there?" She glanced at her watch. "Are you about ready to go, Richard?"

"Well, I don't know." He glanced at McSwain. "Are we wrapping it up here?"

"For now, I think so. I've got your phone number if other questions come up."

"Good," Helen said, "because I want to go home. I've got a headache from yelling at that awful woman."

Moxley touched a thumb to her mascara-streaked cheek. "Maybe you ought to hit the ladies' first, get rid of those zebra stripes. Then we'll take off."

Helen nodded, hoisted herself to her feet, and set off for the rest rooms on the other side of the cafeteria as though she were embarking on a minimarathon. Moxley watched her with the same gaze he'd directed at the blond woman's calves, a look of lust and unabashed ardor. "She's a wonderful woman, salt of the earth," he said. "She's been through hell. Had a hysterectomy when she was thirty-one; then she got pancreatitis. That's one of the most deadly forms of cancer; you know that. But she survived it. Then she was in an auto accident that messed up her back. The other driver turned out to be worth plenty, so she sued and walked away with a couple hundred thou. Couple months back, she slipped in the produce aisle at Albertson's, and she's got a suit going against them." He turned to McSwain, and angled a brow as though challenging him to contest what he was about to say. "You probably think the weight bothers me, but it doesn't. I love her for who she is on the inside, not the outside. The outside's just flesh, anyway, right? It doesn't last. It's the inside that counts."

"No argument there," said McSwain, although he felt uncomfortable with Moxley's need to justify his choice of partners. "Look, how about you give me Kreski's address, and I'll be out of your hair."

"Oh, right. Sure."

McSwain handed him a notebook and pen. Moxley dug a small leather address book out of his back pocket and printed an address in Encinitas. "Guy used to work for UPS, but I think he quit or they let him go. I've cruised past his place a few times—he's always home."

"Thanks, I'll see if I can catch him off guard."

"Guy's a flake," Moxley said. "How 'bout I come along?"

"I think I can manage."

Moxley made a chopping gesture with the side of his hand. "I tell you I used to teach karate? I'm not a bad guy to have around for backup."

"Thanks, I'll handle it."

"Anything I can do for you, Ian—I mean, personal protection, private investigation, it's all part of the same job, right?"

McSwain nodded vaguely and stood. Moxley rose, too. He seemed to want to continue talking, but McSwain used Helen's return from the ladies' room to say his good-byes and depart.

Outside the hospital, he could see commuter traffic backed up on the Coronado Bridge and realized that the five-o'clock rush was well under way. So was the headache that had begun in his temples while he was talking to Moxley and now scraped like a saw behind his forehead. Reaching into his pocket, he pulled out a bottle of Advil, shook out a couple of pills, and popped them down dry, making such a face that a middle-aged woman heading into the hospital stared and then gave him a wide berth.

He was thinking about the strange duo of Richard Moxley and Helen Croft, wondering why his mind kept returning to the woman as though she were a pebble in his shoe, when his cell phone rang.

"Ian?" came a tentative female voice that he recognized after a beat or two as Mandy's. "Can you talk?"

"Sure," he said unconvincingly as he reached his car, unlocked it, and sat down, leaving the door partially open. "What's up?"

"Well, I had a baby-sitter all lined up for tonight, but my plans kind of fell through. I was gonna go to a bar—just for a Coke—but then I thought, maybe that's not so smart; I'm setting myself up if I do that. I get off at six. I thought you and I could maybe get together for a cup of coffee."

McSwain couldn't remember when he'd last eaten and was almost wishing now that he'd taken a chance on the crabmeat cocktail. "You hungry? How about an early dinner?"

"Sure, but you don't have to . . . I mean, just coffee would be fine."

"I was on my way to eat anyway. You at home?"

"At the convenience store up the block actually."

He wondered why she wasn't calling from home, but didn't press it. "You okay to eat in a bar?"

"Yeah."

"There's a place not far from my office called My Brother's Bar. It's on Seacoast a block north of the Pier Plaza. They serve huge, greasy cheeseburgers that'll add pounds to your waist and take years off your life."

"Sure, why not?"

"It'll take me a while to get there, though. I'm in Coronado and traffic's backed up on the bridge."

"See you in a half hour?"

"Sounds good."

McSwain pulled out of the parking lot. He'd been planning to grab some fast food on the way home, but the prospect of a little company sounded good, and he thought it might not be a bad idea to talk to Mandy some more, see if finding out that "Billie" was still alive might have jogged her memory on any details.

My Brother's Bar was a cop hangout and neighborhood institution that McSwain had been frequenting for years. He'd done some work for the owner, an Armenian American who'd had problems with employee theft a few years back. The place consisted of two rooms, a bar with a few tables and chairs, and, through a doorway, a burger, fries, and sassy-waitress joint that could be quiet and cozy or rowdy as a fraternity rush night, depending on the night and what sports event happened to be playing on ESPN.

Tonight was quiet, which suited him fine. He took a booth near the back, facing the doorway so he'd see Mandy when she came in. He started to order a beer, then decided that might be insensitive, considering she hadn't been sober all that long, and went with iced tea instead.

A minute or two later Mandy appeared from the opposite end of the room, coming out of the ladies' room. She wore white capri pants, platform sandals, and a tight black top with a small diamond cut out below the neckline. She looked so good that it took McSwain a moment to recognize her. Then he said her name, and she came over and slid into the booth across from him.

"Hey, thanks for meeting me on such short notice. I really did have a date tonight—a guy I met at a meeting—but he canceled at the last minute. Cold feet, I guess."

"Those things happen."

"Yeah, a lot—when they hear the kids screaming in the background over the phone. That scares a lot of guys off."

The waitress, a platinum blonde with a beehive hairdo straight out of *American Graffiti*, brought McSwain's iced tea and a couple of menus. McSwain knew the menu by heart. He asked for the cheeseburger with Coney Island fries, and Mandy ordered the same.

"You didn't have to order tea, you know," she said when the waitress had left. "If you wanted a real drink, I mean, I could've handled it."

"I wasn't sure," McSwain said, "but I'll remember that."

They talked for a while in generalities—about Mandy's kids and the difficulties making ends meet for a single mother. Then McSwain brought up the subject of Virginia Stromquist. Mandy's shoulders hunched as though a cold wind had touched her, and she seemed to want to curl into herself.

"You sure she doesn't hate me?"

"No, of course not. Didn't Jenna tell you what she said?"

"Yeah, but . . . Jenna didn't actually meet her. You did."

"She said you probably saved her life by luring the guy away. She also said she'd be happy to meet you. She even gave me a card with her phone number if you ever wanted to talk." He started to reach for his wallet. "I've got it here someplace."

"Keep it." A small sigh blew out of Mandy's chest, and it took her a moment to breathe again. "I don't think I could handle it. After what happened, I don't even want to talk to her. I'm too ashamed of what I did that night."

"Look," said McSwain, "all things considered, I'd say you did pretty damned good. You were half in the bag, but you fought off a rapist and escaped—very few women, men for that matter, would've had the balls to do that—but you did. You saved your own life and then you took that life and, from all I can see, you turned it around. Yet you keep beating up on yourself because you didn't metamorphosize into Wonder Woman, beat the guy silly, and rescue Billie, too. You couldn't have pulled that off, Mandy. Nobody could. And to tell you the truth, I get tired of this guilt trip you're on."

"I'm sorry."

McSwain wanted to pound on the table. "No, don't be sorry. There's nothing to be sorry for; that's the whole point. Be proud of yourself. Be happy you're alive and that Billie's alive, too. Isn't that enough?"

The waitress brought the food and set it in front of them, cheeseburgers big enough to feed three and two heaping platters of fries smothered in cheese. McSwain shook salt onto his fries and was passing the shaker to Mandy when he realized she was looking down at her plate, her eyes swimming with tears.

"Mandy, what's wrong?"

She blotted her eyes with her napkin. "Nothing."

"Doesn't look like nothing."

"Just . . . old stuff. I don't want to talk about it now. It's just . . . God, I wish I could have a beer."

Even as she said it, a waitress was passing by with a pitcher of golden, frothy-topped brew, headed for a table of four college-age boys. McSwain was thankful now that he'd ordered tea.

"You can't drink, Mandy."

"I know, I know. I can dream, can't I? Getting loaded's such an easy way to feel better for a little while."

"And a lot worse after that."

"Yeah, but sometimes it almost seems like it'd be worth it. Just a few beers, take the edge off, then stop before I got hammered."

"You know you're kidding yourself if you think it'd be like that."

"Yeah, I know. More is never enough, right? One drink leads to another and another, and pretty soon I'm back at Torrey Pines looking to do a swan dive." She took a bite out of her cheeseburger. "Hey, forget it, okay? I'm not serious. I want to impress you; self-pity's probably not the way to go about it." She forced a smile that was too broad, had too much behind it. It made McSwain wonder if this was how she'd smiled as a little girl, always trying to please somebody, her father maybe, mother almost certainly, never quite making the grade. Not because she wasn't good enough, but because the people she was trying to please didn't really see her, were too wrapped up in their own misery to be pleased by anyone or anything.

"So now that you've found Billie—Virginia, that is," Mandy said, "that kind of closes things, doesn't it? I mean, except for me paying you, which I will—except you'll probably be an old man by the time I get done."

I feel like an old man already, thought McSwain, but didn't say it. "About the money, it's okay, Mandy. Take your time. But about things being closed, no, not really. Because we still don't know who did this to you and Virginia. All we do know is that it's highly unlikely he's stopped. So we have to keep looking."

"It wasn't just a one-shot deal then? Some psycho-fuck, excuse the language, who maybe learned his lesson when I kneed him in the balls?"

McSwain was surprised at her naivete. "It's possible he was somebody with a grudge against Virginia Strom-quist or her husband. That's one angle we're looking into. It's also possible he picked Virginia's car at random. Whichever the case, it's starting to look like you and Virginia weren't this man's only victims—only his luckiest ones."

"What d'you mean?"

McSwain had been debating about how much, if any-thing, to tell her about the bound body at the edge of the drainage ditch west of Jamul. Now he sketched in a few details, leaving out the worst of the horror, but still revealing enough that Mandy's face registered shock.

"This woman they found, how long ago was she killed?"

"Little over a week."

"And you think it's the same guy that hid in Virgin-ia's car?"

"It looks that way, yeah. The location, for one thing—off Otay Lakes Road on the way to Jamul. This guy had rope with him, too, like the man who attacked you and Virginia, and he tied his victim up before killing her."

"He rape her?"

"I haven't seen the forensics report, but yeah, I'd say she was assaulted before she was killed." He watched as the impact of that sank into Mandy's features. "It wasn't an easy death, Mandy. It was long and painful and terri-fying, and she probably wished she was dead long before it was over. She didn't deserve it. Nobody should have to die like that."

"Jesus." She was quiet for a moment, her vision turned inward, scanning some interior vista that seemed to hold no reprieve from what she'd just heard. Whatever image she gazed at in her own mind, McSwain could tell it wasn't a good one, but raw and sore and chafing at her insides. "What you're saying then is that if I'd gone to the cops the night it happened, then maybe nobody else would've been murdered. Maybe the woman in the ditch wouldn't have been raped and tortured and killed."

"We can't know that, Mandy. But it does seem likely that the man who attacked you is still out there and still active and that he may be killing his victims, not just raping them."

"I could've stopped him if I hadn't been afraid to go to the police."

"Maybe, maybe not. It's done now. The important thing is—"

"So I'm to blame, is that it?"

"I didn't say that." McSwain felt the conversation swerving into a nosedive, felt angry at himself for setting it in motion, yet powerless to stop the downward spiral.

"You're saying it's my fault she'd dead."

"Of course that's not what I'm saying."

"Fuck it, you are. I think I'm gonna be sick." She grabbed her purse, slid out of the booth, and walked quickly back to the rest room. She was gone so long that McSwain finished his burger and was starting to get worried about her when finally she returned, a timid smile and fresh lipstick on her mouth.

"Hey, sorry I went off on you like that."

"It's okay, Mandy. You all right?"

"Yeah, I'm fine. Just thinking about that poor woman, though . . . that could've been me." She looked at her plate of barely touched food. "I don't think I can eat this. You want to leave?"

McSwain paid the bill and they walked outside. Traffic was heavy on Clemson, backed up where the left lane was closed for a block due to construction, and car windows were rolled down, radios blaring, squeals and laughter from a sedan full of kids rippling into the cool evening air. The breeze shifted, and McSwain got a whiff of the eucalyptus trees planted behind DeeDee's Florist Shop across the street.

"Something I wanted to ask," McSwain said. "You got a cell phone?"

"No."

He dug into his pocket and produced a small cellular phone. "I got a new one the other day, but this one still works and the bill's paid up a few months. Good thing for a woman to have in her car. You know, in case you get a flat tire or something."

"I can change a tire."

"Well, whatever."

She took the phone, slipped it into her purse. "Thanks. That was nice of you."

"Where're you parked?"

She pointed around the corner. "Over there."

"Come on; I'll walk you."

A soft giggle erupted out of her, completely unexpected given the mood she'd been in just a short time ago.

"What's funny?"

"You're such a gentleman, that's all."

"Because I said I'd walk you to your car?"

"Believe me, a lot of guys wouldn't do that. Kevin wouldn't."

"Your husband."

"Ex."

"Your ex-husband."

She turned toward him suddenly, the knuckles of her left hand brushing his, lingering a second before drawing back. "You're married, aren't you?"

"Yeah."

"Jenna told me you and your wife are separated. I was wondering, if you don't mind my asking, how serious is the separation? You think you and your wife'll get back together?"

"We're getting back together very soon," he said quickly, wondering what else Jenna might have told her. "The separation, it's just temporary."

"You must miss her a lot."

"Yeah, I do."

"How long have you been apart?"

"Couple of years."

She looked surprised. "Long time."

They reached her car and she fumbled around in her purse before finding the key and unlocking it. McSwain opened the door for her, but she didn't get in. She leaned forward suddenly and put her lips on his mouth. "I hope things work out for you and your wife; I really do. But if something happens and you don't get back together . . . or don't stay together, well, I haven't been with anybody since I got sober. Maybe we could keep each other company."

Before he could reply, she put a finger across his lips—"Just something to think about"—and got into the car. It didn't start at first, and she looked up at him and shrugged, but on the fourth try the engine turned over. The Taurus made a chugging sound and lurched away from the curb like a drunk shoving off from a bar stool.

McSwain watched the car until it took a hard left at the corner and disappeared. He put a hand to his mouth, where he could still taste the slightly strawberry tang of her lipstick, where the blood rushed a little bit hotter and faster just for that brief, teasing contact with her flesh.

What he most remembered, though, as he walked back to his car, what he tried to shake, was the sensation that, in that instant when she'd exhaled as she leaned in toward him, the smell of beer had wafted from her breath.

Chapter 19

McSwain felt as though he spent much of that night tossing through a tormented sleep.

He dreamed first of Helen Croft, not as a woman but
as a living, breathing boat, a nightmare frigate made of
skin and bone, organs and tendons and murderous intentions. Her clothes unfurled into voluminous sails, her
many necklaces clanging like bells against her breasts,
and then her flesh transformed into the sea itself, as she
tried to crush the air from his lungs and drown him.

He reached up, trying to claw his way to the surface,
but he made no progress and realized why—the fingers
on both hands were missing.

The dream shifted then, the thread of it beginning to
unravel, but the suffocating sensation of being trapped
still constricting his heart. Then he was sitting at the
kitchen table of his childhood, the yellow Formica
cracked and chipped, silly-looking petunia-patterned cur-
tains flapping stiffly at the open window. He heard his
mother coming up the hall, the familiar scuffle and
scrape of those blue slippers she always wore in the
house getting inside his skull, for some reason making
him want to bolt and run, but he couldn't—his feet were
planted to the floor, his butt grafted to the seat of the
chair.

His mother slumped through the door in that dejected,
preoccupied way of hers, but when she saw him, her eyes
brightened with excitement—they were her Christmas-
morning eyes, her let's-run-next-door-and-take-our-
picture-on-the-neighbors'-porch eyes—and for a second

his heart lurched with hope that something good was going to happen.

His mother's eyes got even brighter, crazy psycho-bitch bright, like she was lit from within with a Times Square's worth of neon. She said, "It was a dog, Ian. I saw it. It was a dog!"

And right on cue a black dog bounded into the kitchen, its black eyes just as wild, just as deranged as his mother's, blood dripping from its mouth onto the linoleum floor. His fingers were in the dog's mouth, and the dog was chewing them—he could hear the crunch of canine incisors on fingernails and bone—and all the while the dog gazed up at his mother with outright ado-ration, looking at her like he could eat her up, too, as if she were his savior, his hero, his god.

The last one, the dream about the dog, was a variation on a dream he'd had before off and on throughout his life, but in recent years he'd been spared it, or at least was able, in some semilucid sleep state, to see the dream coming and wake himself up before descending into the thick of it. This time, though, he woke up slick with sweat and gasping, gripped with the irrational idea that instead of having lost the little finger years ago, he was actually missing all ten, flexing his hands under the sheets to reassure himself.

As he lay there, the sky broke open and rain com-menced to fling itself against the roof, some of it coming in through the partially open window by the bed. When he got up to close it, warm droplets splattered through the screen onto his knuckles, ran like blood down his nine fingers, and dripped onto the sill.

The rain had stopped hours earlier, but sleek, salmon-shaped clouds scudded along the eastern sky, and the humidity draped itself over the city like a warm, sodden cloth as McSwain and Capshaw drove north on Highway 8 to Encinitas the next afternoon. On the left he could see the ocean and a small flotilla of surfers. They bobbed like seals in their black wet suits as they paddled out on their boards before being torpedoed back toward the beach by the mountainous waves.

For the last five minutes, they'd been exchanging theories about Virginia's first husband, Phil Clarion—Jenna had reached him the day before and set up an appointment for later that afternoon—but then McSwain had changed topics abruptly, asking Jenna a question that she was now taking her sweet time about answering, fiddling around with the radio as though searching for a station that held the answer.

Finally she found what she wanted, a PBS station playing classical music, and settled back in the seat with one leg curled underneath her. "Yeah, I told Mandy you and your wife were separated—she asked me your status, okay—but that's it. No details."

"You could've just told her I'm married. That *is* my status."

"What? She come on to you?"

"That's not the point."

"She came on to you."

"I'm afraid she may be drinking."

"Oh, well, then, that explains it." She waited for him to catch the joke, then reached over and slapped his shoulder when he didn't laugh.

"I'm serious, Jenna. I think I smelled beer on her breath."

"Did you call her on it?"

"No, because I wasn't sure."

"How can you not be sure whether you smell beer on somebody's breath? You either do or you don't. It's not subtle."

"They were serving beer in this place. The odor could've been in her clothes, in her hair."

"And you'd told her about the body out on Otay?"

"Just the basics, yeah."

"Why'd you go someplace they were serving beer anyway?"

"She said it wouldn't be a problem, and I took her at her word."

Capshaw didn't say anything, but he could feel her stewing as she lit a cigarette and puffed a small tornado of smoke out the car window.

The road narrowed and curved away from the beach as they approached Encinitas. Traffic was congested, backed up at every light. Up ahead, McSwain saw the Self-Realization Fellowship, a meditation center whose lotus-shaped towers rose from behind high, buff-colored walls that enclosed a meditation garden overlooking the sea. McSwain wasn't much for meditation—he'd tried it and found he got too antsy trying to sit still—but he remembered the garden's tranquil walkways and bubbling waterfalls from a time he'd gone there with Lily.

Arlis Kreski's address was only a couple of blocks away on La Costa Avenue—a small, tidy-looking stucco house with a camper in the driveway and a Ford Bronco parked at the curb. It wasn't quite five yet, and McSwain was expecting the man to still be at work, but he smelled a steak cooking and saw smoke rising from around the side of the house. He looked at Jenna and she shrugged and they walked around back.

A lanky, stoop-shouldered man wearing baggy green shorts and a white undershirt was bending over a barbecue, in the process of flipping a T-bone. With his height and curved shoulders, there was a giraffelike quality to his stance, as though his body were at a perpetual tilt, leaning forward for something just out of reach.

"Mr. Kreski?"

His shoulders jerked and he looked up, startled. He had a broad, pasty face pocked with acne scars and thinning brown hair, and even though McSwain guessed him to be no older than his mid-forties, his eyes looked bleak and weary, the pale, washed-out blue of old denim.

He squinted at them with suspicion. "You two from the union?" Without waiting for a reply he went on, "Because it's about time they sent somebody out. I been waiting on you guys two fucking months now, and nothin's been done."

"You've got us mixed up with somebody else," Capshaw said, pulling out her PI ID while McSwain did the same. Unlike most people, who barely glanced at IDs, Kreski took each one in turn and studied it, looking up at both Capshaw and McSwain to see whether the photos on the IDs matched their faces.

"Private investigators? What, now the damn company's hired an investigator? Why? What the hell's there to investigate? I never touched the guy, there're no witnesses, his word against mine. You wanna investigate somebody, investigate Johnny Sprague; he's a damn drunk who lies through his teeth."

"It's nothing to do with any of that," said McSwain. "We don't know anything about any Sprague. I'm looking into a man named Leland Stromquist. I know you know him, and I wanted to ask you some questions."

At the mention of the name, Kreski tensed and stalked back to the barbecue. He flipped the T-bone high and hard, like someone getting ready to serve a tennis ball. It thunked onto the grill and sizzled as smoke rose from the barbecue.

"Stromquist. What the fuck about him?"

"Your daughter was involved in his organization."

"*Was* involved. Yeah." He speared the steak with a stainless-steel fork and slapped it onto a plate. "See what you've done? Just like that, you took my appetite. This looks like barbecued shit to me now."

"Sorry if we've upset you, Mr. Kreski," Capshaw said.

"Yeah, I'll bet." He marched past them holding the plate with the steak on it, then stopped and looked back at them, scowling. "You wanna talk or not? Come on inside."

They followed him up three cement stairs and through the screen door into the kitchen. A salad bowl filled with greens and a bottle of ranch sat on the countertop next to the sink. Kreski put these in the refrigerator along with the steak. He took out three bottles of Bud. "You do drink on the job, I assume?"

Capshaw said, "No, thanks," but McSwain accepted a bottle.

"Had a rule I never drank before five when I was working," Kreski said, "and I still abide by it, but I swear, five o'clock feels like it's eight or nine by the time it gets here these days."

"You laid off, Mr. Kreski?"

"Suspended with pay pending a hearing. UPS big shots just yanking my chain, that's all. They'll take me back; the union'll see to that. My boss, Sprague, says I got in his face and pushed him, but it's a damn lie. I'da wanted to hurt that asshole, he'd've gotten my fist through his teeth, not a push." He unscrewed the cap on the beer, slugged some back. "Sprague's a nobody, though, a nothing. I don't even hate him no more. But that son of a bitch Stromquist—"

He broke off and headed further into the house, arriving at a living room where a Lakers game was in progress on a big-screen TV. Pictures on the mantel and end tables showed Kreski with a stout, raven-haired woman whose slightly slanted eyes and dark golden skin hinted at Asian origins, and a young girl with hair and skin tones identical to the mother's. In the photos, the daughter aged into a plump but stunningly beautiful young woman, while the older woman grew morose-looking and increasingly corpulent.

Kreski noticed Capshaw eyeing the photos. "My daughter, Adrienne and my wife, Ero. Ero left me a couple of years ago, said my temper made me too hard to live with. Adrienne, she left me for good back in September of last year."

McSwain and Capshaw took seats in two identical patterned armchairs, while Kreski flopped onto a sofa whose springs sagged low and dark like the bags under his eyes. He took a long swallow of beer and looked at them with the laconic, beleaguered expression of the recently bereaved or deeply depressed. When those lifeless eyes swept over him, McSwain felt that odd, flulike chill he always got when a case required him to visit a morgue.

"I know I seen your IDs, but just to get it out of the way, ain't neither of you two cops, right? You have to tell me, else it's entrapment."

"We're not cops," Capshaw said.

"Good, then I don't have to tiptoe around you." He settled back, pulled on his beer. "So you're checking up on Stromquist—what for?"

"It involves a case we're working on," said McSwain. "Stromquist's not accused of anything, but we'd like to know more about him, how he operates, what your relationship with him is."

"Relationship? I got no relationship with that motherfucker."

"Someone close to Stromquist says you've made threats, that—"

Kreski snorted. "You talking about that Moxley schmuck he sent around? Big, goofy-looking guy always has this smart-ass expression, like he knows something you don't? Yeah, he come out here one day, acting the tough guy. Like I'm scared of *him*. Right. I know his kind, all hot air and tough talk, but when push comes to shove, they'll pussy out every time."

"And *did* you threaten Stromquist?" asked Capshaw.

"Hey, c'mon, how dumb do you think I am? He knows what he did, what I think of him. Every time he gives a talk, every time he does a book signing, he sees me right there—front row center—just seeing me's enough to freak him out. He knows what he's done, so it gives him the creeps, I can tell."

"Exactly what is it you think he's guilty of, Mr. Kreski?" asked McSwain.

"He killed my daughter."

"That's what I don't understand. Why you think he's to blame for your daughter's death."

"Adrienne would be alive today if it wasn't for that twisted, family-hating fuck." Dark blotches rose in his ashen cheeks. "She was just twenty-four. A sweet, quiet, God-fearing young woman. She still lived at home until she took one of Stromquist's seminars, and bought into that crap about reinventing herself, about family ties being a noose around her neck."

"So Adrienne changed after she got involved with the Stromquist organization?"

"Changed? Hell, she was a different person. But then that's the whole idea, right? That with Stromquist's help, you get to be a new person, a new, improved fucking version of yourself."

"I don't get that," McSwain said. "An improved version of yourself—how's that different from the goal of conventional therapy?"

Kreski grimaced and his angular frame sagged deeper into the sofa. His torso appeared to go concave under some invisible, overpowering burden that weighed on his chest.

"Regular therapy—not that I've ever done it myself; you ask me it's all a load of crap—but as I understand it, regular therapy you just address certain problems, issues, they call 'em. You're insecure or you always date losers or you got problems with gettin' it up, whatever the hell. You work on this part or that part of your life, maybe tinker a little with a job, a relationship, but that's as far as it goes." He stopped talking, looked from Capshaw to McSwain. "Either one of you ever read his book?"

"I've read it," said Capshaw.

"Well, what d'you think?"

She waited a beat to answer. McSwain knew she was considering the question, taking it seriously.

"I think the stuff about detaching from everything in your past is unrealistic. That it might work for an amnesia victim or somebody who's been held captive by terrorists for the last twenty years, but for the average person . . . it doesn't take into account the bonds people have with their pasts, the fact that for better or worse, people get their identity from their pasts. It's who they are, how they define themselves. You take it away or convince them to give it up all in one wrench, they may be left without much to hold on to. They could fall apart."

"Exactly, exactly," said Kreski, jabbing a finger at Capshaw. "You're sharp, lady. You see the truth. That's what happened to Adrienne. She gave up everything that she was, till there wasn't anything left, till in her own mind it was like she didn't even exist anymore."

"Whoa, whoa," McSwain said, "I still don't get it. What was it Stromquist made your daughter give up and why?"

"You know about the crazy fucking labyrinth, right?"

"Yeah, we've been out there. We've seen it."

"So you know walking the labyrinth is the final initiation that the level fives take? It's like a fucking graduation ceremony, and everything else, all the bullshit lectures and seminars, it all leads up to that. Stromquist gives some pompous, rah-rah talk. Then one by one, everybody goes into the labyrinth. You know what else? You take with you things that are symbolic of what you value, everything that's had meaning in your life, and when you get to the center, there's a pit or a hole or some goddamn thing and you just toss the stuff in, your whole fucking life, symbolically. Then you walk out empty-handed. Reborn, redefined, Stromquist calls it." He paused and the muscles in his tight jaw rolled like ball bearings under the skin. "And you don't go back to being who you were. Ever."

"What did Adrienne leave?" Capshaw said.

Kreski ran a hand through his thinning hair and stared out the window. Across the street, a couple of kids in bathing suits were running through the sprinklers in a front lawn, a woman in a straw hat was bending over, weeding a flower garden.

"She left photos of me and her mother, aunts and uncles, cousins, the whole family. A crucifix, because she said the Catholic religion had poisoned her and was holding her back. Some letters from a boy she'd dated when she was in high school, who still liked her and wanted to get back together. A time card from the restaurant she worked at, because it was a shitty job and made her feel bad about herself. A Polish flag and an Italian one for my side of the family, Vietnamese and Japanese flags for her mother's side, because Stromquist convinced her that ethnic identity is a limiting concept. It holds people back. What else . . . Oh, yeah, a whole shitload of diet books."

"Diet books?" asked McSwain.

"Adrienne thought she was too heavy. Always trying one diet after another, never satisfied with herself. Stromquist told her that wanting to look like society's idea of how a woman should be, that was just another trap, that was bad for her. So she'd decided to hell with it, to eat what she wanted and look how she looked and anybody who didn't like it, screw 'em." He shook his head. "Out of all the bullshit, it was the one thing that kind of made sense to me, that I could understand. That how she looked shouldn't be based on how other people thought she ought to look."

"So after the trip into the labyrinth, what was she supposed to do?" said McSwain.

"Start over with a fucking blank slate. See, Stromquist thinks people are held back by the things they use to define themselves—their family, jobs, friends, background. It's all limiting, supposedly. How do you smash through the fucking self-imposed limits?—you walk away. You just walk the fuck away. 'Cause presto, supposedly you're now somebody else—the person you would've been if things like family and home weren't holding you back."

"Pretty radical," said Capshaw. "Was Adrienne able to do it?"

"Adrienne could do anything she put her mind to, including this. She cut me and her mother out of her life, moved to a new place, got an unlisted phone number. Friends she'd had since she was in kindergarten, she wouldn't contact them. Quit her job, where she could've moved up to management, and ended up doing—Jesus, I still can't believe this—she was working for one of those phone-sex lines, sitting at home talking filth all day long—she said this was supposed to help her get over all the damage the Catholic church had done by inhibiting her sex drive. Can you believe that garbage?"

"Wait a minute," said McSwain. "You said she cut you off. How do you know all this?"

Kreski's gaze drifted back to the window. "There was a girlfriend Adrienne had confided to about where she was living, and I convinced this friend it was in Adrienne's best interest to let me see her. She agreed. So I went to Adrienne's apartment, had it out with her. She said I wasn't her father anymore, that that part of her life was . . . over." His mouth twisted into a horrible grin and his eyes shut tight. He forced his lips around the mouth of the beer bottle and drained it. "She said if her mother and me loved her, we'd respect her decision and leave her alone. I asked her, so what was it with this Stromquist guy, had he hypnotized her, was it some kind of cult, was she brainwashed? She just laughed at me. Said I was one of those people who clung to the past and I couldn't possibly understand. And that was the last time I saw her. A month later she killed herself."

"And you feel sure her suicide was connected to this radical new turn her life had taken?" Capshaw asked.

Kreski raised his eyes to the ceiling as though looking for some answer there. Outside, the kids running through the shower spray were shrieking louder, the joy in their cries a palpable contrast to the despair in Kreski's living room.

"Adrienne left a note. It broke my heart to read it, because you could tell she was so lost and confused. She said she couldn't go forward and she couldn't go back, that she wanted to become this new person but now she felt like she was no person at all. She was empty, a cipher, she called it. She said she'd left her life in the labyrinth." Kreski's hands balled into fists. "Stromquist did this to her, him with his crackpot philosophy. People think he's a great man; I know better. I know he deserves to have somebody sit on his shoulders and ram a gun through his teeth. . . ."

"Stromquist has a wife and son," Capshaw said. "Do you think they deserve to be punished too?"

"For what?"

"By hurting Stromquist's wife, for example, some people might say that'd be a way to get back at him. He took your daughter; maybe if something happened to his wife, he'd understand what it feels like."

Kreski hunched forward, a deep crease bisecting his brows. "What the fuck are you talking about? You think I'm gonna do something to the guy's wife? Oh, no, man, this is between me and Stromquist. When the time comes, it's Stromquist whose gonna pay—no fucking stand-ins or substitutes, no fucking way.

"What you're suggesting—that I might do something to the asshole's wife or kid—that's bullshit. That's a coward's way. Besides, even if I was that kind of person and even if I did blow his wife's brains all over creation, what's to guarantee Stromquist would even give a shit? All I know, maybe he thinks she's a noose around *his* neck. Maybe he'd send me a thank-you note if I offed her." A long sigh rumbled out of his chest and he grimaced as though the air burned his lungs on the way out. He rubbed a hand over his breastbone, shook his head. "Makes me sick, you know, just talking about this. I get headaches, y'know, bad ones, when I get upset. Feels like my skull's gonna explode. I think it's time you people left."

He got to his feet and shuffled to the front door like

a man with logs tied to his ankles. When he thrust out his arm to open it, even though he was a man standing in his own living room, a steak dinner in the fridge, he looked to McSwain like a panhandler, utterly bedraggled and hopeless.

He and Capshaw were almost at the sidewalk when Kreski stepped out onto the porch and called after them, "Hey, wait, wait. Come back a sec, will ya? Somethin' else I wanna say."

McSwain and Capshaw looked at each other, then started back toward the house.

"No, just you," Kreski said, indicating McSwain. "No offense to you, lady; I think you got a lot on the ball, but . . . this is a man-to-man thing."

Capshaw shrugged. "Go do your male bonding. I'll wait here." She walked over to the fence enclosing Kreski's property and leaned against it, watching with an annoyed look on her face as McSwain went back inside the house.

A couple of minutes after he went inside, McSwain strode out of the house, looking disgusted. He was silent as they walked back to the car.

"That was tough," Capshaw said. "I feel sorry for the guy; I can't help it."

McSwain unlocked the driver's-side door and got in. "Don't waste your sympathy. Know what it was he wanted to talk to me about—man to man?"

Her eyes widened. "Oh, shit, he wanted you to . . . some kind of hit?"

"Ten thousand bucks—his life's savings—and the more painful the better. He even had a couple of suggestions—I'll spare you the worst, but kneecapping was the most civilized of them. I told him I'd forget this little conversation and not go to the police, but that if anything ever happened to Stromquist or anybody else in his family, he'd just fucked himself royally."

"Was he deterred?"

"You kidding? Only thing deters a guy like Kreski is whatever it takes to put him in the ground."

"You think he's capable of attacking Virginia or hiring someone to do it?"

"I don't know . . . I can't see it. The guy's a nut, but

I also get the feeling he sees this as a man-to-man thing, something between him and Stromquist. Still and all . . ."

"Anything's possible."

"You got that right."

McSwain checked his watch. "What time's Phil Clarion expecting us?"

"Anytime after six at his office in the Vidmar Building. He said he'll be there grading papers."

"How'd he sound on the phone?"

"Defensive at first, but then his curiosity got the better of him. I got the impression he's still carrying a torch for Virginia."

McSwain was staring at his cell phone, which showed five calls during the period they'd been with Kreski. "Hang on a sec."

As he listened to the calls, McSwain grew concerned. They were all collect calls from CWI. It wasn't unusual for Lily to call him, but it was odd for her to call so often in so short a period.

"Anything wrong?"

"I hope not, but Lily's tried to reach me five times."

"No message?"

"Unless she gets special permission, she can't leave one. Collect only."

"That sucks."

"Tell me about it."

He stared at the phone and tried to buoy his spirits by remembering there were less than two months remaining on Lily's sentence. "God, I'll be glad when she's out of that place. Two years now, and every damn day it feels like I'm locked up, too."

"You haven't said much about Lily lately. How's she doing?"

"Fine, as far as I know."

"As far as you know? What does that mean?"

"Well, she'd like for me to quit the PI business and get into something respectable, but other than that . . ."

Capshaw's eyes widened. "Quit the business? You wouldn't—"

He gave a small sigh, shook his head. "Okay, read me those directions to San Diego State again."

Chapter 20

The first thing McSwain noticed when they entered Phil Clarion's office was the painting of a roomful of naked, bejeweled women languidly reclining around a pool. They were fleshy and doughy pale and gazed out at the viewer with come-hither smiles and deep-lidded, languorous eyes. On the opposite wall two more paintings—nude women being overpowered and abducted by soldiers, another being ravished by a centaur with spectacular phallic endowments. At least one of the paintings was vaguely familiar to McSwain, and he felt sure all three were reprints of great art, but somehow in the cluttered confines of Phil Clarion's office, with the man himself perched gargoylishly on the edge of his desk, the effect was uncomfortably close to pornographic.

"Ms. Capshaw," Clarion said, rising to shake Jenna's hand. He glanced at McSwain, feigning confusion. "On the phone you didn't say there'd be two of you."

"My partner, Ian McSwain."

"Oh. Well, as you can see, it's rather close quarters in here, but you can clear off a chair if you care to."

McSwain lifted a stack of large, expensive-looking art books to the floor and sat down in a chair by the door. To his left, floor-to-ceiling bookshelves sagged under the weight of more tomes. He glanced at the titles at eye level, and saw a number devoted to Asian and East Indian erotica. The books above and below seemed devoted to more conventional art. He wondered if Clarion had deliberately positioned the erotic titles where a visitor would most easily see them.

Clarion resumed his position atop the desk. He was a squat, broad-shouldered man with thinning gray hair, a swooping gray mustache that seemed too big for his narrow face, and the avuncular smile of one adept at dealing with—and charming—much younger people. His navy blue shirt was unbuttoned at the collar, revealing a Saint Anthony's medallion that glinted in the tufts of his chest hair. He saw McSwain looking at the paintings and smiled. "That's Ingres's *Odalisque*—one of my favorites. And you've seen that one, I'm sure. It's Delacroix's *Rape of the Sabines*. Dramatic yet sensuous."

"There seems to be a theme here," McSwain said. "Your female students, do they ever complain about the decor? The absence of nude men, for example? It seems sexist."

"Great art transcends sexism, racism, ageism," said Clarion, with the practiced smile of one who has repeated the phrase many times. McSwain found himself thinking about Leland Stromquist, how Virginia's men—Danny Tibbs included—seemed to share a bent for pontificating.

Clarion wet his lips and steepled his long fingers, gazing back and forth between them as though trying to decide which of two students to call on and relishing the private certainty that neither would know the answer. Finally he swiveled slightly on the desk and directed his comments to Capshaw.

"So I understand that this concerns my ex-wife. You have some questions."

"That's right."

"Since we spoke on the phone, though, I've had a chance to think about this, and I'm not sure I'm comfortable discussing Virginia, at least not without her permission."

"I'm sure she wouldn't mind."

Clarion frowned expressively, fingers steepling again, lips slightly pursed. "Yes, well, be that as it may, I don't think I can—"

"Your discretion's admirable," Capshaw said, "but before you run it into the ground, you ought to know Virginia had no trouble discussing you."

"Discussing me?" Clarion patted his balding dome as though reassuring himself that at least a few errant strands still remained. "What do you mean? What did she say?"

"Only that you two had an affair after her marriage to Leland Stromquist. That, and the fact that you occasionally get in hot water for sleeping with your students."

A patch of red like a rash crawled over Clarion's scalp. He didn't speak for a moment. When he did, he pronounced each word with the exaggerated care of one unfamiliar with English. "Virginia said that? Really? Well, I must say, I'm surprised." He stood up, all pretense at casualness gone, stalked to the other side of his desk, and sat down again, the piles of books and papers providing a kind of fortress between himself and his interrogators. "Her lack of discretion distresses me, but at least I know where I stand."

Capshaw scooted her chair to the left, so she could make eye contact with Clarion behind his barricade of books. "Mind if I smoke in here?"

"Against school policy. Sorry." He picked up a pen, tapped it on the desktop. "What is it you want to know?"

"The affair with Virginia, how long ago was it?"

"Is this really pertinent? I—"

"Mr. Clarion, we just want to see if you and Virginia agree on a couple of things."

"Dr. Clarion."

"Doctor."

"It was three, four years ago. Virginia was lonely, going through a rough time, with Leland being away all the time. I was between relationships. We consoled each other."

"Did Leland know about it?"

"Leland? Not unless Virginia told him, and I can't imagine she did."

"How long were you and Virginia married?"

"Almost three years."

"Not very long."

Clarion shrugged. *"Qué será, será."*

"How did it end?"

The frown lines between Clarion's eyes deepened. "Is this really relevant?"

"Humor me," Capshaw said.

"Well, I'm sure you asked Virginia the same thing. Pray, what did *she* tell you?"

"She said . . . well, these might not have been her exact words," said McSwain, "but she implied, actually, that you were a nice guy, but boring. That about sum it up?"

Clarion's jaw tightened. "Boring?"

"Maybe not boring exactly, but somewhere in the vicinity. Bland, I think. Yeah, maybe that was it. Bland."

"Bland?"

"Bland."

"Well, maybe by Virginia's standards, but she's the type of person who'd probably find the Marquis de Sade tedious."

Capshaw leaned back, crossed her legs, enjoying this. "Sorry, Dr. Clarion, I don't follow."

"She and I had certain . . . Well, the truth is, over time we became sexually incompatible."

"But you were sexually compatible to begin with," Capshaw said. "Then you became incompatible. What happened?"

Clarion seemed to be making an effort not to tear out what remained of his hair. "I'm not going to go into detail. There's no need, and it's none of your business. Just that Virginia's and my idea of what constituted normal sexual relations became increasingly dissimilar. She wanted things that I was unwilling to give, so we divorced—amicably, I might add. End of story. Okay?"

"So you could call it a civilized parting of the ways?"

"Exactly." He leaned forward. "Now let me ask you a question. On the phone, Ms. Capshaw, you told me you aren't working for Leland, that this has nothing to do with divorce proceedings or anything like that. Is Virginia in some sort of legal trouble?"

"No, why would you think so?"

"Well, you're private detectives; you figure it out. She's married to a guy with a degree in business administration, not psychotherapy, who makes a six-figure income writing pop psychology for forty-year-olds who've never forgiven Daddy for not sending them to summer camp and bitter wives who think the only thing that kept them from being on the cover of *Vogue* was being stupid enough to marry hubby and pop out the kids. Hubris and money in large amounts—sooner or later, it usually leads to lawsuits.''

"As far as we know, no one's suing either Leland or Virginia," said Capshaw, "but as you obviously know, Virginia's husband is somewhat controversial—"

"Somewhat?"

"—and there're people who don't wish him well."

"Can't say I'm surprised there. I saw the guy interviewed on TV once. He's a pompous windbag—the kind of guy who all too often ends up in academia."

McSwain saw Jenna cough into her palm, figured she was probably leaving teeth marks in her tongue with the effort not to laugh.

"As far as you know, Mr.—Dr. Clarion, does Virginia have any enemies?"

"No."

"Anyone who'd want to harm her?"

"I believe I just answered that. No. Virginia's very nonconfrontational, an appeaser afraid of other people's anger. Not the kind of person who makes enemies or stirs things up."

"Not the kind of person who'd go to the police if she were attacked?" said Capshaw.

"I don't . . . What do you mean? Has she been. . . .?"

"There was an incident last winter," McSwain said. "A possible attempt on her life."

"Jesus," said Clarion. "Someone tried to kill her? I didn't know about this." He patted the broad, hairless patch on the back of his head. "Details, please."

"We really don't need to go into the details, Mr. Clarion—"

"Doctor."

"Dr. Clarion—except to say that Virginia's all right. What confuses us, though, is her refusal to go to the police. It's almost as though she's protecting someone. That's where we were hoping you might be able to help us."

Clarion polished the bald spot again. "Well, no, I don't think I can, except . . ."

"Except what, Dr. Clarion?"

"Frankly, I don't think Virginia's protecting anyone, but I believe I can shed light on why she won't go to the police. I'm surprised she didn't tell you herself about what happened, except . . . well . . . she has so much shame around it. For years I begged her to get into therapy, but she's one of those people, I'm afraid, who deal with trauma from the past by burying it under distractions in the present."

"I'm not following," McSwain said.

"Do you know anything about Virginia's childhood?"

"Not a lot," McSwain said. "She told me she grew up in El Centro, that the parents used to take her with them to the bars."

Clarion's eyebrows lifted slightly. "Then she told you more than she tells most people. Anyway, yes, the family was poor, both parents drank, the father cuffed the mother around, you get the picture."

"And that's what she's ashamed of?" Capshaw said.

"Not at all. If anything, I think she has some kind of misguided nostalgia for her lower-class origins—those tawdry bars she liked to hang out at—a kind of reverse élitism." He leaned forward, seeming suddenly energized. "Did she tell you about Patrick DeKooning?"

McSwain shook his head.

"I'm not surprised. We'd been married two years before she told me about him." He moved aside a pile of books, so he could see Capshaw's and McSwain's faces, before proceeding. "In El Centro, there was a family in the next block, the DeKoonings, who had a son, Patrick, early twenties, your classic fuckup type who still lived at home. He'd seen Virginia—except she was called Billie then; that was her nickname—he'd seen her around and apparently developed an obsession with her. One weekend, when his parents were away, he got her to come into his house on some pretext or other. Once he had her inside, he held her captive, raping her for two days. Her parents called the police, but only to report her as a runaway. Finally, though, Patrick left her locked in the basement; she broke a window, crawled through, and escaped. Patrick was arrested and went to trial. Virginia testified against him. She was just fourteen at this point, you understand. The defense tried to paint it as mutual consent, statutory rape at the worst, that she had a crush on Patrick and invited herself into his house. Fortunately the jury didn't see it that way—in part because Virginia got cut up so badly crawling through that window that she was obviously desperate to get away. DeKooning got ten years in prison, but you can imagine how traumatic it was for Virginia. Plus DeKooning remained delusional about the nature of what had taken place, that it was some kind of thwarted seduction, not a brutal attack. He vowed to come after her, and she was always afraid that he would."

"So DeKooning would be in his mid- to late forties by now," Capshaw said. "Any idea what happened to him after he got out of prison?"

"Virginia kept in touch with his parole officer over the years, wanting to be informed if he got out. Apparently, when he was released, he went back to El Centro for a while, but except for his mother, what family he had left there wanted nothing to do with him. The parole officer wouldn't give Virginia any other details, only that he was still in the area."

"Did DeKooning ever try to make good on his threat?" McSwain asked. "Ever try to contact her?"

"Oh, of course not, it was just talk. But there'd be the occasional middle-of-the-night hang-up, and a couple of times Virginia found dead flowers stuck under the windshield of her car. I'm sure it had nothing to do with DeKooning, but it freaked her out. She insisted on putting in an alarm system, taking self-defense classes. It would've just been pathetic if it hadn't also been so annoying."

"She's afraid some nut who raped her is going to come back for another try and you find that annoying?" Capshaw said.

"It was over twenty years ago, and the man's well into his forties. That's a long time to maintain an obsession."

"They last—that's why they call them obsessions."

"Look," said Clarion, a note of impatience in his voice, "you say there was an attempt on her life. If she had any reason to think it was DeKooning, then why wouldn't she have told you about him?"

Good question, McSwain thought, but before he could respond, there was a knock on Clarion's door. A young woman with waist-length black hair, wearing a red tube top and capri pants tight enough to interfere with circulation, leaned into the office. "Dr. Clarion?" She glanced meaningfully at her watch. "It's after seven."

"Of course, Julie, thanks for reminding me."

The young woman tossed her abundant locks and stepped back, closing the door quietly. Clarion gazed after her a moment, then turned back to Capshaw and McSwain. "I'm afraid that's all the time I can give you. My students—you understand."

"What happened to summer vacation?" McSwain asked.

"Thing of the past. A lot of kids go year-round now."

"Must make it harder for the professors."

Clarion shrugged. "I bear up."

"Bet you do," Capshaw said. She stood. "Thanks for your help, Dr. Clarion."

"If you think of anything else," McSwain said, "you have our number."

"Absolutely. And when you talk to Virginia, do give her my best. As I said, we did part amicably."

"Amicably, yeah."

Out in the hall, the girl in the tube top was waiting a few feet from the door. When she saw Capshaw and McSwain leaving, she smiled and smoothed her black hair.

"Think she's going to help him grade papers?" Capshaw said as they descended the stairs to the first floor.

McSwain grunted, not really listening. He was thinking how odd it was that Virginia, having suffered a terrifying attack and rape by a ski mask–wearing assailant, hadn't even mentioned the ordeal of her childhood.

Apparently Capshaw was thinking the same thing. "We need to talk to Virginia again," she said. "Find out why, if she's been scared of DeKooning all these years, she didn't mention him to you."

"I agree; it's peculiar," McSwain said. He reached the heavy double doors at the entrance, shoved one open for Capshaw to go through, and followed her outside. A soft, gauzy rain was pelting the walkway and neatly manicured lawn as they cut between the physics building and student union and crossed the street to the car.

McSwain got in first and immediately reached for his cell phone, while Jenna lowered the passenger-side window and lit a cigarette. There were three new messages since he'd last checked. The first was from Mandy, and he listened to it impatiently. She was apologizing for her behavior the previous night and ended the message by saying, "Guess I found out I don't need alcohol to make an idiot of myself." Her voice sounded so shaky that McSwain found himself wondering if she'd been drinking when she left the message.

He decided to ask Jenna to give her a call, then hit play for the second and third messages, both of which were collect calls from the prison that disconnected when no one pressed the appropriate key to accept the call.

So many calls from Lily in one afternoon. Too many. He felt something snag his heart. *It's probably nothing*, he told himself. He tried to remember some other time when she'd called him so persistently, but he couldn't think of any, and the clutching in his heart spread to his windpipe. *This doesn't feel right.*

Capshaw breathed a gray ribbon of smoke out the window and turned toward him, starting to say something. The phone rang and he answered. It was Lily, the recorded voice telling him to push one if he wanted to accept the call.

"Ian?"

"Lily, yeah, what is it? Are you okay?"

She didn't answer right away. He could hear her breathing, and it sounded shallow, fluttery, as though she were breathing with just the top inch or two of her lungs.

"Lily?"

"No, I'm not okay, Ian."

"Jesus, are you—"

"Not okay at all."

"—hurt? What's happened?"

"I've been—"

He saw Jenna looking at him, quizzical and just a little

frightened. He put his back to her, tried to make his face like stone.

"—arrested, Ian."

"What happened? What the hell happened?" As he spoke, he was extricating himself from his seat belt, getting out of the car and walking around to the rear, while her words, coming in snippets, interspersed with small gasps, carved out nicks in his heart.

"It was . . . they found some pills, Ian . . . when I was in the rec room and—"

"Pills?"

"Meth." The word hung in the silence that buzzed between them, ugly and raw. "I had meth on me, Ian."

"You mean you got it yourself, or somebody put it there?"

"I . . . it was me, Ian . . . this woman I know, Sheree, her boyfriend brought it in and I . . . she sold me some. I just thought . . . I just wanted—"

"Jesus Christ, Lily."

"I don't know what's going to happen now."

He leaned against the trunk of the car, his mind reeling, legs feeling liquid, and his voice came out an angry croak, hoarse and choking. "You don't know what's going to happen? You don't? You're going to do more time, that's what's going to happen. What the hell were you thinking? What—"

"I only wanted . . . dammit, I only wanted to feel good for a little while."

"Fine. Great. Was it worth it?"

"Don't use that tone of voice with me. I can't—"

"Was it fucking worth it? Was it—" The phone went dead, but he kept talking into it for a few seconds, unable to believe that she'd hung up on him. That she'd hung up on him in so many ways.

"Ian?"

He felt Capshaw's hand slide up the middle of his back, between his shoulder blades. She held it there a moment, then turned away and leaned against the trunk of the car. He slid the phone back in his pocket and watched a heavyset boy bicycling up the hill toward the campus with a pizza box balanced on the handlebars.

"What is it?"

What it was, he wanted to tell her, was he felt like the world had stopped for him. Everyone else had gone on, but his world had careened to a halt as abruptly as if he'd been hit by a bus or been picked off by a crazed sniper shooting from a rooftop. At the same time, he felt acutely, agonizingly alive, a sense of abandonment he would've imagined only orphaned children could feel, growing clammy and hard in his gut.

But what he said—incredible even to his own ears—was, "Nothing. Everything's fine."

He started around to get back in the car.

"Jesus, Ian, don't bullshit me. You look like a fucking ghost just walked over your grave."

"It's okay, Jenna. Really." He stopped at the driver's side, car keys dangling impotently from his hand. "Maybe we won't leave just yet, though, okay? I think I'm going to walk around the block first. Just to get the kinks out of my legs."

She was looking at him like he was demented, the way she'd probably wanted to look at Kreski earlier that day, but hadn't allowed herself. "Christ, Ian, *what?*"

But he was already striding away from the car, moving fast before she could get in another question. As though by telling her what had happened, it would become more real. As though by holding it inside himself, he could pretend a little longer that he hadn't accepted that collect call, that Lily hadn't told him.

Chapter 21

"They caught Lily with meth."

They were headed back to McSwain's house, Capshaw driving. He'd found her sitting behind the wheel when he got back from his walk, left hand dangling out the driver's-side window, the ashtray crammed with cigarette butts that looked like she'd taken only two or three puffs before crushing them out and lighting the next. She'd told him neither of them was going anywhere until he told her what was going on. Seldom did Jenna give this kind of ultimatum, but when she did, he knew her well enough to give in without an argument. He also understood the futility of trying to pretend nothing was wrong.

"Meth? Jesus, how could that be? She's due to get out in less than two months."

"*Was* due to get out. That's history now. She went in for meth and now she's been caught with it again—you know what that tells the parole board? That she's learned shit from being locked up, that she's no more ready to be released than she was when she went in."

"But why? How did she get it?"

"The why part, who the hell knows. I'm thinking maybe Tibbs had it smuggled in to somebody who sold it to Lily, but he'd've had to move awfully fast. I find out he did that, though, I swear to Christ, Jenna, I'll kill him."

"You don't know it was Tibbs."

"It may not have been. It's easy to get stuff in prison, sometimes easier than it is on the street. Lily should've said no, she should've run in the other direction the minute she even knew somebody had meth to sell. All that matters, though, is everything's fucked. I don't know how much more time the court will add onto her sentence, but it's not gonna be good." He looked at his watch. "Shit, I should call her lawyer, but he's left the office by now. I don't know what to do. I can't believe this is happening."

Capshaw took the off-ramp for Palm Avenue and headed south. She didn't seem to be in any hurry to get him home. For once, she seemed overly cautious behind the wheel. Instead of speeding, she was driving so slowly that a white Cadillac Escalade coming up from behind honked and roared around her, the driver conveying his displeasure with an obscene gesture.

If McSwain noticed the middle finger directed at his partner, he didn't show it. "I can't help thinking maybe I did something—or didn't do something. Maybe Becky was right; I didn't visit her enough, didn't listen to her. That somehow I caused this."

"Oh, Ian, stop it already—it's not like that, and you know it. You didn't screw up; Lily did."

He knew that, too, but found it less painful to be angry at himself—or at his partner—than to direct his anger at Lily. "Hey, don't tell me who did what. It's not your problem, Jenna, and you don't know shit about it."

"Sorry I give a damn." She pulled up behind the Monte Carlo, which was parked in front of the wrought-iron gate, next to his landlords' late-model Lincoln. "You want to blame yourself for what Lily did, fine, go ahead. I'll stop trying to talk you out of it. I'll even agree with you—you did it; it's all your fault, how's that?"

"Sorry I snapped at you."

He got out of the car and started walking up the block. She drove alongside him, lowered the electric window on the passenger side, and leaned over to yell at him, "Aren't you going home?"

"Not yet."

"Where're you going?"

"I just need to walk for a while."

"It's starting to rain."

"Yeah, I noticed."

"Where you going?"

"I'm not sure."

She frowned and ran her fingers up through her dark bangs. "I'll go with you."

"No."

"No what?"

"No, I don't need any company."

"Okay, Ian, whatever you want."

He tried to force his mouth into a smile, but he could tell the attempt was wretched, that his lips drew back and his teeth bared and he must have looked like an animal snarling. "Look, don't worry about me; I'm okay."

"Sure you are."

"I'll see you tomorrow at the office."

"Yeah, see you."

Ten minutes later he was sitting at the bar at Hooligan's, the corner tavern where he'd gotten too much in the habit of drinking during that first year after Lily went away. The bartender, a grizzled older man with Popeye-style forearms and a beer gut, was new to him, but one of the waitresses recognized him and asked where he'd been all this time. He ordered a Scotch and mumbled something about doing a lot of traveling.

One thing he knew but had managed to forget was that, for him, alcohol didn't drown sorrows but amplified them, turned up the volume on personal angst until it felt like banshees were haranguing him from the adjacent bar stools, screeching in his ears. He and Jenna had discussed this one time, and it was clear to him that she no more understood his point of view than he did hers. According to her, as a recovering alcoholic, more booze was never enough, and oblivion was the only destination worth pursuing, and, from the increasing inebriation of many of the people in the bar, she obviously wasn't alone in that sentiment.

Along about the third Scotch, he was fighting the impulse to get in the car and drive straight to Corona. No matter that they wouldn't let him into the prison this time of night or that tomorrow wasn't even a visiting day; he just wanted to be there, and at the same time he wanted to be a thousand miles away. Whatever happened from this point on, Lily wouldn't be getting out—

not in time to celebrate their wedding anniversary in October, not in time to share Thanksgiving or Christmas. She'd fucked up, and she'd fucked them up in the process, and now everything he'd planned and hoped for was going down the tubes.

How much more time would they give her? he thought. How many more days would he have to wait until they could be together again, until he could hold her, make love to her, and how could he possibly wait? The thought of waiting was unbearable and led to a different emotion, a frustrated, angry lust in which he thought about Mandy and the offer she'd made, and even went so far as to pull the free-breakfast card out of his wallet and look at the phone number and address scrawled on the back. Then he realized he was being a jerk, that if he decided to cheat on his wife, it wasn't going to be with a client, and it sure as hell wasn't going to be tonight. He started to pitch the card altogether, but then for whatever reason, he changed his mind and put it back in his wallet.

The bartender leaned a beefy arm on the bar. He had a gold chain with a small cross that dangled into his open shirtfront. "Getcha another?"

"No, I'm done here." He slapped a twenty down on the bar, made his way outside, and headed up the street toward a place where he knew the lost and the grieving were more genuinely welcomed than at any bar—St. Francis.

The neighborhood bar and the neighborhood church—the two seemed to McSwain to be flip sides of the same emotional coin, liquid solace, which usually lasted only about as long as it took the alcohol to pass out of the bloodstream, and the less dramatic but longer-lasting relief offered by the ritual of confession and the promise of heavenly salvation. Two forms of worship, one at an altar and one at a bar, but each equally sacred to the followers of that particular path.

As he came in through the door at the side of the church, he was half hoping Father Takamoto would be there working late, and at the same time afraid of running into him—he knew he reeked of Scotch and self-pity and, as much as part of him would have liked to talk to the priest, the other part was embarrassed about his condition.

Inside, the church was silent, dimly lit, and surprisingly cool considering the dense humidity of the evening. He walked to the altar, dipped his hand in the holy water and sprinkled himself, and genuflected until his knees creaked. He then walked a few feet to the left, where half a dozen candles were still burning, probably lit during the eight-o'clock Mass. He put a few bills into the box marked *Donations,* picked up a taper, and lit two of the candles—one for Lily and one for himself.

He wanted to pray, but found himself obsessing about what Lily had done, about trust, and who, if anyone, could be trusted or not, and he couldn't bring himself to kneel down. He felt jittery, wired, the alcohol churning away in his blood. He was still thinking Father Takamoto might be on the premises, and even called out "Hello" a couple of times, but heard only his own voice echoed back to him.

Twice he paced to the end of the church and came back, started to kneel and then paced again, mumbling to himself like those street people he often saw and felt pity for, deep in debate with their personal demons, and the demons, it seemed to McSwain, were always more eloquent, more Socratically sound. He understood why now. The deck was stacked. The demons cared more. The poor schmuck who debated them had already given up in his heart.

Maybe it was the alcohol, but he found himself thinking about that morning years before when he and his mother had driven north up Highway 1 toward his grandparents' place in San Luis Obispo. McSwain's nine-year-old brother, Andrew, was at a summer camp, but for whatever reason his mother had decided to let Andrew stay at camp while she and her older son headed north.

As they drove, McSwain had watched his mother spiral down into one of her emotional nosedives, murmuring to herself while tears flowed down her cheeks, gripping the wheel as though afraid it would fall out of her hands.

Damn him, she said over and over. *He deserves to be punished. He deserves to hurt.*

On the narrow, winding road, his mother's driving became increasingly erratic. McSwain's eyes never left the road. He was watching it even when his mother swung the wheel violently, and the Buick careened across the left lane, smashed a guardrail, and tumbled twenty-five feet into a stand of oaks, coming to rest on its side with the passenger doors crushed like a soda can, trapping them inside.

They were in the car for almost twelve hours before a trucker stopping to take a leak spotted them. By that time, McSwain's mother was unconscious and close to death from internal bleeding. McSwain had a gash on the side of his jaw and a finger severed at the second joint, sheared off when he was slammed against a piece of protruding metal as the car rolled.

In the hospital later, her voice quavering, tears flowing, his mother had explained what happened. A black dog—a Lab, she thought it was—had bounded into the road, causing her to swerve the car and lose control. She stuck to the story and repeated it so often that it became imbedded in McSwain's mind as a real event, a shared memory. Only years later, as an adult, did he finally admit to himself consciously what on some level he'd known all along—that there was no dog, that in a moment of rage or grief or madness his mother had tried to kill them both.

So much for trusting someone else. Even his own mother.

So much for trusting his own wife.

Such were his thoughts when he finally came back to the altar and knelt down and started to pray. His eyes were shut tight, his hands fisted atop the rail. His breath sounded shallow and labored. When he heard the soft sigh of a floorboard behind him, he experienced the strange sense that his prayer had been answered—he'd asked for help and now it must be here in the person of Father Takamoto—even as, at the same time, a chill sharp as razor wire mounted his spine.

It was that inner alarm that made him start turning around just as something slammed the crown of his head with shattering force. Pain lanced his skull, igniting crimson sparks behind his retinas before it buried him in blackness.

At seven-thirty that evening, the rain that had been pattering the window of Donut Delite had stopped and the pale glow of burnt-orange clouds was visible over the bay. Mandy stuck her card in the time clock next to the kitchen, punched out, and slid the card back into its slot on the wall.

Her boss, AnnaMarie, looked up from the cash register and said, "Remember you're working a double shift tomorrow. See you at ten. No excuses now, no callin' in at the last minute with sick kids."

Mandy bit back a sarcastic retort and headed for the door. Being on time for work tomorrow was the last thing on her mind. Earlier that day she'd phoned her mother—who'd sounded relatively sober, at least—and asked her to stay with the kids for a few hours that evening. Kelly was always eager to baby-sit, so Mandy knew it didn't matter what time she came home, or if she came home at all for that matter.

Her Taurus was parked with the other employee vehicles in the alley behind the shop. As always, there were a few touch-and-go moments before the car's engine turned over and she headed south, past the jumbled collection of fast-food shops, used-clothing stores, and other small, struggling commercial businesses that comprised Imperial Beach's main street. At the freeway entrance she took 5 north, exited at E Street in Chula Vista, and drove another five miles, backtracking twice, before pulling into an Amoco station on the northwest corner of the intersection of Shasta Avenue and H Street.

She parked away from the pumps, went inside, eyed the six-packs of beer in the cooler before buying a pack of Marlboros, then came outside again, walking slowly, acutely aware of her surroundings. The air was heavy with moisture, and a rainbow could be seen disappearing into the low, pink-tinged clouds. Not much light left. About an hour at best.

She got back in the car, lit a cigarette, and tried to remember every detail of that night back in January.

Billie had driven out of the Amoco station heading south
toward Imperial Beach. It was no more than a minute
before the man in the backseat had popped up, his gun
against Billie's head. The car was still heading south,
then the turn while they made their way through Chula
Vista and into Bonita, then onto Otay Lakes Road. No
turns then for several miles. Just driving through an
empty landscape broken only by the rippling gleam of
moonlight on Otay Lake and the rise of dark, feature-
less hills.

How long before he told Billie to turn left, onto the
dirt road? Fifteen minutes max, she decided. She slowed
to thirty-five, thirty. Behind her a trail of cars with impatient drivers had formed, the one directly behind flashing
its lights at her to speed up or pull over. *Fuck you,*
she thought.

She took one turnoff, but found it ended about a quarter mile in at a barn and a lake. The next one, about
three miles farther on Otay Road, petered out in a litter-
strewn clearing that could have been the place where
Virginia left the car before the man walked them deeper
into the hills. She saw a trail leading off into brambles
and scrub and followed that for a while, even though
the sun was down by now, the day dimming out into
twilight, the moist air abuzz with mosquitoes and other
insects drawn to her scent and her sweat.

She tried to see something familiar, even the dark outlines of the hills that rose to the north like the shape of
reclining women, but there was nothing beyond the general sense that this was vaguely similar to the place
where she and Virginia had been marched. Maybe it
even *was* the place, but her memory of that night was
too hazy to be sure.

What the area most reminded her of, though, was the
places she'd partied as a teenager, those seemingly endless, indolent summer nights, the kiss of cold beer sliding
like silk down her throat, and male hands, adolescent
and rough, fumbling with zippers and buttons and flies,
the sweet, languid smell of marijuana that caressed into
life parts of her brain she'd never known existed and
mellowed out other parts of it she knew too well and
wished did not exist at all.

There'd been a group of friends she partied with, sometimes at someone's house, but more often outdoors—at lakes west of the city and beaches near the border and desolate lovers' lanes that were rubble-strewn and forlorn in the daytime, but mysterious and sensual at night when the pot took effect or your blood-alcohol content reached an acceptable high. From the time she was about thirteen till she dropped out of high school in the eleventh grade at age sixteen, she'd drunk and smoked dope almost every weekend night, had the kind of sex those stupid bar drinks were named after—on the beach and in the backseat and up against the wall, and some sex no drinks were named after because the bartenders hadn't even thought of it yet—and all the while she was courting disaster and somehow skirting it, her sister Kendra stayed pristine as snow, good nun material, her mother used to say.

But God has a sick sense of humor, Mandy thought, *and "being good nun material" doesn't mean you live to see the inside of a convent.*

She smacked at the latest mosquito to make a meal from her flesh, decided she'd die of blood loss if she stayed out here much longer, and turned back toward her car, feeling defeated and not terribly bright. What had she hoped to find here anyway? Maybe the rope the guy had tied them with or the gun he'd held to their backs? *Hey, look what I found, Ian; solved the case for you, didn't I? Bet you want to fuck me now, don't you?*

She approached the clearing where she'd left her car and stopped so suddenly the mosquitoes feasting on her arms probably got whiplash. She heard voices and saw a second vehicle, a yellow Ford with a dented rear door, parked next to hers. Four teenagers, three boys and a girl with a ferocious case of acne, gathered around the car, the three boys standing, the girl sitting on the hood, passing around a joint.

It took all her fortitude to ignore their stares, which ranged from curious to surly, and walk past them to her car.

"Evening," one of the boys said. For some reason the girl found this humorous and tittered softly. She raised a bottle of Wild Turkey to her lips, sipped and coughed and passed it to the nearest boy.

Mandy got in her car and tried to start it and—*damn, damn, damn!*—the engine balked and refused to turn over. Now the foursome's attention really was riveted on her as she sat there, an intruder on their evening, face screwed up with angry concentration as she tried to start her car.

Finally, after what felt like half an hour, one of the boys came over and looked in at her through the window until she rolled it down an inch. He had thick brown hair and china-blue eyes and bad skin, though not as bad as the girl's, and looked like if he made it to manhood, he might turn out almost pretty.

"You want a jump? We got cables."

"It'll start."

"Don't sound like it."

"Yeah, it will." She twisted the key in the ignition and the car stalled out as though bent on refuting her.

The boy shrugged. "Whatever." He started to turn away, then seemed to reconsider, as though maybe having noticed that Mandy, while not a teenager, wasn't exactly old. "Hey, how 'bout I give you a ride? That's my car there. I could maybe take you someplace."

"Don't think so."

"Hey, c'mon; we'd have fun."

"Fuck you!"

She turned the key again, stomped on the gas. The engine roared to life and the car surged forward.

"Hey, what the hell's the matter with you?" the boy yelled as she roared away from him, up the dirt track. "All I fucking did was offer you a ride!"

Muddy consciousness seeped slowly back into McSwain's brain, and with it the terrifying conviction that he was never going to escape from the car he was trapped in, that he was going to die in there with his mother. His arms ached, and each time he breathed something clamped itself over his nose and mouth, slowly asphyxiating him.

Then, as his head began to clear, he realized his hands

were bound behind his back and that his head was covered with some kind of silky cloth that was tied beneath his chin. When he swallowed, he could feel the bulge of the knot at his Adam's apple.

I'm suffocating.

He opened his eyes and felt his lashes brush against the cloth, but through the sheer fabric he could see nothing beyond the murky outlines of objects, the looming block of the altar, the hazy flickering of votive candles. He was lying on his side at an angle, the hard edges of stairs digging into his shoulder and side. From where he'd been kneeling when he was hit, he knew he couldn't have fallen that way. His assailant must have dragged him up the short flight of stairs leading to the altar.

His first effort was to try to free his hands, but they were tied excruciatingly tightly, arms almost wrenched out of the sockets, fingers numb as stones.

I can't breathe.

Worry about the hands later, he thought. Air, that was all that mattered. He tried to scrape the hood up and over his head by dragging the side of his face along the edge of a stair, but it wouldn't give, and the effort made his breath come harsher, sucking the fabric tight against his face—he got a mouthful of silk and retched and spat it back out.

He tried to remember everything he'd ever read about people trapped underwater or underground with only tiny air pockets to breathe from, and how you were supposed to make the air last by staying calm, rationing out the breaths, defying the panic that spread like brushfire through your oxygen-starved cells.

He realized that his prone position made it harder to breathe, so he swung his feet around and was trying to stand when the many shades of blackness coalesced into a figure that lunged forward and slammed a fist into his gut.

He doubled over, chest on fire, feeling like the front and back of his lungs met and stuck together with every excruciating breath, and toppled down a couple of steps, thumping onto his forehead and knees.

He heard the heavy scrape of footsteps near his head and braced himself for a kick to the face.

"Thought you were dead." If the voice was one he knew, it was impossible to recognize, muffled by the cloth over his head and distorted by the rasp of his breathing.

Hands grasped his head and forced his face up. He felt the knot under his chin being loosened for a second, then drawn tighter.

"There, that oughta make it faster. Go ahead and die. Wish I could stay to watch, but churches give me the fucking creeps."

Another blow to the head—whether a fist or a foot, he couldn't tell. His whole being was focused on breathing. For half a minute or more he lay still, not unconscious but unable to marshal the energy necessary to do anything beyond struggling for air. Pain blazed through his chest. Tiny, diamondlike lights caromed across the corners of his vision.

Dimly he was aware that the door he'd entered earlier had creaked and then clicked shut. He was alone.

He lifted his head and lurched to his knees, an effort that made the diamonds behind his eyes explode into blinding whiteness. His balance left him, and he thought he might topple forward again, but he stayed upright on his knees.

He tried to visualize the inside of the church, get his bearings. He knew he'd fallen down the stairs that led up to the altar, so he felt reasonably certain that his back was now toward the altar and he was facing the pews. The main door straight ahead would be locked, but the side door locked only with a key, so his assailant would have left it open.

But even if he could crawl to the door, turn his back, and twist the knob with his bound hands, what would he do once he got outside? Shuffle along on his knees, hoping that he'd reach the street and that someone would see him? He knew he wouldn't remain conscious that long. Each breath felt as if he were inhaling fishhooks, and the flashes of light at the edges of his eyes were getting darker, scarlet crowding his vision.

He lost his balance and twisted sharply, fighting to stay upright. His cheekbone thumped against something smooth and hard—he realized it was the edge of the stone basin containing the holy water. If the basin was here, that meant that the votive candles were only a few feet to the right. He started crawling in that direction.

After a few feet, he was close enough to see the candle flames, and he stood up. The movement was too rapid—waves of vertigo and nausea rose from his stomach. His head swam and he thought he might topple over, but after a moment the worst of the dizziness passed. He turned and extended his arms behind him, hoping to burn through the ropes, but he succeeded only in burning his hands. His breathing had become a desperate sucking moan. He tried to exhale the fabric back off his face, but it clung to the roof of his mouth, plugged his nose. He felt the urge to throw up and knew if he did, he was dead. The vomit would be trapped in his throat, and he'd choke.

He turned and bent his head toward the candles, so the top of the hood where the fabric was loosest made contact with the fire. Almost immediately he smelled burning fabric and felt heat singe his scalp.

He felt the fire crawl along one side of the hood, touch the tip of his ear. The pain was galvanizing. He made it the half dozen steps to the basin full of holy water and plunged his head in.

There was a low hiss and he started to cough as air, smoky and stinking of burned cloth, came in through the hole that had been burned through the fabric. It drooped down over one side of his face like a flap of scorched skin. He got his tongue into the tear and then used his teeth to widen it. Then he sank to his knees and flopped onto his back, sucking in sweet lungfuls of air.

How long he lay there McSwain didn't know, but suddenly the sound of the side door creaking on its hinges made him stiffen and arch his back, struggling to sit up. With his wrists bound, he was still helpless. If his would-be killer had come back, he knew he was dead.

"My God, what . . . ?"

He felt hands working at the knot at his throat, the hood being removed. Blinking, he looked up to see the narrow, furrowed face of Father Takamoto staring down at him, his mouth agape, face as white as his wisp of a beard. If he'd had any doubts about how bad he looked, the expression on the priest's face erased them.

"Ian?"

"Anybody for last rites?" said McSwain, trying to make a joke, but unnerved when the priest looked like he might take him seriously.

"What happened? The hood on your head . . . ?"

Now that McSwain could see it, he realized the thing that had almost killed him was a hood ripped off one of the robes that Father Takamoto and the other priests wore during Mass. While he was unconscious, his attacker must have foraged around in the room behind the choir stalls where the robes and other ceremonial objects were kept. For some reason the idea of that room, with its chalices and communion cups, being desecrated almost made McSwain madder than what had been done to him.

"Was it a gang?" said Takamoto, looking up at the walls, his wizened, raisin face lighting up with relief as he saw that the stained-glass windows depicting the Stations of the Cross and the statue of Mary holding the infant Jesus were all intact.

"No, it was one guy," said McSwain.

"Here, let me untie you," said the priest, going to work on the rope that bound McSwain's wrists. "Then I'll call an ambulance and the police."

"No, Father, don't do that. I'm okay. I don't need to waste time going to the hospital or filling out a report for the police. Really, I'm okay."

Father Takamoto finished untying him and he sat up, rubbing the circulation back into his arms. He noticed his wallet lying on the floor beside the front pew and picked it up. His money—a little under two hundred dollars—was gone, but his credit cards, driver's license, and PI ID were all there. Relieved, he slid the wallet back into his pants pocket.

"You sure you don't want an ambulance?"

"Yeah, I'm all right. If you could get me a glass of water, though, while I call my partner—"

He stopped speaking as the floor he was sitting on started to undulate, rippling like a field of wheat in a breeze. Strangely, his head didn't hurt, but his arms felt like he had greenstick fractures all the way from elbows to wrists. Everything started to whirl—a bizarre merry-go-round where the painted horses had been replaced with pews and crucifixes and candles. He took in this wonder with a strange detachment before the speed of it started to sicken him and he leaned forward and threw up onto the floor.

Chapter 22

Fifteen minutes later, after helping Father Takamoto clean up the mess and apologizing so profusely that the old priest finally lost patience and reminded him that this wasn't the first time he'd helped clean up puke, that he did that and tasks more repellent when he worked three nights a week at the homeless shelter on Powell Street, McSwain was sitting on the steps outside St. Francis, rubbing the lemon-sized knot on the back of his head and explaining to Jenna, as best he could, what had happened.

When he got to the part about the hood being on fire, her eyes became huge and she grabbed his forearm with a grip that almost stopped the circulation in his arm. "Jesus, Ian, I don't know whether to laugh or cry. The guy didn't succeed in killing you, but it sounds like you almost ended up killing *yourself* in the process of staying alive."

McSwain shrugged. "It worked, didn't it? I'm okay."

"Barely." She craned her neck to see the top of his head. "What about your hair? It looks like there's a patch missing."

"I didn't know you cared about my hair."

"You kidding? It's your best feature."

"My hair?"

"Yeah, your hair." She shook out another cigarette, her third since she'd arrived, lit it, and took a long drag. Her T-shirt looked rumpled and had some sort of stain near the collar, orange juice maybe. McSwain was pretty sure the clothes she was wearing were the same ones he'd seen her in last.

"By the way, how the hell did you get here so fast?"

"What, you think I was so worried about you, I couldn't sleep and went cruising around your neighborhood in case you were out walking and wanted to talk?"

He lifted an eyebrow. "Well?"

"Don't flatter yourself, Ian." She exhaled sharply and the smoke exploded out of her in a small puff. "Besides, even if I had been doing anything so pathetically codependent, you think I'd ever admit it?"

"Probably not."

"There you have it. The more important question is, Who did this? Personally, I'd say it looks like the guy either followed us back from Phil Clarion's—which makes Clarion a suspect, albeit an unlikely one—or he already knew where you live and was waiting, then saw you go into the church and took advantage of the opportunity. Our guy Josh is one candidate. Or Kreski, for that matter. Maybe he didn't take kindly to having ten grand for a kneecap job turned down."

When McSwain didn't say anything, she went on, "If, for the moment, we rule out the possibility that the attack on you and the ambush in Mexico are connected to some other case—which I don't think is too likely at this point—then it's either someone in Virginia's world or in Mandy's, somebody who'd know we're investigating the assault last winter. My bet's on somebody close to Virginia. Between her and Leland, they seem to know an awful lot of crazies." She frowned and flicked the ash off her cigarette. Tiny sparks, like a horde of incandescent insects, sailed off into the darkness and expired. When McSwain still didn't reply, she said, "Ian, is it the concussion you've probably got from being whacked over the head or are you just ignoring me?"

McSwain looked up. "Tibbs."

"Tibbs?"

"It was Tibbs who tried to kill me tonight. I'm sure of it."

"How sure?"

He hesitated before telling her, in part because he wasn't proud of the rage that gripped his heart like barbed wire, in part because he was still tempted by the idea of finishing Tibbs off once and for all. When he spoke, his voice sounded scraped and husky, as though tiny clamps pinched his windpipe.

"I'm sure enough it was Tibbs that I don't want to go looking for him by myself. I find him, I'm not sure what I'll do. If you're there, even . . . well, it's like insurance."

"Meaning you won't blow out the back of his head if I'm a witness."

"Something like that."

She sighed and glanced back at the double doors that led into St. Francis, big, heavy Santa Fe–style doors with crucifixes carved in the center, doors that looked sturdy enough to withstand a hailstorm of sin and damnation. "This what they're peddling in there these days? Eye-for-an-eye Old Testament stuff?"

"Doesn't matter what they're peddling," McSwain said. "I want to kill the guy, because that's how I feel, and I think I'm justified, but I don't want to act on it. I need you with me to make sure I don't."

"Because you know, partner or not, I'd turn you in to the police in a heartbeat?"

He turned to look at her. "I don't know. Would you?"

"Don't put me to the test." She stubbed out her cigarette and stood up, arms wrapped around herself as if to ward off a chill that only she could feel. "Personally, I wouldn't mind doing Tibbs myself. Just for the record, though, what makes you so sure it was him?"

McSwain had been thinking about that, trying to convince himself the ordeal he'd just been through wasn't making him jump to conclusions. "Right before he left me, the guy made a reference to a church, something about churches giving him the creeps."

"So?"

"So the whole Deacon shtick that Tibbs is so proud of—he'd see the irony in making that kind of remark. Plus when I saw him at VaVoom the other night, he threatened my life."

"A lot of people have threatened your life—both our lives—over the years."

"He *meant* it, Jenna. There's a difference between somebody posturing for effect and somebody cold-blooded enough that when they say they're gonna kill you, you know you need to start shopping for a cemetery plot."

"And?"

"What makes you think there's an 'and'?"

"Just a gut feeling. For you to want to kill Tibbs so badly that you'd actually entertain the thought, I think there's an 'and.' "

He sighed and worried the knot sprouting under his scalp. "I think he might've been behind Lily getting the meth. He didn't just threaten me the other night. He threatened to harm anyone I loved. And he knew about Lily being in prison. He's got enough contacts, he could've set something up, made sure she had an opportunity to use."

"Even if he did that, Ian—and it's a big 'if'—it only means he gave her the opportunity, not that she had to take it." Her voice melted in with the small night sounds, the clicking of crickets and humming of gnats, and hung between them in the moisture-laden air.

"I know that. I know Lily's a big girl, and even if Tibbs set her up, she's the one who took the bait. But I still need to know."

They reached Capshaw's car and she unlocked the door and slid in behind the wheel while McSwain got in the passenger seat. "Look," he said, "for all I know, Tibbs may be anywhere. If he thinks I'm dead, who knows? Maybe he crossed the border to pay another call on Virginia Stromquist? All I'm saying is, I want to check out a few places."

Capshaw started the car and pulled out into the rain-slick street. "Fair enough. VaVoom or Xtreme Ink? Or maybe you got his home address at your last tête-à-tête?"

"VaVoom," said McSwain.

"VaVoom it is."

In the desolate part of National City where the club was located, McSwain stayed in the car while Capshaw went inside. She came back a few minutes later, having sweet-talked the bouncer, to report Tibbs wasn't there.

Around one A.M., after visiting a couple of the bars that McSwain knew that Tibbs frequented from having worked on the Kevin Orlando case years before, they cruised past Xtreme Ink. The place looked deserted, the windows dark except for a gauzy light that could be seen emanating from behind the bars of one first-floor window. When Capshaw pulled into the alley, they saw a bloodred Ferrari with a vanity plate reading DEACON2. It was sitting alone, parked across two slots in Ink's tiny parking lot, and McSwain was astonished the vehicle hadn't been stripped down to a chassis by this point.

Capshaw drove past and parked behind a Dumpster at the end of the alley. "That's odd," she said, reaching into the glove compartment and removing a small plastic case. "Tibbs strike you as the kind of guy who'd leave a seventy-five-thousand-dollar custom ride parked here overnight?"

"Maybe just seeing the license plate scares off the bad guys," McSwain said, though he was wondering the same thing. He watched Jenna open the case and take out her lockpicks. "You don't have to come inside with me, you know. I can use those as well as you can."

He saw her teeth gleam in the dark. "Wanna bet?"

"Almost as well."

They got out of the car, locked it, and walked past the Ferrari to the back door. McSwain slid his hand behind his back, resting his palm on the grip of the .38 while Capshaw crouched by the door. He heard the tiny scrape as she inserted the picks and then a small gasp.

"Door's open."

"Jesus, you *are* fast."

"No, I mean, it was already open. Unlocked."

"That's weird."

"Very."

Capshaw unholstered her gun and went inside, McSwain behind her, the .38 in his hand. They crossed the room with the displays of tattoo designs on the wall behind the cash register and the counter with piercing equipment. McSwain checked the room where Tibbs did his tattooing, saw no one, and turned back toward Capshaw, who was pulling back the curtain that divided the main part of the store from the stage where the performance art took place. A feeble light filtered out from farther back in the room. It clung to Capshaw's features like a thin coating of wax, turning her profile shiny and slightly yellow as she slipped inside. A second later she backed out of the room, almost colliding with McSwain, who was behind her. If the light had given her a yellowish cast before, now her skin looked positively ashen.

"What is it?"

"You were afraid if you came here alone you'd kill Tibbs?"

He nodded.

"Looks like somebody beat you to it."

A half hour after McSwain called the police, half a dozen squad cars, a forensics team, and two teams of detectives had descended on Xtreme Ink, cordoned the building off, and begun the grisly procedure of gathering evidence. Detective DeAngelo, a short, potbellied man with bodybuilder thighs and bad burn scars on his right hand and forearm, interviewed Capshaw and McSwain in Tibbs's tattooing room. He sat on the table in the middle of the room, ham-sized thighs testing the seams of his sweat pants, and took notes on a yellow legal pad.

"Tell me again what you two were doing here?"

"We stopped by to ask Danny Tibbs some questions about a case we're working on and found the door unlocked," said McSwain. "In this neighborhood this time of night, we knew something was wrong, so we came in to look around."

DeAngelo turned to Capshaw, who was on something like her tenth cigarette since she'd walked behind that curtain. "You found the body, right?"

"I was first into the room, yeah. Then my partner had a look. That was it. We didn't touch anything. My prints are on the back doorknob; that's it." She lifted her head, blew a stream of smoke the same color as the smudges under her eyes. "The body looked . . . pretty badly mutilated. The killer used, what, piercing equipment?"

"We don't know yet, ma'am." DeAngelo scribbled something on the pad. The look he gave McSwain suggested he was viewing him in a lineup. "That blood on your collar, Mr. McSwain?"

"My own, yeah."

"Busy night, huh?"

"I was in St. Francis Church tonight, couple of blocks from my house, and got hit over the head. The priest there, Father Takamoto, found me. He can confirm that I was on the floor barfing my guts out earlier tonight."

"And after this brutal attack, instead of going to a hospital, you decide to go see Danny Tibbs?"

"We came here, Detective," Capshaw said, "because we had reason to think Danny Tibbs might know something about the attack on my partner. We thought he might have been the perp. Obviously, we were wrong." She stubbed out her cigarette. "Can we go now?"

"Yeah, you can go," said DeAngelo. "You can go outside to my car and we'll take a ride down to police headquarters." He looked at his watch. "Two-thirty in the morning and I have to be called out because a scumbag who deserved to be killed a long time ago finally got what was coming to him. You two couldn't have waited to find the body till morning?"

Three hours later, they were still sitting in Hank Paris's office, having repeated their account of the events of that night to Paris and two other detectives. The first, Detective Swansea, looked the way you'd expect a man to look who'd been called out of bed in the middle of the night the night before his daughter's first communion. The second, a Latino officer with the kind of burning black stare McSwain imagined could get almost anyone to confess to almost anything, seemed to evince a controlled jubilation over Tibbs's brutal demise.

Around four A.M, when the other detectives left and they were alone with Paris, Capshaw said, "Something I'm almost afraid to ask. Tibbs's penis—did they find it?"

Hank Paris shifted in his seat, took a hit of coffee from the Styrofoam cup on his desk. "The perp has a sense of humor. You didn't see what he did with it?"

"No. Once I got the general idea that it was missing, that was enough."

"Skewered. Fucking shish kebabbed."

McSwain had been drinking coffee, too, but now he lowered the cup and said, "What?"

"Some kind of rod or needle, apparently something

Tibbs used for tattooing, was run through the penis and then into the wall above where the body was lying. Tech who found it didn't realize what it was at first. Thought it was a jumbo-sized rubber."

"Time of death," said McSwain, "any idea?"

"Forensics said the amount of lividity indicated Tibbs died late yesterday afternoon. Probably around five or six, the time he normally closed the place down. Fact that the back door was unlocked and there were no signs of a struggle makes it look like Tibbs knew his killer, let him in."

"I've never seen so much blood," Capshaw said, almost to herself.

"That's because he bled out," Paris said. "I talked to the head of the forensics team down there just before DeAngelo brought you two in. Whoever killed Tibbs first subdued him, then tied him up and put a cock ring around the base of his penis to keep it hard. Then they used a knife or a razor blade to sever it. Blood must've shot out of him like a geyser."

"Meaning the killer got covered in blood, too?" Capshaw said.

"He was probably holding Tibbs's dick away from him when he did the cutting—like aiming a garden hose in the other direction when you turn it on—then he left Tibbs alone to bleed out."

"Wait a minute," said McSwain. "You said the cock ring was put on Tibbs to keep him hard. What do you mean 'keep'? Under those circumstances, how the hell did he get hard in the first place?"

"We don't know. Could be he was having sex when he was attacked, but then what happened to the partner? Maybe he was having sex with himself."

"Or maybe the killer stimulated him," Capshaw said.

"It wasn't a woman," said Paris. "Whoever did this appears to have dragged Tibbs into that room from somewhere else in the shop. That took a lot of strength."

"I didn't say it was a woman," Capshaw said. "A man could have used his hand or his mouth just as well as a woman." She started to reach into her pocket for a cigarette, then remembered smoking was taboo in Paris's office and let her hands fall back to her lap. "Jesus,

Hank, why don't you let us go home? We've told you why we went to Xtreme Ink and how Ian got banged up, and you've verified Ian's alibi with Father Takamoto."

"What about your alibi? You say you got the call from the priest saying Ian was hurt, you went over to St. Francis. But before that you were alone."

"Fine, Hank, arrest me. I'm sure you'd like to believe in my spare time I go around cutting the dicks off of bad guys."

"At this point, I don't know what the hell to believe."

He reached into his desk, pulled out a pill bottle, and shook out a couple of white gel caps, which he downed dry.

"So we can go?"

"Sure. I don't think either of you murdered Tibbs, and I'm sure neither of you's planning to leave town, right, so why not? You can leave now or you can stick around and I'll tell you what Forensics had to say about the woman in the ditch out on Otay Road."

McSwain and Capshaw exchanged glances, then settled back in their chairs. "Not in such a big hurry now?" said Paris.

"All the time in the world," said McSwain.

"We got an ID on her. Name's Maggie Gibson, age eighteen. Last seen leaving a bachelor party for a girlfriend who was getting married. Friends say she was very drunk and upset because she'd had a tiff with the bride-to-be. They quarreled when Gibson cast aspersions on the groom's virginity."

He stroked his jaw, winced almost imperceptibly. "Know what else? We got lucky on the clothing."

McSwain leaned forward. "The perp left it?"

"Not exactly. When the ME looked in Gibson's mouth, guess what he found? An inch of lace. Apparently the perp stuffed her underpants in her mouth to keep her quiet, probably while he was raping her. Maybe it happened when he yanked the gag out, maybe she was in so much pain that she just clamped her teeth down, but she chewed that little bit of lace off and it stayed in her mouth.

"Forensics ran some tests on it and got back to me the other day. They found the kind of oil that's left when perfume evaporates. And just to be on the safe side, in case she was the kind of chick who liked to smell good down below, we checked with the people she was partying with that night. Friends said she never used perfume—she was allergic to it."

Chapter 23

Light was spreading along the lip of the horizon and a woman pushing a shopping cart was having a screaming argument with herself outside the Scientology Center when Capshaw flagged down a cab a few blocks from police headquarters and gave the driver the address of the office in Imperial Beach.

"What about your car?" asked McSwain. "It's still at Xtreme Ink."

"I can get Dave or Ricardo to give me a ride over there later. Right now I want to make some calls."

"Shouldn't you get some sleep?"

She ran a hand through the oily strands of her hair, shook her head. "Finding Tibbs cut up all to hell, the whole bit, it's got me too wired. Besides, if we assume the person in St. Francis last night might be the same person who attacked Mandy and Virginia—"

"Which we don't really know."

"But let's say that it is. With what Hank told us about the perfume, then that means we're talking about the Boy Scout. Tibbs was our best suspect, because he was a vicious son of a bitch who knew Virginia and might have raped her to get back at her for breaking up with him. Now he's out of the picture. I want to find out where Josh and Leland were last night—Kreski, too, for that matter."

"Don't forget Clarion, although except for his tendency for boinking his students, he seemed like a normal enough guy."

"Yeah, normal, that's the word the neighbors always

use to describe a guy after the cops find body parts in his freezer."

"You have a point." He put a hand to the back of his head, where the egg-sized lump under the skin seemed to be forcing the hair out at odd angles. His eyes burned, and his tongue felt like it was coated with lint. The taxi turned onto the expressway, and they joined the earliest of the rush-hour commuters as they swept past downtown and Balboa Park. "There is one other possibility."

Capshaw was reaching into her bag, pulling out sunglasses. "DeKooning?"

"It wouldn't be the first time a perp came back for the same victim years later. And with Virginia's marriage to Stromquist, she's high-profile enough that he wouldn't have had trouble finding her."

"But what about all the other vics?"

McSwain lowered his voice, even though the driver had turned on the radio and was moving his head to the beat of a reggae song.

"Maybe DeKooning's been doing this ever since he got out of prison, but police only realized it was the work of a serial killer in the last couple of years. Maybe it's a fantasy come to fruition. If he's the guy, then I can see why Virginia would have been targeted. She's the one who sent him away."

"His crime against Virginia was too long ago for him to be listed as a Registered Sex Offender," Capshaw said, "but maybe he's gotten in trouble since then. He might be registered."

"Worth looking into."

She leaned back and put her palms over her eyes, massaging the lids. "You sure you don't want to go to the hospital? Get that bump on your head checked out, just to be sure?"

"I don't think so."

"Get some sleep then. You look . . ." She saw his expression, stopped.

"Like what?"

"Like a guy who got beaten up, almost died, then spent the night answering questions at the police station after finding a body with the . . . after finding a body."

"Like shit, you mean."

"Yeah, almost that good . . ."

"Yeah, well, I feel worse. But I'm gonna go home, take a shower and grab something to eat, then drive up to Corona. Visiting hours start at eleven."

"Oh."

They sat in silence for a good five minutes after that. The driver switched radio channels as they took the exit for Imperial Beach, rap taking the place of reggae.

Finally Capshaw exhaled hard, combed back her greasy locks with her fingers, and said, "Visiting Lily . . . maybe you ought to give it some time."

"Time for what?" McSwain was startled by how alien his own voice sounded, strident and self-righteously belligerent, but he couldn't stop talking. "For me to get angrier? More depressed? If I'd been paying attention to what I was doing in that church last night, I might have seen the son of a bitch before he attacked me. No, I need to see her, talk to her. I need to understand why she did this."

"Jesus, Ian, she did it because she's an addict. Addicts use; that's the definition of an addict. Drunks drink and sex addicts fuck. Welcome to the world."

"Thanks for putting it so nicely."

"It's the truth."

"You're an alcoholic and you don't drink."

"And for an alcoholic, that's abnormal. But I take it one day at a time, and by the grace of God, I haven't had to take a drink today. Tomorrow, I don't know. But tomorrow isn't here yet."

"You make it sound so simple."

"It is and it isn't. But for Lily to use, that means she hasn't hit bottom yet. Who knows if she ever will?"

"Meaning what?"

"Meaning she may drag you down with her, Ian. If you let her."

"She's my wife. I won't divorce her." The word left a bitter tang on his tongue, as though just saying it implied that he'd considered it.

Jenna started to say something, then realized they had just passed Dave's Gym. She told the driver to stop and reached for her wallet.

"I got it," said McSwain, grateful that the conversation had been interrupted.

Capshaw got out of the cab, then leaned in the window. "Remember Hank said we're not supposed to leave town."

"We're not?"

She pulled a face. "Jesus, Ian, you're impossible—"

He put a hand to the back of his head. "Hey, it's not my fault if I forget he told us that. I got a concussion, remember?"

Fifty miles south of Corona, the pain medication wore off and the back of McSwain's head felt like an egg somebody'd tapped with a brick. He pulled off at a rest stop, swallowed a couple of Tylenol, and popped a jazz solo into the Monte Carlo's CD player. Gray thunderheads were heaped on the eastern horizon, and they reflected his mood—somber and darkening.

An accident in the northbound lane twenty miles south of Corona slowed traffic to a crawl. By the time he went through the familiar routine of passing through the security check (a joke, he reflected bitterly, considering Lily's situation) and was escorted by a guard into the visiting area, he was half an hour late.

One of the guards, an African-American woman built like a basketball star who'd been watching him show up at visiting hours for two years, greeted him with a subdued version of her normally five-hundred-megawatt smile and left out the usual small talk. McSwain wondered if she knew about the change in Lily's status, and if so, if she pitied him or somehow blamed him, then mentally accused himself of paranoia. He took a seat at a small table next to a vending machine that sold candy and chips, and waited with growing impatience for one of the guards to go back and inform Lily that he was there.

When Lily finally walked through the door, it took her a few seconds to spot him, but he saw her at once, and in that moment his heart rate doubled and he wanted to bolt, to somehow get up and flee without her having seen him, without ever having to pose the questions he'd driven all that way to ask.

As she came toward him, he saw the exhaustion in her eyes. Her face had that haggard, used-up quality he'd already seen too often in too many women, women who needed a private detective because a child had been kidnapped or a husband was cheating or because they were being stalked. They needed help, and often there was so little he could do. Now the woman who needed him was Lily, and before she could even ask him, he knew that he was powerless to help.

Without a word, she put her arms around him, laid her head on his chest, and started to sob. "Ian, I'm so sorry. So very sorry."

In the face of such anguish, he was incapable of delivering the tirade he'd rehearsed on his drive up to Corona. What good would it do to pile suffering on top of suffering? He felt his heart break and said nothing, let her cry.

When she finally pulled away, her eyes widened as she took in the burned area around the edge of one ear. "What happened?"

He put his arm around her and led her over to a table in a corner where they sat down. "It's nothing, Lily."

"Nothing, my ass. What happened?"

"Well, give me another hug, and I'll tell you."

He held her a long time, amazed that just physically touching her could be both intensely pleasurable and exquisitely painful, and at his own reluctance to let her out of his embrace.

"There was a fire at the church up the street from my place," he said. "I helped put it out, but I got burned a little. Nothing serious."

It sounded lame and he could tell that she wasn't buying it, but that, under the circumstances, she was willing to let it go.

"Ian, I—"

"Lily—"

They both started to speak at the same time. "You first," she said.

He took a deep breath and realized he'd forgotten everything he'd planned to say, everything he'd rehearsed on the drive up. So he blundered in, saying whatever came into his head, realizing it was probably all wrong and would get things off to a bad start but unable to stop himself.

"Look, driving up here, I had time to think. And what I thought was, I want to be able to tell you I'm not mad, that it'll be all right. I want to do that, Lily, but I can't. Because I am mad, and that's just the start of it. I'm half out of my mind. What the hell happened, Lily? How could you do this? Jesus Christ, meth? It'd have been bad enough if you'd used that shit after you got out, but to do it inside a prison? What were you thinking?"

She shook her head. "I don't know, Ian. I didn't think. Or I did, but only as far as how good it would feel to use again. I didn't take it as far as the consequences. I didn't think there'd *be* any consequences."

"How'd you get the stuff?"

She shrugged. "Does it matter?"

"Yes, it does."

"Like I told you, one of the women . . . she has a connection on the outside and had it smuggled in. She was willing to sell me a half ounce."

"Had she done this before?"

"Yes."

"But you didn't buy from her?"

She turned her head away.

"You mean this wasn't the first time? Then you lied when you told me you hadn't gotten high in two years."

"I didn't mean to use, Ian. It just happened."

"Jesus, that's what all the junkies say."

"I only did it a few times. It wasn't like she had stuff all the time."

"This woman, they bust her, too?"

"Of course. The guards suspected her all along. They were watching her."

"So you've got nothing to offer the DA. Nothing to deal with."

"I guess not." The way she said it, as matter-of-factly as a woman reporting there was no more coffee left, infuriated him. She went on, "I talked to my lawyer this morning. He says that up until now I've been a model prisoner, that what I need is drug counseling. If things go well, he says I could be looking at three to four years with parole in two."

"Another two years?"

"I know it's a long time, but—"

"Jesus Christ, what is wrong with you?" He felt as if a hammer were pounding the back of his head, as if her words were nails driven into his scalp. His burned ear itched so fiercely he wanted to rip it from his head. "You talk about two years like it's two weeks. Like it's a normal thing to have a chance at getting your life back and then to throw it away like so much garbage. After the hell you've been through—that we've been through— because of drugs, and you used? How could you? It makes no fucking sense."

She bit her lip hard enough that he thought she'd draw blood. When she spoke, there was an edge of ice in her voice he hadn't heard before. "I didn't use. The meth was found in my possession, while I was giving her money. If I'd had time to use it, I wouldn't have gotten caught, now, would I? I'd've gotten high and I'd've felt happy and safe and on top of the world for a little while and everything would've been fucking fine."

He just stared at her, amazed and appalled at her addict's logic, that she could even say such a thing, let alone believe it.

"How can you say that? How can you talk about that damn drug like it's a solution, like it's some kind of savior?"

"You don't understand."

"No, you're right. I don't. I don't understand how getting high could mean so much to you that you'd throw your life away, throw our marriage away. I don't understand how you could be so goddamned stupid."

She looked as shocked as if he'd struck her. In a way, he felt as though he had, and hated himself for doing it, but he pressed on. "Look, I never told you this, but when I was eighteen, I stole a car along with another boy my age, and we got caught. And I got sentenced to a month in jail. Now, I know to some people that doesn't sound like much—a lousy thirty days, that's nothing, right?"

She started to interrupt, but he held his hand up, silencing her.

"But you know what I learned in that month? I

learned that the definition of pure hell is not being able
to walk outdoors whenever you feel like it, not being
able to go to the fridge and grab that Snickers bar you
put in the freezer the day before; it's smelling the stink
from your own armpits, but not being able to take a
shower, because nobody's given you permission, or
wanting to call a friend or walk your dog or take in a
movie or, hell, jerk off in private, but all of those things
are as remote as the moon. And what I learned was that
there is no crime in this world I'd be willing to commit,
no drug I'd be willing to take, if it meant even a chance
I'd piss away my freedom. Nothing is worth that. And
I've never understood how a person who'd been locked
up for even one day could ever go back. For anything."

"Maybe it would be a better world if we were all like
you, Ian? Is that what you mean?"

"Of course not, no. It's just that I don't understand
how any drug could mean so much to you that you'd
throw away your freedom."

"Are we that different, Ian?"

"I don't know."

"Then you tell me, what do you do to stop the chatter
in your head?"

"Chatter?"

"You know, the mental noise, the tapes that play in
everybody's head all the time, monkey mind, the Bud-
dhists call it."

He shrugged. "I don't know. I've never thought
about it."

She gave a low laugh, more like a chuckle, rife with
bitterness. "Never thought about thinking. Why does
that not surprise me?" Before he could protest, she went
on, "The tapes that play in my head aren't uplifting
ones. They're full of anxieties and self-recrimination, of
you-should-haves, and you-could-haves, and why-didn't-
yous and what-ifs. It's like having a TV set that's stuck
somewhere between the nag-you-to-death channel and
the horror channel twenty-four hours a day, and you
can't shut the damn thing off; you just have to listen.
Do you remember that day in Encinitas, when I dragged
you to the meditation garden?"

He nodded. "You said it would calm my mind."

"Well, maybe your mind didn't need calming. But mine did. It's always one of two places—in the past, regretting things I've done or didn't do, or in the future, dreading what might come and feeling afraid. The present, that might as well not exist."

"That sounds like hell."

"Exactly. Meth takes that away. I feel on top of things, in control. And I needed to feel that way, Ian, because I've been so afraid of what could happen when I got out—if I couldn't get a job, if we couldn't afford a house, if you realized after all this time being apart you didn't love me anymore."

"Jesus, Lil." He didn't know whether to shout at her or take her in his arms, but he did neither. "How could you think such a thing? For two years, all I've done is think of you and dream of our being back together. I loved you, Lil." He saw her expression and realized what he'd said. "I love you."

"Enough to see this through with me, to wait?"

The question hit him like a rock. He hadn't expected her to be so blunt. When he spoke his voice sounded muted and hoarse, as if he were speaking through gauze. "Another two years?"

"I know it's too much to ask. Becky's already said she's washed her hands of me, that she can't take it anymore." Tears crawled from the corners of her eyes and glimmered in the etchings of crow's-feet. "I know I can't expect you to wait for me again, but . . ."

"But what?"

"I need you to be there for me. Now more than ever. I need to know that when I get out of here you'll still be there."

He couldn't answer. He watched the tears fill and overflow her eyes and cascade along her cheeks. He realized that, at forty-one, she was beginning to look old; at forty-five, he knew he already did. They had talked of growing old together and, until the day before, he'd still dreamed of that—the rosy fantasy of two still-in-love old people enjoying twilight years full of quiet pleasures and shared memories. Part of him still clung to that fantasy, but another part couldn't bear to take the risk of being hurt again.

"Lily, I . . . I don't think this is fair. For you to ask me this now. It's too soon. I can't tell you. I don't know myself."

"You said you still love me."

"I do."

"Then . . . don't walk away. Give me another chance."

He desperately wanted to. It would be so easy to believe her again, to fall into the trap of thinking this next time everything would be different. But there was something too familiar about this conversation, and he realized why: It was almost exactly what Lily had said the first time he'd caught her using meth, the same thing she'd said after being arrested. He felt some kind of trap being set and his own mad desire to leap into it, realized maybe the only difference between their mutual capacity for denial and self-deception was that, at least at this moment, he was able to recognize his. He pushed the chair back as though it were on fire and got to his feet.

"I'm sorry, Lil. I have to get out of here."

"But . . . visiting hours aren't over . . . it's—"

"I have to go." He leaned down and kissed her on the mouth. "The things we've said . . . I have to think about them. I need time . . . to decide what I'm going to do."

"Don't . . ." She held out a hand to him, but he was already walking away, catching the eye of one of the guards, who would escort him through the metal doors and back into the free world.

On the way home, he tried to distract himself from thinking about Lily by focusing on the case—the attack on him the night before, the murder of Tibbs. His mind kept returning to Mandy, to that last phone message she'd left him. She hadn't sounded good at all. He wondered if he'd told her more about the Boy Scout, about the woman's body in the ditch, than she'd been able to handle.

I ought to call her, he thought. And that was when it hit him. An image came suddenly to mind: the card from Donut Delites with the doughnut logo next to a phone number and address and, on the back, Mandy's first name printed in childishly large letters above her phone

number. She'd handed it to him, and he'd stuck it in
his wallet.

He yanked the wheel to the right, cutting off a white
Toyota Tundra as he swerved into the breakdown lane
and stopped the car.

His fingers didn't want to function. They were too big
and slow to match the urgency he felt as he pulled his
wallet out of his back pocket. He started flipping
through the credit cards and driver's license in their plastic pockets. Looking for the card Mandy had given him,
not finding it.

His stomach suddenly felt like he'd swallowed a bag
of ice, tendrils of cold creeping into his throat as he
realized that now the man who'd tried to kill him last
night had Mandy's phone number and knew the location
of her work. He could find her now with no trouble at
all. He could follow her home or intercept her on the
way. He could find her children.

He called Information, suffered through the hour-and-
a-half-long two minutes that it took the operator to get
the number for Donut Delite, and then dialed it. No one
picked up, although he let the phone ring twenty times.
Then he called the office and got his own voice asking
him to leave a message. He told Capshaw to call him
back at once, then tried her on her cell phone. While it
was ringing, a call came in—Capshaw calling him back
from the office.

"It looks like Josh is in the clear as far as last night.
I just got off the phone with the limo driver who took
him and Leland to a speaking gig in LA. That's the bad
news. But the good news, Ian, you won't believe what
I—"

He cut her off. "Is Mandy at work now?"

"I don't know. Maybe. What's going on?"

"She gave me a Donut Delite card with her name and
her phone number on the back. It was in my wallet, and
now it's gone. The guy who hit me last night took it. If
he's the same person who attacked her and Virginia—"

"Then he knows where she works."

"We need to get to her before he does. Donut Delite
isn't answering, but I'll keep trying. In the meantime,

see if you can get her at home. If you reach her, tell her to stay there, not to open the door to anybody until one of us gets there, and most important, don't go to work. If you don't get her, go over to her place anyway—she might be out on an errand. I'll head over to Donut Delite."

"I'll call the AA club, too. There's a meeting there she told me she hits when she's not working."

"Great."

"Where are you now?"

"Just passing the exit for Rancho Bernardo. Traffic keeps moving, I can be at the doughnut joint in thirty minutes."

"I'll call you back if I get her."

"Good enough." He started to hit the off button, then thought of something. "You said there was something I wouldn't believe. What . . . ?"

"Tell you when I see you. First let's find Mandy."

Chapter 24

Mandy's Thursday shift started at six P.M. She arrived ten minutes late and left five minutes after that, screeching out of her parking spot behind the building so fast that she almost clipped a Honda Civic that was turning into the alley behind her. At the first intersection, she ran a caution light, made a harrowing left turn that avoided oncoming traffic by inches, and turned a few hairs white on the head of a pedestrian who was still several feet shy of the curb when her Taurus careened past.

Somewhere amid the anger, fear, and frustration stewing in her mind, she was dimly aware that it was foolhardy to drive so chaotically. Imperial Beach had more than its share of vagrants and petty criminals and thus more than its share of cops. They were mostly out to thwart holdups and interrupt drug deals going down, but happy enough to deal with something less dangerous to them personally, like a careless and reckless woman driver.

What she needed, Mandy realized, was something to help her relax, calm her nerves.

The I.B. Bar and Grill was quiet and dark when she walked in, with patrons widely spaced along a horseshoe-shaped bar and occupying a handful of booths. She ordered a draft with a vodka chaser, watching the bartender drawing the beer from the tap and pouring the shot with rapt fascination. It wasn't exactly her first drink in recent days. That had been the Miller Lite she swigged down at My Brother's Bar when Ian thought she had gone to the rest room, gulping it so fast and so

desperately that stars had lit up behind her eyes. After
that one drink she'd stopped, though, knowing she'd
crossed over into enemy territory, yet surprised when
the urge to binge didn't seize her at once, when she
didn't even bother to open the bottle of Stoli she'd
bought at a liquor store later. Because she wasn't riddled
with craving at that point, she'd thought she might not
even be an alcoholic.

   Yeah, right.

She knew differently now, understood that stopping
after the one beer had been easy because she knew,
deep in her heart, that she wouldn't stay stopped. The
line had been crossed, and she would drink again. Not
a question of if, only when.

Now her skin felt electrified, and her mind simply
wasn't *there* anymore. Like a stopped clock, her thoughts
hung suspended, knowing she was only seconds away
from the sublime first swallow.

And it *was* sublime, the beer sliding down golden and
glorious, delicious foreplay to the kick of the shot when
she knocked it back. Like a head-to-toe orgasm, almost
heart-stopping and definitely mind-stopping, and she
thought, like one taken back into the body of a lover
after a fierce quarrel and long separation, *What the hell
made me ever stop doing this? Why the hell did I give
this up?*

   And then: *I want more.*

She signaled the bartender for a second shot, but held
back the impulse to down it immediately when the glass
with its clear, fiery liquid was set in front of her. There
was a phone call she needed to make, and it was important to her not to sound loaded when she did so. She
wanted the person she called to understand that what
she said wasn't fueled by alcohol, but was the decision
of a sane, sober mind.

Well, almost sober anyway.

She got up and threaded her way through a tight cluster of tables and into a short hallway that led to the rest
rooms and a pay phone. She took down the receiver and
started to dial; then, realizing she was on the verge of
making a stupid mistake—the person on the other end
might have caller ID and thus know her location

immediately—she hung up again, got out the cell phone McSwain had given her, and made her call.

When she went back to her stool, she saw that her shot glass and beer mug had multiplied by two while she was gone. The bartender, a bored-looking bottle blonde with a tattoo of a rose on her neck and a wad of gum padding her cheek, gestured with her head. "Guy over there sent you a drink."

Mandy glanced toward the end of the bar farthest away from the door and saw several men, one of whom looked back at her and nodded. She couldn't really see him and didn't smile or nod back—he could have been Brad Pitt, for all she cared, she still wasn't interested. She almost told the bartender to tell the guy no thanks and pay for the drinks herself, but then thought, *What the hell?* Some dude wanted to buy her drinks, go for it, honey. Just don't expect her to stick around for lame chitchat till she got hammered enough that a blow job in the parking lot could be viewed as a sensible first step in a budding relationship.

She was slamming the second shot, feeling the alcohol kiss and soothe every nerve ending in her body, when it occurred to her that she might have just screwed up bigtime. The phone call she'd made with her cell phone—could it be traced? Would the person she'd given her message to even take her seriously enough to try to trace it? And what about star 69, did that show the location of the call or the identity of the caller? She couldn't remember, but it was one of the two. *Shit,* she thought, *I could be fucked before I get started.*

"Dammit, I'm a fucking idiot!"

The bartender looked up from the cooler, gave a cynical grin. "Right, hon, you're the first fucking idiot ever walked in the door."

"Here, take this; I gotta go." She threw some money onto the bar, grabbed her tote bag, and bolted for the door like the bomb squad had just pulled up, yelling that the place was about to blow sky-high in thirty seconds. Her speed surprised even her—maybe the vodka was actually speeding up her reaction time rather than bogging it down.

Behind her, as she went out the door, there was movement at the other end of the bar—the man who'd sent her the drinks getting up, too, fumbling for his wallet—but she was moving too fast to notice.

McSwain walked into Donut Delite about twenty minutes after Mandy had left. There were only a couple of customers, a man at the counter and a woman sitting alone at a booth. A young African-American girl was wiping down the counter with a cloth while an older woman with a wrinkled brow and a nose that dominated her face like a forklift in an empty lot sat parked behind the cash register reading a paperback.

The cashier was closest, so McSwain approached her first. "Is Mandy Sutorius here?"

The woman took so long in responding that McSwain wondered if she understood English. Finally, as though it required tremendous effort, she said, "No, she's not here."

"She scheduled to come in later?"

"Nope."

McSwain caught the counter girl rolling her eyes. He walked past the cashier, stepped behind the counter, and briefly consulted the row of time cards. Mandy had punched in less than a half hour earlier.

"According to this, she should be working now."

"Should be don't mean she is." The woman got up, strode back to where McSwain was standing, snatched Mandy's time card out of its slot, and tore it in half. She offered the two halves to McSwain. "There, now she's not working here, is she?"

McSwain fought to control his temper. "What happened? Where is she?"

"What happened is that I fired her for being late. Where is she, your guess is as goddamned good as mine."

"Thanks for your help," said McSwain, but he was thinking maybe this was a blessing. Work was the least safe place Mandy could be—if she was headed home, her getting fired just might have saved her.

Intending to call Jenna to tell her Mandy might well be on the way home, he trotted back to his car and was reaching into the console for his cell phone when it rang in his hand. He checked the caller ID, saw the word *unidentified,* and walked outside to take the call.

"Mr. McSwain, Virginia Stromquist. Thank goodness I got you."

His first thought was that he needed to question her about Patrick DeKooning; his second was that he didn't have time to deal with this now. "Look, we need to talk, Mrs. Stromquist, but now isn't the time. How about if—"

She interrupted him. "I just got the strangest message—from Mandy. It sounds scary, and I didn't know who to call, but I thought you should know."

"What?"

"Leland's receptionist, Fern, just reached me at home. Mandy called Leland's office looking for me, and when Fern wouldn't give out our home number—standard procedure—she left a message. I'm repeating this secondhand, of course, but Fern said that Mandy sounded upset, that she wanted me to know how sorry she was for what happened. She'd hoped one day to tell me that in person, but she can't do that now, because she's going to do, and I quote, 'what I should've done fifteen years ago.' She said she was calling to tell me to have a good life and to say good-bye and that she wants me to forgive her.

"After she said all that, Fern realized how serious it was and tried to give her the unlisted number, but she'd already hung up."

"Jesus."

"I don't know how well you know this woman, but I thought you might know how to find her. Or how serious she might be about . . . doing something to herself."

"Did Fern have any idea where Mandy was calling from?"

"I don't think so, no, but she did have the presence of mind to hit star sixty-nine and get the phone number." She then repeated a number that McSwain recognized immediately, because it had once been his own. "I've tried calling the number, but no one answers."

"She's calling from a cell phone. She may have it turned off or just not be answering. Look, I'd better get off the phone. I—"

"There's one other thing. Fern said she said to tell me

that what she was going to do wasn't really about me; it was about someone named Kendra. Does that mean anything to you?"

McSwain tried to recall. "I think she mentioned a sister once, but . . . no, I have no idea. I need to go; I've got another call coming in. Maybe it's her."

Virginia hung up and he took the call—Capshaw, saying she was at Mandy's apartment with Kelly and the kids. Kelly had assumed Mandy was at work, and Jenna was keeping it casual, not letting her know anything more serious than a mixup in schedules was involved.

"Stay there," McSwain said, "in case she calls or comes in. Try not to upset her mother, though. I'm going to keep searching."

"Where?"

"Torrey Pines."

"Torrey Pines? Why—"

"Remember what Mandy said that day she first came to the office? She used to go to Torrey Pines when she was a teenager and fantasize about throwing herself off the cliffs. Then when she got drunk again after the incident with Virginia and she came out of the blackout, she was driving around up there. Not only that, but I just got a call from Virginia Stromquist. Mandy tried to reach her, said something about asking for her forgiveness and telling her good-bye."

"Jesus, you think she's planning to go up there and kill herself?"

"I hope not. But she mentioned Torrey Pines again the other day, something about going up there to do a swan dive. I can't think of any better place to look."

He snapped the phone shut and started the car. As he was pulling out, the rain started, fat drops splatting slowly onto the windshield at first, then speeding up, making the road go liquid and fuzzy as he watched it through the bars of the rain. He thought of his mother and the way the mascara had tracked black bars down her cheeks as she drove into the dark that night, the night when both of them were due to die, but somehow didn't, and he hoped that if Mandy were as foolish as his mother had been, that at least she would be as lucky.

Chapter 25

Speeding north on I-5, Mandy took the Carmel Valley Road exit and turned into the reserve just west of Pacific Coast Highway. The park would be closing in less than an hour and, with rain starting to fall, few people, if any, would be going in. Rather than risk being noticed, she parked near the water, reached under the seat, and pulled out the fifth of Stoli she'd stashed there. She popped the seal, unscrewed the cap, and took a deep gulp that burned down her throat and filled her blood with tiny, nicking razors.

She took another pull, then screwed on the cap, tucked the bottle inside her denim jacket, and started off into the park on foot. Climbing the sandy embankment that led up to the road, she walked a half mile and then crossed into the park well out of sight of the ranger who sat in a booth taking entrance fees and handing out maps.

The road leading through the park was steep and winding, glistening with rain and sloppy along the shoulders. She passed a handful of cars going out, but saw none coming in, and no one on foot. She trudged doggedly upward, but even with the vodka providing the illusion of warmth and encouragement, she was soon soaked and breathless. At one point, a jeep marked with the park service insignia cruised by, and she stepped quickly behind some trees, but the vehicle passed by.

She crossed the Guy Fleming and High Point trailheads and kept going until she saw the turnoff for parking for the Razor Point and beach trails. The two trails ran parallel at first, but split off from each other quickly, the beach trail winding three quarters of a mile down to Flat Rock, the other continuing to the cliffsides for a dramatic view of gorge, badlands, and wildflowers.

As a kid, Mandy had hiked these trails many times, but never under these conditions, with wind blowing the rain almost sideways and the sandstone paths that cut through the chaparral turning muddy and slick. Up ahead, she could see the stark outline of high sandstone walls, eroded and pockmarked, topped with Torrey pines bent under the wind.

The trail was no more than two-thirds of a mile long, yet she was startled by the suddenness with which the railing for the main viewing platform appeared. When she peered over, she saw below a muddy ledge about five feet wide and a trail that zigzagged dizzyingly along the cliffside before dropping off into the sea. Small shrubs grew up along the edge of it, leaning out at odd angles over the drop.

Holding on to the railing, she shimmied under it and let herself drop down to the ledge below. Here she was shielded somewhat from the rain, but not from the vertigo-inducing view of the dropoff and the sandstone cliffs rising to the north, pounded by a wind-whipped sea.

Despite her jacket, she was thoroughly drenched now, water sloshing inside her tennis shoes. It jogged memories of the stream that she'd waded through, trying to get back to Otay Lakes Road, the stitch of pain in her side and the rasp of her breath.

With that memory came another—Kendra getting into the midnight-blue El Dorado with the gray-eyed man, then looking back at her through the window with that tentative smile, that slightly scared, slightly questioning look. *Should I really be doing this? Is it really okay?*

And the look on her sister's face, that missed moment of opportunity when she could have opened the car door and pulled Kendra out; in spite of Kendra saying *I don't need you, I'll get home by myself,* it entered her ear like a knife and scraped the inside of her skull, and she knew no amount of vodka or anything else was going to anesthetize that memory out of her soul. Nothing short of death itself would stop it.

To try shaking the memory, she swigged some more vodka and risked leaning out over the drop. The wind was so strong now that it seemed to be pushing her back, thwarting her intention to leap, but she knew all she had to do was step forward for gravity to claim her. Below her, the roar of the ocean seemed to challenge her; she thought of crowds gathering to watch the drama of a suicide, feeling cheated when they were made to wait too long, yelling, *Jump.*

Between the rain and the salt spray, the air seemed half-liquid now, clinging coldly to her lips and lashes, seeping under her clothes.

For the first time since she'd eased her way down from the viewing point onto the ledge, fear punched past the vodka haze and gripped her. The wind came in fierce gusts, like a boxer throwing combinations; the rain made it hard to tell where the ledge that she crouched on ended and the open air began. Below her, the water looked cold and fierce, launching itself against the cliff base like a wild, hungry animal.

I can't do it, she thought. *I may want to die, but not like this. Not sinking deeper and deeper with that cold black water closing over my head. I've got to get out of here while I still can.*

First, though, she realized she needed a little warmth, a little encouragement. She uncapped the vodka and sucked down a good inch. A woozy warmth flooded her while the terror seemed to seep out of her skin and spill away like dirty water spiraling down a drain. She thought of Dakota and Em back at home, and her longing for them felt so deep and so visceral that had they been in her arms, she would have wanted to eat them alive if she could have done so without harming them.

All right, I have to get out of here. Before I really fuck up and slip over the edge and die anyway.

She took a deep breath and twisted around to her right, but the rock behind her angled, too, and the rain fell in dizzying corkscrews that poured into her mouth and tasted like vodka, and she realized suddenly that the bottle she was tilting to her mouth was nearly empty.

She shivered, the cold creeping into her bones again, and tried to climb back up the incline toward the viewing platform, but her foot failed to find purchase. The smooth soles of her tennis shoes slid backward in the mud. She tried again, managed two more steps, then slid back, landing on her knees with a force that made the liquid in her stomach lurch bitterly into her mouth.

As though her change of heart had altered it, too, the wind had now changed direction, was sweeping in from the north. No longer pushing her away from the drop, now it seemed determined to buffet her over it. Looking for a handhold, she saw nothing except the railing on the viewing platform above. When she stood on her toes and reached up, her hand missed the bottom rung by tantalizing inches.

Swiping the rain and her wet, windblown hair out of her face, she tried to focus on the trail and the rock wall beside it. The wall was smooth sandstone with only a few stunted shrubs growing out of cracks here and there, and she couldn't imagine trusting her weight to them. The trail was slick and muddy, but it still seemed to present the best possibility for climbing up. Rocks protruded from the mud in several places. She put her foot up on one of them, testing it with her weight. The rock held and she got halfway within grabbing distance of the rail before, on her next step, the rock she'd chosen for a foothold popped out of the mud like an olive pit spat onto a plate.

Arms flailing, she went down. This time, though, her momentum was greater—instead of sliding, she fell all the way backward, landing on her back with a jolt.

The fall punched the breath out of her, and the vodka percolating in her bloodstream urged her to stay put, so she lay there for a second, blinking up at the rain, feeling rivulets of cold, muddy water streaming into her hair and inside her jacket and blouse.

When she heard a voice calling her name, she thought that she'd passed out and was dreaming—until the same voice yelled again.

"Mandy, it's Ian! Are you here?"

"Ian? I'm down here!"

She got to her knees and was about to yell out again when she heard something that made the cry die in her throat—above the steady drumming of the rain, the crack of a gun going off.

McSwain put a hand to his chest and thought he was too damned old and out of shape to be doing this, jogging two miles up the steep, curving road that led to the trailheads at Torrey Pines. He'd arrived when the reserve was already closed, with chains across the entryway and exits, so he'd parked his car along the road and hiked up. Along the way he kept an eye out for park rangers who might be patrolling, but he hadn't seen any and figured that, in this weather, they probably weren't too worried about the most likely kind of trespasser, horny kids looking for a place to party.

The rain was coming down harder now, the sky darkening. At the Razor Point trailhead, he stopped to catch his breath and saw a single car, a compact parked at the edge of the lot. He took a flashlight from the pocket of his windbreaker and shone it on the car, a blue Taurus. If he'd had any doubt that it was Mandy's, the ONE DAY AT A TIME bumpersticker and open, empty box from Donut Delite in the backseat confirmed it.

She'd been here for some time, too, he concluded. A back window was down a couple of inches, and rain had soaked the seat and floor next to it.

He'd hoped his hunch about Mandy was wrong. Now that it was confirmed, he felt anger lodge in his heart. If she'd been there in front of him, he would have screamed in her face: *What were you thinking of? What about your kids? Just because you had a shitty childhood, you want the same thing for them?*

Anger galvanized him, and he moved quickly, trotting across the road to the trailheads, where a map of the area was displayed—the Razor Point trail, which climbed to the west, and the beach trail, which took a circuitous, zigzagging route to the water.

Given her purpose in being there, he assumed Mandy would have taken the Razor Point trail. It was also possible, he realized, that she hadn't taken either, but had left her car at one trailhead to confuse patrolling rangers and walked up or down the road to a different one. Nevertheless, he figured Razor Point to be the best bet.

As soon as he set out along the trail, he regretted not having a larger flashlight. The rain and the darkness made the going painfully slow, and the light illuminated only a few feet in front of him. Every few feet he stopped and yelled Mandy's name, but against the drone of the wind and staccato beat of the rain, he wondered if she would be able to hear him.

For the first hundred yards or so, the trail was relatively flat. Then it steepened abruptly and forked. McSwain hadn't been expecting this. He decided going left would be more likely to intersect with the beach trail and continued climbing. In the steepest places, steps had been cut into the stone, but these were muddy and treacherously slick.

He came to an open area with wooden steps leading up to a viewing platform and a telescope, and though it was impossible to see beyond a few feet, he knew what the view would be on a clear day: trails winding through the chaparral against a background of massive sandstone cliffs eroded with time and weather, and beyond that, the point where the cliffs ended in a sheer, dramatic drop to the sea. That would be Mandy's destination, and, if she were still alive, that was where he'd find her.

Another fifty yards along, the trail veered left and skirted the edge of what looked like a flat monolith rising out of the blackness. McSwain trained the flashlight on it and saw a broad sandstone cliff pockmarked with so many indentations it resembled a gigantic chunk of Swiss cheese. What looked like terraces of darker, fluted rock topped portions of the sandstone.

Past that, a hundred yards or so farther on, he could just make out the guardrail that skirted the edge of the cliff. If Mandy had intentions of jumping, she couldn't have picked a better place.

He cupped his hands to his mouth, yelled her name, and was starting toward the edge when a bullet fired from somewhere up above ricocheted off the rock wall behind him.

He cut off the flashlight and pulled his gun, but the rain was lashing down so hard that the shooter would have had to be standing three feet away for him to get off a decent shot. He was sure he'd heard Mandy's voice and wanted to call out again, but knew that would give away his position.

Ahead, he saw the dark outline of the viewing platform.

"Mandy?"

"Down here!"

He dropped to his belly and leaned under the rail, saw her balanced precariously close to the edge of what looked like a sheer drop.

"Can you climb up?"

She shook her head. He inched as far as he could under the railing and extended his arms to her, but even standing on tiptoe, her hands missed his by a good eight inches.

He was debating whether to climb down or not to try to help her when a gunshot made the decision for him. A bullet cut through the sheets of rain, struck the steel railing over his head, and ricocheted off. Mandy gave a cry and covered her mouth. McSwain aimed his gun in the general direction of where the shot seemed to have come from, but he didn't have the benefit of the shooter's voice to guide him.

"What's happening?" Mandy said, and before McSwain could even lean down to tell her to stay quiet, the shooter was honing in on the sound of her voice, firing again.

The bullet shredded the elbow of McSwain's jacket and nicked the skin underneath—hot pain stung the edge of his forearm. There was no place to hide, and he knew the shooter was advancing. With his gun drawn, he eased himself under the guardrail and dropped to the ledge next to Mandy, who had wrapped her arms around herself and was shaking uncontrollably.

He leaned toward her ear and whispered, "We're sitting ducks down here. We need to take the trail down to the water, but we need to throw something to distract him."

"How about this?" She reached into her jacket and pulled out a bottle of vodka with maybe two swallows remaining. McSwain took it.

"Wait!" To his amazement, she uncapped the bottle,

drained the contents, then handed it back to him with a shrug. "Sorry, can't let it go to waste."

McSwain hurled the bottle as far as he could toward the sandstone wall that projected out to the north. The sound of it shattering was immediately followed by a blast of gunfire. "Okay, come on." He grabbed her hand and they started descending the trail.

Within a short distance, McSwain realized he was going to have to use the flashlight or get both of them killed. The trail narrowed in places and almost disappeared. In others, switchbacks ended so abruptly it would be easy to step off into the air.

He turned the light on, and almost wished that he hadn't. Ahead sloped an even steeper stretch of rain-slick sandstone; below, black waves frothed and rolled, pitted with rain.

About twenty feet above the water, even the narrow trail they were on petered out into a dead end.

He cut the light off and turned toward Mandy. "Take off your shoes and your jacket."

"What?"

"We have to jump. It's deep enough here and there's a beach a few hundred yards up."

"How the hell do you know if it's deep enough?"

He didn't, not really, but he was already shedding his shoes and jacket. "Mandy, take off the goddamn jacket. It'll drag you down and you'll drown."

"I'm too cold."

"Fucking do it!"

She began removing the jacket and shoes, but moving too slowly, as if she were already underwater. He didn't know how much alcohol she'd consumed, but knew that it wasn't helping any.

"Hurry, Mandy. He's up there looking for us."

He could see the terrible irony of it hitting her—she'd come here intending to kill herself by jumping off the cliffs and now was terrified to make a jump that might save her life. "I can't do it. I'm too—"

A bullet fired from above whizzed past them.

He grabbed her hand, felt her pull back and yell "No!" and he jumped, pulling her with him, and they fell toward the water below.

He tried to hold on to her, but the force of hitting the water tore her hand from his grasp. As soon as he hit, he V'd his legs to slow his descent and started kicking back up. The shock of impact and the coldness of the water stopped his mind momentarily. When he surfaced, he didn't know in which direction to swim. Then he saw the far-off lights of the beachfront homes in La Jolla and knew that was south, the direction of the beach.

Before he could locate Mandy, though, a wave that felt like a frying pan struck him in the face and he went under, then surfaced gasping and spitting out water as he turned in a circle, looking for Mandy. Her head popped up a few yards away from him, and he swam to her, reached her just as a wave toppled over them like a brick wall, pushing them apart. The next time he surfaced, he saw Mandy ahead of him, realized the wave had pushed them toward the beach. He yelled at her to go on, but she was already swimming, and he followed her, trying to keep her in sight, breathing in as much rain as seawater.

A few hundred yards up, the waves pounded them with less force, and McSwain found himself touching bottom. A wave shoved Mandy into him and he grabbed her around the waist and started hauling them both up the beach, although his legs felt like they were only minimally controlled by his brain, like they might turn around and walk him back into the sea if he weren't careful.

Once out of the water, Mandy dropped to her knees, shivering so violently that it seemed she would shake apart. She looked up at him, lips blue as shadows on snow. "We're alive?"

"For the moment." He saw headlights and heard traffic moving up above on the Pacific Coast Highway. "Come on; we have to get up there."

"Jesus," she said, although her teeth were chattering so hard that it was hard to make out her words. "Jesus, but I need a . . ."

She saw the look on his face, rolled her eyes. ". . . a hot shower, that's what I need. A hot shower and about twenty-four hours' sleep."

Chapter 26

Around one A.M. McSwain called Capshaw's cell phone from a pay phone on Carlsbad Boulevard and found she was still at Mandy's apartment with Kelly and the children. He gave her a rundown on what had taken place; then Mandy got on the phone to tell her mother that she was okay. Fortunately Kelly had to take her word for that, because, had she been able to see her daughter, soaked and shivering, with blue lips and cuts and bruises on her arms and legs, she might have doubted just how "all right" she really was.

When McSwain got back on the phone, Capshaw asked where they were, and McSwain told her. "I'll come pick you up."

"No, stay there." He walked a few feet away, lowering his voice so Mandy wouldn't hear. "I have a feeling I was the shooter's target more than Mandy was—but I do think he followed her to Torrey Pines when she left work. If he's figured out where she lives, he may show up at her apartment next. My car's a couple of miles from here. I'm going to go get it, but first I'm going to put Mandy in a cab and send her over there, so you need to watch for her. I'll tell her not to get out of the cab till she sees you come out of the building to meet her."

"Is she okay?"

He looked over at Mandy, who was sitting on the edge of the curb, knees drawn up to her chest, arms scrunched tightly around them, and he thought the only way she could've looked more utterly forlorn would have been curled on her side in a fetal position.

"We're both pretty cold and miserable, but—"

"I mean is she drunk?"

"Not anymore."

"Shit."

"Look, don't give her a hard time, okay? She's had a hell of a night."

"The guy who shot at you, you know by now he's probably found your car and he's—"

"—waiting for us to come back to get it. I know. That's why I don't want Mandy with me."

"Okay. Be careful, will you?"

"I'll see you soon."

McSwain hung up, then called a cab. When it finally arrived, he gave the driver money and told him Mandy's address. The driver, a bushy-bearded man with skin the color of coffee beans and a beard pleated like an accordion, stared at the wad of soggy bills as though unsure if they were really legal tender, then reluctantly accepted the money.

McSwain got in the cab and let the driver take him to within a few blocks of his car, then got out and walked the rest of the way. He surveyed the car for several minutes before finally determining no one else was watching it. On the drive home, he checked out the bloody scrape on his forearm where the bullet had grazed him and determined it was nothing that couldn't get by with a good cleaning and bandaging. At home, he showered, changed into dry clothes after taking care of the wound, and drove to Mandy's apartment. There he scouted the neighborhood, cruising through the alley and then around the block a few times before finally parking and getting out of the car.

As soon as he parked, he saw the door to the apartment building open and Capshaw trotted down the front steps. She wore a T-shirt and shorts, and her hair clung to her face in damp strands, as though she'd just stepped from the shower.

"Long walk back to your car? I was getting worried."

"I went home to shower and change clothes. Guy shot a hole in the arm of my favorite sport coat."

"Your sport coat? What about you?"

"Bullet grazed my elbow, but nothing serious. I've had

mosquito bites that looked worse." He saw her frown and said quickly, "How's Mandy?"

"Well, her lips aren't blue anymore and she's stopped shaking, but she's scared and exhausted. And mad at herself. She's going to have to pick up another white chip at the next meeting."

"A what?"

"Because of the most recent slip."

"Yeah, well, after what happened tonight, I'd say drinking is the least of her worries."

Jenna didn't argue, but he could see the that's-what-you-think look on her face as they headed into the building.

On the first-floor landing, she stopped and turned back to him. "So aren't you even going to ask me?"

"Ask you . . . ?" His brain felt like a few crucial synapses had been jarred loose when he plunged into the cold water, but suddenly it came to him. "On the phone . . . you said there was something I'd never believe. . . ."

"DeKooning."

"DeKooning?"

She rattled off a street address in Brawley.

"His?"

"Yeah."

"How did you . . . ?"

"Remember I said if he'd been arrested for any sex offenses after he got out of prison, he might be in the Sex Offenders Registry? Well, guess what? In ninety-one he was picked up for exposing himself to two young girls who came to his door selling tickets to a school play. He did three years, got out, registered at the address in Brawley. Now who knows if he's still there, but . . ."

"Hey, it's the best lead we've got. Let me get Mandy settled, and we'll head up there this afternoon."

On the third floor, after using Mandy's key to get into the apartment, they found her huddled on the sofa, bundled in a yellow terry-cloth robe and staring at the silent, flickering images on the muted TV screen. The baby, Dakota, slept on her lap, while Emily lay asleep with her head on her mother's thigh, a plump thumb plugging her mouth.

Mandy looked up long enough to nod to McSwain, then her gaze returned to the TV.

McSwain said, "Why don't you throw some things in a suitcase and I'll take you and the kids to a motel."

Mandy looked at the sleeping children. "I can't go anywhere tonight. I just can't. The kids are asleep and I . . . I'm still cold and I feel like my head's the size of LA. I just want to stay still." She must've seen something in his expression, because she said, "You're mad at me, aren't you?"

"For getting drunk and almost getting yourself killed?" He shrugged. "It's your life, Mandy. But next time you decide you're going to throw it away, I'd think about those kids first."

Capshaw came over and sat on the arm of the sofa, massaging the back of Mandy's neck while shooting him a look that Mandy didn't see. Intended to remind him, he supposed, that he was the one who'd told *her* not to go too hard on Mandy.

"Speaking of the kids," she said gently, "if you're going to stay here tonight, shouldn't they be in bed?"

"I want them here where I can touch them, hear them breathing. After what happened tonight, I thought I'd probably never even hold them again."

"Okay," Capshaw said, "but at least go to bed. Let the kids sleep with you."

Mandy nodded sleepily, but she didn't move to get up off the sofa. Instead she flopped over sideways, dug her head into a pillow, and gathered the children against her. Soon her breathing deepened, and she began to snore.

"I'll stay here with them," Capshaw said. "You go back home."

McSwain looked at his watch. "What for? It's almost morning. There a second bedroom?"

"The kids' room. There's a couple of twin beds, and you'll have to move a bunch of stuffed animals, but yeah, get some sleep if you can. I'm going to stay up."

McSwain nodded and then walked through the back of the apartment, checking windows and the back door.

In the small kitchen, he didn't like the window over the sink, which overlooked a fire escape and provided easy access. He found Kelly in Mandy's bedroom, fully dressed and sleeping, one flabby arm thrown across her eyes.

The window next to her bed was open, and McSwain crossed the room to lower and lock it.

Kelly uncovered her face and sent him a squinty-eyed glare. "Whatcha close the window for? It's like the fuckin' Amazon jungle in here."

"Safer this way."

"Anything in here look like it's worth climbin' in a window to steal?" She yawned and struggled to a sitting position. "When're you people gonna leave, anyway? It's"—she lifted her wrist and frowned at her watch—"middle of the goddamn night."

"We'll be gone soon," said McSwain, "and Mandy and the kids are going with us. You might consider coming along or going home, but you shouldn't stay here."

"And why not?"

"It could be dangerous."

"Oh." Her mouth twisted disparagingly as she propped herself up on one elbow. "You mean the big, bad man Mandy says was after her last night. Look, honey, she always thinks somebody's after her, and there usually is, but it's not some cloak-and-dagger chase scene. They're after her because she owes 'em money or slept with their boyfriend or something."

"Does Mandy have a sister?" asked McSwain.

Kelly gaped at him like she didn't comprehend the words. "A sister?"

"Yeah, you know, a female sibling born to you and her father?"

"Hey, don't get smart-mouthed with me."

The way her face hardened reminded McSwain of the craggy cliffs up at Torrey Pines. He knew he would get no useful answer.

"Mandy's my only kid. And I thank God, too, since she gives me enough trouble for six." She gave a harsh smoker's laugh and flopped back down on the bed. "And don't let the door hit you in the ass on your way out. I need my beauty sleep."

*   *   *

Mandy barely spoke at all the following morning, drinking cup after cup of black coffee and turning grass green when Capshaw returned from the McDonald's up the block and waved an Egg McMuffin in her face, but in McSwain's car, with the baby on her lap and Emily in the backseat, she stared out the window and said, "It was the guy who raped Virginia that night, wasn't it?"

"Did you get a look at him?" McSwain had asked her that same question the night before and she'd told him no, but she'd also been drunk then, so he was hoping for a different answer this time.

"No. But he followed me . . . why else would anyone follow me out there with a gun if he wasn't trying to kill me?"

McSwain had thought of another possibility that he didn't want to voice. According to Mandy, the gunplay hadn't come into the picture until McSwain entered the scene. He believed the man's original intention had been not to kill Mandy, at least not there in the park, but to get her back to his car and take her somewhere else for a more leisurely disassembling.

"It was probably the same man," he said finally.

"I think he must've followed me when I left Donut Delite. And I'm pretty sure he was at the bar when I made the call to Virginia. But how did he know where I worked?"

McSwain winced but he told her the truth, giving an abbreviated version of the attack in the church and the loss of the card Mandy'd given him.

"Jesus." She lifted Dakota off her lap and held him tightly to her chest as though suddenly afraid someone would snatch him away. "What about Virginia? I mean, if the guy could find me then for sure he can find her, with her husband being famous and all. Shouldn't you warn her?"

"Jenna called her husband's office while you were showering. Virginia left last night to join Leland and his son in LA. We're trying to get in touch with her."

He checked the rearview mirror for the third time in as many minutes, making sure that they weren't being followed as he exited the freeway and headed toward the parking area under the overpass near Torrey Pines where Mandy had left her car. As he speeded up to pass a slower vehicle, he noticed a sticker on the rear window that said, CAREFUL, BABY ON BOARD, and felt a small prick of shame at the unsafe way he was transporting Mandy's children. "We really shouldn't be driving like this . . . without child seats, I mean, and an air bag on the passenger side. But under the circumstances—"

"Yeah, I know. Cop stopped me a few months back, told me I had to get car seats for the kids, or I'd get wrote up. I been trying to, but, you know, they're not cheap."

"Important, though."

"Yeah." She brought a hand across her mouth and giggled softly. The giggling grew until she removed her hand and laughed out loud.

"What's so funny?"

"Nothing. It's just that . . . what a crazy world, huh? Somebody's out to kill both of us, we could've both got shot or drowned last night, and we're worrying about car seats for the kids. And here neither one of us may make it till midnight."

"True, but we're sure as hell gonna try."

He took Mandy back to her car and waited to make sure she got it started—the engine didn't want to turn over, and before it finally caught, he thought he might have to get out his jumper cables—then he headed south again toward Chula Vista with her following in the Taurus.

McSwain had once spent a month's worth of Wednesdays staking out the Motel Eight in Chula Vista, where a client's husband was supposedly shacking up every Wednesday afternoon with his girlfriend. It took three rolls of film to convince the client of what McSwain had realized the first time he saw the big-boned "girlfriend" walk out the door after the husband had gone in alone carrying a suitcase—that the man was meeting no one at all at the motel, only using the room to transform himself into a well-coiffed, stylishly dressed, if butt-ugly (in McSwain's opinion) woman. He would spend a few hours out on the town, generally lunching in the Gaslamp District and spending the afternoon shopping at

Horton Plaza, then return to the room so "Jeanine"—
the name McSwain once overheard a saleslady call
him—could change back into the staid and decidedly un-
stylishly dressed Jeffrey.

McSwain therefore knew that the motel was both reasonably priced and conveniently located and that he
could rent a suite, consisting of a bedroom and living
room area, for less than he'd pay for a regular hotel
room at many places. It was hardly the Ritz, but a couple
of steps up from the kind of fleabag establishment where
Mandy would have to worry about the pimps plying their
trade at the ice machine.

He stopped outside the office, waited until Mandy
pulled up behind him, then went inside and paid for a
week's stay. He figured he and Jenna could take turns
staying at Mandy's apartment and hope whoever had
come after her last night was as adept at getting her
home address as he'd been at finding her workplace.

The room was on the third floor near a stairwell with
a sweeping view of the rear parking lot and an empty
field that backed up to it, where a woman was tossing a
Frisbee to a golden Lab and a smaller mutt of more
dubious ancestry. McSwain checked the windows and
door and found the locks to be adequate for keeping
out small kids and the elderly, but probably not anyone
else. Still, he didn't think there was any danger here.

"You okay?" he asked Mandy when she came back
into the living room after unpacking her bags and getting
the kids settled in front of the TV in the bedroom.

"Yeah, I guess. But . . . how long we gotta stay here?"

"Let's see how it goes."

She shrugged. "Not like I have a job to show up at."

"Jenna's real concerned about the drinking. You get
drunk, you won't be able to protect yourself or your
children."

"Yeah, I kind of proved that, didn't I?"

She folded her arms and shifted her weight onto one
hip, seemingly impatient for him to leave. Instead of
doing that, however, he surprised her by sitting down at
one end of the beige-striped sofa and putting his feet on
the coffee table.

"You called Virginia Stromquist last night."

"Yeah, I told you that. And Virginia called you, and you guessed where I was and came looking for me." She gnawed on the corner of one ragged nail, where a fleck of pink polish remained. "Guess I didn't even thank you or anything. For going to all the trouble. So thanks."

"Who's Kendra, Mandy?"

She winced almost imperceptibly, a retraction of muscle, a shrinking of size. "How do you know about Kendra?"

"From you. Your message to Virginia, you said this wasn't just about her, it was about Kendra, too."

"I did?"

McSwain couldn't tell if she was lying or if she honestly couldn't remember what she'd said.

"What happened? You got drunk last night, and it sounds like it had something to do with your sister. Where is she? I need to know."

"Christ, what for?"

"Look, Jenna and I can't protect you if we don't know what's going on with you."

"Why do you care?"

"Because we do. So what happened to Kendra, Mandy? Where is she?"

"Well, she was supposed to be in the ocean somewhere—she wanted her ashes scattered at sea—but Mom's such a great one for following directions that she had her buried in a plot at Rosemont Cemetery." She took the armchair across from McSwain, pulling her legs up underneath her. There was a TV set in that room as well, and for a moment she stared at it as though an image played on the screen, something cast there by memory.

"What happened to her?"

She lifted her right hand and pantomimed firing a gun into her temple. "She offed herself; that's what happened to her, and I was the cause. She was shy and liked books, a real Goody Two-shoes, you know, and I wanted her to be more the way I was, to drink and screw around with the boys. One night I took her with me to a party up in the hills around El Cajon. A lot of drinking, smoking pot. I was sixteen and there was this guy I liked, Jimmy somebody—I don't even remember now—but I wanted to hook up with him, and he wasn't there yet. Kendra didn't like all the drinking and drugs. She wanted me to take her home, and I said, 'No fucking way, I'm not ready to leave.' So we're out on the road having an argument. She called me a selfish bitch and I shoved her, and she fell down—right there on the side of the road.

"And this car pulls up. It was a midnight-blue El Dorado, and the guy driving it . . . he was either a priest or some guy pretending to be a priest; he had the collar and all—and he offered Kendra a ride. He was old, like in his fifties, and he had these really kind-looking, crinkly eyes, like if he'da been fat, he could've played Santa or something. So Kendra asked me was it okay, should she go with him, and I knew it wasn't okay, I just knew, but I wanted to get rid of her so I could be with this boy, and I told her to go on. I told her to get in the car."

"And?"

"And what do you think? He raped her. Let her go the next day, but she was never the same. They never caught the guy, either. And a month or so later, she gets hold of the gun Ma kept around the house for protection, and she kills herself. And she did it because I told her it was okay to get in the car."

"She did it because of what happened to her."

"Same thing. Wouldn't have happened if I'd told her to stay put, that I'd drive her home."

She glanced toward the bedroom, where Emily could be heard explaining something on the TV to her brother, and wrapped her arms around herself as though permeated by a deep chill.

Some of Mandy's behavior was starting to fall into place for McSwain—the alcoholism and history of promiscuity, the terrible guilt she still felt for running away when Virginia Stromquist started screaming for help. He thought about Jenna's husband, and wondered if people who committed suicide could begin to guess the suffering they left behind or if, at times, imagining that devastation was part of the motive.

"I'm glad you told me," McSwain said. "It helps to talk about these things."

"Yeah, well, my mom and I used to talk about it

sometimes, but you've met her, so you know she checked out a long time ago. God, life is so fucked-up, isn't it?"

"Sometimes, yeah."

"And getting loaded's such an easy way out."

He stared at her. "How easy was last night?"

She didn't answer.

"Look, I have to go, but Jenna or I will stop in and check on you, let you know how things are going."

"And if that guy doesn't show up again? Will it be safe to go home?" She looked at the door as if she were considering grabbing the kids and running. "How long do we have to stay in hiding?"

"We'll find the guy," said McSwain. "I promise you. Soon."

A few minutes later, after saying good-bye to Mandy and taking the stairs down to the first floor, he made a couple of calls to the *Union-Tribune* building over on Camina de la Reina. The first one was to the paper's morgue to verify what he already guessed—that the paper kept CD-ROM records dating back only to the early nineties. If DeKooning's attack on Virginia had occurred when she was fourteen and if she was in her mid- to late thirties now, then the crime would have taken place in the mid-eighties.

The second call was to Darwin O'Shea, a crime reporter with the *Union-Tribune* whom McSwain had met when O'Shea was covering the Heaven's Gate suicides back in ninety-seven and McSwain was trying to track down a client's missing daughter, who'd been involved with one of the cult members. The girl turned up safe and sound working at a resort in Baja, and McSwain and O'Shea had been casual friends ever since, getting together for the occasional drink or hockey game.

McSwain told O'Shea he needed to get into the morgue and look through the microfiche. O'Shea made a call to the morgue librarian and, a little over an hour later, McSwain had made the drive to the *Union-Trib*'s Mission Valley headquarters and was settled in a cubicle in front of a computer, searching for articles on Patrick DeKooning from eighty-four through eighty-nine.

He got nothing, though, and then spent another hour

searching the paper for the following year with equally frustrating results. Finally he went back a year to 1983 and hit pay dirt.

The first entry was for May 8 and read:

El Centro Man Charged with Kidnap, Rape

Police arrested an unemployed carpenter, Patrick DeKooning, 24, and charged him with the kidnap and rape of a fourteen-year-old girl who said DeKooning stopped her to ask if she'd help him decide on a birthday gift for his mother. When she went into the house, she said he held her captive and raped her over a period of two days.

During one period when she was left alone, she escaped and ran for help to a neighbor's, who called the police. The girl told police DeKooning kept her tied up much of the time she was held captive and that he told her he planned to eventually let her go but would kill her if she ever told anyone what had happened.

DeKooning's parents, who were out of town at the time, say he has a history of emotional instability but has never been violent. The girl was treated at the El Centro Hospital and released to her parents.

On June 10, another story appeared under state news:

Man Accused of Kidnap/Rape Held without Bond

Judge Edward Tuttobenne ordered Patrick DeKooning, 24, of El Centro, held without bail until his trial for the kidnapping and rape of a fourteen-year-old girl in an El Centro neighborhood last May. The girl told police that DeKooning lured her into his home while his parents were away, then held her captive, raping her, until she managed to escape two days later.

The next article McSwain found was dated December 2 and read:

DeKooning Sentenced to Ten Years

A jury sentenced Patrick DeKooning, 24, to ten years in prison without possibility of parole for last year's rape of a fourteen-year-old El Centro girl.

DeKooning's father and stepmother, Ralph and Leonore DeKooning, were present at the sentencing. DeKooning's stepmother became distraught upon hearing the sentence and had to be removed from the courtroom. The victim's family was not present.

In a sometimes emotional testimony, interrupted frequently so the girl could regain her composure, she described how DeKooning lured her into his home, then held her captive over a period of two days, keeping her tied up much of the time when he wasn't sexually assaulting her. She said DeKooning told her he was in love with her and that he was holding her prisoner only until she could learn to love him, too. She testified that DeKooning gave her one of his mother's rings and that he sprayed her heavily with perfume, saying it would make her "clean."

Jesus.

McSwain braced his hands on the edge of the cubicle and leaned back, absorbing what he'd just read.

DeKooning had sprayed Virginia with perfume, just as the man who assaulted her and Mandy had done, which meant that the man either *was* DeKooning himself or someone close enough to Virginia to be familiar with her history and want to terrorize her in an especially sadistic way. Now he thought he understood why Virginia hadn't wanted them to know about her assault as a young girl. It would rule out the possibility that the attack had been a crime of opportunity committed by a stranger and point the finger at someone she knew.

Either way, McSwain thought as he left the newspaper building and headed back to his car, she had been the biggest impediment to bringing her own rapist to justice.

He called Jenna at Mandy's apartment and, after filling her in on what he'd learned at the newspaper, told her he was going to drive to Brawley.

"Where are you now?"

"Getting ready to leave the *Union-Tribune* building."

"Stay there. I'll drive over and go with you."

"What about Mandy's apartment? I thought we wanted it staked out in case whoever tried to kill us shows up there."

He heard Jenna exhale a long, tired sigh and knew a trail of smoke was wafting up with it. "As far as I'm concerned, the apartment is staked out—by her mother. I can't get the old bat to leave. She's zoned out on the sofa watching TV and smoking grass. I threatened to call the cops on her—she just laughed and offered me a toke. A minute ago I heard her on the phone inviting some friends to come over and to be sure to bring plenty of booze, because she feels like partying. Nobody's going to try breaking into this place when it sounds like Mardi Gras's going on."

"I take it she's not scared of whoever's after her daughter?"

"No, but much more of this and she's gonna have to be scared of me. I'm about ready to take that remote away from her and ram it up her—"

"All right, I'm parked in the *Union-Tribune* lot. Meet me here as soon as you can. We'll go for a ride in the desert."

"Isn't that what the Mafia hit guys always say before they off somebody?"

"Hey, you wanna get out of there or not?"

"I'm on my way."

Chapter 27

For some reason, McSwain was surprised when Jenna told him she was familiar with El Centro, Brawley, and the whole Imperial Valley area southeast of San Diego. He knew people went out there to bird-watch at the Salton Sea, which was California's largest lake, and to bounce through the desert in dune buggies and ATVs, but except for a brief trip to Calexico, on the border with Mexico and the United States, to pick up a bail jumper a few years back, he'd never spent time in the area.

"Actually Larry and I had our honeymoon out here," Capshaw said.

"In the desert? Funny, I'd always figured you for a basking-in-the-sun-on-a-beach-in-Fiji type."

"Well, you can't drive to Fiji, and Larry got nauseous going up in elevators, so flying was out. But you can't say we didn't get plenty of sun and sand."

"No, you can't say that."

He stared out the window, where the passing landscape reminded him of his conception of where men went to join the French Foreign Legion. Flat, sun-blasted scrub stretching to a horizon where shimmering heat waves created the illusion of a luminous blue-green sea. He wondered how many people who got lost in the desert for one reason or other had succumbed to that illusion only to realize, perhaps as they died, that there was only sand and more sand, that there had never been anything except sand.

"We camped a couple of nights north of here at

Glamis and then a few more at Superstition Mountain near El Centro."

"What's there?"

"Nothing."

"Nothing? Then why go?"

"Because there's nothing there. Well, other people, sure, but not if you go out far enough to where all you can see is the badlands and dunes. You sleep during the day when it's too hot to move, but at night you can look up at the stars and feel like you're the only two people left in the universe. You're so alone it feels almost scary." She sighed and he wondered if talking about it made her sad. "Of course, on a honeymoon, that's exactly how you *want* to feel. And it was great till the bombs started falling."

McSwain thought he'd misheard. "Bombs?"

She laughed. "There was a military bombing range nearby, and we were right on the edge. I don't know if this was Larry's great idea or mine—where we'd camp—but in the middle of the night"—she made a whistling sound—"ka-*boom*!"

"So the earth really did move."

"Oh, definitely. And we were moving, too—fast in the opposite direction."

They were headed east on I-8, just passing the tiny farming community of Octillo, about twenty miles west of El Centro, where Virginia Stromquist had grown up. From there, the town of Brawley, where Patrick De-Kooning now lived, was a half hour north on State Road 86.

"Did you call Paris and tell him DeKooning's our man?" Capshaw asked.

"No, because one, we don't know that for sure it's DeKooning, and two, we still don't have any assurance Virginia will testify to what happened. She didn't bother telling us about DeKooning or the perfume."

"She didn't, did she? I mean, do you remember that afternoon she turned up at your house and told her version of the story—did it include the fact that the assailant sprayed perfume on her?"

"It didn't. We heard about the perfume from Mandy.

This morning I went back and reread my notes from the conversation with Virginia. She never mentioned it."

Capshaw leaned forward and tried to turn up the air conditioner, but it was already cranked up to maximum. "So to say she's impeding the arrest of whoever raped her is an understatement. On the other hand, you said she talked about the trauma of having to testify to sexual assault—that comment about a jury thinking the lack of vaginal abrasions indicated enjoyment of the rape—that's the statement of somebody who's been through hell on the stand. And she was only fourteen. If she's not willing to talk about what happened to her back in January or testify against her attacker if we find him, I see that as maybe gutless but still understandable."

"The fact that it's understandable doesn't make it right," McSwain said. "It just leaves a proven killer on the street who's going to come after some other woman. Who probably already has."

They were just passing the WELCOME TO BRAWLEY sign, when McSwain spotted a Wal-Mart and pulled over. He went inside, bought a map, and located Gecko Road at the north end of town.

"One thing I don't understand about DeKooning," Capshaw said when they were en route again.

"Only one?"

"Well, aside from how he grew to be a rapist and child molester, what puzzles me is why he's living here in Brawley. I mean, it's what, a half hour up the road from El Centro, if that. I'd think once he got out of prison, he'd've wanted to put as much distance between him and this area as humanly possible."

"Maybe he had friends, family?"

"A child molester?"

"They do."

"Once he got out of prison, he wouldn't have been able to leave the state, but that doesn't mean he had to move within spitting distance of where his victim and her family lived."

McSwain shrugged. "Maybe he didn't. Maybe he's been living somewhere else, but moved back to the area after enough time had gone by that he figured no one would remember him." He stopped at a traffic light, watched an old man hobble past, wiping sweat from his face and scowling up at the sky as though he held the sun personally responsible for the sweat streaming down his gnarled face.

"Another reason DeKooning might have moved so close to El Centro," Capshaw said. "Habit. People return to what they know, what they're familiar with, even if it was traumatic. Look at the women who divorce one abuser for another. They're caught in a cycle. No matter how terrible it is, they seem compelled to act out the same drama."

"Yeah, and molesting kids is a habit, too," McSwain said, "one that pedophiles are familiar with. A child-raper isn't going to control his preference for children. Rehab doesn't work with these guys—only Death Row."

He drove another block, passing fast-food eateries, before turning left at the corner, but he wasn't paying much attention to the route except when Jenna, consulting the map, gave him directions. Something he couldn't quite put his finger on was bothering him. Something about the idea of Patrick DeKooning trapped in a sick cycle of addiction to children, of the many child molesters he'd heard or read about who claimed they were powerless to stop and, the ultimate irony to McSwain's way of thinking, that the majority of pedophiles had been victimized by pedophiles as children themselves.

Were they seeking to take control of an unbearable situation by perpetrating it on someone else?

"Whoa, you turn right here," Capshaw said, and he filed the thought away as something to mull over later.

Gecko Road was a bleak, sun-bleached mile of standardized housing on a flat tract of parched, pebbly land. The houses backed up to a broad hill with a railroad track running across the top. Unlike the rest of Brawley, which from what McSwain had seen so far had unexpectedly lush greenery for a desert town, the few trees here looked beleaguered and stunted, their limbs rising like the dehydrated arms of men expiring from heat prostration. Puffs of dust, fine-looking as talcum, floated down the hill toward the backyards. Someone had gone to great effort to ensure that no neighbor would feel outdone by another—from what McSwain could see the houses varied only in whether the bay window was set to the left or right of the front door and which of three pastel colors—robin's-egg blue, yellow, or an odd shade of green that seemed more appropriate to the hallways of some sort of institution—had been used for the paint job.

When they located the block with DeKooning's house, McSwain drove past once while Capshaw looked for the number.

"I don't like this," she said.

"What?"

She took off her sunglasses and stared at the passing houses, most of which had their street numbers in large numbers on the mailbox. "I'm hoping I just read the numbers wrong, but I don't think I did. If that's De-Kooning's house we just passed, it's got a For Sale sign out front and a lockbox on the door so the realtors can show it."

"So his house is for sale. That doesn't mean he's not there."

"I just got a feeling when we drove past. That house isn't being lived in, Ian. It looks empty."

"So do all the other houses in this neighborhood." He finished circling the block and parked opposite the house with the street address they were looking for. As they crossed the street, he realized Capshaw was right—there was nothing, not a flowerpot on the porch, not a curtain in the bay window—to indicate habitation.

"Damn," said Capshaw, who'd walked ahead and was bending over, shielding her eyes as she peered in the front window. "It's empty. He's gone, Ian."

Out of the corner of his eye, McSwain got a glimpse of movement around the side of the house. It might have been a product of the shimmering, fierce heat playing tricks on his eyes, but he started to walk in that direction.

"Are you for real or are you just looky-Lous?"

The question came from a young girl who suddenly popped from around the side of the house like a small, chubby jack-in-the-box. Her appearance was so sudden McSwain almost jumped back. From the sly expression on her round face and the unexpectedness of her appearance, he figured she'd been watching them, probably since they got out of the car.

"You live around here?" he asked.

She jerked her head toward the lemon-yellow house next door. "There."

"And what is it you just asked if we were?"

"For real or looky-Lous."

As she spoke, the girl kept playing with a strand of her brown hair, first winding it around an index finger, then popping it into her mouth and sucking on the wet end.

"I think she means are we serious real estate investors or just your garden-variety busybodies who like an excuse to peek in someone else's window," said Jenna, coming around the corner. She smiled at the child. "What's your name?"

"Hannah," said the girl, not smiling back. "My mom wants to know if you're gonna buy this house. She likes to know who's gonna be living next door to her."

"I don't think we'll be buying it," Capshaw said.

"Looky-Lous," Hannah said in a singsong voice. "Just a couple of looky-Lous." She didn't smile at all, but kept the same flat stern stare as she sang. McSwain thought this odd. He wondered how old she was and guessed her to be about ten or eleven, but she might have been younger—the extra weight she carried on her plump arms and midsection might have made her look larger and therefore older than she was.

"We are interested in the house, though," McSwain said. "Is your mom around? I wonder if she'd talk to us for a minute."

"You want me to wake her up?"

McSwain didn't need to look at his watch to know it was only a little after two. Well, maybe the kid's mom worked the night shift. Before he could respond to the question, though, Hannah spat the strand of hair out of her mouth, dashed across the lawn, up onto the porch, and into the lemon house.

A minute passed, then another, while the heat pummeled them like hurled bricks. Jenna lit a cigarette. McSwain pulled out his notepad and jotted down the

name, number, and company of the real estate agent
who was offering the house, thinking he could call later
to ask who was selling it.

"You woke me up for what?" he heard a woman's
voice say. "Jesus, you coulda at least asked what they
wanted."

Hannah reappeared on the porch, the look of bland-
ness and detachment still on her face despite the fact
that she was evidently being scolded. A woman with
fried-looking yellow hair not too dissimilar from the
shade of the house and the darkest tan McSwain had
seen outside a surfer movie followed Hannah outside.
She wore tight white shorts and a white halter top, the
better to show off both the mahogany skin and the gold
ring piercing her belly button. She looked young, late
twenties maybe, but there was something old in the set
of her mouth and the hard jut of her jaw, a furious
disappointment in the lines etching her eyes.

She appraised Capshaw and McSwain with disdain.
"My daughter woke me out of the first half-decent sleep
I've had in a couple of days—you better want something
besides directions out of town."

McSwain thought this might be a good time to pull
out his PI license and swap introductions. The woman
studied his license and Capshaw's for a long moment
before handing them back.

"Private detectives, eh? And you found something
worth detecting in this armpit of a town?" She ran a
hand through brittle-looking bangs. "Okay, I'll bite."
She extended a hand so dark it might have spent time
in a broiler. McSwain thought he saw a tattoo on the
wrist, but the skin was so dark he couldn't be sure.

"Susan Walmsley. Pleased to meet you."

"The man who used to live here," Capshaw said, ges-
turing toward the house with the For Sale sign, "how
well did you know him?"

"Oh, Patrick, sure. I knew him." A hesitation crept
into her voice, and something in her manner seemed to
change. She glanced behind her at Hannah, acknowledging the child for the first time since she'd left the house.
"Hon, I want to talk to these folks alone, okay? How
about you play outside for a while?"

Hannah was sucking on a strand of hair again, but removed it long enough to say, "Okay."

McSwain glanced around. There were no trees in the yard and no other children in sight. With the sun slamming the earth like an anvil, he wondered what exactly Susan Walmsley expected her daughter to do.

"C'mon inside," said Susan. "I don't know a whole hell of a lot—he kept to himself pretty much—but I'll tell you whatever I can."

They entered a cheaply furnished living room with a couple of generic landscapes—cutesy cabin in the woods, rustic cottage with morning glory vines. An exercise bike sat in front of the TV, and McSwain noticed a couple of sets of dumbbells lined up beside the red recliner. Two huge balls, the kind McSwain knew were popular with chiropractors, rested under a window.

As if responding to McSwain's unasked question, Susan said, "Reason I'm here at home, I'm an aerobics and tae kwan do instructor and a personal trainer. Most of my work's in the late afternoon, early evening. Believe it or not, this is a pretty good town for promoting physical fitness. God knows, it's too hot to do anything outdoors, so anybody wants to stay in shape they join a gym, take classes, get a trainer." She made a slight downward gesture with one hand and, either consciously or not, flexed her abdomen, which immediately contracted into abs worthy of a fitness infomercial. "Well, go ahead and sit down."

McSwain took the recliner next to a door that connected into the kitchen, Susan settled herself on the sofa, and Capshaw straddled an exercise ball.

"Those are great for your back," Susan offered.

"Yeah, I'm thinking of getting one for my office." She bounced up and down a couple of times, then said, "So you know Patrick DeKooning? How long since he put his house on the market?"

"Well, he didn't really put it on the market."

"How long since he moved away then?"

A look of confusion crossed Susan's hard features before she said, "You don't know, do you?"

"Know what?" said McSwain.

"Patrick's dead."

"What?"

"He killed himself Christmas Day."

Almost a month before Virginia and Mandy were attacked, thought McSwain. He looked at Jenna, saw she was obviously thinking the same thing.

"See, reason I didn't want Hannah in here while we talked is that she doesn't know. It was two days after Christmas, for God's sake, and here's cop cars up and down the block, like all the fugitives on *America's Most Wanted* were holed up in that house. After I found out what the deal was, I told Hannah a burglar alarm must've gone off and I took her to spend the rest of the day at her dad's place. I mean, she's just a kid. What's she need to know about this kinda thing, right?"

"You ever tell her?" asked Capshaw.

Susan shook her head. "Someday maybe, when she's older." She shrugged. "Or maybe some nice people with kids will move in next door and she'll forget all about Patrick."

"How long have you lived here, Mrs. Walmsley?"

"Coupla years."

"And was Patrick DeKooning living next door when you moved here?"

"Yeah, I think he'd been here a few years already."

"Did you know him well enough to have any idea why he would have done this?" asked McSwain. "As far as you knew, was he in any trouble with the law?"

"Patrick? No, he seemed like a pretty straight arrow." She chuckled and sat back further on the sofa, getting more comfortable with the situation, folding her hands on her washboard belly. "For someone who was gay, that is."

"Gay?" Capshaw gave up on the ball and took a seat in the chair next to it. "Who said anything about De-Kooning being gay?"

"Well, not that he ever came out and said as much, but I can put two and two together."

McSwain leaned forward. "What do you mean, Mrs. Walmsley?"

"Well, first off, the guy's, what, in his mid-forties and not married and he has no women come to see him that

I ever saw. Second, he doesn't, you know, notice women. Always kept his eyes at face level, know what I mean?"

"He never made a pass at you, is that it?"

"Not once. And I sunbathe in some bikinis that would have most guys leaning out the window with their tongues hanging out." She reached down and adjusted the halter top, tugging at the tiny bow that tied underneath her breasts. McSwain found he had no difficulty keeping his gaze at face level and felt extremely certain he wasn't gay.

Anxious to move the conversation along, he said, "You said he didn't appear to have women visitors. You mean he had men coming and going?"

"No, he didn't have men visitors either that I ever saw. Only person I ever saw over there was this older lady—had the same kind'a long, hound-dog face as he did, so I figured she had to be his mom."

"Did DeKooning have a job, Mrs. Walmsley?"

"Yeah, he worked at the meat-packing plant in El Centro. Hey, look, what's this about? He owe somebody money or something? His face on a Wanted poster somewhere?"

Capshaw leaned forward, scribbling notes and speaking at the same time. "You called DeKooning a straight arrow, Mrs. Walmsley. Why?"

"'Cause all he seemed to do was go to work and putter around in his garden on weekends. That's another reason I figured him for gay—I mean, single guy puttering around with his snapdragons and his marigolds—come on."

"Did he ever mention anyone named Virginia or Billie?" Capshaw asked.

"No. Look, I knew the guy; I didn't say I conversed with him beyond 'How ya doin', hot day we're having,' that kinda thing." She reached over and rolled the ball Capshaw had been sitting on over toward her, used it to prop her feet up. "Except for the one time when—"

They heard what sounded like the top of a soda can being popped and dishes rattling around. "'Scuse me a sec," said Susan, getting up. From the gist of the somewhat one-sided conversation that followed, McSwain gathered Hannah had come in the back door and was in the kitchen making herself a snack, which apparently she wasn't supposed to be doing.

A minute or two later, Susan came back into the living room and straddled the exercise ball, legs wide, rocking back and forth in an agitated way. "She eats too damn much," she said, "and the kids at school make fun of her. I told her this summer she was going to slim down, like it or not. Hard to do that, though, when you're eating a sandwich with an inch of peanut butter and jelly on it. Now school starts in two weeks and not only has she not lost any weight, she's put on pounds." She tapped her own cast-iron-looking midriff. "It's not like I don't set a good example of staying fit, but on the other hand, she may feel like she'll never measure up to her mom, so why even try, know what I'm saying?"

"It's tough following in the footsteps of perfection," Capshaw said, keeping a straight face.

"You said most of your interaction with DeKooning was pretty mundane, but there was one exception?" prodded McSwain.

"Yeah, right. When he came over here about the brooch."

"The brooch?"

"I think he must've stolen it."

"What happened?"

"Hang on a sec." Susan got up, checked the kitchen, which apparently was empty, then came back and sat down on the sofa.

"Well, Patrick used to give Hannah little gifts occasionally. Nothing expensive, just cheap, discount-rack-at-Target type stuff. Like one time he gave her a little bracelet with charms, and another time it was a pair of earrings—cute, too—they were little yellow-and-blue plastic parrots. Then about a month before Christmas, I guess it was, Patrick shows up at the door. He says he hates doing this, but he needs to ask Hannah if he can have his brooch back. I say, 'What brooch.' And what ten-year-old kid wears brooches anyway—they went out with gramophone records.

"So I went and asked Hannah and she brought it out. Gorgeous piece of jewelry, not the tacky junk he'd been giving her, but an expensive piece. She didn't know the difference, of course. After he gave it to her, she'd just stuck it back in a drawer somewhere and forgot about it. I mean, she sure as hell wasn't going to wear it. So Patrick apologizes all over the place and says this really belongs to somebody else, but he thought they didn't want it anymore so it'd be okay to give it to Hannah. Well, he was wrong and apparently this person did want their brooch, and now he had to ask Hannah to give it back. Which she did, of course. I mean, I'da known about it, I'd never have allowed her to keep it."

"So the brooch was stolen," McSwain said.

"Yeah, you know what I think—I think it was his mother's and he kind of snuck it out of her jewelry drawer, thinking she'd never know, and she did notice and raised hell over it. So then he was up the creek and had to try and get it back."

"Between that incident and Christmas, did you see his mother come back to the house at all?" asked Capshaw.

"Didn't see her, no. Maybe she was still pissed at him—if it was her jewelry he stole. Who knows?"

"And he killed himself Christmas Day."

"But they didn't find the body till two days later. A UPS guy came by with a package to sign for and he saw the body in the living room."

"He shot himself?" McSwain said.

"Nope." She tilted her head to one side and pantomimed yanking on a rope. "Hanged himself from a beam in the ceiling."

For a moment there was almost complete silence during which McSwain tried to envision Patrick DeKooning's last moments—the self-pity he might have felt as he secured a rope over the beam at a time of year when everyone else was hanging ornaments on Christmas trees, fully aware of the nasty surprise awaiting whomever found him. He tried to feel sorry for such a lonely and terrible end to what must have been a lonely and terrible life, but years of dealing with the sordid, dark, sometimes vile side of humanity had depleted his store of compassion when it came to perpetrators like DeKooning. Especially like DeKooning.

He broke the silence, saying, "Mrs. Walmsley, were

you aware that Patrick DeKooning served time in prison
for the kidnapping and rape of a fourteen-year-old El
Centro girl?"

The nut-brown skin over Susan Walmsley's cheekbones took on a sallow sheen as every hint of chatty
self-absorption drained from her eyes. "You're saying
Patrick was a . . . a pedophile?"

McSwain let the awful echo of the word hang in the
silence a moment before saying, "A pedophile, a rapist,
and a kidnapper."

"No, that can't be. There must be some mistake."

"There's no mistake, Mrs. Walmsley."

"But he and Hannah, they were friends. I mean if . . .
if he . . . what you say he was . . . then Hannah . . ."
Her voice dwindled down to a grainy whisper, then disappeared entirely, and her eyes seemed to look inward
as all the awful implications and possibilities rolled past.

There was a pleading in her voice as she said, "You're
sure there's no chance you're wrong?"

McSwain shook his head. "No, Mrs. Walmsley, we're
not wrong. I'm sorry to have to tell you, but it's the
truth."

"Jesus."

"You might want to sit down with Hannah and have
a talk about her friendship with Patrick, the gifts he gave
her. Or have her see a therapist, in case there're things
she needs to talk about."

Susan nodded, but her whole body seemed to sag so
that, for a moment, she looked in danger of sliding right
off the sofa onto the floor. Finally she blinked hard,
maybe banishing whatever images were wheeling past
behind her eyes, and shook her head as though waking
from a deep, drugged sleep. "No, I don't think he, you
know, did anything. He really seemed like a very nice
man. How long ago was it when . . . when what you say
he did happened?"

"He was twenty-four."

"Oh." She gave a nervous laugh and let out her breath
with a soft whoosh. "That long ago . . . that means he
could've changed. He could've, you know, outgrown it."

"Or found God or a grown-up girlfriend or had himself castrated," said Capshaw, "but you can't count on any of those things."

"Were there any other gifts that you know about?" McSwain asked.

Susan rocked back on the sofa. Deep ridges crawled across her forehead as she shut her eyes, thinking.

"Just the one time, back last summer, he gave her a little bottle of perfume."

McSwain saw Jenna flinch and felt a sick coldness crawl through his own stomach.

"Mrs. Walmsley," Capshaw said, "Hannah needs to talk to someone about her visits to DeKooning. A therapist who specializes in sex—"

"Don't say it," hissed Susan.

"Will you call someone? Will you promise me that you'll get help for your daughter?"

The three of them sat in silence for a long moment. Finally Susan nodded mutely, her eyes still tightly shut.

They saw themselves to the door.

"So it couldn't've been DeKooning in Virginia's car," Capshaw said as they drove back toward San Diego. "But it *was* somebody who knew her well enough that she'd have confided about the perfume. Which points to Leland or Phil Clarion or even Tibbs, if you think it's possible that the man who raped Virginia and the one who tried to kill you and Mandy last night are two different guys."

"I don't think so," McSwain said, and told her the theory he'd been keeping from Mandy, that the man at Torrey Pines hadn't intended on killing her there, but on abducting her and taking her somewhere else. "Which makes me wonder if he was really interested in eliminating a possible witness—a witness to something that happened months ago, in the dark, with him wearing a stocking over his face—or just out for some sick fun and payback."

"You mean because Mandy's the one who fucked him up and got away?"

"Yeah, that makes her unfinished business, an obsession. How can he go after new victims when a woman who should have been dead is still out there?"

"Meaning you think our guy is definitely the Boy Scout?"

"Well, Paris told us Forensics found perfume in the fabric of Gibson's underpants. That sure points to the Boy Scout, as far as I can see."

"And he'd have as much reason to consider Virginia unfinished business as Mandy. He raped her, yeah, but she's still alive. Doesn't that put her in the same category?"

"At this point, I'm not sure what category Virginia fits into," said McSwain.

"What do you mean?"

"I was thinking about the conversation we had driving up here. About why DeKooning settled a half hour up the road from El Centro instead of going someplace where no one would know him."

"Because people are creatures of habit?"

"You said something about people who get caught up in a sick cycle, like a woman who grows up with an abusive father and then, as an adult, spends years with an abusive husband or a succession of them. It's almost like the trauma sucks them back in, compels them to repeat it."

"Are you saying that what happened in January, that Virginia might have unwittingly set it in motion by . . . I don't know, talking about DeKooning's assault with somebody sick enough to want to then act it out?"

"I'm not sure what I'm saying at this point. But when Phil Clarion was tiptoeing around whatever it was Virginia wanted him to do sexually—"

"I figured he meant a threesome with another guy maybe, something like that," Capshaw said.

"Yeah, I did, too, but now I'm wondering. You take a guy like DeKooning who's into little girls, and almost everything I've ever read or heard about that, it's that pedophiles aren't just born; they're created by the people who molest them when they're kids. Maybe DeKooning created something inside Virginia. Maybe she has a compulsion, too."

"Jesus, you think the reason she didn't go to the police . . . it wasn't fear of her attacker, but complicity?"

"All I know right now is that I want to have another talk with Phil Clarion. Go with me?"

"Sorry, but you better drop me off at my car. I want to go over to the motel, check on Mandy."

"You think she'll drink?"

"Who knows what anybody will do. And yeah, I know I can't control what she does. But I thought maybe if I kept the kids, she could get to a meeting, admit she's had a slip and share about it."

"After what she went through last night?"

He hit the brakes as traffic slowed to a crawl, four lanes merging into two to avoid an accident between a delivery truck and a Porsche in the right lanes.

"All the more reason," said Capshaw. "Besides, she talks about what happened, even a little of it, maybe somebody else will stay sober."

"Kind of the opposite of Stromquist's philosophy, huh?"

"Do unto others before they do unto you? Yeah, I'd say." She twisted around to see the wreck blocking the lanes, three police cruisers already on the scene, a man in a neck brace being loaded into an ambulance, a woman sitting in the cab of the truck with her head in her hands.

"I hope I'm wrong about Mandy, that's all."

"Wrong? How so?"

She gestured toward the passenger window. "That her life's like that—that mess out there. And it's never going to change. One accident after another and the next one just waiting to happen."

Chapter 28

McSwain drove Capshaw back to her car, and she headed over to the motel to check on Mandy. He then took 8 north to San Diego State, located the Vidmar Building, but found Phil Clarion's office locked. He waylaid a student carrying an armload of art-history books, who told him Dr. Clarion was teaching a class a few rooms down the hall.

When he heard Clarion's voice from outside the door, McSwain charged into the room in much the same way he'd once entered his brother's eighth-grade class and given the bully who'd been harrassing Andrew a face-plant onto his own desk. Clarion was standing, just walking back from the window where he might have paused to look out at the soft mound of cumulus clouds that, from this distance, seemed to be just touching down on the Coronado Bridge. In midsentence when McSwain marched in, he was saying something about a sixteenth-century artist named Caravaggio who evidently had done time in prison when he wasn't painting canvases of saints. Two dozen or so undergraduates listened with varying degrees of attention, from one raptly wide-eyed girl up front to a guy nodding off in the back.

Clarion's eyebrows canted when McSwain walked in, but he continued talking, unfazed.

McSwain walked up to him and said in a low voice, "We need to talk in your office. Now."

Very slowly, as though he were explaining the situation to a blind man who'd just blundered in by mistake, Clarion said, "I am in the middle of teaching a class."

"So I see."

"If you must, come back later."

McSwain was getting tired of whispering. "I don't think you heard me," he said in a normal voice. "I said *now*."

He and Clarion now had the room's undivided attention. The guy taking a nap in the back came back to life, and a couple of kids pulled out cell phones just in case, McSwain presumed, a fistfight or something worse broke out and they needed to summon authorities. Or maybe they were just getting ready to call their friends.

"How dare you," hissed Clarion. "How dare you come into my classroom like this and interrupt me when—"

"Okay, that's it with the lecture," McSwain said. He grabbed Clarion's wrist and twisted it behind him at the same time he clamped his other hand on the back of the man's neck and shoved him toward the door.

"What the hell are you doing? How dare you . . ."

McSwain turned his head toward the classroom. "Dr. Clarion will be back to finish up with Caravaggio in five minutes. Consider this a study break."

Inside Clarion's office, McSwain slammed the door and shoved Clarion into a chair.

"McSwain, I ought to have you arrested," the man sputtered, "barging into my classroom, putting your hands on me—what do you imagine my students are thinking? How do you expect me to keep their respect?"

"They're thinking it's great to get a break from class. Their respect you keep by going back and acting like nothing's happened. Because nothing *has* happened— yet. All I wanted was to talk. You're the one who didn't have the time."

Apparently adrenaline affected Clarion in much the same way as a double Scotch. Since he took McSwain to his office, he hadn't stopped babbling, alternating outrage at McSwain with predictions of dire consequences for having physically ejected him from his classroom.

When he started into another rant, McSwain banged a fist on the edge of the desk so hard that a couple of books lying close by lifted an inch into the air.

"Shut up!"

Clarion's mouth knit into a petulant seam, like a kid

about to unleash a tantrum, but he nodded finally and sat back in his chair. "What the hell is it you want?"

"The other afternoon you told us that you and Virginia were, and I quote, sexually incompatible. You said after you got married you wanted to please her, but that she was asking too much, more than any normal man would countenance. When you wouldn't say more, I assumed you meant she wanted other partners, maybe for you to watch her with them or participate, something like that. Now I think I assumed wrong. What was she into, Clarion? What was it she wanted that you thought a normal man couldn't be expected to go along with?"

Clarion gave a long-suffering sigh. "This is none of your business, McSwain. If you want to know my ex-wife's intimate secrets, I suggest you take it up with her."

"But I'm not, am I? I'm taking it up with you. And I'm asking you one more time, What was it she wanted?"

"Fuck you, McSwain. I don't have to tell—"

Before he could finish, McSwain reached over, grabbed Clarion by the knot of his burgundy tie, and yanked him halfway across the desk.

"Yeah, Dr. Clarion, you do have to tell me, because I'm not leaving until you do. And this could be a very long afternoon."

Sweat glistened in the silver at Clarion's temples. His eyes bulged and the color in his face began to rival that of his tie.

"All right, McSwain. Jesus, let go."

McSwain released his hold. Clarion plopped back into the chair, panting and loosening his tie.

"Virginia asked me once never to reveal her erotic tastes to anyone, and naturally I assumed I'd have no trouble honoring that request. The idea of being under duress never entered my mind. However, under these circumstances . . ." He paused and tilted his head back, gave a rueful laugh. "Ah, well, not my fault. This is more than I bargained for."

"Go on," said McSwain.

"Before we were married, Virginia made all sorts of

oblique references to enjoying various forms of unorthodox sex. I assumed she meant your more commonplace forms of unorthodox sex, if you will, doing it outdoors or in the back pew of a church, hell, hanging from a trapeze, whatever. I'm not averse to a little spice in my lovemaking. I figured I'd have no problem accommodating her.

"At first, we actually did those things—well, perhaps not the trapeze—but we were, in my estimation, a sexually adventurous couple. Then I could see Virginia was getting bored." He paused, consulted the fingernails of one hand as though suddenly searching for dirt. "I wanted to please her, you understand. I loved her. I asked her what would make her happy, what would excite her. At the very worst, I expected her to say she wanted other men, and I was bracing for that, so when she told me what she wanted, I suppose at first I felt almost relieved."

"Because it wasn't other men she wanted, was it?"

Clarion shook his head. "You seem to be ahead of me on this. What she wanted was for me to beat her, really beat her, rip her clothing off, humiliate her. She wanted to be tied up, and she was very specific about it. Not spread-eagled to a bed like you see in porn movies, but tied standing up, her arms behind her. What we needed, you see, was a column, and the designers of our home hadn't seen fit to put one in our bedroom, so I had to improvise. I installed an iron ring in the wall and I tied her to that. She wanted me to talk dirty to her, and again, she was very specific. She did everything but write out a script and hand it to me to memorize. Once she was tied up, she wanted to be sprayed with perfume, not just a puff here and there, but over her whole body, her crotch, her face, everywhere. God, you couldn't get the smell out. Our bedroom smelled like there'd been an explosion in a Chanel factory."

Clarion's eyes glazed over and he gazed at the wall behind McSwain's head. McSwain thought it was as though he were seeing what he was describing, Virginia the helpless victim and, at the same time, the puppetmaster who made the rules and set the limits, who orchestrated every slap, every obscenity, who choreographed her own violation with the deft attention to detail of a society matron organizing a ball.

"So you did what she wanted?"

"At first, yes. I didn't enjoy it. I felt uncomfortable and cruel and a bit silly and . . . this is the hardest part to explain . . . I felt badgered. Here I was playing the role of the rapist, the sadist, the thug that she's begging for mercy from, and yet the whole time she's subtly giving me orders and cues. She's making . . . *demands.* I'd hit her, and she'd moan and I'd do it again and she'd say 'harder,' so I'd try to hit her harder, but how could I . . . I mean, I always held back."

McSwain thought about the makeup Jenna'd found in the condo in Mexico. "She got bruised sometimes, though, didn't she? And wore heavy makeup to cover it."

Clarion nodded. "I hated hitting her. But sometimes when I didn't do it the way she wanted, she'd look at me with . . . God, I still remember . . . this look of such loathing and contempt. Like I was nothing. Jesus, I tell you, once when I was in college I went to bed with this girl I'd been aching to fuck, and maybe it was nerves, whatever, I couldn't get it up. And I tell you the feeling I had then, being twenty years old and impotent with this girl I wanted so much, this was nothing—*nothing*—compared to how I used to feel when she gave me that look.

"Virginia kept saying I was holding back, that eventually I'd find the whole scene as big a turn-on as she did. She said all men get off on sexual power trips—some just repress it. She implied I wasn't enough of a man if I didn't find this incredibly erotic. But how could I? Knowing what I knew about her—that she was getting me to reenact this horrendous thing that had happened to her?"

A note of anguish crept into Clarion's voice. "You know what it reminded me of? A Jewish man I read about once—the only way he could have an orgasm was by pretending he was in a camp and his partner was a Nazi."

"Last January," said McSwain, "did you decide to

show Virginia that you were man enough? Did you follow her, hide in the back of her car, and show her what it was like when she wasn't the one controlling the action?"

"What are you talking about?"

"Or maybe it was consensual? Maybe it was a game you and Virginia had played before, making it more realistic every time. You just hadn't counted on another person getting involved."

"I don't—"

"The way I see it, only a very few people would have known about Virginia's sex fantasies. You being one of them."

"What about DeKooning? Did you ask him?"

"He killed himself before the attack on Virginia ever took place. Leaving you, Leland, and anybody caught up in Virginia's fantasy as likely candidates for the man who hid in the backseat of Virginia's car and later raped her."

"You told the police this?"

"Not yet."

"Jesus." He leaned forward and ran both hands through his hair with such savagery that flecks of dandruff leaped from his head like lice. "You've got to believe me, McSwain: I didn't assault Virginia. What we did together when we were married, I didn't even enjoy it." He looked up, and McSwain was surprised to see tears running along the crevices on either side of his nose. "I'm just a regular man with a normal sex drive. She was the one who insisted I do those things. *I* was the one who got hurt."

McSwain's cell phone rang while he was descending the stairs between the third and second floors of the Vidmar Building. He yanked it off his belt, hit talk, and barked hello as he descended the stairs.

"The necklace Wynn was wearing—I got a more detailed description."

He recognized Hank Paris's voice and stopped on a landing, leaning against the wall as a stampede of students thundered past him.

"What'd you find?"

"This Carol Yates who was the last person to see Wynn alive—she got picked up last night in I.B. for soliciting. I sent one of my people over to talk to her again."

"And?"

"She says what Wynn had on that night, what she always wore, was a jade pendant about the size of a silver dollar. Symbol for the Hindu word *Om*."

"*Om*? Like what the Hare Krishnas chant?"

"You say so; I don't know what the hell they chant."

"What did it look like?"

"I'm coming to that. Detective who interviewed actually had her draw him a picture. Looks like a three with a couple of curlicues, like a comet, on the right. And the very end of the comet's chipped off. She musta dropped it or something."

"Would you say it looks like the number three?"

"Yeah. That mean anything to you?"

"Maybe everything."

Chapter 29

Helen Croft's home was a two-story stucco with a Spanish-tile roof and a high wooden fence running around the property. From what McSwain could see, it was the only home in the upscale neighborhood with a large, sloping backyard, and he guessed that she, or whoever had built the house, had purchased two lots together. The house sat about halfway up a steep, curving hill lined with silk oaks and elegant old magnolias. McSwain parked several houses up on the opposite side of the street, where he could observe any comings and goings at the front of the house.

He didn't see Moxley's car, but there was an oversize blue SUV in the carport that he assumed must belong to Helen, if only because the dimensions of the vehicle seemed appropriate to her own. While he waited, clouds gathering on the western horizon smothered what little light remained, and darkness converged so quickly that McSwain had the impression of a lamp being unplugged. In Croft's home, lights came on in three first-floor windows, which he guessed to be the living room and possibly a kitchen or dining area.

Fifteen minutes after he'd begun his surveillance, Capshaw drove past, kept going, and turned right at the bottom of the hill. She circled around and parked higher up the hill, several car lengths behind McSwain, who got out of his car, walked quickly to Capshaw's vehicle, and got in the passenger side.

"What do you mean, there might not be anybody on the desk?" she was saying into her cell phone, "I want to make sure that she gets this message." She swore and hung up, then turned to McSwain. "I waited for Mandy in the motel room for the past two hours. She still hasn't come in."

"Her things, were they still there?"

"The bag with the kids' stuff was gone, but she left everything else."

"So maybe they just got bored and went somewhere. The zoo, I don't know."

"We told her to stay put."

"That means something?"

"I don't like this, Ian. She's got the kids with her. What if she goes on a binge?"

"You can't control what other people do. You've told me that enough times."

"You're right," she said grudgingly. "So fill me in. What've we got here?"

"Croft's in there, but I haven't seen any sign of Moxley. That doesn't mean he's not with her, though."

Capshaw pulled out her cell phone. "You still have Moxley's phone number?"

McSwain took out the card Moxley had given him and read Capshaw the number while she punched it into the phone. Apparently Helen Croft answered, and Capshaw pretended to be calling from a dentist's office to reschedule an appointment Moxley had made. She mouthed *Not there* at McSwain, told Helen Croft she'd call back the next day, and clicked off the phone.

"Unless she's covering for him, I think she's alone."

"Good enough," said McSwain.

They got out of the car and walked down the hill toward Croft's house in the deepening dark. As they turned up the walk, McSwain saw a stone Buddha, about a foot high, nestled against the trunk of a jacaranda tree in the front yard. A bird had crapped on the Buddha's head, giving the appearance of a small, rakishly tilted skullcap above the closed, slanted eyes and serene visage.

He rang the bell, and a few moments later Helen Croft opened the door. Her hair was down today and it flowed over her shoulders in a rich cascade of auburn. She carried a cane and wore an emerald caftan with silver stitching along the neckline and sleeves and matching slippers. A treasure trove of silver bangles and rings bedecked her chubby fingers and wrists.

She blinked at Capshaw and McSwain. Then recognition set in, and deep furrows bisected her forehead as she looked from one to the other.

"We're sorry to bother you," McSwain started, "but—"

Her small, dark hazel eyes seemed to widen to the size of marbles, and she said in a breathy voice, "Has something happened to Richard?"

"No," McSwain said, "but we need to talk to him."

"Can we come in?" Capshaw asked.

"Oh, of course, of course," Helen said, stepping back from the door. "I'm sorry, but you startled me. I was doing my breathing exercises. Come in, please."

She led them into an entrance hall decorated with photos of people McSwain presumed to be family members, a few of Helen and Richard together.

"Why would you think something's happened to Richard?" Capshaw asked when they were inside.

"Well, when you both showed up at the door, looking so grim, if you don't mind my saying so, I thought maybe you were here to give me bad news. You know, like cops do on TV."

"I'm sorry," said McSwain, "I'm not following you."

"Well, I know you and Richard are working together on that case, and he said he'd be on a stakeout with you tonight, so I just thought . . . if he isn't with you, then where is he?"

"We were hoping you could tell us," Capshaw said.

Helen stared at her. "Your voice—you called here a few minutes ago."

"Ms. Croft," said McSwain, "the other day when we met, you were wearing a very distinctive pendant. I believe it was a Hindu symbol."

Helen nodded and smiled "You mean *Om*?"

"Could we see it?"

"See it?" There was suddenly a hesitancy in the woman's manner that hadn't been there before. "I don't understand. Why do you want to see it?"

"If you don't mind, Ms. Croft, this will only take a minute," Capshaw said. "Then we'll be out of your hair."

"That doesn't answer my question."

"Ms. Croft, if you want to help Richard, you'll go get it."

Helen Croft's eyes narrowed. A fleck of mascara, dark as soot, clung to the end of one lash. "Richard wasn't going to be on stakeout with you tonight, was he?"

"No," said McSwain.

She smoothed the folds of her caftan, her slender bracelets tinkling like wind chimes, and swallowed hard, an action that made her chin disappear into the folds of her neck. She seemed to be trying to compose herself.

"I'll let you look at the pendant, but I still don't see the point of this," she said finally. Planting her cane ahead of her on each step, she moved slowly to the end of the hall and began a laborous climb up a flight of stairs. She was gone for a long time, and when she returned her eyes looked different, smaller and slightly swollen, as though she'd had a brief, hard cry once out of their sight. She handed the pendant to McSwain, who examined it and passed it to Capshaw.

Helen held out her hand. "Are you satisfied? Can I have it back now?"

"Did Richard give you this?" asked McSwain.

Helen Croft's pink, pouty lower lip started to vibrate. Her nostrils flared rapidly and then her whole face seemed to collapse on itself and crumple inward, like a ripe apple withering with age under time-lapse photography. For a few seconds her throat worked silently. Then words started to gush out.

"I knew Richard would get into trouble over this necklace. He told me where he got it, and I knew it was wrong, but I swear to you, he's never done anything like this before. It's my fault anyway. I've been a student of Vedanta for years, and jewelry with Sanskrit symbols holds a special fascination for me."

"There's a chipped place down at the bottom," said McSwain. "Didn't it seem strange to you that Richard would give you damaged goods?"

"No, not at all. It's still a beautiful pendant. Look, I

hope you aren't going to cause trouble for Richard. This was just an impulse thing on his part."

Capshaw said, "An impulse thing? Ms. Croft, what is it that you're referring to?"

Helen gulped and seemed to lean a little more heavily on the cane. "Because Richard stole the necklace, isn't that why you asked to see it? He told me he happened to be in the house one day and he saw it and knew it was something I'd love and that it would never be missed, that it was probably something some woman left behind making a fast departure from that awful man's bed."

McSwain held up a hand. "Who are you talking about? What awful man?"

"Why, the son, of course; he was always picking on Richard, first one thing and then another, and Richard didn't even work for him. Richard found the necklace in his house. Josh Stromquist."

McSwain's cell phone rang just as he was trotting back up the hill toward his car—Capshaw, who had reached her vehicle a few yards up ahead and was calling from there. "Ian, I just got the strangest message from Mandy's mother. She called to say she thinks it sucks that you and I would tell Mandy to go into hiding and not to let anyone, including her own mother, know where they're going to be."

"Go into hiding? What's she talking about?"

"I don't know. Kelly's not answering the phone over at Mandy's place. But obviously somebody called and talked Mandy into leaving the motel with the kids, saying it was our idea."

There was silence on the line for a moment, then Capshaw said, "Ian, you don't think . . . Why would Moxley have told Helen he was going to be on stakeout with us tonight?"

"Any number of reasons—he's got something going on behind her back, he's trying to impress her that he's moving up in the world from being Stromquist's lackey—or he's the one who took that necklace off of Harriet Wynn's dead body and now he's convinced Mandy to meet him someplace with her kids."

"Jesus."

"On the other hand, if Richard told Helen the truth about stealing that necklace from Josh's house—"

"Then Josh is our guy."

Chapter 30

Mandy got the kids out of the car and squinted up at the carriage house nestled amid a grove of eucalyptus trees. A wooden trellis covered an entire side of the house, and the ivy covering it looked so green and crisp that the leaves reminded Mandy of artfully folded hundred-dollar bills. Of which she was sure it had taken more than she'd seen in her lifetime to construct this house.

"You live here?"

Virginia squatted down and felt under the porch rail until she located a magnetized box that held the spare key. "No, this is my stepson's house. The place we passed on the way in, that's where Leland and I live."

"Jesus, I thought it was a hotel."

Virginia laughed until she realized Mandy wasn't joking. "Leland and I try to keep our address private, but because of the success of the book, a lot of reporters and other people have come here, Leland's private clients, for instance, so I thought Josh's place might be better if we're going to, you know, lie low for a bit."

"Your stepson, he doesn't mind us using his place?"

"He's not here, is he? I won't tell him if you don't."

"Ian said the secretary told him your husband gave a talk last night, and you and your stepson went with him."

"Yeah, Leland spoke in Burbank, and I drove up to join him." She rolled her eyes. "Boring as ever. When will I learn? So I decided to skip Leland's book signing tonight and come home. That's when I got the message from Ian that you were in danger. He said I should bring you here as soon as possible and not to ask any questions."

"I wonder why Jenna didn't say anything when she called this afternoon."

"Maybe she didn't know. Ian sounded rushed, like he couldn't talk. He just said, 'Get Mandy over to your place and the two of you stay together.'"

She turned the key in the lock and they went in. Emily immediately pulled free of Mandy's hand and sprinted off to explore. "Em, come back," Mandy called. "Oh, Lord, I hope she doesn't break anything."

"Don't worry about it," said Virginia. "Come on back to the kitchen. I don't know about you, but I could use a stiff drink."

"Nothing alcoholic."

"Don't tell me you're a teetotaler now?"

"Yeah."

"Then I'll have the stiff drink and I'll make lemonade for you and the kids. That okay?"

"That'd be fine." While Virginia took some glasses and a blender down and went about making the drinks, Mandy looked around the ultramodern kitchen with its chrome fixtures and butcher-block table, everything as pristine-looking as though no cooking had ever been done here.

Virginia filled the blender with water and then poured in what looked like enough sugar for a large cake. Way too much sugar, Mandy thought—maybe this was the first time she'd ever made lemonade—but she didn't want to be rude by saying anything.

Dakota squirmed in Mandy's arms, and she put him down, then looked around and realized Emily wasn't in sight. "Em!" She stood up. "'Scuse me a sec. I gotta find her."

"She's okay," said Virginia. "I'm sure Josh doesn't have anything she can break."

Mandy made a face. "You don't know Emily. She loves to take things apart. Probably grow up to be a brain surgeon or something."

Virginia smiled and started the blender as Mandy went out into the hall. She found Emily giggling as she bounced up and down in a leather armchair. Mandy grabbed her by the hand and led her back into the kitchen.

"Sure you don't want a real drink?" said Virginia, who was filling a highball glass from a bottle of Wild Turkey. Mandy felt her mouth go dry and her throat close up with something very close to unrequited lust as she imagined the sweet, burning bite of the alcohol.

"No, thanks, lemonade's fine."

Emily went over to the refrigerator and started opening and closing the door—*ka-bam, ka-bam*—peering inside each time as though expecting her favorite food to appear by magic.

"Stop doing that, Em. It's annoying."

Virginia removed the top from the blender and filled three juice glasses, one for Mandy and one for each of the kids. She then opened the pantry door next to the stove, wrinkling her face with distaste. "The kids must be hungry. I was going to fix us something to eat, but I swear, when it comes to food, unless you can put it in a blender and mix it with booze, it's not here."

"Young guys, you know how they can be."

"He hired a Mexican girl to cook for him a few months back, but I have a feeling the only cooking was what went on in the bedroom."

Mandy smiled, sipping her lemonade. "Maybe we should call Ian and Jenna, let them know we got here okay."

"Good idea." Virginia gazed into her highball glass, letting the amber liquid slosh alluringly against the ice cubes, before downing half of it in one swallow. "Maybe we'll get food sent over later. I know Josh keeps a whole drawer of takeout menus somewhere."

Watching Virginia drink activated Mandy's thirst. She drank some more lemonade, the sugar granules coating her tongue, thickening it. Noticing Emily was missing, she twisted around in her chair. "Em, stay here where I can see you."

"Relax," said Virginia, as she undid the top button on her silk blouse and stifled a yawn. "I'll go get her."

Mandy looked up at her and saw a second, translucent, Virginia superimposed slightly to the right of the first. The first Virginia was lifting that glorious golden drink and smiling a sleek pink smile that didn't show any teeth. The second, fainter Virginia wasn't smiling at all. Mandy found this very strange.

She blinked a couple of times and the illusion faded. The two Virginias merged back into one.

She started to get up. "No, I'll get Em."

"Shit," said Virginia, putting a hand to her forehead. "I'm not feeling so good all of a sudden."

"What is it?"

"I don't know, just . . . dizzy or something." She laughed weakly. "I knew I shouldn't drink on an empty stomach, but—"

"Maybe you ought to lie down."

"Yeah, I think you're . . . right." She started to stand up, thumped back down hard into the chair, looked at Mandy, and rolled her eyes as though this was too funny.

"Where's the phone?" Mandy said.

"The phone?"

"Something's wrong with me, too. I think maybe we should call someone."

Virginia leaned forward. "I think I'm gonna be sick." Then she looked up at Mandy, her mouth cracking into a lopsided grin. "Hey, that was your line, wasn't it?"

Before Mandy could respond, Emily came running into the kitchen, sneakers careening on the tile floor as she barreled into her mother's arms.

"The man," she said, gasping.

"What man?" Mandy asked. To her own ears, her voice sounded strange and hollow, as if she were a ventriloquist projecting her voice down a well.

"The upside-down man." Emily said. "Why's he upside down?"

"Don't be silly," Mandy said. "Nobody's upside down."

Except me, she thought.

She turned back to Virginia, who had a twin sister now and a double of Dakota on her lap, and thought how interesting it was, amazing actually, that without a drop of alcohol, she felt drunker than she'd ever been in her life. One thing she knew, as the chair melted away from under her and the cool tile floor bumped her cheek: She never, ever wanted to feel this drunk again.

* * *

At the point where he could see the back of Josh Stromquist's house on a rise a few hundred feet away, McSwain pulled off the road and got out of the car. Capshaw had pulled her Suburu off the road about fifty yards ahead of him. Now she got out and beckoned him toward her.

He jogged back to the dirt road and followed it until he came to the brick wall that encircled the rest of the property. A locked steel gate allowed visitors to be buzzed through, but there was no guard. He saw no evidence of surveillance cameras or motion detectors, but rather than take the chance, he stepped back a few feet, took a run at the wall, and got his hands over the top. He clung there for a moment, gathering strength to hoist himself up, then slowly swung his body from side to side until he could get a leg over the top of the wall. From there he pulled himself up and dropped down to the other side.

The carriage house was backed by thick foliage, and he was crouched there, trying to determine the best mode of entry, when he felt the vibration of his cell phone signal a call. He glanced at caller ID, and saw it was Jenna.

"What is it? I'm almost ready to go in."

"Don't."

"Why? What's happened?"

"I just called the Hyatt in Burbank again to be on the safe side. Josh checked out this evening. The desk clerk doesn't remember exactly when, only that it was before six. Ian, if he's come home, he's had plenty of time to get there. He may be inside the house now."

"There's no sign of a car."

"He could have parked it at the main house or inside the garage."

"Look, I'm going to go in. Keep an eye out and let me know if you see anything."

"Sure you don't want backup?"

"You are backup."

"Not if I'm in my car."

"I'll call you if I need help."

"I'll give you twenty minutes. I don't hear from you, I'm coming inside."

He clicked off, came through the trees around the side of the house, and stood in the shadows, surveying it from the front. No cars were parked outside. A couple of lights were on inside, but no more than most people left on when they went away. The moon was in and out from behind the clouds, making him feel more exposed and vulnerable as he skirted the side of the house, checking the back and side windows as he went, trying to determine the best means of entry. He found a sliding glass door that opened onto a sun porch at the rear of the house, tried it, and smiled to himself when he found that the latch was faulty. It popped open easily when he exerted some pressure.

Gun drawn, he moved quietly into the house.

The fragrance.

That was the first thing she was aware of.

Before she even thought of her children, before she tried to figure out why she was on the floor in the dark with her head pounding like someone had used it for an anvil. It was the odor she sometimes smelled in her dreams, the odor she knew she would take to her grave. She had read somewhere that smells could trigger memories more powerfully than anything else. The smell—and the realization that the man who had attacked her had come back—unleashed in her a panic that was almost incapacitating. The odor seemed to seep into her very skin, immobilizing her at the very time she most needed to move. She had to find the kids and get them out of there. But where were they? Where was *she?*

Getting to her feet, she bumped her head on the low ceiling that sloped above her. She put a hand up and followed the slant of it, which went from a height of about five feet to less than four. She remembered the dormer windows on the roof and decided she must be in a storage space in the attic. Someone had carried her up there.

She was groping along the wall for a door when something thin and silky swung against her face. She thought, *Spider,* and lost her balance as she flung herself backward, falling against a stack of boxes. Immediately she realized what she'd felt had to be a string leading to an overhead light. She found it again, but the bulb, if there'd ever been one, had been removed from the overhead socket.

She felt her way back to the boxes and ripped open the top one, hoping to find something to use as a weapon, but she could tell by touch that they contained only clothing—jeans and sweaters and the like.

She then ran her hand along the wall until her fingers hit a vertical crack indicating the edge of a door. There was no knob, which meant that there would be a latch on the outside. Whoever'd put her in here had probably locked her in.

The thought of being entombed in an attic storage space sent her into a spiral of panic that precluded all rational thought. She hurled herself against the door, expecting to be met with resistance, but it gave at once, and she tumbled out hard onto the floor.

She had been right about being in the attic. The room was dark, but she could see the outlines of three dormer windows to her right and leafy branches silhouetted against the pale, pewter glow of moonlight. The branches bent against an unseen breeze and made a hollow scraping sound against the panes.

The perfume was even stronger now, coming not just from her own body but from farther back in the recessed gloom of the attic. As her eyes adjusted to the dimness, she made out objects shoved against the wall, an armchair and a miniature pool table with skis leaning against it, a desk piled high with stacks of books or magazines and a blocky, light-colored rectangle that had to be a small refrigerator.

As she watched, the area of darker shadows next to the refrigerator uncoiled, sprouted limbs, and swiveled around to stare at her with terrified eyes. Adrenaline hummed in her veins, and a small *oomph* sound punched its way through her lips.

A voice scraped so raw with fear that she scarcely recognized it whispered, "Help me."

"Virginia?"

She moved forward toward the white block of the refrigerator, saw Virginia with her arms tied so brutally tight behind her back that the sinews in her forearms quivered like plucked bowstrings. The rope was looped around her wrists, knotted and looped again, then tied around the refrigerator. She was wearing the skirt and blouse Mandy had seen her in earlier, but now the blouse was shredded down the front, strips of it hanging down, revealing the tops of her breasts and the lacy edge of her bra.

Oh, Jesus God, oh, God.

"Mandy, thank God you're okay."

She tried to respond, but her tongue felt cottony and twice its size.

"Untie me. Hurry. Before he comes back."

"Who?"

"The man who raped me. He's here. He drugged us."

"Emily and Dakota, where are they?"

"I don't know. Untie me. We'll find them and get out of here."

Her head swam with a hailstorm of thoughts. She tried to remember the last image she'd had—Virginia sitting at the table with Dakota on her lap, Emily babbling about an upside down man. Where were Emily and Dakota now?

She pushed her arms down between Virginia's hands and the refrigerator and dug at the knot with her fingers, but it was like trying to chip away stone.

Virginia twisted around, struggling against her bonds, making it harder for Mandy to work. Against the pallor of her skin, her eyes looked wild and feverish.

"Wait," hissed Virginia. "In the windowsill . . ." But the words didn't register on Mandy. She clawed at the ropes, gasping as one of her nails snapped off. Blood seeped out and dripped into the palm of her hand.

"It's too tight. I'll get help. I've got to find the kids."

"No! No, listen to me—in the windowsill—behind you—I saw a box cutter—"

"I'm sorry, I've got to . . ." The words died in her throat as a thought hit her like a knife to the neck. The refrigerator Virginia was tied to—what if the children were inside? Like photos she'd once seen in a tabloid paper of children who'd crawled inside an abandoned refrigerator and not been missed, then were found hours later, suffocated and dead. She could see it all with breath-stopping clarity, the assailant carrying Emily and Dakota up the stairs, stuffing them inside an airless, lightless tomb.

She battled her way past boxes and ski equipment to get to the window, where a dusty pair of box cutters lay on the sill. She grabbed them and, with two hasty swipes, freed Virginia's hands, then attacked the ropes encircling the refrigerator. They snapped and slithered to the floor. She yanked the door handle open with both hands and saw—

Behind her the door to the stairwell opened.

—an ancient box of baking soda and a can of Miller Lite.

She whirled around, the air hissing out of her chest, dropping the box cutter to the floor as the silhouette of a man filled the doorway.

McSwain slid the sliding door back and stepped to the side, gun ready. Silence reverberated from the rooms beyond. He crossed the sun porch and went up a short flight of stairs into a darkened kitchen, passed through it into a hallway, where he heard the faint hum of static coming from the first room on the right. Opening the door, he saw the gray-lit rectangle of a big-screen TV and realized he was in Josh's workout room, remembered the exercise equipment and the entertainment center that ran along one wall.

Slowly he moved into the room and ran his hand along the wall, feeling for a light switch. He found one and flicked it on, but nothing happened. Likewise with the standing lamp he bumped into as he made his way around the perimeter of the room. Someone had removed the bulb just as they had apparently removed the bulb from the light fixture overhead.

He flicked on his penlight, and a yellow beam opened up a thread of light in front of him. Checking the TV, he saw that someone had put a video in the VCR and let it run down but hadn't cut off the machine.

He slid the video back into the slot, hit the rewind button, then waited while the images flicked past. At a point he expected to be about midway into the video, he hit the play and mute buttons simultaneously. A picture came on—two young women, one nude, one wearing peach-colored lingerie—having sex with each other. At first he took it to be a standard porn video, grainy and poorly produced, when suddenly a naked Josh Stromquist sauntered into the frame. The girl in the lingerie turned away from her partner, and he pushed his penis into her mouth, hands clasped in her hair as he worked her head to control the rhythm.

McSwain watched long enough to determine that the video was nothing more sinister than amateur porn, then turned the VCR off and continued his search around the perimeter of the room. He was following along the wall opposite the TV when his toe hit something with a force that slammed the bones in his foot together like a multicar pileup on the freeway. Pain jolted into his shin. He shone the penlight ahead of him to see what he'd kicked and immediately launched himself backward, colliding with the wall as adrenaline hammered his bloodstream.

Josh Stromquist hung from the steel inversion machine, feet held in place by the ankle clamps while his limp arms dangled downward, knuckles grazing the floor in a stance that seemed grotesquely simian. He wore gray sweatpants and a loose-fitting black T-shirt that hung down over his face. McSwain reached down and lifted the shirt up with the end of the penlight. A piece of scalp drooped from the crown of his head, and there was an indentation the size of a fist in the exposed skull. A camcorder lay a few inches away—one end of it smashed and covered with blood.

"Long time, no see, Mandy."

The man made a *tsk* sound and cocked his head to one side. He wore jeans and a patterned short-sleeved shirt that hung untucked at his waist. Sweat shone on his broad, high forehead, and a tight, hard smile played on his slit of a mouth. In one hand he held a coil of rope.

"You do remember me, don't you?" He nodded toward Virginia, who shuddered as though she'd been struck and rubbed her wrists together surreptitiously behind her back. "Billie there remembers me *real* well. But then, she got to know me a little better than you did."

"Where are my kids?"

As soon as the words left her mouth, she felt sick at her own stupidity. What had she done? Maybe the man didn't even know the children were there. Maybe after she and Virginia passed out, Emily and Dakota had simply wandered off somewhere, were playing or napping in some other part of the house, oblivious to the danger that their idiot of a mother had just made worse.

"Kids? You think I'd hurt your kids?" The tight smile split into a grin. "Fuck, what kind of a monster you think I am? No, sweetheart, this is between you and me. That kick to the balls you gave me—that hurt for a week when I took a piss."

A drop of sweat slid down his face and clung to his stubbled jaw. When it fell, the silence was so intense, Mandy thought she heard it plink upon the floor.

"Please don't hurt us," Virginia said. Out of the corner of her eye, Mandy saw that she'd picked up the box cutter Mandy had dropped and was holding it by her side.

Virginia was going to fight back. Just knowing that helped Mandy get her wits about her enough to start making a plan. The man was enjoying toying with them now, but sooner or later he'd have to go for one of them. If it was Virginia he came for, she'd try to sprint behind him to the door that led downstairs. If he came toward her, she'd fight back and pray Virginia wouldn't hesitate to use the box cutter.

Even as she was thinking this, the man eased his way forward. There was a jut to his hips, a sauntering self-assurance that frightened Mandy almost as much as the rope that swung from his hand. For an instant his eyes darted toward Virginia and the thin lips pinched into a smile.

Mandy bolted, cutting left toward the door as Virginia moved to the right. The man seemed to lunge for Virginia, then changed his mind and whirled around toward her. His hand closed in her hair, yanking her back so violently that she lost her balance, stumbled, and would have plunged headlong down the stairs if she hadn't thrown her arms out and caught herself against the wall.

An arm that reeked of perfume went around her neck,

and the point of the box cutter popped through the skin in a spot between her skull and her jaw.

"All that guilt you felt for running away and leaving me tied to a tree," Virginia said. "Still sorry you didn't come back to untie me?"

Chapter 31

McSwain was reaching for his cell phone to alert Capshaw that he'd just found Josh's body when he heard a sound that made the hair on the back of his neck prickle. More death rattle than scream, it seemed to come from the upper floor of the house. It was human, but unlike any scream he had ever heard—a tortured shriek that ended with a harsh explosion of air, as though the person making the sound were in the process of suffocating.

Unholstering his .38, he ran for the stairs.

He had reached the second floor and begun a search of the bedrooms when he heard a thumping noise overhead and a repetition of the same cry, only weaker and more abbreviated, and he realized that the noise was coming from the attic. A flight of stairs at the end of the hallway, which he took three at a time, led him to a locked door.

Quietly he went back down half a dozen steps and took a run at the door, landing his foot a few inches above the knob. There was a crack like an ax splitting kindling, and the door buckled inward. He stepped into a low-ceilinged attic whose only light source was a single bare bulb overhead and the moonlight that filtered in through the three dormer windows. A blizzard of dust motes, stirred by the crashing of the door, swirled in the air. The smell of perfume was gaggingly strong.

As his eyes adjusted, he saw Mandy's contorted body in the far corner of the room. She was hog-tied next to some packing crates, her wrists and ankles bound together behind her back. A second rope looped around her neck and then was tied to the first, forcing her to hold a painfully arched position or choke to death. As he approached her, she arched even harder, rocking forward and back. A wet, gargling noise came from her throat.

A few feet away, Virginia cowered against the wall.

"Help us," she said, as Mandy's head jerked back, trying to make eye contact with McSwain.

"Virginia, get away from her. Hands where I can see them. Move!"

She backed off and he rushed toward Mandy, was within three feet of her when Moxley stepped from behind the packing crates and held a small, snub-nosed revolver to her head.

"Drop your gun, Ian, and step away from it."

"Richard—"

"Do it!" He yanked Mandy's head back so that her jaw dropped open, and he forced the barrel of the gun into her mouth. Her eyes rolled in her head and she made a hideous wheezing sound.

"All right, Richard. Take it easy." McSwain held his gun out by the barrel and dropped it on the floor, where Virginia retrieved it.

With his free hand, Moxley removed a handkerchief from his back pocket and used it to wipe the sweat off Mandy's forehead before he removed the gun from her mouth.

"Here, you look like you could use this, too." He wadded the handkerchief and tossed it idly in McSwain's direction, where it unfurled like a tiny parachute and fluttered to the dust-caked floor.

Stepping around Mandy, he came toward McSwain. "And here you tried to tell me being a PI wasn't exciting. That it was all humdrum shit. I think you were just being modest. Too bad you didn't take me on as a partner like I wanted you to—playing PI might've been fun for a little while—till it got boring and I had to start killing people again."

"You're not bright enough to be a PI, Moxley. You had Helen Croft walking around wearing a necklace from one of your victims—how stupid is that?"

"Hey, I'm still free, aren't I? This one over here"—

he gestured toward Mandy—"she shoulda died back last winter, or the other night when I nearly had her in Torrey Pines. And you, Ian, you shoulda suffocated with that robe over your head in St. Francis. But it's all okay, y'know—'cause you're both here now, and you're both dead. Now tell me who the fuck's stupid."

"How'd you find me in the church that night, Richard?"

"You made it so simple. Virginia'd told me where you lived, and I thought I'd cruise by, just take a look. Lo and behold, there you were, walking up the street in the rain, looking like your dog just died. I coulda had a brass band with me that night and you wouldn't have noticed. It was too good an opportunity to miss."

He thought about Capshaw, wondered how much of his twenty minutes was up, how much longer Mandy'd be alive if he didn't do something quickly.

"How long have you been killing women, Richard?"

"Depends on how you look at it. The Boy Scout only started killing a couple years ago—when he hooked up with the lovely Mrs. Stromquist here. Richard Moxley, he killed a girl when he was fifteen, but that was it for the next twenty years." He gave a tight smile, showing no teeth. "Then Virginia came along and reinspired me. Guess you could say she was my muse."

"She inspire you to kill Tibbs, too?"

Moxley laughed. "Come on, Ian. You ever meet anybody who needed killing more than that douche bag?"

"Just you, Richard."

"I'm flattered. Too bad you won't get your wish."

"The police know all about you, Richard. Before I came here, I called a detective I know and told him about the necklace you gave Helen."

"Know what, McSwain? You talk too much. And know something else? If you're here, I bet that means your partner's here, too. Downstairs? Maybe waiting outside? Am I right?"

"She drove up to Burbank to hear Leland's talk," McSwain said. "Have a little chat with Josh afterward."

Moxley lifted an eyebrow. "Did she now? Well, be that as it may, I think I'll go have a look around downstairs. Virginia?"

"Yes?" She turned toward him, her gaze rapt and excited as she cradled McSwain's gun in her hands.

"Keep him here. Shoot him if you have to. He tries anything, looks at you the wrong way, shoot Mandy over there first."

He tucked the revolver inside his belt. "Oh, McSwain, that partner of yours? I find her, I'm gonna bring her up here and put on a little show. I get through with her, it'll take a whole forensics team just to figure out which parts go where."

As he listened to Moxley's receding footfalls, McSwain looked over at Mandy, saw her eyes were clenched tight, head thrown back in an agony of effort to breathe. Her face and body were drenched in sweat. Short, sharp gasps came from her mouth, but the intervals between them seemed to get longer and longer.

He turned to Virginia. "Let me untie her, Virginia. We aren't going anywhere. Moxley comes back, he can shoot us both if he wants to, but at least she doesn't have to suffer."

Virginia shrugged. "*My* suffering didn't bother her until after the fact—when she hired you to find me. She left me to die, remember?"

"Then why did you call me to say Mandy had left that message with Fern, saying she was going to kill herself? Why try to help her?"

"To cover my ass. How could I possibly have known you'd know where to find her? Or that Richard was following her? Besides, Richard didn't want her to kill herself. That would deprive him of the pleasure."

"How about the pleasure he's going to derive from killing you? Your turn's coming, Virginia. You think he's not going to kill you? Why wouldn't he? In his eyes, you're just another victim—killing you's just a longer, more drawn-out process. Or maybe he figures you're actually easier to kill than the others, because so much of you is already dead. Looks to me like your body's the only part of you that escaped from that house in El Centro. The rest of you is still back there. The only time you feel free is when you get to act out what happened and survive it—if you can consider somebody as sick as you are to have survived."

Her eyes went cold, and for a second he thought he'd played it all wrong, that she was going to shoot him dead on the spot. "How do you know about what happened in El Centro?"

"I saw the newspaper articles. Know something else, Virginia? DeKooning's dead. He killed himself."

"Too bad he didn't do it sooner."

"At least, at the end, he finally had the decency to take himself out of the game. Using yourself as bait to lure other women to their deaths . . . a lot of people would say you deserve to die more than DeKooning."

"Who the fuck are you to judge me? Just shut up and pray that Richard doesn't find your partner. If he does, he'll make her fucking scream. I've watched him work on other women; I know what he can do. Want to hear something funny, Ian? Richard actually was a Boy Scout as a kid. A fucking Eagle Scout, no less. When the media started calling him that, we had some good laughs."

"I'm curious about something, Virginia. The night that you and Richard put on your little show for Mandy, how'd you let him know you had a victim? And how'd he get into your car at the gas station without being seen? I've been by there, and it's a well-traveled, well-lit area."

"The Amoco station?" She paused, distracted by the sound of tree limbs tapping on the dormer windows. McSwain held his breath, ready to lunge if she turned her head even a fraction, but neither her gaze nor her gun hand ever wavered. "I stopped at the Amoco station because I'd forgotten to get gas earlier. Richard was furious with me. He'd been hiding under a blanket in the backseat the whole time. Mandy was like all of them—too drunk to notice what was going on around her."

"The murdered women—did you help Richard kill them or did you just watch while he did all the work?"

She gestured toward Mandy with the gun. "Stick around and you'll find out. It'll be interesting how Richard handles this. We've never had an audience before, and he likes to take his time."

"Like he did with Tibbs?"

She nodded.

"Tibbs died with a hard-on, Virginia. Do you get credit for that or does Richard like boys, too?"

"I was the distraction, you might say, but killing Danny wasn't my idea. Richard went crazy when I told him about the ring left on my pillow. He drove down to Ensenada that afternoon."

"And Moxley was inside the condo waiting for you during the time we had it staked out?"

"An unexpected bonus, yeah. Too bad Richard wasn't able to finish you and your partner off after he ran you off the road."

"In Helen Croft's SUV?"

" 'The Tank' is what Richard calls it. Anything not reinforced and that pig he's fucking would have crashed through the floorboards."

McSwain didn't allow himself to look directly at Mandy, but he knew from the sound of her breathing—of the gaps between breaths—that she was close to losing consciousness. As soon as she did, her body would relax, her head would drop forward, and she'd be strangled by the tension of her own legs on the rope. Except for the occasional scraping of tree limbs against the windows, the dry wheeze of her tortured breathing filled the attic. McSwain realized she was dying less than ten feet away from him.

"Moxley said you inspired him to kill. Is that how you two got started?"

"We have similar tastes. Maybe we inspired each other. Maybe we gave each other courage to do things we never would have done alone."

"Soul mates, maybe? The way I see it, you two were lovers before you became killing partners. How'd that happen, Virginia? You got Moxley to act out your rape fantasies like you did with Phil? Probably with Tibbs, too, I guess. But then you'd have reached a point where you couldn't go any further, am I right? Where the next logical step in the game would be the one where Moxley killed you. So in order to escalate the game, you decided to bring in other women. Women who were expendable. Like Mandy."

She directed a look of detached scorn at the woman

on the floor. "Yeah, she's as expendable a woman as I've ever seen."

"What about Leland? Where does he fit into all this?"

"Leland's the perfect husband—wealthy enough to pay the bills and self-absorbed enough to pay very little attention to what I do."

"You think you'll just walk away from this, Virginia? That the cops will think you're just a victim here once again?"

"Why not? Richard isn't going to talk, because he'll be long gone. And as for where I was tonight, I've got an alibi."

McSwain had a hunch and he played it now. "I don't think so, Virginia. I think your alibi came home early sometime before you and Mandy arrived and got his throat cut."

"What are you talking about?"

"Wasn't Josh your alibi? He didn't hate you because you were cheating on his father. He hated you because you refused to fuck him. Tonight you told him you'd changed your mind. He was going to meet you somewhere, only he came back here first for some reason—maybe he wanted to use his camcorder to preserve your romantic moments. He walked in on Moxley before you and Mandy showed up, and Moxley had to kill him."

"Josh isn't even here. He went out of town with Leland."

"But he came back. I told you."

"You're lying. Richard's not stupid. He wouldn't kill Leland's son. He wouldn't do that to me."

"You don't believe me, look downstairs—the video room. Check out the inversion machine."

"Richard wouldn't—"

"He would. He did. Go take a look."

Doubt crossed her face and her eyes flicked toward the door. McSwain launched himself at her, both hands going for the gun. She didn't fire, but her left hand came around in a low, sweeping arc. Something that felt like a wasp sting burned his forehead. Suddenly the side of his face was on fire and hot blood flooded one eye. He grabbed the gun, but it slipped through his fingers and fell to the floor, and her hand was coming around again, the blade of the box cutter glinting between her fingers. He ducked, trying to clear the blood from his eyes, and when he could see again, she was in a shooter's stance a few feet to the side of him, a look of manic rage twisting her face.

"I'm going to kill you now," she said. He heard the gun cock, and he thought about Lily and what this would do to her. *Lily, I'm sorry, I—*

The gunshot exploded a few feet from his face. Virginia's left shoulder disintegrated in a bright cloud of blood as the force of the bullet lifted her off her feet and hurled her across the floor. Tiny missiles of glass imbedded themselves in his exposed skin. He heard more glass shattering and saw Capshaw kick out the pane in the right dormer window and start to slide through.

He grabbed his .38 off the floor and ran to Mandy. She wasn't breathing as he turned her onto her side and tore at the rope that was strangling her. When the knot gave, she flopped forward. A wet hitching sound came from her throat.

Capshaw squatted next to him. She was panting hard, and the front of her black T-shirt was soaked with blood. She saw the blood sheeting down his face. "Jesus, she shot you?"

"She had a knife . . . something . . . I don't know." He looked at her blood-spattered clothing. "You're hurt?"

"Virginia's blood. She's in bad shape."

She reached over to check Mandy's pulse just as Moxley appeared in the doorway, gun drawn. He took in the sight of Virginia crumpled in a bloody heap with no reaction or shock, but coolly aimed the revolver and squeezed off a shot. The bullet slammed into a packing crate behind McSwain's head, wood splintering and dust powdering up. Capshaw had her SIG Sauer out and aimed, but Moxley was already gone, pounding back down the stairs.

"Your twenty-two," McSwain said, "give it to me." She set the larger gun aside, unholstered the .22 from the ankle strap under her pant leg, and handed it to him.

"Get help for her. I'll be back."

Halfway across the attic, he picked up the handkerchief Moxley'd thrown and used it to wipe blood out of his eyes. A few feet away Virginia lay on her back, blood pumping out of the gaping hole between her biceps and collarbone. Her feet thumped rhythmically on the floor, as though the lower half of her body were trying to run away even as the upper half bled out. She looked at him with eyes bright with terror.

"It's all right," he said. "Help's coming."

He had just reached the first floor when he heard the rumble of the garage door opening and a chugging whine that was familiar to him—it was the sound of Mandy's Taurus struggling to start.

He had no time to wonder why Moxley was taking Mandy's car—it didn't seem to make sense—but saw the car lurch forward out of the garage as he came out the back door. Hunkering down in the shadows next to the porch, he fired shots into the front and rear passenger side tires. Air hissed out of the tires, and the car rocked back and forth. Moxley hurled himself across the front seat and used his gun to shatter the right front window. As McSwain ducked and rolled into the deeper darkness under the porch steps, Moxley fired three quick rounds.

McSwain started to return fire, then saw Moxley getting out of the car on the driver's side and reaching into the backseat. When he pivoted and straightened up, McSwain realized why he'd jumped into Mandy's car instead of his own vehicle—he was holding one of Mandy's children under each arm. They were silent and limp, and he could see the white-sneakered feet of the baby dangling down.

"Moxley, let the kids go. We can work something out."

For a response, Moxley juggled the baby to his other arm and squeezed off a shot that passed so close to McSwain's head he could feel the shock pierce deep into his eardrum. Still holding both children, Moxley sprinted toward the rows of orange trees at the side of the house.

Despite Moxley's speed, he was slowed down by the weight of the children. McSwain was easily closing the distance between them when he saw Moxley stop just beyond the orange grove and then disappear, swallowed up behind what looked like a wall of blackness. McSwain stood there a second, blinking blood out of his eyes, as he realized Moxley had gone into the labyrinth.

Chapter 32

Using the same entrance as Moxley, McSwain found himself in a tunnel of greenery so narrow that in places the innermost leaves snagged in the weave of his shirt and caught in his hair. Despite the stippling of moonlight, he could see almost nothing ahead, but was quickly aware that, soon after he entered it, the design of the labyrinth ceased conforming to the traditional layout. He remembered then the trap Leland set for his students—they went in expecting a labyrinth and instead found themselves in a maze.

He stopped, wiping blood off his face and staring at a fork in the path. As he listened for any sound that would give away Moxley's position, his ears rang from the bullet that had passed so close to his head. He wondered why neither of the children was crying, wondered if they'd been drugged or worse, and he told himself it was fear keeping them silent.

Finally he did notice something—the odor of perfume that had permeated the attic. It seemed stronger toward the right, so he took that fork for about forty paces, turned left and then left again, before the path dead-ended and his outstretched hand disappeared elbow-deep in the dry, prickly wall of hedge.

He turned to retrace his path—two right turns, then straight back to the fork. His breathing was hard, almost labored. Occasionally he looked up at the night sky to reassure himself that he wasn't really enclosed, that all the air and space in the world was right up there over his head, and he told himself to stay calm and keep breathing. But when he reached the fork again and took the opposite turn this time, the hedge seemed to close in around him like a giant green fist, squeezing the air from his lungs. He told himself this was only the illusion of a claustrophobic, but the next time he stopped, illusion or not, his heart was bouncing around inside his ribs like a fly in a jar.

He put a hand on his chest, inhaled deeply. The scent of perfume wafted into his nostrils.

"Don't quit now, Ian. You're almost there."

The voice floated out to him from deep within the maze, light and singsongy. A breeze stirred and he caught a sharp whiff of sweat mixed with the perfume.

He didn't speak, afraid to give away his position, but crept along, making two more turns before hitting another dead end. Rather than retrace his steps again, he considered dropping down and belly-crawling under the hedge, but decided to do so would make too much noise. Moxley would probably be waiting there, ready to fire a bullet into his head as soon as he emerged.

Halfway back to the point where he'd made his error, he saw an opening in the hedge so narrow he'd missed it before and turned sideways, inching through as quietly as possible. A spiderweb passed across his face and he slapped it away. Gnats, drawn by the blood, worried the wound on his forehead.

"You in the part I call the Devil's Dick yet, Ian?" Moxley called. "That real narrow stretch before you get to the hard part?"

He stopped and listened, trying to gauge where the voice was coming from, but the twisting hedgerows seemed to both muffle and amplify sound. Moxley could have been two feet behind him or twenty feet up ahead. He held his gun at the ready, wondered how the hell he thought he'd be able to use it with Moxley holding Mandy's kids.

A few feet farther on, the corridor opened up into a broader space, roughly triangular, and this in turn offered a choice between two more paths.

"You believe some of those idiots Leland sends in here don't even make it as far as you have? They get lost and scared and I have to go in and lead them the rest of the way in, and the fools are blubbering and hugging their pathetic bundles of shit they're going to throw away—their photos of their mean mom and their bullying dad, the wedding rings that started out being gold bands on their fingers and ended up being nooses around their necks, their statues of Saint this or that who never answered their prayers, their fucking Stars of David. Like Leland's little game can make them free! What fucking morons!"

Moxley's voice sounded much closer now, as though only a couple of hedgerows might be between them. He crouched low, expecting a bullet to explode through the greenery at any moment. Then he realized Moxley couldn't possibly know his exact position and probably wouldn't want to waste the ammunition shooting blindly.

The damp breeze changed direction. He could smell the cloying gardenia smell of the perfume more strongly, and with it the stench of his own body—a dank stew of clammy sweat and naked fear. He put a hand to his heart—it seemed to have split into a trio of smaller hearts that were beating wildly in various parts of his body.

Faced with another choice, he took the left path, which widened almost immediately. He was actually looking at Moxley a moment before he realized what he was seeing—in the darkness, the outline of Moxley's body blended with the hedge, making him almost invisible. He was holding a limp child in each arm, and only when he shifted the baby higher up on his shoulder did McSwain actually see him.

But Moxley seemed to have no trouble seeing him. He called out, "You made it, Ian. Good for you. Now the real fun begins."

He gestured broadly with his left arm, as though the baby were a platter of hors d'oeuvres that he was offering to pass. Then he laughed and pulled the child back against his body.

"Don't know about you, Ian, but I never liked kids. Never saw what they were good for. But now maybe I'll have to change my mind."

A few feet in front of Moxley, McSwain was able to make out the dark oval of a hole and, next to it, a metal disk that resembled a manhole cover. This was the pit that Kreski'd talked about, the place where people threw away the symbols of what they considered bondage.

"Put the kids down, Richard."

"I could do that," Moxley said, and he swung the baby out over the hole. "I could put them both a long way down. But are you sure you want that? Got any idea how far it is, or all the sharp, jagged shit that's down there?"

"What's down there, Richard?"

Moxley grinned, obviously relishing the question. "Discarded lives of fucking fools, that's what. Hole didn't used to be that deep, either. Then Leland found out some of these buttholes—after they pitched Mama's heirloom crystal or the album of the wedding photos—whaddaya know, they changed their minds. Came back here all sentimental trying to salvage what they'd already thrown away. Got old, so Leland made the hole deep and put a padlocked cover on it—wetback who cleans the thing out every month or so gave me the combination."

Sweat and blood poured down McSwain's face. He started to reach into his pants pocket for the handkerchief.

"Hold it right there!" Moxley snarled, all pretense of civility vanished from his voice. He bounced the baby in his left arm and stepped closer to the pit.

"Lotta broken glass down there, Ian. Be a shame if I dropped this kid."

McSwain held his hands up, palms out. "Hold on, Richard. Just reaching for a handkerchief. It's a fucking sauna back here, and I'm bleeding like a stuck pig, you haven't noticed."

"Yeah, Virginia got you good, didn't she? Okay, I'll give you a break. Toss me your gun. Slowly. Remember I got a gun, too, and more important"—he bounced the girl over the drop this time—"I got the bitch's rugrats. That don't mean anything to me, but I know it does to you."

"Fine, Richard. No problem."

He held the gun up by the barrel so Moxley could see it. Then he bent and threw the weapon in a low, underhanded toss, like he was lobbing a ball to a child. It fell to the ground and Moxley kicked it into the hedge.

"Very good, Ian." He hefted the little girl higher up over his shoulder and bounced the baby in his other arm. "Kids're getting heavy, though. Might have to drop one anyway."

McSwain mopped his bleeding face. "Do yourself a favor, Richard. Let them go."

"Tell you what, Ian. I'll make a deal. How about I give you one of the kids—in exchange, you give me your car keys."

"No deal, Richard. I want both children."

"Oh, no, no, no, nooo. Don't overstep your bounds. Besides, I kind of like the idea of making you decide— McSwain's choice—maybe they'll make a movie out of it. A tearjerker. Wonder which of the brats McSwain will choose?"

"You don't need either of them, Richard. They'll just slow you down."

"Yeah, but not as much as the bullet I'll get in the head soon as I walk out of here by myself. Your cunt partner's called the cops by now—only reason a SWAT team hasn't charged in by now's they probably know I got the kids." He made a juggling motion with his extended arms, the girl going up, the boy down, then reversing it as he gazed down into the hole. "My arms are getting tired, McSwain. You don't choose fast, I might just drop 'em both."

"But then you wouldn't have any hostages."

"Well, hell, let 'em shoot me. Maybe I don't care."

"I think you do."

A smile twisted his lips. "Well, maybe I do care. Just a tad. I make it out of here, I can make a few adjustments, start over someplace else. Won't have Virginia to be my bait, but so what? That was getting old anyway. So throw me the fucking car keys. Then tell me which kid should go into the hole."

McSwain held up one hand. "Okay. I'm going to reach into my pocket now to get the keys."

"Wait." Moxley knelt down and let the little girl slide off his right arm onto the ground. He then pulled the gun out of his waistband and pointed it at McSwain.

"Slowly. You try anything, I'll kneecap you and bash both their heads in before your eyes. Got that?"

"Real clear." He tried to see if the little girl was moving, if she was even breathing. He couldn't tell. "What's wrong with them, Richard? What'd you do to them?"

"Ask Virginia. She made the lemonade. Now, the keys, please."

"Wish you'd put that gun away. You're making me nervous."

"Too fucking bad. Now take a few steps closer, Ian. When you toss those keys, I want to make sure I can see them."

He approached Moxley until he was within fifteen feet of him and Moxley told him to stop. He then glanced at the child on his left arm, the gun in his right hand. From his expression, McSwain could tell he realized a choice had to be made if he was going to have one hand free. After a second's hesitation, he came to a decision and slid the gun under his waistband.

"The keys, Ian. But hold them up first. Let me see them."

McSwain reached into his pants pocket, took out his car keys, and held them up. Moxley nodded and held out his hand.

He lobbed the keys high and to the left, saw Moxley's eyes track them. His right hand was already out when he realized they were on an arc headed directly for the pit. Automatically he twisted to the left and reached across his body with his right arm. McSwain's hand went to his pocket. He yanked out the blood-soaked handkerchief with Capshaw's .22 concealed inside and sighted down the barrel, aiming for the center of Moxley's chest. Moxley's body was off-center, leaning left, but he saw McSwain's gun and brought his right hand to his waist, swinging the baby across his body as he did. McSwain's finger was already depressing the trigger when he saw Dakota come into his line of fire. He lifted his hand a quarter inch and fired. Moxley's head jerked back and his gun went off. McSwain fired again, aiming for the juncture of Moxley's thigh and torso, clipping him at the hip. Moxley's left foot stomped at open air and then his body twirled in a spastic pirouette before he crumpled into a "V." The baby was still gripped against his chest as he dropped with a whooshing sound into the hole. There was a crunching-scraping sound as he hit the bottom.

McSwain held his gun in both hands and approached the edge. He listened for any sound below, the sound of Moxley trying to climb back up or the gun being cocked again.

But all he heard in the swelter of the hedgerows was the baby's cry. It started out thin and hesitant, then rose into a scream that pierced the summer night.

Chapter 33

On a Monday morning ten days after the shoot-out with Moxley, McSwain drove up to Riverside to attend Lily's sentencing hearing. Since her arrest and arraignment, she'd been held in the Riverside County Jail, but her final destination—as they both knew—was back to CWI. The only question now was for how long.

He'd driven up the week before to visit her at the jail and had left as exhausted as if he'd gone twelve rounds with the best sparring partner at Dave's Gym, burned out by a conversation steeped in anger, contrition, and promises. She wanted him to have faith in her again. He didn't know if he could or even wanted to, if he could afford to take the risk.

He also had to face another possibility, one he'd encountered before in his dealings with criminals: that she had unconsciously sabotaged herself out of fear of being free and facing the hardships and responsibilities of freedom.

Now he was wearing a groove in the marble floor of the Riverside Courthouse hall, glancing up now and then at the clock and at the bank of elevators at the end of the hall, expecting to see Capshaw, who'd said she'd try to drive up for the sentencing. He half hoped to see her and, on the other hand, half wished she wouldn't come, that he could get through this ordeal the same way Lily would be getting through it—alone. Like everything else these days, he felt ambiguous about it.

His forehead burned and itched where he'd been slashed with the box cutter, each of the forty-four stitches that had been used to close the wound feeling like an African ant had sunk its pincers into his flesh, so he bought a diet Coke at the snack bar just beyond the metal detectors and washed down a couple of Advil.

A bailiff that he questioned told him Lily's case wasn't scheduled until after lunch. The man then did a double take and asked if he wasn't that San Diego detective who'd taken out a serial killer the week before, and how'd that feel anyway, to kill somebody, and McSwain said, "Like it always does," just to see the guy's reaction before he walked away.

He bought a local paper because he felt reasonably sure it wouldn't contain any mention of Moxley or Virginia or the shoot-out that had gotten his picture in the *Union-Tribune* three days in a row, and he was right— the events that had taken place on Stromquist's property were old news now, at least outside the immediate San Diego area, where the reporters were still salivating like starved jackals over murder and mayhem—less than a decade after Heaven's Gate, no less—in posh Rancho Santa Fe. He couldn't concentrate, however, and wound up simply turning pages, staring at headlines that might as well have been written in Mandarin for all his distracted brain was able to decipher.

A little after noon, after he'd given up on trying to read the paper, he was thumbing through a brochure on fishing expeditions in Baja that he'd picked up at a tackle shop in I.B., when the elevator door *ping*ed open and Jenna strode out. She wore a pearl-gray suit with a burgundy blouse and gray, low-heeled pumps, and her hair was pulled back and tamed down dramatically from its usual explosion of curls. Under one arm she carried a folded newspaper. McSwain thought that if she was trying to impersonate a lawyer she was doing a pretty good job.

When she saw him, a look of relief crossed her face and her heels clicked with renewed vigor along the corridor.

"Is it over?"

McSwain shook his head, surprised when he realized how pleased he was to see her. "Lunch break till one.

Lily's case is on the docket for this afternoon, but there're
four other people. I don't know what order the judge
will take them in."

"Sorry I'm so late. Getting Mandy checked into Harmony took longer than I expected. Paperwork and everything, and she wanted me to go with her to look at
the room. I think she expected it to look like a room in
a reformatory, but it was actually nice. Kind of a college-
dorm atmosphere."

"How's she doing?"

"Scared. Twenty-eight days is a long time to be away
from her kids. But she needs to be in rehab. Otherwise,
after everything she's been through, she'll almost certainly drink."

"Those kids . . . please tell me she didn't leave them
with her train wreck of a mother."

"Thank God, no. Her ex-husband was a possibility of
last resort, but it turned out he didn't want the kids,
after all. He's got a new girlfriend, and Mandy said she's
allergic to children. But the ex has a sister who supposedly thinks her brother's a jerk, and she's agreed to take
them for now. Mandy seemed okay with that."

"So both kids check out okay? No ill effects?"

"Not physically. That's something huge Mandy's got
to be grateful for, and she knows it. The chloral hydrate
that Virginia put in that lemonade to knock them out—
it could just as easily have killed them. By the way,
Mandy said to tell you she's going to start paying us
in installments as soon as she gets out of rehab, finds
a job."

"Yeah? That's . . . good."

"You're not listening to me, are you?"

"Sorry, I was just thinking . . . I ever tell you I tried
to get Lily to go to Harmony a few years ago? She
wouldn't do it. Said she could kick drugs by herself."

"Famous last words."

"No shit."

"So maybe now she realizes she needs help. I never
thought I'd hear myself quoting Stromquist, but that
French saying of his, in this case, I think it's right on
the mark. With addiction, the door's either open or it's

closed. You either use or you don't. There's no middle ground."

"I think Lily was always searching for a middle ground."

"Aren't we all?" She sighed—a little wistfully, McSwain thought, then dug in her purse and came up with a pack of Parliaments. "I gotta have a cigarette. Want to walk outside?"

He shrugged. He knew that pacing the hallway while his heart jumped through hoops and puddles of sweat formed in his palms wasn't doing him any good, but he hadn't known what else to do. Trying to eat anything more substantial than antacid pills was out of the question.

"Sure, I can always use a little secondhand smoke."

She frowned. "I'm going to quit one of these days."

"Unless your lungs quit on you first."

She elbowed him in the ribs. "Enough already. You're starting to sound like Hank Paris."

"Mea culpa."

They took the stairs down to the first floor, past the metal detectors, then exited through a side door and walked down some stairs to the street. Capshaw pulled out a lighter and lit up, exhaling with an appreciative sigh.

"So Lily, how's she holding up?"

"Depressed. Scared. Her lawyer thinks she'll get four to six, reduced down to two or three. Which means with good behavior, she could be out in another two."

"That's not ancient, Ian."

"Of course not. If she gets her shit together, she can still build a good life for herself."

He started to go on, hesitated. Jenna looked at him. "But . . . ?"

"Dammit, she wants me to wait for her, but how can I? How do I know she won't do this again? At the same time, I don't know if I can *not* wait for her. I mean, even if I divorce her and start dating again, go through the motions, I don't know if some part of me won't be hanging back, waiting for her to get out while I waste some other woman's time."

"You still love her."

He grimaced. The word *love* had that effect on him now. "Depends on what time of day you ask. Sometimes . . ." He realized he was clenching his fist. "It varies."

"She's sick, Ian. Maybe she'll get well this time; maybe not. It's a crapshoot."

"That's not very comforting."

"Wasn't meant to be."

They sat in silence awhile. McSwain saw a guy in a white Camaro double-parked outside the courthouse as a curvy, dark-skinned woman in tight jeans bounced down the steps and hopped into the car. The two kissed fiercely; then the man put the Camaro in gear and they roared out of there like they were leaving the site of a bank heist. Future uncertain, perhaps, but both of them free.

He turned back to Jenna. "You didn't have to come here, you know. You told me you had plans."

"Yeah, tonight. But if I'm too tired by the time I get home, I can always cancel. Being here, this is important. Helps me keep things in perspective."

"Your date tonight isn't important?"

She shot him a look. "You *are* kidding, right?"

"This Ray guy you've been seeing—"

"It isn't Ray. That ran its course. This is someone I met at the gym."

"Oh."

"Why the interest in what I euphemistically call my love life all of a sudden?"

He felt embarrassed now. Couldn't believe he'd asked h   bout Ray or that he'd even remembered the guy's   , but he'd started this and now he felt compelled to continue.

"I guess I'm envious. I mean, over the years, I know you've seen a lot of different people. You drop them or maybe they drop you—"

She raised an eyebrow. "Excuse me?"

"Like I said, you drop them and then you go on to the next one like nothing's happened. You don't get attached and you don't get hurt. You just move on. I wish I could do that. Tell you the truth, it pisses me off that I can't."

"Then we're even, because sometimes it pisses me off that I can't stick around long enough to have anything beyond a good time. I fell in love once—with Larry. Whether or not I'll ever be able to do it again, I don't know. I do know I'm missing something. Missing a lot. But I try not to think about it. Sleeping around is sort of like a consolation prize."

"Not a bad one. Maybe I ought to try it."

"Don't, Ian. You're not that kind of guy."

"How do you know what kind of guy I am?"

"Oh, I know," she said, and held his gaze a bit too long, both of them looking away at the same time, the moment growing awkward.

He looked at his watch. "We should go back in. It'll be starting soon."

A few minutes later court resumed. McSwain found a seat at the end of a bench occupied by family members of other prisoners who were there for sentencing. Capshaw squeezed in between him and an overweight teenage boy with greasy black locks tumbling over an acne-stippled forehead.

Lily was sitting a few rows ahead with her lawyer, a hunched, mousy-looking man who kept shoving his gold-rimmed glasses up higher on his thin nose. At one point, she cast a worried eye over her shoulder, looking for him, perhaps, but she didn't twist around quite far enough and turned back before McSwain could try to make eye contact. He noticed that her hair was starting to grow out again, fanning out across the back of her neck in feathery blond curls. Something about those curls, perhaps the memory of crushing them in his hand while they made love, made him want to weep, and he looked away.

When her turn came—a little over an hour later—she and her lawyer stood and went before the judge.

The lawyer made a brief, predictable statement, pointing out that this was his client's first offense while in prison and playing up the magnitude of her remorse, but to McSwain, he sounded detached, almost perfunctory.

The judge, a rail-thin fellow with the most unexpressive eyes McSwain had seen outside a morgue, pored over his notes for a minute and then, with all the emotion of a man ordering fries to go with his burger, he sentenced Lily to three years, one of them suspended, banged the gavel, and called for the next case.

A lifetime later, but only a couple of minutes in clock time, McSwain got up, wandered outside alone, and walked around the block a couple of times, a headache swelling up behind his ear like he'd been thumped on the head with a brick.

On his third swing past the courthouse, he heard the heels clicking behind him.

"That was it?" Jenna said.

"That was it."

He heard her sigh and realized, maybe for the first time, that this was painful for her, too.

She slid her arm through his. "You okay?"

"Sure, I'm great. Never better."

She pulled back, stung. "Hey, don't cop an attitude. You know what I mean."

"Sorry."

They walked to the corner, where McSwain had left the Monte Carlo. The meter was expired, and a yellow ticket flapped from underneath the windshield wiper.

"Terrific." He yanked it off, stuffed it into his coat pocket.

Capshaw leaned against the bumper of the car. "Want to hear the latest on Virginia? You won't like it, but it might get your mind on other things."

"Shoot."

"I talked to Hank this morning. He says Leland's getting her a crack team of lawyers, and she's probably going to plead not guilty."

McSwain was incredulous. "Not guilty? She was two seconds away from killing me."

"You know that and I know that, but her story is that Moxley brutalized her to the point where she was unable to think for herself; she was paralyzed with fear."

"But not too paralyzed to open my head with a box cutter, I guess."

"Apparently not. She was, and I'm quoting Hank here quoting the DA, 'in thrall to Richard Moxley,' endquote. Plus her attorneys are going to bring up the whole De-Kooning thing, and argue that, because of what happened to her as a kid, she suffered post-traumatic stress disorder."

"Jesus. She's a cold-blooded, premeditating murderer. She got her thrills helping Moxley pick out a victim and kill her."

"You know it and I know it, but—"

"What about Mandy? She can testify Virginia held the box cutter to her throat and helped Moxley tie her up. She heard Virginia as much as admit that the whole rape scene last winter was staged."

"And Virginia's lawyers will undoubtedly say, yes, she did do those things, but she wasn't responsible. PTSD, Stockholm syndrome, whatever."

"So even with all the testimony against her, she could walk?"

"Unlikely, but not impossible."

"Jesus, Jenna, she'll do it again."

"I doubt it. She needed Richard. Without him, I expect it'll just be Virginia alone with her sick fantasies."

He realized his hands were balled into fists and took a deep breath, then relaxed them. "Dammit, sometimes I wonder if Lily was right about me getting out of the business. Not because it doesn't pay enough, but because of the human swill we get involved with. People like Virginia, Moxley, Danny Tibbs. Sometimes I want to just buy a fishing boat and go down to Mexico, take charters out fishing for marlin, make enough money to get by, call it good."

"It sounds nice now, but you'd be bored silly in six months. Face it, Ian; that human swill, it keeps our adrenaline going. Chasing scumbags is a rush, and you know it." She gave a wry smile. "Almost as good as a double vodka on the rocks."

"You make it sound like an addiction."

"Excitement? Maybe it is, but so what?"

He thought about that a few seconds. "Yeah, well, I wasn't entirely kidding about the fishing. I'm gonna take a week or two off. Drive down to Baja. Hang out in the sun for a while."

Jenna's brow furrowed. "A lot of work coming our way now. Since all the publicity around the Stromquist case, the phone's ringing off the hook. Mostly your standard bail jumpers, background checks, and the like, but a couple that sound really interesting."

"More bad guys to chase?"

"Endless supply, it would seem."

"Do you consider that good or bad?"

"Mostly bad, but"—she gave him that great smile—"hey, it keeps life interesting."

"Interesting, yeah." He unlocked the door to the Monte Carlo. "See you back in the city?"

"See you."

On the drive back, he thought about what Jenna had said, but mostly he thought about Lily. Whether to hang in there and wait for her or say to hell with it, make a new life for himself. By the time he hit the outskirts of San Diego, he'd reached a decision of sorts. Something he'd have to rethink and mull over in the days to come, but nevertheless, a choice that he thought he could live with.

As long as he kept his mind occupied.

As long as there were bad guys to chase, as Jenna put it. As long as he could find just enough danger to keep his adrenaline pumping.

He found himself hoping those cases Jenna said might be interesting involved a reasonable amount of danger. Hell, maybe a lot.

Jesus, she's right. I'm addicted, he thought.

Maybe Baja could wait.

HUSH

Anne Frasier

"INTENSE...This is far and away the best serial killer story I have read in a very long time."
—Jayne Ann Krentz

"CHILLING...Don't read this book if you are home alone."
—Lisa Gardner

Criminal profiler Ivy Dunlap is an expert at unraveling the psyches of the most dangerous men alive. She understands the killer instinct.
But even Ivy has her limits. And the Madonna Murderer will test them...

0-451-41031-9

To order call: 1-800-788-6262

S641/Frasier/Hush